THUNDER
IN THE SUN

First Published in the UK 2015 by Belvedere Publishing

First edition: 2015

*Any reference to real names and places are purely fictional
and are constructs of the author. Any offence the references
produce is unintentional and in no way reflects the reality of
any locations or people involved.*

A copy of this work is available through the British Library.

ISBN: 978-1-910105-47-4

Belvedere Publishing
Mirador
Wearne Lane
Langport
Somerset
TA10 9HB

THUNDER IN THE SUN

BY

ELIZABETH REVILL

The terrifying Inspector Allison psychological thrillers:

Killing me Softly
Prayer for the Dying
God only Knows
Would I Lie To You

Llewellyn Family Saga:

Whispers on the Wind
Shadows on the Moon
Rainbows in the Clouds

Stand alone novels:

Against the Tide
The Electra Conspiracy
Sanjukta and the Box of Souls
The Forsaken and the Damned

Dedication

For my dear friend Hayley Raistrick-Episkopos who is always there for me.

Author's Acknowledgements

Well, here we go again!

I have had so many requests for more after the Llewellyn trilogy that I have written number four in the series, Thunder in the Sun; and I have many more planned to follow on from this one.

I hope you all like this latest offering and would like to thank my amazing publisher, Sarah Luddington, a notable author in her own right who has been a constant source of support and advice throughout my publishing journey and her excellent team at Belvedere.

Similarly, I have a number of friends who have pressed me for more in this series, the lovely Karen Gulliford, Lynne Haylock Moore, Pamela Hamer, Heather Stamp, Sarah Kettel and Pauline Dorrans.

Again I must thank my husband Andrew Spear for his support and my gorgeous son, Ben Fielder who wrote the amazing "Land of the Awoken." Watch out for more from him.

If you do like my work, check out my Facebook author's page:

https://www.facebook.com/pages/Elizabeth-Revill/221311591283258
And click 'like'.
Similarly do visit my website: www.elizabethrevill.com
Thanks one and all. Keep reading and I'll keep writing.
If you like my books please click 'Like'. Thank you.

Terms and colloquialisms used in

Thunder In The Sun

bach:male term of endearment - dear.
blas:flavoursome, tasty.
cariad:term of endearment – my love, little
one.
Cawl: Welsh stew.
Cwtch: cuddle.
Cwat lawr : Shut up!
Dera nawr: come on, now.
Diolch: Thank you.
Duw: God.
Dadcu:Grandfather.
esgyrn Dafydd:bones of David - an exclamation.
fach:female term of endearment - dear.
fy merch 'i:term of endearment - little lady.
Goody-oo: nosy, interfering, idiot.
ie:yes.
iechy dwriaeth:an exclamation.
Jawch:an exclamation like crikey.
Jib: unpleasant expression.
Mam-gu:Grandmother.
nawr yna:now then.
paid:don't - stop it.
potch:soaking wet.
rhwyn dy garu du:I love you.
tschwps:a lot, cried the rain.
twp: stupid, dull.
Wuss:friend, mate, pal - local to the region
not what it means today.
Yerffyn darn!:An exclamation like, damn it.
Yfflon: tatters

CHAPTER ONE

Difficult Days

Little Timmy Noble was confused; nothing seemed to make any sense. He and his sister, Marion had their cases packed and were dressed in their Sunday best even though it was a Tuesday. They had brown luggage type labels threaded through the lapel buttonhole of their coats displaying their name and address. At the top in typed letters was the official stamp of Hackney Borough Council. The back of the label detailed medical information, which stated Timmy's age and that he was asthmatic. His sister Marion had no such problems and the label was clear except for her birth date.

Timmy's mother, Martha was struggling hard not to cry. She stooped down and crushed her five-year old son to her, "Now you are to be a brave boy and be good. You must be on your best behaviour."

"But, why? Where are we going?"

Martha sniffed hard and removed a grubby handkerchief from her apron pocket and blew hard.

"Are you okay, Mum?" asked her daughter, Marion, solemn faced and just nine years old.

"I'm fine, really," affirmed Martha. "You'll have a lovely time. Like a holiday. Wish I could come with you."

"Then why can't you?" asked Timmy beginning to look and sound fearful.

"Someone has to look after the shop. Keep it going until you come home. With Daddy gone I need to be sure you will be safe."

"But, where are we going?" asked Timmy starting to cry.

"Somewhere lovely. Into the countryside where there are green fields and pretty meadow flowers. You'll see animals such as you've never seen before. As soon as the war is over and it's safe to come home, you'll be back and even before then I will come and see you when I can, I promise."

"But where? How will you know where to find us? I don't want to go," howled Timmy.

"The people will tell me and I'll write and I'll expect you to write to me. It will be a real adventure for you, you'll see." There was an official sounding knock on the door. "Quickly now. Have you got everything? Your identity cards?"

"In our pockets," said Marion stoically.

"You must promise me you'll look after each other. Don't let them split you up. Promise." Marion's eyes welled with tears as she nodded. There was another sharp rap on the door. Martha stood up, "Let me look at you both." She eyed her offspring critically and in approval. "Perfect. Come on. And here, for the journey…" She took out two bags of sweets and gave a bag to each child. "Remember to share. Put them in your pockets, now. That's it. There are sandwiches in your satchels and a bottle of pop."

Martha walked to the front door in Clifden Road, Hackney and opened it as a large bearded man was just about to knock again.

"Ah, Mrs Noble. I see they are ready. The bus is waiting."

The family stepped out onto the street where other children were assembled with anxious mothers watching.

The day was bright and sunny this warm summer morning. A few cumulous clouds puff balled across the sky and the gentle breeze rustled the fingered leaves of the horse chestnut tree on the corner of the street, bedecked in blossom and promising a rich bounty of conkers, but with the children leaving there would be no one to harvest the burnished treasures.

A stern-faced woman with a clipboard was ticking off the names of the children standing in regimented lines. She looked up and saw the two newcomers and her face softened, "You must be Timmy and Marion. Come along. It's time to go."

Some mothers stood back reluctant to engage with their children for fear of upsetting them while others openly wept. The children were ushered onto the waiting green single decker bus.

Marion took her brother's hand and led him to the queue waiting to mount the steps to the coach. All the while Timmy gazed back at his mother with a look of loss and abandonment etched on his face. Martha wiped her eyes and stepped back from the pavement and watched as the children clambered aboard and found a seat. Her eyes scanned the bus to see where hers had sat and she nodded reassuringly at them willing her bottom lip to stop trembling.

As the last child was loaded onto the bus and all of the luggage had been stowed away the driver started the rattling engine. Martha stepped forward and stopped the portly bearded man from the church, "When will we know, Mr Barton? Where they've gone?"

"As soon as they're placed we will be wired and let you know. Don't worry. You're doing the right thing," he asserted seeing the worry manifesting on Martha's face. "They'll be fine."

Martha not trusting herself to speak merely nodded. The mothers crowded around to wave at their children as the bus pulled away and headed down the road. They stood there a moment and watched the bus rumble along the asphalt, clouding the dusty street air with its diesel fumes. Martha turned away sadly as others stopped to chat and bemoan their fate.

As soon as Martha stepped inside she was horrified to see Timmy's one-eyed teddy bear sitting crookedly on the hall chair. "Oh my!" She snatched it up and raced out running after the bus waving at it to stop but the bus trundled on, rounded the corner and disappeared from view. Defeated Martha stopped. She studied the teddy in her hands speaking to herself. "He can't sleep without it."

"Don't worry, Mrs Noble. You'll be able to send it on to him. It'll be all right," said her neighbour, Mrs Kenyon. "Do you fancy a cuppa?" Martha shook her head. Her neighbour continued, "Me, I'm looking forward to a bit of peace and quiet with my three gone. Not that I won't miss them. But I won't miss the noise and the mess." But Martha smiled half-heartedly, sadly retraced her steps and entered her house closing the door behind her with a weary sigh.

She leaned against it clutching the small teddy. The house was already too quiet without them and with her husband,

David, at war. She knew she would have to get used to that but she also knew she would miss their laughter and their cheeky chatter, and a stray tear rolled down her cheek. This was no time to let down her defences. Martha knew she had to get to the shop and open up. Life had to go on as normally as possible.

Four streets away in a terraced property Janine Clarke was impatiently waiting for her brood of four to come downstairs. Ten-year-old Naomi with her huge soulful eyes and long dark hair came slowly and silently down the stairs.

"Where're the others?" screeched Janine. "Tell the little bleeders to hurry up."

Naomi turned and ran back to the landing, "Hurry up! Mum says to come on. Quick!"

Three subdued children emerged from the bedroom in their outdoor clothes that were worn and had seen better days. The six-year-old twins Katy and Sally were hesitant. Their brother, eight-year-old, Gerald barged past whooping in glee. He ran screaming down the stairs. His mother caught him by the arm and shook him before striking him behind the ear.

"Ow," cried Gerry breaking down into tears.

"Don't 'ow' me. If you don't stop your snivelling I'll give you what for and something to cry about. Wipe your nose."

Gerald drew his nose across the sleeve of his coat and his mother railed at him again, "What do you think you're doing? Use your handkerchief. We don't want folks to think you're a scruff. Now get outside with the others and wait for the bus."

Gerald slunk off looking morose. He picked up his case and exited the house leaving the front door wide open. Janine gestured to her daughters, "Well, come on. Hurry up or you'll miss the bus."

The light spilled through the doorway like a promise filled path to a new world.

The girls moved silently down the stairs. Janine inspected them, "You'll do! Come on," and she led them outside into the street milling with children and families all bidding their offspring goodbye.

Janine hugged each child in turn ordering them, "Now, you

4

behave and do as you're told. I don't want no reports of bad behaviour. Understood?" The children nodded, gravely. "Now, I may speak a bit sharp and I may be hard but it don't mean I don't love you, cos I do," said Janine gruffly and she hugged her daughters to her but Gerald stood back. "Come here, Son." Gerald stepped forward warily, "Come on, I'm not going to bite." She opened her arms and drew her son into her, giving him a big kiss on his cheek, which he hurriedly wiped off.

Janine watched as her children boarded the bus and put on a brave smile. "It will be grand, you mark my words," she called out drawing nods from other parents and murmurs of agreement.

Janine waved as they climbed aboard before sniffing and retreating indoors where she berated herself and rubbed at the unexpected tears that rolled down her cheeks. "Daft. That's what I am. Daft!"

The fleet of buses drove to Hackney Town Hall where an official waited. He boarded each bus and gave the intended destinations for each child. The Clarkes and the Nobles along with thirty other children were to be transported to Paddington Station where they would board a train to take them to South Wales, Glamorgan to a place called Neath. They would assemble at a large church hall where people from the town and neighbouring villages would gather and select a child or children to stay with them for the duration of the war or at least while the Blitz of London continued. Now that the Japanese had bombed Pearl Harbour on December 7th 1941, the war had escalated and the Americans had finally come to the aid of the Allies. The conflict that had been expected to come to an end within a few months of starting in 1939 had continued to drag on and it was now summertime 1942.

The bombing of London and major cities had brought many families to the decision that their children would be safer away from the cities and it would be better if they went into the countryside. Where they were dispatched was a lottery. The Nobles and Clarkes were headed for Wales. Other children were destined for Oxford, the Cotswolds, Yorkshire Dales and various places in the South West and more.

The children were silent while they contemplated their fate as the bus rumbled through the traffic to Paddington Station. Sunlight like strobe lights flickered through the windows as the bus travelled along a tree-lined avenue.

The children were filled with both trepidation and nervous excitement. None of them had ever been on a train or visited a railway station before and they were in awe of the huge concourse with its big clock and stared in wonder at the domed glass ceiling and the many pigeons that fluttered on the platforms.

It was the smell of steam that most excited them as the huge iron horse chuffed into the station. Clouds of white marshmallow vapour smoke signalled up and the harsh hoot of a whistle set the children chattering with glee. Light filtered in through the opaque glass and pooled like spilled milk on the stone floor.

Feeling dwarfed by the size of the station Timmy Noble looked up, his eyes as large as pork pies, and he let out a huge sigh. "Cor!" He turned around on the spot with his head lifted up watching the swooping, fluttering pigeons that cooed and puffed out their iridescent shining pink breasts, so much so that he became giddy and fell into his sister, Marion.

"Oi, watch it!" she warned.

Timmy staggered light-headedly as his head still swum and again he muttered, "Cor!"

The driver of the bus who had unloaded them onto the platform assembled them into some sort of order but Timmy continued to fool around and set off after the pigeons, chasing them into flight with a look of delight on his face as he saw them rise into the air. "Cor!"

"Will you stop saying that," chided his sister, Marion. "You sound like a crow."

Timmy immediately began flapping his arms and running around the other children shouting, "Caw! Caw!"

The driver put his hand out and grabbed the lad. He caught him by his ear and yanked him into place on the line as Timmy yelped. The other children giggled and suitably chastened, Timmy became quiet and stood as he should.

He gazed around the building noting several groups of

children waiting quietly heading off to wherever. The Tannoy system blared out with a male voice that spoke in a pukka and impeccable English accent. It announced the departure of a train from platform three that was headed for Bristol and beyond. The driver gathered his motley band together and marched them to the platform where a guard stood inspecting tickets for the journey. The luggage was taken collectively, by porters, to the guard's van as the children were waved through to walk the length of the platform to the third class carriages. They were silent as they passed the impressive train and obediently boarded on instruction, walking along the corridor until they found vacant seats.

Timmy finding an empty compartment struggled to slide open the door, somewhat stiff on its runners, and Marion tugged on the door, too. Reluctantly it gave in and he clambered inside with his sister. He bagged a seat by the widow and bounced down. Marion scrambled in after him followed by the Clarke children. They eyed each other warily.

Naomi Clarke stared at Marion but as soon as Marion caught her eye she looked away. There was an uncomfortable silence in the carriage as each child weighed up the others. Marion dug into her pocket and pulled out a white three cornered paper bag shaped like a triangle. It was filled with small red gummy sweets. "Would you like a cherry lip?" she asked.

Naomi hesitated. Her brother Gerald shouted, "I'll have one."

Naomi piped up, "You'll wait till you're asked. Remember your manners."

Marion smiled, "It's okay, he can have one, the others, too."

Gerald beamed and dived into the bag, "Don't mind if I do. Ta!" He stuffed a couple into his mouth."

Marion passed the bag around and the twins, Katy and Sally, smiled shyly thanking her. Marion held out the bag to Naomi, "Go on; take one. Take a couple."

Naomi dipped her hand in the bag and took two, "You won't have none left," she said quietly.

Marion popped a couple in her own mouth and returned the

sweets to her pocket. "They're my favourite, cherry lips. Mum doesn't let me have them often because they stick to my teeth. Must make sure we all clean our teeth when we can."

There were a few minutes silence as the children chewed happily.

An elderly lady with silver grey hair tied back in a bun, dressed all in black, using a walking stick, came along the corridor and peered in. She frowned distastefully at the seats all occupied by children and walked on, her stick tip tapping as she went.

Her voice could be heard in the corridor as she remonstrated with the guard, "But I can't be expected to stand all the way and I haven't the money to pay the extra for a second class seat. Third class is bursting with children, it is."

The guard's words were inaudible. The tap, tap of the stick was heard returning and Marion stuck her head through the door. "You can come in here if you like, we can budge up and take it in turns to sit on each other's laps, can't we kids?"

The other children nodded and smiled their teeth slimed with red and gummed up with the juice from the cherry lip sweets.

The old lady didn't know what to say. "Um, well… thank you, I think."

"Excuse us. It's the sweets, cherry lips, make our teeth stick together."

Marion pulled Timmy onto her lap and moved into Timmy's seat, leaving hers free. The old lady entered the compartment not knowing quite what to say and squeezed into the vacated seat. Her stick rested against her legs. The children stared at her curiously.

"Say, Miss," said Gerald. "How come you use a stick?"

The lady gasped at the boldness of the remark and then a twinkle came into her eyes, "I have a condition, I do, and sometimes it's difficult to walk. The stick helps me."

"Oh."

"Where you going?" asked Timmy.

"Neath and you?" she replied in her singsong tones.

"Neath," they all chorused.

"Well, we will be neighbours, then we will."

"What's your name?" asked Sally curiously.

"Mrs Gregory. Phyllis Gregory, and you?"

There was a babble of chatter as all the children blurted out their names. Phyllis Gregory felt a rare smile tug at her lips as she struggled to remember their names. She banged her stick, "Duw, Duw! One at a time, please." The children fell silent at the school ma'am type of authority built into the request. She looked around at the crew and Phyllis felt a warmth flood through her veins with the recognition of feelings normally alien to her. "Now, let me see if I can remember." She paused and studied the children's faces. "Now, you, you are Marion, Marion with the cherry lips. Do you know; they used to be my favourite sweets?"

"Would you like one, Mrs Gregory?" asked Marion.

"Why, in a moment, yes, I would. Thank you."

"What's my name?" asked Timmy.

Mrs Gregory sighed and thought for a moment, "You are Marion's brother... is it Jimmy?"

"No," screeched Timmy howling with laughter. "Try again."

"If it's not Jimmy, then it must be Timmy!" she said trying not to laugh.

"Yes!" said Timmy delightedly.

"And you?" she turned to Gerald.

"I'm Gerald but mum only calls me that when I'm in trouble otherwise I'm Gerry."

"Then Gerry it is," smiled Mrs Gregory.

The twins, Katy and Sally sat silently, lifted their eyes and stared uncertainly at the old lady.

"And you, two... you must be sisters, you are so alike. But that's impossible. Are you first cousins? Or am I seeing double?"

Katy began to giggle.

"No? Then you are just good friends, you are?"

Sally began to chortle, then, "No, silly. We're twins!"

"Twins? My, my, who'd have thought it?"

"Why do you wear black?" asked Naomi tentatively.

"Well, you see... I lost my husband."

"Where? Where did you lose him? In London?" asked Timmy.

"In the war," sighed Mrs Gregory.

"This war?" asked Marion.

"No, the first one." Mrs Gregory stopped and her eyes misted over.

Marion took out her bag of sweets again, "Cherry lips?"

The old lady looked at her and smiled as she accepted one from the bag. "I haven't had one of these for years."

"Take a few, please."

Mrs Gregory took a couple more and popped them in her mouth with a serene expression on her face. She began to chew and soon her jaw became gummed up with the sticky sweets. She began to make the most extraordinary faces as she tried to unstick her teeth, which Marion noted must be false as they moved up and down as she chewed and she tried not to laugh.

"Oh, my... now I remember why I stopped eating them," mused Mrs Gregory. She took out a pristine white handkerchief and removed her top row of teeth, digging at the deep pink glue like substance to get rid of it. The children watched in fascination.

"How do you do that?" asked Timmy amazed and he attempted to remove his top teeth. His sister, Marion tried to warn him and nudged him in the ribs.

"Timmy, don't. It's not polite."

Mrs Gregory laughed and assured her, "It's all right. There's a lesson to learn, so there is. You look after your teeth and you won't have to take them out to clean them."

"Didn't you look after yours?" asked Timmy.

"Well, I did and I tried for many years but I had problems with my gums."

Timmy couldn't take his eyes off her face, "Is that why you talk funny?"

"Talk funny?"

"Yes, repeating words and saying them differently," persisted Timmy.

"Oh, you mean my accent?"

Timmy looked at his sister, "Is that what I mean?"

Marion apologised, "I'm sorry, Mrs Gregory. He doesn't mean to be rude."

Timmy looked puzzled, "I only asked a question."

"And a very good question it is, too." The children all looked expectantly at her. "Well, you see in different parts of the country people don't sound the same. Take your accent…"

"Our accent?" asked Naomi.

"Yes, you don't always sound the ends of your words, sometimes you drop your aitches. Your voice goes up and down in different places. You have London accents."

"My mum says we're cockney, born within the sound of Bow Bells," said Naomi.

"And other people have different accents."

"How different?"

Mrs Gregory cleared her throat and smiled, "I can show you if you like?"

"Yes, please," exclaimed Timmy.

Much to the children's amusement, Mrs Gregory began to speak in varying accents and urged the children to guess where she was pretending to be from. She was accomplished in Irish, Scots, Birmingham, Black Country, Yorkshire, Lancashire and many more.

"Cor!" said Timmy. "How do you do that?"

"That's my secret," said Mrs Gregory. "I may tell you, one day if our paths cross again."

The children were having a fun time and so was a surprised Mrs Gregory. She couldn't believe that the journey was passing so quickly. They chugged into Bristol Parkway and idled at the station before setting off on the Newport and Neath line.

The children had now settled down and fell quiet as they struggled to keep their eyes open with the regular chugga, chug, chum, and soporific sound of the wheels on the rails. The countryside rumbled by with green fields and animals in pasture but nothing more could excite them and they all slumbered peacefully lost in a world of dreams.

Mrs Gregory studied the children and their clothing. One group, she could see were not as healthy looking as Marion and Timmy and she felt her heart warm toward them all before she, too, closed her eyes and slept fitfully until the piercing hoot of the whistle announced their arrival in Neath Station.

11

CHAPTER TWO

Changes

Carrie bumped down the mountain track on her newly acquired bicycle. Her flame red hair glistened in the mellow sunlight as it fought to escape the constraints of her district nurse's hat. Vaseline or no Vaseline her hair never seemed to survive the trip down the hill from Hendre into Crynant and tangled out like Moses' burning bush. Her titfer was a navy felt round hat with a braided ribbon and badge, which Carrie had secured with one of her mother's oversized pearl hatpins.

She freewheeled down the stony track and whizzed out onto the road, her medical bag bouncing in the basket on the front. Today was to be relatively easy with a few simple calls in the morning, but this afternoon she was to collect the expected newly arrived evacuees assigned to their village and surrounding areas. For this she had to go to Neath. The newcomers would need a medical assessment and it would be Carrie's job to check on children fostered out to members of the community. But, first, she had to look in on old man Price. It was her first call to the man who had previously been attended to by the last District Nurse who had moved onto another area in Wales. Mr Price was an elderly widower who was suffering from an ulcerated leg and needed his dressing changed.

Carrie cycled along the main road waving at the few people she saw and recognised until she arrived at Pleasant View Cottage next door to the butcher and his wife, Gwyneth Hughes, who was a piano teacher and well loved by everyone in the village. She was the one that had taught, Jenny, her sister-in-law, to play so beautifully and had worked on her voice to help her sing like a nightingale.

Carrie braked sharply and stepped off her bike, walking it to Mr Price's front door. She picked up her medical bag, propped the cycle against the wall and knocked.

"Oo, oo! Mr Price? It's only me, District Nurse, Carrie Llewellyn."

A feeble voice called out, "Door's open, Nurse Llewellyn or may I call you Carrie?"

"Carrie is fine, Mr Price. Where are you?"

"I'm out back in the kitchen. Come in," he wheezed.

Carrie pushed open the door and walked along the dark dusty passage past the parlour to the kitchen. The house could do with a good clean thought Carrie, but she was there to help not criticise. She opened the squeaky door to the kitchen where old Mr Price sat in his fireside chair, his leg resting on a footstool. He was studying a newspaper, reading the print through a large magnifying glass.

"You'll ruin your eyes, reading through that," quipped Carrie.

"They're already ruined that's why I need it," said the old man.

"Why don't you get yourself a proper pair of specs?"

"Can't afford them, Carrie fach. Glasses are for rich folk not someone like me."

"I know Dr Rees gets some old glasses donated by patients. I'll have a rummage and see what I can find."

"Thanks, Nurse," said Mr Price gratefully.

"Now, down to business. How have you been? How's your leg?"

"Not good. It hurts to walk. Falling apart, I am."

Carrie smiled sweetly, "Let's take a look and I'll get that dressing changed." She opened her bag and looked around the sparsely furnished kitchen. Dishes filled the sink, and newspapers cluttered the floor. She studied the old man. It seemed to her that Mr Price had not changed his clothes in a while and it looked as if he had been sleeping in his chair. He smelled none too fresh. "First of all, I'll clear this lot," she said bravely, taking off her coat and rolling up her sleeves. She piled the crocs on the side and swilled the enamel washing up bowl out; it was covered in grease. Carrie covered her distaste with a smile and took the kettle from the range to dissolve the solidified fat. She hummed as she got to work on clearing the debris.

Mr Price began to cough. Carrie dried her hands and stooped down. He definitely smelled bad and unwashed. "So. Mr Price, when was it you last had a bath?"

The old man rubbed his rheumy eyes, "I can't remember…"

"Then, I'd better get the water on and run you one. You'll have to keep your leg out of course – can't get that wet."

The old man didn't protest and Carrie ran up the stairs to the bathroom, which Mr Price was lucky to have. It had an old copper geezer that heated the water. Carrie checked the colour of the flame on the pilot light, which looked healthy enough and as she turned the brass taps the heater exploded into life. Roaring blue flames went to work and hot water trickled out.

She opened the window ever so slightly and went into the main bedroom. It was obvious that no one had slept in there for many days or even weeks. She collected some clean fresh clothes and towels and took them into the bathroom and laid them out on the wicker chair that stood there before she ran back down stairs.

Mr Price had fallen asleep and his chest rattled with mucus. He dribbled and drooled over his grubby shirt and waistcoat. Carrie spoke brightly and cheerfully to the old man who snorted in his sleep waking himself. She began to unwrap the dressing and revealed the extent of his wound. It was not good. Carrie did her best. She cleaned up his leg with warm salted water and mild disinfectant, applying colloidal silver to the lesions before wrapping it up again. All the while she chattered animatedly to him. "I really think in time it would be good to leave your leg to the air for a while but I'll wrap it up for now. Next time I come I hope to have some of these new antibiotic drugs, which should kill the infection, but first let me check the bath and then I'll come and get you."

Carrie dashed back to the bathroom and stopped the bath. She checked the temperature of the water as she would for a baby and satisfied that it wouldn't burn or hurt him she ran back down to her patient. "There we are. Now you can have a lovely warm bath. Come on. I'll help you up."

Carrie struggled to manoeuvre the old man into a position

14

where he could stand. She pulled a kitchen chair out for him to lean on and was surprised to find how light he was. Carrie frowned in that engaging way she had and the old boy beamed at her as he struggled to bear his weight with a grunt and a groan.

"Mr Price, you should smile more often. Smile like a beacon, you have. It lights up the whole room no wonder your wife fell in love with you."

"Ah, Carrie, I miss her I do. She was my world."

"And I'm sure you were hers, too." She encouraged him to lean on her and they edged to the stairs, "One step at a time, let's count."

They mounted the stairs and, as with a little child, counted each step up to the landing. She took him into his bedroom and sat him on the bed, "Come, let me help you with those," and she began to help him undress.

She had a towel at the ready to cover his modesty but as the old boy removed his clothes she was horrified to see he was skin and bone, not only that, there were pressure sores on his bottom and Carrie could clearly see bruises on his arms and torso. She helped the old man up and to the bath. "Careful now. We mustn't get your leg wet."

It was a fine balancing act in getting his good leg into the water and easing him down allowing his injured leg to hang over the side. Carrie held onto his arm and passed him a flannel and soap to wash over his body as best he could. "There, there. We'll soon have you squeaking like newly born piglet, all pink and clean." Carrie continued to chatter, "And we'll have a look at those pressure sores on your bottom, ease the discomfort with some soothing ointment and a nice soft cushion. They must be really uncomfortable."

"Aye, they do sting a bit."

"So, Mr Price, when did you last eat anything?"

The old man thought a moment and shook his head, "I can't remember."

"Does anyone come by to help you?"

"My son used to do what he could but he's gone to war now. In the Navy, he is."

"Then who looks out for you?"

Mr Price hesitated, "My daughter-in-law does what she can but she's a busy woman."

"Looks like she can be a bit rough with you," commented Carrie.

"She does her best, got little ones to care for and having to look in on me doesn't help much," he said evasively.

Carrie pursed her lips; she knew cruelty when she saw it. "When we've got you clean and changed, we'll see what there is in the house to eat. See if I can rustle something up." Then she asked casually, "Who is your daughter-in-law, then?"

"Jacqueline Price, was James," he said.

"Oh, I know. Works in the drapers in the village."

"That's the one."

Carrie stored away the information and as gently as she could she helped the elderly gent to get clean. "I'll leave you to do your bits and pieces and then we'll get you out."

"Aye, better had, Nurse or I might give you a shock."

"Go on with you."

"Can't have you bragging to the village now, can I?"

"Bragging?"

"Aye. About what an impressive man I am," he joked.

Carrie was pleased to see he had a sense of humour in spite of everything, "I can't keep calling you Mr Price..."

"But that's my name," he teased; then noticing her arched eyebrow, he laughed, "It's Howard. Howie to my friends."

"Let's hope I come into that category then, Howie."

Howard Price was now spruced up and clean. Carrie's nose detected that he certainly smelled better. She bundled up his niffy clothes, which desperately needed washing and took them out to the scullery and outhouse. She piled them on the old table wondering how they could be dealt with when she had an idea, but first she needed to get some food inside him and hunted through his cupboards for something nourishing to feed him. There was very little there but she managed to find a tin of Spam, a tub of lard, some tinned peas and a few old wrinkly potatoes. Carrie set about peeling the spuds, removing the eyes and sprouting shoots and chopping them up. She popped the peas in a saucepan and melted a chunk of lard before tossing in the potatoes to fry with the spam. The kitchen began to fill with the aroma of hot food and Carrie dished up a plate for the old man, putting the remainder into the larder under a cloth.

"There you go," smiled Carrie. "This should warm you up… tell me, where is your ration book? I can't see it and you need some shopping. It's out of everything you are, no essentials…"

"Jacqueline took it," he said.

Carrie pursed her lips again. "Did she? Think I'll pay her a call and get some shopping for you."

Howie flinched and frowned, "Don't see her. She'll only shout."

"Not to me, she won't." Carrie could feel her famous temper rising. "Now eat that all up, there's a good boy."

"You sound like my mother," grinned Howie but he tucked in nevertheless and Carrie was gratified to wash up a clean plate. The old boy relaxed in his chair now more comfortable with a strategically placed cushion.

"Right, I'll be off but I will be back. I have a few things to do before I go to Neath to meet the evacuees. You rest. Would you like me to put the wireless on for you?"

"Aye, that would be splendid. Thank you. You're a good girl, Carrie Llewellyn much better than the last one. She frightened the life out of me."

Carrie laughed she had heard that her predecessor was a monster of a woman in size and manner. She switched on the old valve wireless and waited for it to warm up before sliding through the whistles, bleeps and burps of tuning until she found the BBC Home Service that was transmitting Jack Warner in Garrison Theatre. Howie Price sighed contentedly. "Thanks, Carrie, gal."

"I'll be off now."

"There's a spare key behind the pot on the mantelpiece, take it, just in case."

"Thanks, I will." Carrie picked up the key and made for the door with another idea forming in her mind. She closed the door firmly behind her and stepped out into the golden sunshine, which played on the ground like molten gold continually shifting and moving in patterns through the leaves on the trees.

She went next door and stepped inside onto the sawdust floor of the butcher shop and was greeted by the burly figure of the butcher Joe Hughes, "Good morning, Nurse Llewellyn. How can I help?"

"Um, is your wife in?"

"Yes, she's out back. Gwyneth!" he shouted.

Gwyneth limped in, she wore a built up shoe a result of contracting polio as a child but had a decidedly lovely face, big nut-brown eyes and a smile as wide as the viaduct. "Carrie, hello." She sounded surprised but pleased to see her.

"Sorry to bother you, it's old Mr Price next door. He's in a bad way. No food in the house and unable to get himself up to bed with his leg."

"I thought I hadn't seen him. I used to pop in once a day to make sure he was okay until his daughter-in-law stopped me. Didn't like strangers in the house, she said."

"Well, I'd take no notice of that. He's as scrawny as a liquorice stick and covered in bruises. I cooked him a meal but his ration book is missing. He needs someone to keep an eye on him."

Gwyneth Hughes hesitated, "I don't know, his daughter-in-law was pretty adamant about not wanting anyone in the house. Besides, there should be food. She uses it to shop here for his bits of meat. She was in this morning, I believe."

"As I suspected... Leave her to me. I'm off to see her now."

"Good luck with that one, she's a mouth like a hornets' nest, not to be trusted and carrying on with that man while her husband's at war." Gwyneth tutted in disapproval.

"I'll leave the key with you. I can fetch it when I need it and you can let yourself in."

"I don't mind making him a bit of supper. I always have something left over. Pity to waste it."

"It's nourishment he needs and help to rise and to go to bed. I'll be popping in regularly till his leg's better. I would like you to be my eyes when I'm not here."

Gwyneth nodded, "Of course. I like the man, got a wealth of stories tucked under his jersey. He can be very entertaining, but I don't want to cross that woman."

"You won't. It'll be on my head," smiled Carrie. "Thank you… he also has some clothes that could do with a wash."

Gwyneth nodded, "I'll see to that."

"They're balled up on the table in the scullery." Carrie smiled a goodbye and went to collect her bike. She hopped on her cycle and pedalled to the draper shop and dismounted. Leticia Parish was coming out placing a small brown paper bag into her basket. She nodded politely at Carrie who took a deep breath and holding her head high in her signature style, reminiscent of her mother, she entered. The lively shop bell clamoured in her wake and Carrie stepped boldly to the counter where Jacqueline Price was winding some braid back onto its reel. She looked up and saw Carrie and pasted a smile on her face.

"Good morning, how can I help?" her tone was ingratiating.

"You are Jacqueline Price?"

"I am."

"I've come about your father-in-law, Howard Price," said Carrie curtly.

"What's he done now?" she asked rolling her eyes.

"I need his ration book. There's no food in the house and I want to get his shopping."

Jacqueline Price paled, "I haven't got it. He must have lost it," she said tartly.

"No, not lost. I have it under good authority that you have it. You used it at the butchers to buy his meat."

The woman coloured up, "I do sometimes but not recently."

"Really? I hear you were there this morning and yet there is nothing in his larder." Carrie held the woman's eyes in a steely glare.

"Oh yes, I remember now. I did."

"Then you won't mind me taking his ration book and shopping." Carrie held out her hand.

Jacqueline Price stooped down behind the counter and lifted her handbag to the counter. She searched through it, "I must have misplaced it."

Carrie persisted, "Look again."

The draper's assistant sighed in annoyance and rummaged through it again, "No, definitely not here."

Carrie put her hand on the open bag. "Let me."

"How dare you?"

"Oh, I dare," and she peered through the contents and lifted out a book, "Well, well. Here it is. It must have escaped your attention." Carrie looked through it, "Ah, here we are. I see, you have his butter, dried eggs, bacon and tea. I'll take them for him."

"You don't understand," began the woman.

"Oh, I understand all right. You just thought you'd take his rations for yourself."

"He said I could have them. For the children."

"I don't think so. Someone else will be looking after Howard, now. I suggest you stay away. I will be watching."

Suddenly, Jacqueline Price flipped. "You know nothing about it. Dirty old man, can't even keep himself clean."

"Because he can't walk…"

The owner of the draper store came from the back of the shop, "Is everything all right here? Oh… Hello, Miss Llewellyn."

"Mr Bevan," Carrie nodded curtly and turned back to Mrs Price. "I don't want to see any more bruises on him, do you understand?"

Jacqueline became quiet and nodded. Carrie continued to glare at Jacqueline until the woman was forced to look away. She picked up her shopping from under the counter and passed it across to Carrie. It was only then that Carrie turned away and with her head held aloft she marched out of the shop.

Carrie picked up her bike and cycled back to the butchers. She handed over Mr Price's shopping and his ration book. "I think you should look after this, Gwyneth. You are far more trustworthy than his daughter-in-law. I'm sure she's been snaffling the old man's rations as well as her own."

"Don't worry, Cariad. I'll do what I can."

"I know you will," smiled Carrie and she set off for the station.

Hendre Farm nestled against the mountainside of the lush

green Dulais Valley. The yard was glowing in the sun's rays, which streamed its honeyed ribbons on the out buildings and grain silo. Jenny, John's wife, and a beautiful soprano, sang lustily as she squinted up at the dazzling sun. She cast her eyes down as she went to feed the chickens and collect the eggs. Bethan toddled cheerily after her mother. Jenny had a lovely dimpled smile that radiated happiness, which could rival the beaming grin of the sun. She chuckled as Bonnie, the farm's black and white border collie, ran past her sending the little one onto her bottom. Bonnie immediately danced around the child, licking her in a frenzy, as if to ensure she was okay. Bethan leaned onto the collie and clung to her fur to haul herself up and she waddled off again quite happily whilst Bonnie chased the chickens sending them scuttling and clucking in the yard.

Jenny collected the eggs in her basket and made her way back to the house as Laura one of the Land Girls emerged from Old Tom's cottage complaining, "I can't believe I've overslept! If my alarm clock doesn't wake me then your rooster most certainly does."

"Aye, Korky's got a crow like a rusty nail on metal. Come to think of it. I haven't seen him this morning. I hope nothing's happened to him."

"What could happen to him here?"

"Well, Korky refuses to roost in the henhouse preferring to perch in a tree. We've had a few chickens go missing recently courtesy of Mr Fox. John caught him sneaking into the henhouse last week. He managed to frighten old Reynard off. But I thought he'd repaired the hole in the wire. Anyway, never mind all that why are you in such a rush?"

"We've got two new Land Girls arriving later. One's to go to Michael Lawrence and the other to us. I'm supposed to be meeting them at the station with Ernie. He hasn't gone has he?"

"Not as far as I know, but then you can never tell with Ernie," and so saying Ernie came out from the barn his beret askew and whiskers sprouting.

"Iechy dwriaeth, I missed my wake up call this morning. Korky usually rouses me and what with been up half the night with Gladys and her piglets, making sure she didn't squash none, I slept like the dead."

Jenny wrinkled her nose, "Duw, you niff worse than the slurry. It's clean clothes and a good wash you'll be needing or the Land Girls will think we're tramps."

"Aye, you're right. Don't want to put them off. I'll get cleaned up." He turned to Laura, "Can you be set to go in an hour?"

"I can. And at least that gives me time to get some breakfast. I'm ravenous. Will you give me a shout, Ernie? And if John wants me for anything at all tell him to knock."

Jenny laughed and nodded her head sending her wild curls, so like Carrie's, flying. "That I will. Here, Laura have yourself a couple of fresh eggs, the hens have laid well."

Laura dipped her hand in the basket, "Mm, still warm. You can't get fresher than that," and she returned to the cottage.

Jenny continued back to the farmhouse still singing a pretty ditty, she rinsed off the eggs and put them in a bowl laced with straw before picking up the trug and calling to Bethan, "Come on, my lovely, it's mushrooms we must be picking now. Come and help mammy. No picking toadstools now or anything else."

Bethan obligingly giggled and tottered after her mother and Bonnie. They crossed the yard and walked to the gate by the meadow. She lifted her daughter over and picked up her skirts and climbed into the field, where Bonnie's mother, Trixie, and Carrie had often romped together. Bonnie scrambled under the gate and ran on ahead enjoying the wind in her fur. The breeze was sufficient to move the grass in waves like flowing water and Jenny headed for a crop of trees close to the hedge where the mushrooms grew.

As they walked on, Bethan caught her mother's hand and they skipped together in the grass still wet with dew. The drops glittered like small jewels in the increasing sunshine and Jenny's heart was filled with love.

"Oh, no!" Jenny stopped abruptly as she came across a mess of tawny feathers that littered the ground. "Korky!" Her worst fears were realised, their strutting cockerel that was filled with personality plus had indeed been 'got'. "Oh, dear!

At least we know what happened. Now, we must get another, if we are to have new chickens, and not get one that refuses to roost in the henhouse."

Jenny sighed sadly and moved onto the trees where mushrooms stood proud like chalk white stones embedded in the earth. She began to gather some and sang a plaintive sad song in respect of the rooster's death.

Bethan scrambled onto the lower branches of one of the trees, "You be careful now. I don't want you falling and hurting yourself," Jenny said. But Bethan continued to clamber up the trunk of the old apple tree with its many leafy spreading branches.

Jenny shook her head, "No further, please. You wait while I gather the mushrooms."

"But, Mammy, I want to help."

"Then you better get down."

"I can't."

Jenny sighed and set her basket on the ground. She held her arms out to Bethan who managed to crawl down a little lower before launching off a lower branch and into Jenny's arms almost sending her flying. Bethan chuckled delightedly and even Jenny giggled. The two of them set to picking some large open capped mushrooms and Jenny sang again this time more lustily as Bethan attempted to join in her favourite nursery rhymes.

Mushrooms gathered, hand in hand, mother and daughter danced out of the meadow full of love and happiness.

CHAPTER THREE

The Collection

Carrie was settled in the old Bethania Chapel Hall in Neath. At the back was a large desk that would be the focal point for anyone in the room. It stood out as a base from which to take charge. She had stowed her bicycle in the corner, laid out seats around the room and opened up the very small side room where medical examinations could take place. She placed her nurse's bag and all her accoutrements in there.

Christine Figgis, a wholesome plump midwife, with short mousey hair, had stopped by to help, as this was the first group of children to be sent to this area. Other groups had been routed to Monmouth, Newport and Tenby. Carrie had been around the villages of Crynant, Tonna, Cilfrew, Seven Sisters, Resolven and Ystradgynlais knocking on doors with the ministers of the parishes to try and find homes where the youngsters could stay. Christine had been more than helpful in putting forward her own list of those who may be prepared to give the evacuees a welcome. It was very different from some parishes, where the children had arrived with no guaranteed placement and then they had been carted around the streets whilst nurses and the clergy had invaded houses trying to find someone to take them on the spot.

It had been the result of discussion with Dr Rees and they both thought the sensible way to go was to arrange their accommodation before hand, if at all possible. Carrie just hoped that everyone she and Christine had on the list would be prepared to keep his or her word.

The hall with its dusty wooden floorboards was somewhat cold and forbidding and Carrie yanked at the drapes to allow more light and warmth into the barren church hall. The sun managed to probe its honeyed fingers in through the thick grimy glass. Dust motes floated in the air like dandelion parachutes and the old creaking floor was mottled with golden pears of sunshine.

Carrie forced her hat on her head for the umpteenth time and re-pinned it, "I hope the foster carers all turn up. It'll be a tragedy if not all the children are taken. What time are they arriving?"

Christine beamed, "Should be any moment now if the train's punctual. We'll have time to check them off and make sure they are all well and up to date with vaccinations before the families arrive to select them."

"We must try and keep brothers and sisters together."

"Although, it may not always be possible," advised Christine with a wry smile.

"Then if that happens we must ensure they at least are billeted in the same village. Agreed?"

"Agreed. Now, let's open the door make it look a little more welcoming. In fact, I can hear footsteps outside, now."

Christine marched briskly to the big oak door and opened it wide and a flood of children streamed inside. They looked around the room in awe as their chaperone instructed them. "All of you find a chair and sit down. If there aren't enough chairs then sit on the floor. Children from one family sit together and leave a gap until the next one so we can clearly see who belongs to who."

The children scattered suddenly finding their voices and squealed with excitement. Timmy Noble whooped and pounced on Carrie's bike and tried to clamber on but it clattered to the floor where he insisted on ringing the bell in a flurry of excitement. His sister, Marion, caught hold of him by the scruff of his neck and dragged him away, apologising profusely, at which point Gerry took his turn in ringing the bell. Carrie marched professionally to the bike and removed the child's hand from the handlebars and bell, and wheeled it behind the desk at the back of the room and propped it up again.

Carrie faced the assembled company, "Welcome. I am District Nurse Carrie Llewellyn and I will be here to see you settle in. This is Midwife, Christine Figgis who will be helping me."

"Ha! Figgis! Sounds like a Christmas pudding," chortled Gerry. "Looks like it, too!" He stared about him for confirmation and a number of the other children sniggered.

Christine smiled coolly at the child, "Ah yes, figgy pudding, as if I haven't heard that one before. But I tell you I am not as sweet and I will not put up with rudeness or nonsense. Is that clear?"

"As mud," screeched Gerry holding his sides with laughter.

His sister, Naomi tried to shut him up but he continued to make faces and stick his tongue out at Christine.

Carrie opened her bag and removed a pair of surgical scissors, "Looks like your tongue is too big for your mouth. It could do with a little trimming," and she snapped them together rapidly in succession and slowly approached the child who clamped his hand over his mouth and scuttled behind his sister.

The room became subdued and the evacuees stared wide-eyed at Carrie, who winked at Gerry's sister, Naomi, who in turn tried to hide a smile of understanding. The room became hushed.

The chaperone passed over his clipboard with the names of all the children and their home addresses and bade his charges goodbye retreating, it seemed, almost gratefully and he ventured back toward the road and station.

Carrie checked off all the children's names, dates of births and other necessary data and then one by one they were to be assessed in the small room. Carrie left the group in the capable hands of Christine Figgis, who gathered them around the desk and sat them on the floor. There were a few dissenters complaining of the dust but most sat down eagerly to listen to the story that Christine had promised them.

Carrie took up residence in the small room. Each child was filled with trepidation after the scissor incident and hardly dared to speak as they entered to be given the once over. Hair was inspected first!

Time marched on. The children were now getting hungry and thirsty; the lucky ones, like Marion and Timmy, had been provided with something by their mothers, but many had just been packed up and packed off without any sustenance at all.

People had been trickling in and out of the hall all afternoon, selecting children and taking them to their new homes. It seemed most were prepared to accept one child but not two or more and, as suspected, not everyone had turned up. Messages had been received saying that some volunteers had changed their mind.

Carrie was dubious about some of the volunteer carers but had no choice in the matter as they had all passed the cursory vetting, which Carrie assumed was not as stringent as it should have been. Now there were just six children left, the Nobles and the Clarkes. Most prospective foster parents had been put off by Timmy's boisterous behaviour and Gerry's cheekiness.

Carrie whispered to Christine, "If we're not careful we'll be taking some home with us!"

"No, thanks. I have enough problems with my own lot without taking on anymore. What about you?"

"I don't think so," said Carrie.

Just then there was a tap, tap of a stick. A lengthy shadow loomed through the door. Carrie and Christine both turned around to see an elderly lady dressed all in black. Timmy Noble jumped up from his seat and ran to her. "Mrs Gregory!"

"Can I help you?" asked Carrie surprised to see the old lady in the hall and a small flush of guilt coloured her face as she remembered a past scrape involving the old woman.

"I hope so, I'd like to take this child."

"And you are?"

"As Timmy said, I am Mrs Gregory; Mrs Phyllis Gregory."

Carrie ran through the names of would be foster parents, "I'm sorry... I can't see your name on the list..."

"Oh, it's not. But I have a large house and plenty of room. I could do with the company and I already know the children."

"I'm sorry," said Carrie apologetically. "The children can't be separated. They are brother and sister."

"And I'll happily take them both, Timmy and Marion."

The two children's faces lit up and Marion jumped up, joined her brother with the woman and they snuggled into her.

"Please, Nurse Carrie. We'll both be good, I promise," asserted Marion.

"That's not the point…" Carrie began.

"I am of good character, you can check my background and I am more than capable of looking after them."

Christine interrupted, "Carrie, there's only two more people due and we have six children…"

Carrie could understand what Christine was saying. She hesitated and then made a decision, "Mrs Gregory, do you mind if I go over a few things with you? In here…" Carrie indicated the small room.

"Of course, I wouldn't expect any less." The old lady tip tapped into the room and sat down. Carrie entered and closed the door firmly.

Carrie remembered the old lady from her childhood and she seemed to look exactly the same as she had when Carrie was just eight years old. She flushed with embarrassment again as she remembered the uncharitable acts she and her friends had performed against Mrs Gregory in their ignorance. But she pushed those memories away and began to ask sensible questions about welfare and what the children could expect with their care.

About ten minutes later the door opened and Carrie shook hands with Mrs Gregory and beckoned to Timmy and Marion. "Right, now, collect your cases and go with Mrs Gregory. You are to be going to Crynant. That's my neck of the woods and I will be checking up on you."

"You won't bring your scissors, will you?" asked Timmy fearfully.

"That depends," said Carrie with another wink. "Off you go! And be good."

The children skipped off happily and Timmy slipped his hand into Mrs Gregory's.

"Hope I'm doing the right thing," sighed Carrie.

"I'm sure you are," assured Christine. "They look happy enough." She looked at her watch, "The others are late aren't they?"

"I think some had to wait until they'd finished work. Who's left on the list?"

Christine picked up the clipboard and scanned the remaining names. "There's a Mrs Price from Crynant."

"Mrs Price?" Carrie's eyes narrowed, "Which one? Where does she live?"

"Uh…"

"I'll answer that," said the draper's assistant that Carrie had crossed swords with earlier. "Jacqueline Price. Twenty-two Neath Road." Her voice was surly and challenging. "I offered a place to a child out of the goodness of my heart. I have children myself. They'll be company for each other."

Carrie tried to bury her rising misgivings about the woman. "The children left are an entire family."

"Hence the reason they're still here," came the reply. "I'll take her." She pointed at Naomi who sensed an undercurrent of something unpleasant in the air. She lowered her eyes.

Carrie looked at Christine who shrugged, "It's your choice."

Carrie did something she never did; she dithered as she tried to make up her mind. There were four children and it was unlikely anyone would take all four. She was relieved when two more people entered the church rooms. Fortunately, they, too, were from Crynant. Mrs Powell, a young woman in her thirties whose husband was down the mines and Mrs Griffiths, a reasonably well to do woman who lived at the top of The Crescent.

The children looked at their prospective foster parents, Gerry grinned toothily at Mrs Griffiths who smiled back tentatively.

Carrie addressed them, "At least you're all from Crynant, but is there anyone able to take all four. They're from the same family." The women shook their heads. "Then, I'm sorry but I'll have to split you up. But only then on the proviso that they will be able to meet." Carrie searched each woman's face in turn.

The women seemed to agree and Mrs Powell, said, "I can take the twins. They are twins, aren't they?"

Carrie nodded, "Then, can you speak to Christine to complete the rest of the paperwork?" Mrs Powell smiled and approached Christine.

That left Gerry and Naomi. "Very well, Mrs Price, if you would take Naomi and Mrs Griffith, Gerry."

"Oh, I never expected a boy... but then, hmm... okay. Let's give it a try."

Naomi turned to her little brother. "You be good, Gerry. Don't give the lady no trouble. Understand?"

Gerry nodded and took Mrs Griffiths' hand. He beamed up at her and grinned again.

Naomi spoke again, "He's a good boy at heart. He can be a bit of a so and so at times but he means well. He doesn't ever do anything nasty or hurtful just a lad being a lad."

Mrs Griffiths nodded and went to Christine to complete the paperwork, which left Carrie and Jacqueline Price staring at each other. "I shall be checking on Naomi as I will all the children," she said sternly.

"Of course."

"Very well. Christine will take the details." Carrie turned to the children, "Your parents will be notified of your address and you'll be expected to write to them and tell them how you are getting on."

The children nodded solemnly but none of them smiled except for Gerry who seemed to be quite taken with Mrs Griffiths.

They left the hall to get the train back to Crynant. Carrie collected her bike and the signed forms from Christine, put them in the basket and moved to the door. Christine called out cheerfully, "Well that went better than I thought. Last time I did this it was a nightmare. Let's hope it bodes well for the children."

"Let's hope," agreed Carrie not seeming convinced. They left the hall and Carrie locked up.

"I'll take the keys back, if you like," offered Christine. "It's on my way home."

"Thanks." Carrie handed her the keys and pedalled off toward the station, not certain why she felt so unsettled.

She looked up at the innocent baby blue sky, now with no sign of any clouds and wondered whether any long overdue rain would fall.

CHAPTER FOUR

Working it out

Carrie sat at home around the kitchen table with the family detailing the events of her day's work, "I could have smacked the woman right across the chops," she said vehemently.

"Good job you weren't at the fishmongers then," chortled Ernie.

"Why?"

"Knowing you, you'd have picked up a piece of cod and sloshed it across her face," said Ernie with a wink.

"Go on with you, although I must say that would have been extremely satisfying, don't you think?"

"Aye. But you don't want to go losing your job, now do you?" said John, her brother, pushing his unruly quiff of hair back from his brow. "You must learn to curb that temper of yours. I've suffered under it many times."

"Oh yes? When?"

"Do you want me to count?" laughed John.

"Now, now," said Jenny, wisely. "Let's eat up or it will be cold and there's nothing worse than cold food."

There was a moment's silence while the family tucked into their cottage pie. Ernie was the first to speak, "Seems to me, you need to keep an eye on the children, a close eye. Oh, some of them will be fine but some may not," he said cryptically.

"Oh, Ernie, don't be so mysterious. What do you know? Tell me?" pleaded Carrie.

"Nothing yet. It's just a feeling."

"And we all know what that means," said Jenny. "It's a pity, if we had more room, I'd have taken one of them in."

"Yes, you could do with some help with Bethan and it sounds like they could do with some love and security. It must be hard being ripped from home and dumped with strangers," said John.

"Maybe, we could sort the loft out. Make it into another bedroom?" mused Jenny.

"That was going to be a playroom for Bethan, for when she's older," said John.

"Well, perhaps the war will be finished with by then and so if we do it now then the work will have been done... It's a thought," said Jenny.

"Hmm," muttered Ernie. "You be careful with ladders, doing that. Don't want you breaking your leg pottering about up there, or coming through the ceiling."

"Are you trying to tell me something?" asked John.

"No, just saying be careful that's all. Duw, Duw why is it everything I say has to have a hidden meaning?" complained Ernie.

"Because it does," smiled Carrie. "Changing the subject, what are the new Land Girls like, John?"

"Jawch! I don't know. Ask Ernie. He went with Laura to meet them at the station. I ought to pop across and see them. I'm sure Laura will have it all in hand, though," said John. "What do you say, Ernie?"

Ernie tapped his nose, "I'm saying nothing. You can make up your own minds."

"Isn't one of them going to Michael?" asked Carrie.

"Yes, one here to replace Daisy and one at Gelli Galed," confirmed John.

"Oh my gosh! Michael! I promised I'd go up to see him when I got back."

"Then you'd better shape it, girl."

"Aye, and don't go getting green eyed," said Ernie.

Carrie finished her mouthful of food and sucked the fork, "But, I've got green eyes ... Now, what's that supposed to mean? Speaking in riddles again."

"Nothing, nothing at all, Cariad."

"Do you know, you can be an infuriating old curmudgeon at times?"

"So you've said."

Carrie scraped her chair back, "No time to change. I'll have to go in uniform. Where's Bonnie?"

"Out by the water butt, she was," said John.

Carrie raced out of the kitchen, her spangled curls flying as she tried to shove them under her hat. "See you later!" she called.

John laughed, "Esgyrn Dafydd, she'll never change."

"Nor would you want her to," added Ernie as he helped himself to another portion of cottage pie.

Carrie stepped out into the fresh air and beamed as the sun bathed her face in golden warmth. She called to Bonnie, who upon seeing Carrie rose, stretched and padded toward her. "Come on, Bonnie. Let's go."

The black and white Border collie bounded after her before running ahead on the stone track. Every so often she would stop and run back to Carrie before lolloping off again.

It wasn't long before Carrie's energetic brisk walk had slowed to a dawdle on the steep trail. A few cotton wool clouds tumbled across the sky and the face of the sun, and for a moment Carrie felt a chill run through her as if the bones of the dead had stopped to dance with her. She dismissed the feeling and clambered gaily on, wishing she had changed as her uniform now felt sticky and hot.

She sighed with relief as the farmhouse known as Gelli Galed, Hard Living, came into view. Boots, Michael's small terrier, came hurtling towards her whimpering in ecstatic delight at seeing her. He danced around her until she stooped and fussed the little dog that began a game of chase with Bonnie up and down the track. By this time, Carrie was puffing and turning quite pink. "There's glad I don't have to do that climb every day, at least not yet," she murmured as she pushed open the small gate, which led to the path of the house.

Carrie found the energy to run up the steps of the veranda and was about to knock, when the door opened and a smartly dressed willowy brunette with a wasp waist and ample cleavage emerged followed by Michael.

Carrie stopped and looked at the young woman in surprise and then back at Michael.

"Ah, Carrie. This is Sarah, the new Land Girl. She has a first class honours degree in Science but more recently has been involved in fashion."

"How do you do?" said Sarah who had a husky voice like roasted whiskey.

"W… Well…" stuttered Carrie. "And you?"

"I'm just dandy, thank you," she purred seductively, and fiddled with her beautifully manicured fingernails sporting scarlet nail polish.

"Good… er well, that's all right, then," said Carrie for want of something else to say.

Behind Sarah, stepped Sam Jefferies, Michael's farm manager, who tipped his hat to her, "Miss Llewellyn. Come this way, Sarah and I'll explain the layout of the farm." Sam steered the young woman down the steps. Her legs appeared to go up to her armpits and she swayed as she walked with a wiggle like a fashion model. Carrie stopped and stared after her so rapt in what she was seeing that she didn't hear the next thing Michael said to her. She then, felt his hand on her jaw closing her mouth that had dropped open in wonder.

"Sorry, what did you say?" said Carrie finally coming to.

"I said that the new Land Girl is a surprise to us all."

"I should say so. Did you see her hands? Can't see her lambing sheep. She looks as if she belongs on the front cover of Vogue." Carrie's jaw dropped again as she watched the girl sashay across the yard to the barn.

Michael once more closed her mouth and planted a kiss on her lips so ready to pout. She broke off breathlessly and he twirled her around, "Love the uniform. Very smart. Did I tell you I fell for a girl in uniform, when I saw her in Aberystwyth?"

Carrie turned back to see the young woman disappear inside the barn as Michael continued, "It was just a pity she had buck teeth, crazy hair and no sense at all…"

Carrie said nothing but then realising something was expected of her said, "Mmm." Suddenly, Michael's words rose from her subconscious and she connected with what was said. She turned, "What did you say?"

"I thought you weren't listening. Come inside and let's talk it seems an age since I saw you."

"Michael, it was yesterday," said Carrie following him inside and tripping over the threshold as she turned to look back once more.

He caught her before she fell and helped her inside, "We don't want you twisting your ankle again. It is not a good idea. What has got into you?"

Carrie pulled off her hat releasing her cloud of curls, "Nothing, nothing at all," she said in a voice that contradicted her true feelings.

Michael pulled the kettle off the range trying not to laugh, "Really? Sure it hasn't got something to do with young Sarah?"

"Of course not," blustered Carrie. "Why would it?"

"Well…" mused Michael.

"Just because, she's beautiful, willowy, with legs that go on forever and a voice that would melt honey."

"Can't say I'd noticed," quipped Michael.

Carrie turned and looked at him giving him *that* look. "Do you think I'm twp?"

"No."

"Or a goody-oo?" She turned away.

"No!" protested Michael trying not to laugh. He poured hot water into the teapot and swilled it around. The silence between them was clamouring. Michael put down the kettle and pot, walked across to her, spun her around and kissed her on the tip of her freckled nose before crushing her into her arms. "You are the most delightful, adorable, infuriating, obstinate, fascinating woman I have ever met," and he kissed her again.

Carrie blushed till her face matched her hair and for once she was speechless.

"And now, Miss Llewellyn, let's be civilised about this, share a cup of tea and talk about our future wedding."

*

Naomi stared about her new 'home'. Still in her coat and hat she stood stiffly in the unfamiliar surroundings clutching her battered case. Jacqueline turned and attempted a brittle smile, "The children will be in soon. I'll expect you to help me with them. You should be used to that. They've been with their grandmother. Relatives help me out when I work. You'll be able to that now, once you're settled." Jacqueline put away her few bits of shopping. Naomi stood there watching.

Jacqueline whirled around. "Well, don't just stand there. You'll need to learn where everything goes. Then when you've done that there's some washing up to be done. Hm… Better show you where you're sleeping, I suppose. We are upstairs. You are down here."

Jacqueline opened a cupboard door and steps led down into a basement. She switched on a torch, which partially illuminated the rickety stairs. "Bring your case," ordered Jacqueline.

Naomi stood on the top of the stairs and tentatively looked down. She hesitated to speak but finally found her voice, "They told us we would be staying in a proper family home and …"

"And so you are. This is a family home. Hurry up!" she snapped.

Naomi slowly descended the stairs into the murky gloom. Jacqueline took an iron key from her pocket and unlocked the cellar door and flashed the light around the space. There were no windows and water dripped down the bricks in the corner. There was a makeshift canvas camp bed against one wall with a sleeping bag thrown over the top of it, an orange box stood at the side with a candle and holder, and matches.

"There are more candles in the box. You can put your clothes over there." Jacqueline indicated another wooden box. She studied Naomi's shadowed face, "Don't look so glum. You'll only be sleeping here. The rest of the time you'll be in the house with us. It's not so bad, you'll see. And it's only temporary."

Naomi stared at her in disbelief. "But…"

"Oh, you dare to argue? You ungrateful child. That's not very nice, is it? Here's me welcoming you in and all you can do is complain. Unpack your things, quickly now and then come into the kitchen and do the washing up while I prepare tea." Jacqueline Price flounced off, back up the stairs.

Naomi stood in this barren dungeon and blinked back a tear, "Oh, mum, I don't like it here. I'd rather be home, chores or no chores," she whispered aloud. "I hope the others have fared better than me."

*

Marion and Timmy Noble gaped in wonder at their surroundings. Mrs Gregory lived in what they would describe as a palace. It was an enormous house. It had a fine entrance and gardens front and back. There was a beautifully polished tiled passageway through the porch and into the entrance hall. There was a lounge, a dining room, a drawing room and breakfast room not to mention the kitchen, utility room and scullery plus a magnificent conservatory filled with all manner of exotic plants and a grand stairway such as the children had never seen before with a long curved banister. It resembled something of a film set such as where great musicals were filmed. Mrs Gregory had a butler, a maid and a cook. Marion couldn't understand then why she had travelled third class on the train and said so.

Mrs Gregory explained, "There is no point in wasting money. Third class is just as good as any other and I can use the money for other things, you see."

"But, you said you couldn't afford another class," said Marion.

"Did I? I suppose I did, but then it's not good to advertise the fact otherwise people take advantage, so they do. I've had that happen before. I have learned to be wary. But your act of kindness touched me. You shared a seat when you had no need to."

"Yes, we did. We couldn't leave you to stand all that way. Our mum would have given us a right telling off if we'd sat and done nothing."

"Then your mother must be a very good woman, I would think."

"She is," smiled Marion.

"Now, you must settle in properly, so you must."

Mrs Gregory rang a bell and her butler came and bowed, "Yes, Milady?"

"Basil, take the children to their rooms and let them unpack. Show them the playroom."

"Playroom?" yelled Timmy.

"Yes, out of bounds to grown ups, where you can play and imagine to your hearts' content." Timmy whooped in delight, "That is a most unfortunate habit, but I am getting used to it," she smiled. "Be ready and washed for dinner in time. Be in the dining room at six o'clock prompt."

The children followed Basil up the stairs and Timmy fell back on his favourite expletive of "Cor!" He then whispered, "I thought dinner time was midday…"

Basil overheard and explained, "Midday is considered to be lunch, four o'clock is afternoon tea and dinner can be served anytime between six and eight."

"Cor, eight o'clock's my bedtime, ain't it?"

"And I'm sure Madame will adhere to that," said Basil.

"You don't talk funny do you? You speak posh," noted Timmy.

"Timothy," warned Marion as they continued up the stairs to the first floor.

Basil opened a door to a fairy tale room with a huge bed and indicated to Marion, "This is your room, Miss Marion."

"Cor!" said Timothy. "It's bigger than the whole downstairs of our house!"

Naomi stepped inside and her face broke into smiles. Basil put down her case, "Would you like to see your brother's room?"

"Yes, please," beamed Marion.

Basil walked down the landing and indicated another room, "This is Mrs Gregory's room and this is for young Timmy," said Basil and opened the door.

It was a room of equal size to Marion's and Timmy twirled around gazing up at the high ceiling, "Cor!"

"Along here is the playroom," he led them to an oak panelled room filled with an assortment of toys, including a rocking horse, a type of two seated rocker, a dolls house, a ride on engine, china dolls, teddies, cars, a bookcase full of books and all sorts of other items. The children were wide-eyed and stunned into silence. Timmy ran to an adjoining door and tried to open it. It was locked.

"What's in there?" he asked.

"Nothing to concern you and if I may advise you, don't try and gain access to it. It is locked for a purpose and must stay that way."

"Why?" asked Marion.

"I expect Mrs Gregory will tell you in her own time, but for now just pretend that it doesn't exist," said Basil. "Now, unpack and remember to be downstairs promptly at six o'clock."

"Yes, Basil," affirmed Marion. "Come on, Tim. Let's get cracking."

*

Gerry and Mrs Griffiths were sitting around the kitchen table. Gerry had a glass of milk and a slice of home made cake. Mrs Griffiths took pleasure in watching him devour the slice and lick his fingers, "That was lovely. Can I have some more?"

Mrs Griffiths tutted, "That's enough for now and we like to use the words, please and thank you in this house. Do you see?"

Gerry nodded, "This is a big house, bigger than ours at home. Can I go and play?"

"First of all we'll go to your room and take your things up. Come on, I'll help you unpack," said Mrs Griffiths kindly. "This way."

Gerry followed Mrs Griffiths up the wide staircase and she showed him to a room with a neatly made up bed. Gerry's eyes opened in wonder. "Is the bed all for me?"

"Why, yes. Now, let's put your things away."

Gerry hooted with delight and ran to the bed letting himself flop onto it with a sigh of delight. "Never had a bed to myself, or a room. You must be rich!"

"Not really," smiled Mrs Griffiths. "But, my husband is away…"

"In the war, like our dad?"

"Yes."

Gerry wandered to the enamel washbasin in the room and ran his hand over it, "It's even got a bosh!"

"A what?"

"Bosh, sink"

"Oh yes, all the bedrooms have."

"Where are your kids?"

Mrs Griffiths sighed, sadly, "Alyn died. Diphtheria over a year ago now."

"Dip…? What's that? Is it catching?"

"It's a horrible disease," her eyes clouded over. "We thought it was just a bad cold or nasty case of flu…"

"Did you only have one?"

"No, no, " Mrs Griffiths sniffed. "Lizzie my eldest is in Cardiff. She comes home from time to time. She's teaching in a school there."

"Oh, a brain-box."

"You could say," smiled Mrs Griffiths. "And Angela… well, I'm not sure where Angela is now." She didn't say anymore.

Gerry sat up curiously as Mrs Griffiths opened his scruffy case. She took out the worn, faded and patched clothes that had seen better days. "Is this all you have?"

"If that's what's in there, then that's what it is. Mum usually gets my clothes from the jumble. The girls are luckier they have hand me downs." Gerry was totally unfazed and spoke honestly, which moved Mrs Griffiths. She placed the items in the drawers and wardrobe. The few shabby garments looked forlorn in their places and most drawers in the Tallboy were empty.

Mrs Griffiths made a decision, "Wait here."

Gerry sat on the bed and bounced up and down, before leaping up and dashing to the window to look out. There was an enormous garden, with trees, shrubs and flowers, a greenhouse and a garden shed. He couldn't believe that there was this much free space. It looked inviting as the sun played through the trees creating ripples of light on the grass. He turned back with a yell and dived onto the bed just as Mrs Griffiths returned carrying a washing basket filled with clothes and a few coats slung over her arm.

"Here, these aren't doing much good where they are, you may as well have them. I'm sure they'll fit."

Mrs Griffiths filled one drawer with vests, pants and socks. Into another went an assortment of woollies. The coats and jackets were hung up along with, trousers and shirts. Gerry looked on in amazement, "Them for me? Some of them look brand new. Ain't never had nothing new before."

"They were Alyn's. Now, they're yours."

"Really?" Gerry was thrilled, "Ta! I mean, thank you."

Mrs Griffiths smiled, "Tea is at four, make sure you wash up before you come down."

"Can I go outside and play?"

"Well... er... yes!"

"Whooo!" Gerry bounced around the room in glee. "What time's four o'clock?"

"Can't you tell the time?"

Gerry looked down somewhat shamefaced, "I never learned..." he added softly, "Can't read, neither."

"Well, now, Gerry Clarke. We'll have to fix that now, won't we?"

"What do I call you?"

"Why don't you call me Aunty Madge? It's a bit less formal. And here," she took a child's watch from her pocket and strapped it on his wrist. You have to wind it up every day and look at the hands, you can read numbers can't you?"

"I can count to fifty," he said proudly.

"Very well, now look at the clock face. When the big hand is on the twelve and the little hand is on the four that's when it's four o'clock.

"Okay." Gerry studied it. "So do all the o'clocks work like that?"

"Yes," said Mrs Griffiths pleased. She talked him around the dial. "Now remember to wash and brush up before tea, so you need to come in when the big hand is here, and the little hand there; that will give you time to get cleaned up."

"Hmm! Think I've got it. Can I go now?"

"Of course."

Gerry cheered and raced out of the room, he jumped on the banisters and slid down to the bottom and fled into the garden. Madge Griffiths sighed wondering if she had taken on more than she could cope with. But, no, she told herself. This was just what she needed.

*

Sally and Katy entered Mrs Powell's house somewhat nervously as a huge white Alsatian came rushing to the door barking furiously, "Settle down, Prince," remonstrated Mrs Powell.

41

The girls froze and held each other's hands tightly. Behind the dog came a ten-year-old boy who eyed up the girls with a surly expression.

"Ah! This them?" he asked.

"Emrys, this is Sally and Katy. They're twins."

"Which is which?"

Mrs Powell looked quizzically at them, "Well?"

Katy nudged Sally who said, "I'm Sally and this is Katy."

"There you are, Emrys. Sally and Katy."

Emrys shrugged and walked away. Prince sniffed around the two girls. "He won't hurt you," said Mrs Powell. "He's an old softie, really he is."

Sally and Katy were not convinced until Prince padded over and licked Katy all over her face setting her into fits of giggles.

"There you are, I told you so. Now you are introduced p'raps you'd like to see your room."

The twins nodded and smiled. They followed Mrs Powell through the house and up the stairs to a bedroom with twin beds. It was a pretty room with patchwork curtains to match the coverlets on the beds. There was a tall chest of drawers and matching wardrobe and an ottoman by the window.

Mrs Powell put down their cases; "You can put your things where you want. Emrys is next door and I am just along the landing next to the bathroom."

"Bathroom?" said Katy.

"Yes, bathroom. Don't you have one at home?"

"No," said Sally. "We have a tin bath, and take it in turns once a week."

"And a piss pot under the bed," added Katy.

Mrs Powell frowned, "That's not polite language, not in a God fearing house. I don't want to hear it again." There was a distinct change in Mrs Powell. Her face became pinched, her voice tart and her manner brittle. "Put your things away, wash your hands and come downstairs."

The twins looked at each other uncertainly, their initial enjoyment of the house had vanished.

CHAPTER FIVE

Letters

Carrie dashed downstairs buttoning her uniform as she went. She breezed into the kitchen and snatched a piece of toast that Jenny had just buttered and held out to her. Ernie chortled, "Duw, Duw, she'd be late for her own funeral. It looks like Korky's absence is affecting everyone. We need another cock bird to rule the roost."

"And act as an alarm clock," observed Jenny. "It seems there are more than a few who relied on his timely crows."

"That there are, me included," said Ernie. "Where's John?"

"Gone to meet the new Land Girl at the cottage," said Jenny taking another piece of bread off the toasting fork and buttering it. She placed it on the hot plate on the range.

"You haven't said a word," accused Ernie studying Carrie as she forced her hair into a topknot to put under her hat.

"I'm doing all the listening," said Carrie impishly. "Can't get a word in!"

"Jawch, there's more cheek in you than an ox and some to spare."

"Go on with you," smiled Carrie. "Let's hope the new arrival is a worker not a model."

"What's that supposed to mean?" queried Jenny.

"Well, the one at Gelli Galed is like a film star, all legs and brains to match her bust... big. She's a waist so tiny you could fit one hand round it."

"Like to know how she does that," said Jenny.

"Me, too," agreed Carrie. "She's a charm offensive, a voice to lean into and hair that's... how lucky to have such manageable hair."

"Sounds like a little note of envy creeping in, Cariad," smiled Ernie.

"Not me. I just can't see her getting her hands dirty," Carrie defended.

"Well, she'll have to on a farm," said Jenny as John entered with a smile on his face.

Carrie and Jenny turned to him, "Well?"

"Well what?" he said puzzled at the question.

"The new Land Girl," said Ernie. "They're keen to know if she's a glamorous debutante."

"What?"

"Let Carrie explain," said Ernie with a wink.

Carrie blushed, "He's making a boulder from a pebble, so he is. Take no notice."

"So, what's she like?" pressed Jenny.

"Seems nice enough," said John noncommittally.

Ernie probed, "That's no good, Wuss. They want to know if she's tall, short, slim or stout, brown hair, blonde hair and if she's a looker."

"I don't know," said John helplessly. "She's a girl…"

"What's her name?"

"Rose. That's all I can tell you."

"Looks like you'll have to wait and see for yourself," said Ernie mischievously, chuckling to himself.

There was a cry from upstairs of 'Mammy', "Bethan's awake. I'll see to her, slept late she has, Korky's affected her, too. Help yourself. Bacon's warming in the oven."

Ernie and John began to serve themselves and Carrie started for the door.

"Oh, I almost forgot, Cariad. Some letters arrived for you yesterday. Here." John stepped up to the mantelpiece and rummaged behind the ormolu clock. He handed her three letters.

"No wonder I didn't see them, hidden by there. You usually put new post by the candlestick."

"Sorry," said John sheepishly.

"Thanks," said Carrie, rushing to the glasshouse to fetch her bike.

She hurried out into the summer sun, slipped the letters in her basket and squinted up at the bright cerulean sky. It was to be another fine day.

Naomi looked miserable. She was in the kitchen tackling

the washing up and watching two young children who were waiting to be collected by their grandmother, Margaret James, Jacqueline's mother. Then she had a list of chores she had to complete before Jacqueline returned from work. She sniffed back a tear.

Jacqueline's children, Ted, two and a half and Mary four were squabbling at the table, fighting over a cuddly toy. Ted began to scream and tugged hard at the stuffed toy knocking over the glass of milk on the table, which pooled and ran across the table and dripped onto the floor.

Naomi rushed across with a cloth to mop up the spillage and right the glass. She looked in horror at the children's clothes now stained with milk. Mary had begun to cry and Ted not to be outdone just began to grizzle, which then turned into a wail, just as Jacqueline's mother arrived.

"Oh dear, dear, dear, whatever is wrong?" The two little ones stopped crying immediately and beamed at their grandmother. "What happened?"

Naomi tried to explain and Margaret James nodded in understanding, "Don't you worry now. It can't be helped. Accidents happen. And what's your name? Jacqueline didn't tell me."

"Naomi," she answered shyly, surprised at the kindness.

"Well, Naomi, you pop upstairs and fetch some clean clothes and I'll get them changed. Do you want to come along to my house, too?"

Naomi would have loved to say yes. Mrs James seemed a very warm and pleasant woman. But she said nothing.

"Don't be shy. It'll be more fun than being here alone until Jacqueline gets home."

Naomi didn't know what to say and blushed with embarrassment. "Um… I have some chores to do…"

"Chores? Oh well, all right. Another time perhaps?"

Naomi nodded vigorously, "I'd like that."

"Good. Now run and fetch their things."

Naomi rushed up the stairs to the respective bedrooms and rifled through the drawers to find something suitable for the children. She grabbed some items and ran back down. Mrs James was already putting coats and jackets on. She took the garments and smiled. "I'll change them at home. A little dampness won't hurt. I'll take care of the washing, too. Don't worry."

The anxiety vanished from Naomi's face, and Mrs James frowned, "The things you have to do … are they things you need to do? For yourself?"

Naomi hesitated. "Or are they things for my daughter?"

Naomi lowered her eyes and nodded. "I see…" her tone was measured. "Well then, Naomi I'll see you later." She smiled brightly, "If you need anything, anything at all I am at number forty-four, not too far," and she left with the children.

Naomi sat at the table and thought a moment before jumping up. "If I get all the chores done I can go to number forty-four and play," she said aloud. "That's what I'll do." Naomi skipped back to the sink and renewed her efforts with the washing up, feeling much happier.

Carrie pedalled along the road to The Crescent. She parked her bike outside Dr Rees' house and strode up to the entrance. She knocked and the diminutive Mrs Millicent Rees opened the door to admit her, "Good morning, Carrie."

"Morning, Mrs Rees."

"Come in, the doctor is expecting you. If you'd like to sit in the waiting room? He's with a patient at the moment."

"That's fine, I have letters to read to keep me occupied."

Mrs Rees smiled and Carrie walked through and sat down. There were a few people waiting who acknowledged her with a nod and a smile. Carrie took the first envelope postmarked Burma and opened it. She had recognised the handwriting as belonging to Megan. It was full of exciting news. Megan and Thomas were married and it detailed all that had happened with Grainger Mason, who had been obsessed with her and more. Carrie grimaced at the man's name. She had her own memories of the sinister and evil, Grainger Mason and the plague of diphtheria he had brought with him to the region. Carrie thought Megan must not have heard of his death and resolved to tell her the whole story when she wrote back.

Carrie gasped as she read on and saw that Megan thought she might be pregnant as the result of her and Thomas' wedding night. If so, then it would no longer be viable for her to continue in the service and once this tour was over she would return home. But nothing was confirmed yet. If she was, she wanted Carrie to be her baby's Godmother. But that news was to be kept secret from everyone until she was sure and she knew for definite.

Carrie flushed with pleasure, her excitement was apparent. She tucked the letter back in its envelope. That would be one to read to the others at supper but omitting the speculation of a baby. She took the next missive and recognised Pemb's neat round hand and curly writing. She eagerly read the contents and began to giggle as Pemb related a story regarding Lloyd on his last trip to London. 'He arrived so late he had nowhere to sleep. His B&B was locked up tight, so Kirb and I smuggled him in to the new Septic Block, which had just been painted. He seems to make a habit of this, doesn't he?'

Carrie giggled aloud and continued reading. 'Unknown to us, Matron had arranged for a tour of the block by some visiting dignitaries. Hearing footsteps approaching Lloyd turned out the lights and scooted under one of the beds. At first, no one entered the isolation ward and believing himself to be safe he began to crawl out from underneath the bed when the door opened and the light was switched on. The nurse on duty caught sight of him and let out a scream to rival any opera singer that could hit top 'C'. Fortunately, it was someone he knew and he managed to quiet her, whispering to her not to worry, as it was only him, Lloyd. Her scream brought the officials and matron rushing across. Lloyd scooted back under the bed and when questioned the nurse, said she'd seen a mouse. Can you imagine, Carrie, Lloyd a mouse? Matron ordered the porter over to catch the vermin. Poor Lloyd had to stay there for over an hour while Matron explained the benefits of the new annex. Good job he didn't sneeze.' Carrie chuckled as she read on and sighed. In truth, she missed her nursing friends and would have loved to be back there with them. She felt that in London she had made an important difference.

The last letter also had been posted in London. She turned it over curiously in her hand, as she didn't recognise the writing. She was about to tear open the envelope when Dr Rees' door opened and the patient he'd been treating emerged. The doctor saw Carrie and beckoned her.

Carrie beamed as she entered the doctor's office. "Morning, Dr Rees."

"Morning, Carrie. I trust all is well throwing you in the deep end like this after Muriel's sudden departure?"

"Of, course. I'm used to getting up to my neck before I realise what I've done! Seems to be a habit. Although, I must admit, I do miss the camaraderie of other nurses on the wards. It's strange working alone"

"I'm sure it is, but you'll get used to it. There are plenty behind you in the background willing to help if you need it."

"I'm sure there are. Let's hope I don't need them."

Dr Rees passed a list of people for Carrie to see through the week and received Carrie's report and update on some of the patients. "Thanks, I'll go through this after morning surgery. You know where I am if you need me."

"Fine, I just need to collect some items from the dispensary and see if you have any donated reading glasses that I can offer to Mr Price."

"See Millicent about all of that and we'll talk again at the end of the week."

Carrie smiled once more and left the office as tall Dr Rees with half spectacles perched on the end of his nose opened the door and called "Next."

Carrie collected the items she needed and went outside to her bike. She picked up the last letter and turned it over, puzzled. The handwriting was unfamiliar... Her heart skipped a beat – it couldn't be, could it? Carrie gazed up at the benevolent blue sky and her thoughts swum away on a wave of imagination. The confusion she had felt in France came hurtling back to her. She toyed with the idea of not opening it but quickly dismissed that thought and taking a deep breath she ripped open the envelope.

'Dear Sweet Carrie,

I have fought against writing to you but my next mission is taking me to France and from France into the heart of the enemy in Germany and I have no way of knowing whether I will come out alive. It is for this reason I am compelled to write to you to share my feelings for if I should die without telling you what is in my heart I will never rest and if I survive at least I will know that I have admitted the strength and truth of my feelings no matter what you decide.

I have to tell you that my love and heart is yours. Never before have I felt such a connection; never before has my heart leapt so joyously on seeing someone. You have captured me totally and my life would be so much more bearable and I would have a better determination to come through this hateful war if I knew that there just might be a chance with you.

You told me I could write and I am baring my soul to you, my beautiful, sweet, Carrie. You have led me to understand that you love another and he is a very lucky man but I have one request before I leave and that is to see you one more time. I will be in Cardiff for two days recruiting some new SOEs. If at all possible and you can find it in your heart to answer my request I will be staying at The Angel in Castle Street on the fifth and sixth of this month. After that date I will be in France preparing to travel to Germany. Please leave a message at the hotel for me if you are able to make it and I will be there whatever time you wish.

Yours longingly,

Matthew.'

Carrie flushed guiltily as if reading the words seemed to constitute infidelity to Michael in some way. She hurriedly replaced the missive and tried to calm her confused jittering and racing heart. Her hand was shaking. His letter had disturbed her and she was concerned at the way his letter had made her feel.

"Stuff and nonsense," she blurted aloud. And to her anger a tear forced itself from her eyelids. She blinked hard, tossed the letters in the basket and tied them with a stout elastic for keeping transported items secure, hopped on her bike and pedalled away to complete her rounds. The wind blew in her face taking her colour back to normal. Normal! She needed to behave responsibly and attend to her job. Her first stop would be Mr Price.

CHAPTER SIX

Raising concerns

Carrie breezed into Mr Price's kitchen and nodded agreeably. "Well, well, Mr Price and how are you today?"

"Better than I was, Carrie fach. Better than I was."

"Well, you have more colour in your cheeks that's for sure. Now, let's see your leg and get something more on it to kill the bugs. Have you eaten today?"

"Yes, Gwyneth made me porridge and toast, this morning. She's popping back at lunchtime with something else."

"And your daughter-in-law, Jacqueline?"

"Not seen her today, reckon you scared her off. But, to tell you the truth I'm glad you did. Not the most pleasant of women, if I'm allowed to say. Got a jib on her like an ogre."

Carrie pursed her lips, she didn't want to tell the old man she'd banned his daughter-in-law from visiting. Instead, she did what she did best and cared for him, making him comfortable.

"Now, let's take another look at your leg and get some more of this on the lesion." Carrie brandished the bottle of colloidal silver and placed it on a side table before unwrapping the bandages. "It's good stuff this. Did you know that no germs can survive in it?"

Carrie was accomplished at disguising her feelings on the nursing front but as she unwrapped the bandages she was still concerned by what she saw. The wound appeared somewhat better and cleaner, but she could see more clearly the extent of the lesion, which had been hampered by crusting and oozing matter that Carrie had been unable to completely clean for fear of hurting the old man. At the very least, she needed some sort of anaesthetic before prising off some of the deeper encrustation. Carrie was concerned that the ulceration may have spread too far, but the old man's demeanour gave her cause for hope. Carrie cleaned the leg again. This time, equipped with ether, she could numb the edge of the ulcer and remove the sticky matter without causing too much discomfort. She used the colloidal silver again paying special attention to the edge of the wound to try and prevent it getting any bigger.

"How's it looking, Nurse?"

"Well, it's not good. I won't lie to you."

"But, I'm feeling better…"

Carrie didn't like to say that his improvement was probably due to some better nourishment and getting a good meal inside him. "I'll not tell any tales," said Carrie. "But I will have to refer back to the last nurse's notes regarding measurements of this sore. We may be lucky, and now I have some more effective treatment we could slowly be doing it some good. We will start you on a course of antibiotics, which must be taken regularly and you must complete the course. I'll ask Gwyneth to monitor that. However, I would like Dr Rees to take a look, just to be on the safe side. And if you don't mind, I'd like to take some blood to make sure there are no other complications."

"Like what?"

"Any number of things, diabetes for instance."

"My mam was diabetic."

"There you are, then. It's a good idea to check."

"If you say so, Cariad."

Carrie set to and did all she needed before making him a cup of tea and sitting down with him. She knew that spending time with her patients was important. Carrie intended to do her best for them all.

Ernie was struggling to catch a handsome rooster strutting amongst his harem of hens at neighbouring Gelli Galed. There were two cockerels at the farm and it was causing problems as each time they confronted each other they fought. "Esgyrn Dafydd!" exclaimed Ernie as he tried unsuccessfully for the umpteenth time to sneak up on the unsuspecting bird, nab it and bag it. He slid on his knees catching the cloth of his trousers on the sharp small stones that the chickens had scratched about.

Sam Jefferies strolled past and chortled, "Not caught the blighter, yet, then?"

"Na! Eyes in his tail feathers he's got. No sooner do I get within striking distance than he scoots away as if his feet are scorched. Look at me. Carrie and Jenny will wear my ears out with complaints at my trousers. The bird's bringing rags to my backside, so he is."

Ernie stood up and rubbed his back as Sarah sauntered from the barn pushing a barrow with hay bales to the field. Even in her working garb of check shirt, dungarees and headscarf she looked like a Hollywood starlet. Sam Jefferies was so taken with staring at her he walked straight into the washing line strung across the yard almost strangling himself in the process. The prop fell down and the line dipped almost dropping the clean garments into the dirt. Sam floundered around trying to rescue the prop and right the line to its correct height. It was Ernie's turn to chuckle. "Can't see much serious work being done round here with yon," he indicated Sarah with a nod of his head and a roguish twinkle in his eye.

Sam had the good grace to blush as he brushed himself down and hissed at Ernie, "Quick, Ernie! While he's not looking."

The troublesome rooster was scratching and calling the females to come and taste the juicy titbits he was raking up just as the master cockerel, a large white bird with a proud crop and puffed out chest, came around the corner to see the usurper trying to find favour with what he considered to be his wives. The cock bird came strutting across angrily to face his rival, which just gave Ernie time to drop a Hessian sack over the elusive bird. He flung himself into the dirt and grabbed it. "Gottcha! Duw, Duw there's a fight I've had." At that point the white rooster known as Wilfred fluttered at the squirming sack its claws outstretched and caught Ernie's hand. Fast as a warning whistle Ernie rolled away clutching his bundle and scrambled up. Wilfred unable to see his opponent proudly approached his hens and took over from the other cock bird and Ernie limped away his hand pouring with blood from Wilfred's spurs.

Ernie called out to Sam; "I'll get this chap back and

introduce him to his new ladies. See you at the meeting tonight."

Sam acknowledged with a three-fingered salute and went on his way as Ernie started back down the slope to Hendre with the rooster safely in the bag.

Carrie was washing up the cups for Mr Price and ensuring he was comfortable before leaving for her next visit. "I'll have the doctor call by later, Mr Price."

"Jawch, call me Howie, remember?"

"Of course! Howie – sometimes I'm too formal for my own good."

"Nothing wrong with that. It's good to show some respect. Something lacking these days."

"Aye. You're right there. Sometimes it's hard to know what's right or not."

"Whatever do you mean?"

"Oh, nothing," said Carrie colouring up remembering the letter she'd received from Matthew. "Sometimes, I don't know what I mean, myself."

"Is there anything you want to talk about? Anything at all? I'm a good listener."

"I'm sure you are, Howie. But this is something I must figure out myself. But, for now is there anything I can get you before I leave?"

The old man shook his head and then murmured, "Perhaps, a book from the shelf and an eye glass."

Carrie walked to the bookcase. He had an impressive array of novels, "Anything in particular?"

"Aye, Jock of the Bushveld, been a long time since I read that. Oh, and the eyeglass is in the top drawer of the dresser."

"That reminds me, I almost forgot. Hold tight…"

"I'm not going anywhere, Nurse," smiled the old man.

She was back in the time it took to say, 'mouse and whiskers'. She carried a brown paper carrier containing four spectacle cases. "I have these, let's see if any of them will do while I find your book. Jock of the Bushveld, you say?"

"Yes, by Sir Percy Fitzpatrick."

Carrie found the book and retrieved the magnifying glass

for him just in case. The first glasses he tried were no good. "Here you are." Carrie handed him the book and watched as he tried the rest of the various donated spectacles.

Howie tried on another two pairs that were wrong but wearing the next pair, he beamed. "These are perfect, and it will be so much easier to read with these. Thank you. You're an angel that you are!"

His pleasure was obvious and Carrie patted his hand, "Then that's grand. I may see you later with the doctor. You behave yourself now. Don't go getting into any mischief."

Howie laughed. His chuckle was like crackling brown paper. She bid him goodbye and moved on.

She needed to visit some of the evacuated children to make sure they were faring well. Next stop would be Jacqueline Price to see Naomi.

Back at Hendre Ernie was introducing the new rooster to the chickens. He set the proud male bird free and after an initial strut around the yard he began to engage with the girls scratching up tasty morsels and calling his new harem to sample his offerings.

Ernie nodded in satisfaction, "There you go. This is better than fighting all day, isn't it, now? We'll just have to get you to roost in the house and not up a tree then you'll be safe." Ernie spread a handful of corn and watched the chickens cluck and scurry toward the food.

He looked across as Rose came across the yard followed by Sarah. His eyes narrowed and an unnatural cold shiver spread through him in spite of the warm sunshine and clear skies. He had a feeling, some misgivings and hoped for once he would be wrong.

Ernie retreated to the roundhouse where the grain was stored. Bonnie followed him curiously. He stooped down to fuss her and watched. Sam Jefferies had come down from Gelli Galed. He caught up with the girls and casually placed his arms around their shoulders as Laura emerged to join them. Sam dropped his friendly arms and beckoned her. He took out a list from his pocket and began to relay the jobs to be done. The girls made for the barn and Sam fell into step behind them as they went to collect their implements to take to the fields.

They came out giggling at something Sam had said and Ernie thought he detected a flash of something in Laura's expression, as she looked first at Sam and then at Sarah.

Sarah, Ernie decided was like a peacock spreading her tail for appreciation. It seemed to Ernie that she was the sort of girl used to getting her own way and who enjoyed the limelight and attention her model looks could attract and he wondered how many hearts she had broken, just because she could.

Carrie hammered on Jacqueline Price's door but no one came to answer it. She was just turning to leave when the woman from next door popped her head out and addressed Carrie, "Mrs Price is at work. Won't be back till around five o' clock."

"I see. What about the children?"

"Gone with their grandmother. She picks them up and takes them to her house and so on."

"Oh, I see. Do you know where that is?"

"I'm not sure. It's along this road somewhere but I can't tell you the number. Sorry. You'll have to knock on the doors."

"Oh, I see. Thanks, diolch yn fawr." Carrie retrieved her bike and pushed it back down the path. "Well..." she spoke to herself. "Change of plan. I'd best visit Mrs Gregory..." she consulted her list, "And Timmy and Marion Noble."

Carrie tucked the list back into her bag, mounted her bike and headed for the posh house at the top of the village known as Four Winds. It was hard cycling uphill and Carrie was puffing and panting by the time she arrived at the massive wrought iron gates and extensive grounds of the Manor House. She dismounted, pulled her hat down to imprison her escaping curls and walked the bike through the impressive entrance and up to the front door.

Carrie remembered with some shame the times when she and some of her school friends had thought the old lady to be a witch as she had always dressed in black and walked with a stick. She remembered being dared to ring the bell and when she complied being transfixed in fright as the bell pull came out in her hand and she heard the tip tap of the stick approaching the front door. Carrie had dropped the bell and ran away as fast as she could. There had been all sorts of stories about old Mrs Gregory. Carrie knew now that they were nonsense but she couldn't suppress the shiver when she thought back to the time she believed the old woman ate children for her supper. She always remembered her friend, Megan, telling her that the dogs, the huge bloodhounds that used to roam the grounds were fed the bones so that no evidence would remain.

Carrie propped her bike against the ivy clad stone wall and attempted to negotiate the old bell pull for the second time in her life but this time she was more gentle and the bell clamoured loudly making her jump.

Crisp footsteps were heard as Basil opened the stout oak door. "Yes?"

"District Nurse, Carrie Llewellyn. I've come to see the children, Marion and Timmy Noble."

"Ah, yes. We've been expecting you. Come in. Would you like to see the children first or their rooms?"

Carrie was taken aback at the open generosity of the offer, "The children, please and Mrs Gregory, if that's possible?"

"Certainly. Come in. They are in the kitchen."

Carrie entered the spotlessly clean tiled hall and followed Basil. The sound of a child's scream assailed her ears and she quickened her step. The scream was followed by gales of laughter. Basil turned to her and explained, "They are learning how to bake Welsh Cakes."

Carrie followed Basil along the corridor and down three steps into an enormous kitchen. The children were on tall stools around the table wearing voluminous aprons and covered in flour. Mrs Gregory sat at the end of the table laughing as the cook, Milly, a pleasant faced jolly woman with dark crisply permed hair and chubby cheeks, was demonstrating how to whip up a cake mixture. Timmy seemed more interested in dipping his fingers in the mixture and licking them. He was giggling happily as was Marion.

Carrie laughed, she could see the happiness in the children's faces and any misgivings she might have had vanished. "Well, well, it looks like you are having a fine time."

The children stopped and stared. Timmy's eyes opened wide, "You're not going to take us away are you?"

"Good heavens, no. I just called to see if you'd settled in comfortably. That's all."

"It's heaven!" said Timmy. "Do you want to see our rooms?" Timmy scrambled off his stool and flour billowed through the air in a white cloud as he tried to remove his apron.

"Here, let me," said Mrs Gregory kindly.

The children took off their pinnies and Marion turned anxiously to Milly, "Can we come back and finish off afterwards?"

Milly nodded and smiled, "Course you can, my handsome. Duw. It's lovely to have children's laughter in the house again."

Timmy grabbed Carrie's hand and rushed her along the corridor. "This way. You should see my room it's huge!"

The children chattered happily as they ran up the elegant staircase.

Mrs Gregory called out; "Don't run! I don't want you falling and hurting yourselves."

"We've got jobs to do, too!" babbled Timmy enthusiastically. "I go with Milly to collect the chickens' eggs. They're out back by the vegetable patch."

"And we're learning to make cakes," added Marion. "I help to hang out the washing and bring it in and make the beds."

Carrie was swept along by the children's sheer exuberance.

Timmy slid along the polished floor and opened his door with a flourish and said proudly, "Look!"

Carrie had to agree that the room was more than sufficient for his needs and was a little in awe at the ample space and toys scattered around. "It looks wonderful."

"It is. We love it here, don't we, Marion?"

Marion nodded shyly, "Come and see my room."

Carrie dutifully followed the girl to her equally impressive bedroom. The tap of a stick was heard and Mrs Gregory appeared in the doorway behind them.

57

"Does it meet with your approval, Nurse?"

"Most definitely," smiled Carrie delighted at what she'd seen. "About school…"

"All in hand. The new term starts September the second and I have made an appointment to see the headmistress and register these two. Their names are down. I just have to go through the usual formalities."

"Then there's no more to be said. I am delighted to see they are all getting on so well. Thank you, Mrs Gregory. I'll continue on my way and call back in a week or so."

"Please do," said Mrs Gregory, graciously. You will be more than welcome, so you will."

Carrie made a note in her book and the children raced from their rooms and scurried back downstairs to the kitchen. She shook hands with Mrs Gregory, "Thank you. It's lovely to see them looking so happy. It seems they are the lucky ones."

"No, I am the one who's lucky. These children are bringing me a joy I'd forgotten. I'm happy to have them here."

"Children can be mischievous and awkward at times and at others downright naughty. I hope you are prepared."

"Rest assured, Nurse Llewellyn. I remember how they can be, too. After all, believe it or not I was a child once myself and I have a long memory. I am hoping that giving them time and things to do, will enable them to learn so that they may not have the need to be naughty. From my recollection it is boredom and idleness that wreaks havoc more than healthy energy and high spirits, so it is."

"There's a lot of truth in that," nodded Carrie.

"How are the other children?"

"I don't know. You're the first I've seen. I hope they'll have found their feet like these two. Have they written home yet?"

"That is something we will do together this evening." Mrs Gregory affirmed, "Basil will see you out. Maybe next time, you'll stop for a cup of tea and sample some of the children's cooking."

"Maybe I will," smiled Carrie. "And now I must be off. As my Auntie Annie would say, this dawdling won't knit the baby a bonnet."

Carrie followed Basil down the stairs and out as more shrieks of laughter filtered through from the kitchen making her smile.

Naomi sat miserably in her dungeon of a room. The last candle had nearly burned down and she was afraid of the dark. She had heard the earlier knocking on the door and had shouted to try and make someone hear but alas no one did. And she knew the cellar door was securely locked.

Jacqueline Price had made her slave away like Cinderella, washing dishes and cleaning. She had slapped her hard when she broke a breakfast bowl and shoved her down the cellar stairs and locked her in to make her think about her sins. The children had been collected by their grandmother and Mrs Price had gone to work. She was instructed to wait for Lewis Owen to arrive, who would let her out. Lewis was a friend of the family, or so she was told, and often helped Mrs Price.

Naomi had no idea of the time, she didn't have a watch and there was nothing in the windowless cellar to tell her what the weather was like or the time of day. Naomi tried hard not to cry. She thought about her little brother Gerry and the twins and hoped they were with better people than with those she had been billeted.

Naomi strained her ears to hear a sound, any sound and she was somewhat relieved when she heard movement upstairs. She waited quietly until footsteps could be heard descending and she held her breath just as the candle gave up its sputtering flame to utter darkness and she stifled a cry. There was no hope of seeing anything in this pitch-black netherworld.

Someone fumbled with the stiff bolts on the door and the metal grinded against the iron hasp. The door creaked open and light filtered through from the stairs. A beefy looking man stood silhouetted in the doorway.

"Naomi? It is Naomi, isn't it?"

Naomi looked up fearfully and nodded. The man's voice was soft and warm, "Come now, come on out there's a good girl. Let's have a look at you."

Naomi glad to be released from her dungeon prison sat up and stepped forward tentatively.

"Duw, Duw there's dark it is. Where's your light?"

"The candle's gone out and I don't have anymore," she said quietly.

"Well, we can't have that. There's more in the kitchen. You come out now and we'll replenish your supplies."

"But…"

"Don't you worry none about Jacqueline. I'll sort her out. Don't know why she's shut you in down here. It's not right, so it isn't."

Naomi stepped out slowly and faced Lewis Owen. His voice was pleasant enough and he was a big chap with a pudgy face as if he'd eaten one bun too many. He extended his hand to her, which Naomi took. It was dry like parchment and Naomi felt the urge to pull away but so grateful was she to get out from the hellhole that she didn't and she trustingly went up the stairs with the stranger.

Lewis seemed to be very kind. He chattered away to her, making excuses for Jacqueline as he foraged for a box of candles after sitting her at the kitchen table. "I'll just take these down the stairs and then you needn't be afeared of the dark again."

Lewis returned to the cellar room giving Naomi time to adjust to the bright hissing, gaslight in the kitchen that made her eyes twinge. Why they were lit she didn't know, as it was light outside.

It wasn't long before he was back and reassured her, "You won't be in the dark anymore, Naomi. I promise you. I have put the extra candles and some more matches on the orange box. I don't know why you are shut away there anyway. I will speak to Jacqueline. It's a disgrace, it is. I'll see what I can do. Maybe you can stay with me instead."

Naomi managed a half smile as Lewis fussed over her making a warm drink and giving her a biscuit. "Tell me what was it you did to make her so cross with you?"

"I broke a dish when I was drying it. I dropped it," she said quietly with her lashes lowered.

"Sounds like an accident to me, it does. The woman's being too hard on you. Leave it with me, Naomi."

Naomi gasped as she heard the front door open and

footsteps approaching the kitchen. Jacqueline opened the kitchen door and glared at Lewis and Naomi. In a voice filled with icy menace she said, "What's she doing in here?"

"Come on, now, Jacqueline. Don't be hard on the girl. She was locked in the dark. Her candle had run out. She did all your chores." He turned and winked at Naomi. "If you don't want her she can always stay at my place."

"She was being punished. She broke a dish."

"Yes, but accidents happen. Bet you've broken one or two in your time. It wasn't deliberate… Give me a smile…"

Jacqueline's face softened as Lewis continued to talk and win her around. "I've bought you a fresh rabbit for the pot, bagged it this morning … Remember it's tough for her, a strange place, leaving home and not knowing what's going to happen. She's a sweet enough kid and will help you around the house. Doesn't do any good to be so tough with her, does it?"

Jacqueline grudgingly replied, "I don't suppose so."

"Good. Good. Now then, Naomi, why don't you pop the kettle on and we'll all have a nice cup of tea. Don't expect you've had any lunch, have you?"

Naomi shook her head.

"Girl needs something to eat. Not right to starve her," Lewis admonished.

"I'm not starving her. I was cross that's all."

"And I know how you can be when you get cross. Give her something now and she can see to the kids when they come in. Have you enrolled her in school yet?"

Jacqueline shook her head.

"She'll have to go. They'll be checking up on you, you know. Tell you what; I'll take her tomorrow. It'll look good that she's registered. She'll be able to see the other kids, too. You got brothers and sisters, Naomi?"

Naomi nodded and smiled. She began to lay out the tea things as Jacqueline took off her coat. The little girl believed she had at last found a friend in Lewis and was less afraid…

Lewis watched her a moment and then turned to Jacqueline giving her a brilliant smile. "That's settled then," and he continued to beam.

CHAPTER SEVEN

Further afield.

Megan, Carrie's best friend, had been drafted into another show headed for Egypt and Palestine. The journey across the water gave her time to think and write letters home. She placed her hand on her stomach where there was a strange fluttering like moth wings inside her. Megan closed her eyes and sighed, this was not a complete surprise. She needed to double-check her diary and she knew she must write to Thomas. He was going to be a father or so she thought. She wasn't sure how he would feel about that or indeed how she felt about it either. She had confessed all this to Carrie in her recent letter and then wondered whether or not she had done the right thing. Perhaps she should have said nothing. She determined to write and remind her friend again not to divulge her secret; after all, it wasn't yet confirmed. But, knowing Carrie, as she did, she knew she could trust her, and surmised the letter reading to the whole family would omit that piece of information. She trusted her secret was safe as long as Carrie let nothing slip or said anything that could be heard by Megan's own mother.

Megan sat in her cabin that she shared with another singer and dancer, Penelope, and wiped her forehead. She had been more tired of late and the increasing heat hadn't helped. The cabin was small and stuffy and she ached for the fresh green hills and mountains of Wales and for the first time ever Megan began to feel homesick. She was glad this would be her last tour of duty.

Megan pushed her conker coloured tresses from her eyes and reached for a small headscarf to tie up her lustrous hair and keep it off her face. Sweat was beginning to bead on her forehead and neck, and her hands felt clammy in the sticky, airless cabin. Megan made up her mind to go out on deck once she'd finished her correspondence. She stretched out on her bunk bed and began to pen a missive to Thomas, her wonderful new husband. They had shared one night of bliss after marrying and she prayed that they would both come through the war together. News from the battlefront was scarce but now the Yanks had come to fight alongside the Allies she hoped they would be done with this messy war sooner rather than later.

For some inexplicable reason, Megan felt highly emotional and a tear dropped on the paper spreading her newly inked words in a watery pool. She decided it had to be something to do with her hormones. She was already noticing changes in her body. Her breasts were fuller, firmer and her nipples were darkening and becoming much more sensitive. She reached for her diary and counted back. She had missed one period. It had to be. She was convinced she was going to be a mother. Conflicting emotions ran through her and argued in her mind. She needed to know for certain. There were after all other reasons why she could be late; changes in routine, the travelling, excess heat and more.

Megan rolled over and stared at the cabin ceiling. She hadn't heard from Thomas in a while. She knew he was aboard another vessel and on a top-secret mission. All she wanted was for God to keep him safe. She bowed her head and began to pray.

Thomas stood on the deck of HMS Welshman and thought it ironic that he should have been transferred to a ship bearing a name that reflected his nationality. He stared out across the water and allowed his thoughts to drift to his homeland and to his beloved wife, Megan. Their time together had been so short and he could only hope that he would come through this mission and live to see her again.

The ship easily mistaken for a destroyer was an Abdiel class minelayer and had transferred from the Home Fleet to the Mediterranean Fleet and in view of the strategic importance of Malta it was to protect convoys and alleviate the threat to Egypt and the Suez Canal. Protection was needed to transport supplies, personnel and fuel to North Africa and to free the blockade around Malta. Disguised as a French destroyer and carrying two hundred and forty tons of stores and RAF personnel they were taking part in an American and British mission, 'Operation Bowery'. They were hoping to deceive the enemy aircraft after the Armistice had been announced between France and Germany, which allowed the French free movement due to the German occupation of their country.

HMS Welshman had sailed from Gibraltar carrying much wanted Spitfire Aircraft to Malta, which were desperately needed to bolster the island's defence against strong Axis air raids. Thomas didn't know all the details he just obeyed orders and he was finding war was not the glorious experience he had been led to believe from the cinema and novels. Thomas felt less like a hero and more like someone caught in a trap.

He sighed as he gazed out to sea. It was hard to believe on a day like today with the scorching sun burning down on the aqua blue sea with its rising troughs, furrows and white water that there was anything wrong in the world. He turned his head as another seaman joined him at the rails. "Jonno!" He acknowledged the other sailor.

"Getting some air while you can?" said Jonno taking a cigarette from his pack.

"Yes. Although everything looks clear and safe, you just never know. I've been caught out before."

"Me, too, the buggers can appear from anywhere. Especially the U Boats," groaned Jonno stripping a match from the cardboard book.

Before he had a chance to light it a claxon sounded and reverberated around the ship as enemy aircraft had been sighted approaching their vessel. Sailors scrambled to their places all over the ship. With the French flag flying and British uniformed sailors out of sight. It continued to sail as if unconcerned in the sparkling seas.

The aircraft dipped and flew around the vessel and seemingly assured that it was indeed a French vessel they flew off leaving the ship to cruise onward. Thomas heaved a sigh of relief as the deception had apparently worked but how many times would they escape detection was a question Thomas didn't want to ask.

In Hackney, London, Martha Noble had parcelled up Timmy's teddy. She copied the address from the official letter she'd received detailing where they were staying and she smiled as she pored over the exuberant note from Marion and Timmy. She pinned the drawings they had enclosed onto her notice board in the kitchen. It was filled with enthusiasm for the place they were staying and all about Mrs Gregory.

Martha sighed and a single tear squeezed out and plopped on the table as she sat. She had done the right thing. The children were safe and more importantly they were happy. Surprisingly, Timmy hadn't even mentioned his teddy but Martha was going to send it anyway. She decided there and then that she would try and visit them at the weekend. She would close the shop early and take the train to Neath. If Mrs Gregory was as kind as they said and the house was so large Martha was sure she would be allowed to stay one night. Martha made up her mind to take some sweets for them all.

Happy she had made a decision, she took a hankie from her sleeve and blew her nose hard. She had time to get to the Post Office before opening the shop. She picked up her parcel and purse and made for the front door when the bell rang.

Martha popped her package on the hall table and opened the door wondering who was calling at this early hour. A shiver ran through her as she stared at the solemn faced telegram boy in his Post Office uniform standing on the doorstep. He removed his hat and said quietly, "Mrs Noble?" Martha nodded; her mouth was so dry she was afraid to speak. The young man handed her the brown buff envelope pasted in type written strips and the word 'Priority' leapt at her from off the page. "I'm sorry."

He walked back to his motorbike and set off down the road as Martha turned the envelope over and over in her hand. She stepped back inside her spotlessly clean, highly polished hallway and the parlour beyond.

After she was seated, she found her voice, "Please don't say, he's..." She stopped and crushed the message to her before steadying her ragged breathing. Finally, and with shaking hands, she tore open the packet of doom and read:

'From Wing Commander D A Garner
Royal Air Force Station
Kirmington
Lincolnshire
Dated 24th August 1942

Dear Mrs Noble,

May I be permitted to express my own and the squadrons' sincere sympathy with you in the sad news concerning your husband Sergeant David Noble.

The aircraft of which he was the Flight Engineer took off in the battle of Dieppe 19th August 1942, where we lost 96 aircraft.

You may be aware that in quite a large percentage of cases aircrew reported missing are eventually reported as prisoners of war, and I hope that this may give you some comfort in your anxiety.

Your husband was a most proficient Flight Engineer and his loss is deeply regretted by us all.

It is desired to explain that the request in the telegram notifying you of the casualty to your husband was included with the object of avoiding his chance of escape being prejudiced by undue publicity in case he was still at large. This is not to say that any further information about him is available but is a precaution adopted in the case of all personnel reported missing.

Your husband's effects have been collected and will be forwarded to you in due course through Air Ministry channels.

Once again please accept the deep sympathy of us all, and let us hope that we may soon have some good news of the safety of your husband.

Yours very sincerely,

Donald A Garner'

Martha stifled a sob as she let the telegram flutter to the floor. She dropped her head into her hands. Then she pulled up drawing in a deep breath, and reassured herself, "He could still be alive, don't give up hope." She picked up the telegram and put it back in its envelope and placed it on the table. She would deal with it later and see what she could find out.

After drying her eyes, Martha returned to the hall, picked up her package, bag and keys, and left the house in Clifton Road. She stepped out into the dazzling sunshine and wondered how such a glorious day could mask such gloom and upset. Martha headed for the Post Office on the Chatsworth Road where market traders plied their wares she was greeted by name by some of the barrow boys.

Martha slipped in and out of the Post Office feeling somewhat better now she knew Timmy would be getting his beloved teddy back and pleased she had enclosed a letter and some treats for him and Marion. She reached the newsagent and sweet shop that she had run with her husband until he had received his call up papers. June Barnes, a friend, and her assistant had already opened up and taken in the newspapers, which were placed in their piles for customers to pick up.

"Sorry, I'm late."

June, an amply bosomed brunette with an engaging smile, chirped cheerily, "That's okay, love. I was glad to get in early today. Ma was blistering my ears with her shrieking and jibing. Had too much gin yesterday, can't hold her liquor well and takes it out on us girls. My sister Maisie is seriously thinking of joining up."

"Surely not. The war must be over soon," said Martha as she removed her coat.

"Huh! We thought that three years ago. It just keeps dragging on. What's worse are these nuisance raids that stop us sleeping. I'm so tired I could sleep on a clothes line."

Martha gave her a brief smile as she moved behind the counter. June studied her friend's face and frowned, "What's wrong, kid? You've a face like nine pence."

Martha took a deep breath to steady her nerves; "I had a telegram this morning…"

"What? Oh, no… I'm so sorry, Martha."

"It might be all right. David's missing in action. He could have been taken prisoner. There I've said it."

"Oh, Lordy. That's not good. Still, we have to be optimistic especially for the kids. Do they know?"

"No, and I'm not going to tell them. No sense in upsetting them unduly. They seem to be having a good time in Wales and if you can hold the fort here Saturday I'd like to go visit them?"

"Of course, you can give them my love from their Aunty June."

Martha managed a real smile this time, "Thank you. Don't know what I'd do without you."

Katy and Sally, the six-year-old twins, were confused. One minute it seemed Mrs Powell was sweetness and light and another she could flip and change her mood as quickly as a ladder could run in a stocking. They were playing outside and being hounded by Emrys who bullied them at every opportunity. He was very much like his mother in as much that one minute he would pretend to be friendly and the next he was sadistically cruel. His favourite ploy was to grab one or the other's arms, as if taking them to show them something interesting and either twist their wrists or give them a Chinese burn. His cruelty didn't stop there and the twins noticed that Prince avoided the boy whenever possible, but the German Shepherd had taken a liking to the small girls who, once over their fear of the large Alsatian, had lavished love and affection on the animal.

Prince was with them now but Emrys was wielding a catapult and loading it with sharp stones to fire at the girls who squealed in dismay as they were hit. Sally began to cry as a pebble caught her cheek drawing blood.

"Cry baby, cry baby," chanted Emrys as he danced malevolently around them. Prince moved closer to Sally as if to soothe her and Emrys smiled wickedly, "So, you're taking my dog, now, are you? He's mine and he will come with me. Prince, here boy, Come. Now!" His tone was angry and uninviting. Prince refused to move. He stayed at Sally's side.

Katy bravely stood in front of the animal, "Leave him alone!"

Fortuitously, it was then that Mrs Powell opened the back

door to call the children in for tea. She was smiling and pleasant and the twins ran to her followed by the dog, while Emrys scowled sullenly. He raised his catapult once more and fired. This time the stone hit his mother and she blazed at him. "Emrys, get in here right now. I'm going to burn that thing."

"No, Mammy. I'm sorry I didn't mean to hit you. It was an accident, honest," he blustered.

"And just who did you expect to hit?" Mrs Powell shouted.

"No one. I just misfired that's all."

"Get inside now, or else...."

Emrys skulked back to the house and followed the other children into the kitchen taking his place at the table. Mrs Powell dished up three small portions of stewed steak and mashed potato. The children sat quietly and waited while Mrs Powell said Grace, "Lord, bless this food that you have provided for us and grant us the ability to share together in your love that your will may be done. Amen."

That was the signal for the children to begin eating, which they did in silence, knowing that chatter at the tea table only annoyed Mrs Powell, or Aunty Edna as they had been instructed to call her. They remained quiet trying to ignore Emrys's wandering foot that would occasionally kick at their shins. Gentle Prince watched with knowing eyes and settled at the twins' feet preventing further strikes from Emrys.

His mother noticed the blood on Sally's cheek and glared at her son. "That was you, wasn't it?" Emrys said nothing. "You'll finish your tea and get to your room. You just wait till your father comes home. He'll have something to say about this. That thing will go in the bin." She snatched the catapult from his pocket and snapped the 'V' shaped twig and chucked it in the rubbish bin.

Emrys scowled. His face looked bestial and he glowered at the girls. Katy and Sally exchanged worried looks fearing the boy's retribution.

Ernie looked up at the sagging grey sky laden with rain. The weather had taken a dramatic and unexpected turn for the worse as swollen clouds rolled and gathered threatening the worst. The animals seemed to sense the change in the air.

Senator whinnied in his stable and the ducks and chickens went running for shelter as the first drops of a potent shower plummeted down. Ernie retreated to the barn entrance and watched as John returned with the tractor with its open cab and the three Land Girls in the trailer.

He hurriedly parked the machine and hastened to the house as Sarah ran to Old Tom's Cottage. He couldn't help but notice that Laura and Rose hung back somewhat and it was plain to see that Laura had been crying. Her eyes were red and puffy and it seemed that Rose was sympathising. Ernie wondered what was wrong and endeavoured he would find out, but now was not the time as the heavy skies dumped their wet load with ferocity and Bonnie beat a hasty retreat from the water butt and scooted through Ernie's legs, nearly sending him flying, and into the barn where she showered him with water droplets from her soaking coat.

"Jawch, Bonnie, you'll have me over. I'll look as drenched as a knitted suit rinsed in the sea. Iechy dwriaeth, I'm potch!" Bonnie looked up at him in that engaging way that all collies have. "All right, all right. I'll forgive you. Don't look at me like that as if I've pinched your bowl of scraps."

Bonnie whined softly in her throat and as Ernie bent to ruffle her wet coat and pet her, she shook herself once more dowsing him yet again. This time Ernie laughed and took off his beret to shake it revealing the wiry tufts of steel wool grey hair, which sprouted above his ears. "Yerffyn darn! I can't win." He moved further into the barn and picked up an old towel to dry the sodden dog and sat talking with her as he rubbed her down. The rain tamped down on the metal galvanised roof like thundering ball bearings and eclipsed all other sounds.

Ernie sat on a bale of straw and looked at the dog. "Well, well, Bonnie. This is just the sort of trick your mother would have got up to. Duw, you are so like Trix. If only you could talk, I'm sure you could tell me things that no one could ever guess at."

Ernie rose and went to the ladder, which led to the hayloft. Bonnie whined softly in her throat as she watched Ernie climb up the wooden steps. "I'll not be long, Bonnie fach. I'm just going to check the roof. See there's no leaks to spoil my quarters."

Bonnie put her head on one side watching Ernie climb up when the barn door flew open and John rushed inside to shelter. "Wise dog," said John as he saw Bonnie sitting there. Bonnie rose wagging her tail and nosed toward John begging for a fuss and John duly obliged. He jumped as Ernie began to descend the ladder. "Duw, nearly frightened me out of my pants you did. What are you doing up there?"

"Making sure no rain is coming in. Nothing worse than wet straw for a bed and it makes for mould and mustiness if it gets damp. Not good for old bones."

"Don't know why you won't come and sleep in the house with us. We've got the room."

"I know, I know. But I'm nothing if not set in my ways. I'm used to the barn. It suits me and it's easier when we have a cow to calf or a sheep to lamb."

"I suppose," said John accepting his explanation. He indicated the gloomy conditions outside. "I hope this is just a temporary setback in the weather, after all the lovely sunshine we've had."

"What else do you expect? What is it visitors say?"

"I know. It always rains in Wales. But it doesn't."

It seemed no one had told the rain, which continued to deluge from the lowering sky. It was unbelievable that there was anymore left up above to drown them.

John opened the barn door and looked out at the ominous bruised heavens. "I don't like the look of this. Too much water in too short a time. If the water spreads from the streams to the fields we'll be in trouble. The sheep grazing have got young and no shelter. We all know how dangerous the Black River can be if it becomes too swollen." John was remembering how his own father, Bryn, had tumbled into the raging river after persistent rain and the river had taken his life.

Ernie sighed. He knew what John was thinking and feeling. "If you're planning on inspecting the flock. Take the tractor, it will be safer and load up with some grub for them, they can't eat mud and that's what the meadows will be if we get a flash flood. Do you want me to come with you?"

"Na. You get in and have a good hot bath. Get out of those sopping clothes. I'll be all right."

"Make sure you are."

"You worry too much, Ernie. Sometimes you're worse than Mam-gu."

John pushed open the barn door and fled across the yard to the house. The yard now resembled a pool and the ducks waddled and paddled, quacking happily and the rain continued to fall steadily.

John dived indoors with Ernie close on his heels. He shook himself like Bonnie and removed his outer clothing. Jenny was busy with Bethan and tutted loudly, "Don't go bringing the wet in here. Leave your outer clothes in the glasshouse." She took one look at Ernie, "And what have you been doing? Swimming in it?"

"I've been ordered to have a hot bath and change my clothes."

"Well, you're lucky I did the washing before the heavens opened. Go on upstairs and run a bath. Take your clean clothes with you."

Ernie didn't argue; he looked forward to the treat of hot running water and use of the proper bathroom that John and Jenny had finally put into Hendre with Michael Lawrence's help, and money from Jenny's mother and father. As planned they had turned Carrie's old single bedroom into a family bathroom to be proud of; not only that they had placed a proper roof on the glasshouse and built another two bedrooms on top so they didn't have to lose a room and also had a spare. Hendre had become a real family home; even the landing was large enough to support another bed, if occasion needed.

Ernie scooted up the twisted stairs through the door from the scullery, snatching the clean dry clothes from the guard by the range as he fled.

"There's fresh towels in the cupboard," called Jenny. "Help yourself." She studied her husband's face, "What are you up to? I know that look."

"I need to check on the flock. Don't want them washed away. It could cost us hundreds of pounds if we lost them."

"Surely not? It's only been raining a few hours."

"But it's been heavy and continuous. It shows no sign of stopping. Better to be safe than sorry." John changed his shirt for a clean dry one and donned his heavy waxed cape and boots. He pulled on a brimmed hat that made him look as if he'd escaped from the set of the Gene Autry film, 'Cowboy Serenade'.

"You be careful now," warned Jenny as she set Bethan down from her seat at the table and onto the floor to play.

"I'll be fine." John opened the door against the wind that had built up in the murky and dismal weather. He raced for the tractor in the yard and climbed aboard as Rose emerged in wet weather gear from the cottage.

She called above the cacophony of the howling wind, "Where are you going?"

"I need to check on the flock."

"I'll come with you. Better to be two of us than you alone."

"Climb up," urged John and Rose clambered up the steps and held onto the side of the machine as John began to negotiate his way out of the yard to the track now slippery with mud, stones and water as the rain continued to lash down.

Carrie hadn't anticipated such a dramatic change in the weather and the ferocity of the unexpected wind and torrential downpour had prevented her from visiting the other children evacuated to the village. She was satisfied with Marion and Timmy Noble's placing with Mrs Gregory and intended to call on Mrs Griffths to check on Gerry Clarke at the top of the Crescent before returning to Dr Rees with her report and request that the good doctor visit Mr Price soon. She also needed the distraction. Matthew's letter troubled her. There was no doubt there had been an underlying attraction between them when they were thrown together in a life or death situation but Carrie believed it was the severity of their situation in France that had confused her emotions. She shook her head; she didn't want to think about it. But, then again with Matthew coming to Cardiff she needed to face up to that and what she should do. The outpouring of love in the letter was disturbing to say the least. But, now she had to focus on completing another visit and getting home in the atrocious weather.

Carrie took another sip of her much-needed cup of tea and looked out through the enormous glass window, graced by brightly coloured gingham curtains the gaiety of which belied the angry storm raging outside. Raindrops hammered like bullets hard and sharp enough to crack the pane. The street was awash with water. The drains seemed unable to cope with the increasing flow, flooding the road and lapping against the kerbside. A lightning strike crisscrossed the heavy drooping grey sky followed by a splintering crack of thunder that rumbled and grumbled on, growling like a rabid wolf.

Carrie drained the last of her tea and stood up.

"Surely, you're not going out, yet?" said Mr Segadelli. "Wait till it eases up. It can't go on forever. Besides, if the storm does continue the metal on the bike is a prime target for the lightning…" Mr Segadelli shook his head. "I would hate for anything to happen to you. You could get a nasty cold out in this lot."

"Thanks, Mr Segadelli but I have visits to make and work to do. A lot of people are relying on me. A bit of water won't stop me."

"Always stubborn, like your mother, your dad used to say. Often think of him I do, and your mam."

Carrie sighed, "I still talk to them, even though they're not there. Keeps the link I say," said Carrie, pulling her hat firmly on her head.

"You just be careful. I haven't seen anything like this for many years. This rain is vicious, evil. We are a narrow valley and I am fearful of a flood."

"Come, come. It's only Mother Nature doing what comes naturally."

"I don't know. It seems unusually heavy and persistent. Still, you be careful out there."

Carrie smiled. "I will. I promise," and with that she left the small café and stepped out into the sheeting rain."

Carrie's face dripped in water and she looked as if she'd fallen in the River Dulais itself, so called locally the Black River because of the coal dust that filtered into the waters from the colliery at Maes Mawr that stained the water black.

Carrie wheeled her bike through the water massing in the

74

road. She ventured to take a look at the thundering river, normally as benign as a babbling brook, but she had seen before how dangerous this water could be, when she had witnessed the death of her father, Bryn, when he slipped from Bull Rock. She shuddered as she thought back to that fateful night and the misery that Jacky Ebron had wreaked upon her family as she ventured closer to the bridge, which led to the road on the other side of the village, passing the way to the primary school and playing fields, and she looked down.

The usual bank of stones, which always lay bare in the centre of the flow were now covered with rushing water. The fierce coursing river was excavating the bank at the mountain's edge and racing to explore the valley side with greedy waves that bit into the land. Carrie turned away and hurried back from the bridge, along the road to the square, up the hill and toward The Crescent.

The street, which sloped down to her grandmother's and Doctor Rees' dwellings was almost like a waterway itself. She approached the large house at the top of The Crescent belonging to the Griffiths' family and knocked on the door.

Mrs Griffiths opened the door a crack to stop the driving rain forcing its way into her polished hallway. "Ah, Nurse Llewellyn. Come in, please. There's dreadful it is."

Carrie propped her bike up outside and gratefully stepped inside the impressive entrance with its polished wooden floor and ornate plant stand with a fronded fern.

"Take your coat and hat off, do. I'll hang it on the line to dry in the scullery by the range. You're sopping wet."

Carrie removed her outer coat, which Mrs Griffiths received and shook. She then took the felt hat and walked through to the scullery putting Carrie's dripping hat by the range and her sodden coat over the big fireguard. "Bit heavy for the line. The guard will do just as well."

"Thanks, Mrs Griffiths. I don't know where all the rain has come from after all our lovely weather."

"Aye. It's as if someone has waved a wand. It's changed in an instant. That makes mountain roads dangerous and slippery and the farmers won't be none too pleased caught in the middle of the harvest. They'll need the sun out to dry everything up again. The children start back to school next week. Nothing worse than bad weather for making them act daft."

"It's the child I've come to see you about. You took Gerry Clarke, didn't you?"

"Yes, come through. He's in the parlour."

"How's he getting on?"

"Oh, he's a proper boy, has his moments like any lad, but I think we rub along well enough together."

Carrie followed Mrs Griffiths along the passageway to the parlour. Gerry was on the floor playing with some toy cars. A flicker of alarm crossed his face as he saw Carrie. "Not taking me away are you, Miss?"

"No, not at all," laughed Carrie. "I came along to see how you were faring."

"Faring?"

"Doing..."

"Oh, it's grand here. I got my own room and Aunty Madge has given me lots of new clothes and look," Gerry scrambled up and brought a play clock to Carrie, "Turn it, to a time, any time at all," he said proudly.

Carrie turned the hands to four o' clock.

Gerry snorted, "Pooh! That's easy all the o'clocks are, try something harder." So Carrie turned back the big hand to the nine. "Easy peasy, quarter to four. Do something harder."

Mrs Griffiths nodded at Carrie who turned the big hand all the way round to the four and looked expectantly at him.

"Twenty past four," said Gerry with confidence. "I could never do it before. Aunty Madge is real clever; she's even given me a watch. Gerry proudly showed Carrie the child's watch he was wearing.

"Why, that's lovely," said Carrie beaming.

"She's going to teach me all sorts of other stuff, too, aren't you?"

Mrs Griffiths blushed as she nodded. "That I am. He did so well on the time, learned really quickly."

"That's cos you made it fun and easy!" said Gerry before turning back to his cars.

"Is it all right if I see his room?"

"Of course. This way. Gerry, you don't mind if the nurse sees your room do you?"

"No!"

Carrie couldn't believe the startling change in the boy from when she had last seen him. He was promising to be an awkward little monster but whatever Mrs Griffiths had done she seemed to have tamed the lurking beast within.

Carrie followed Mrs Griffiths out and up the stairs. She was impressed with his room and the array of clothes he'd been given. Mrs Griffiths went onto explain, "My Alyn was the same age when he... when he passed... At first I was none too sure about taking him on but he's a lovely boy underneath the bluster and bravado. I feel I really can make a difference to him."

"I'm sure you can. I must say I'm impressed with what I've seen. Has he seen his sisters yet?"

"No. I tried to arrange for Naomi to come to tea but Mrs Price said it wasn't convenient and I'm hoping to fix something up with his twin sisters before they all start school next week."

Carrie nodded, "I haven't managed to see Naomi, yet. But if all else fails then I shall have to see them all at school. This dismal weather is not helpful when it comes to making visits."

Carrie smiled and shook Mrs Griffiths' hand. She had a firm grip of which Carrie approved.

"I will have him reading, too. His schooling has been sadly lacking but I hope to change that and make him want to learn."

Carrie beamed in pleasure, "Well, I'd better get on. I need to see Dr Rees before I go home."

"Good luck with that in this weather. Why don't you have a cup of tea before facing the wet again?"

"Much as I'd love to, I can't. But thank you."

"Your coat won't be anywhere near dry, neither will your hat."

"But it will be better than when I took them off, I'm sure." Carrie retrieved her things that were still steaming from being in front of the range and put them on. "At least they are wet-warm," she smiled.

They walked to the front door and Carrie gasped, The Crescent was more like a river than a road. It looked as if the water from Olchfa and Pwll Alyn from the waterfalls and deep pools up the mountainside had travelled down and were hurtling to meet the River Dulais; this combined with the heavy rain had caused a flash flood.

"I don't think you'll be getting to Dr Rees or home until this lot has subsided. Come back in. You'll have to sit it out."

Carrie reluctantly agreed. She managed to drag her bike inside from the clutches of the water, which threatened to steal it away. Mrs Griffiths nodded for her to bring it into the hallway. "There's glad I am to live at the top of The Crescent. We're on a hill here. But the folks below are going to have to watch they don't get flooded."

Carrie nodded a worried look on her face, both her grandmother and Dr Rees lived at the bottom. She thought that if anybody were likely to be flooded it would be them.

CHAPTER EIGHT

Flood

The rain continued to tumble down and rush down the mountainside filling small streams and spilling over onto the land dragging stones and twigs in its path. The roots of new saplings were winkled free and joined the bubbling frenzied dance of water, which fled from its usual travels and broke new ground.

Great swathes of land were carved from the mountainside where streams met and coursed to the river. The ground was unstable and threatened further landslips. The flat fields of the valley by the riverbanks resembled lakes and water birds had arrived in the deluge to enjoy the new wetlands whilst sheep and cattle struggled to find dry ground and shelter in the stampede of the bullying rain.

Higher up the track where peat bogs lurked, the ground was even more dangerous as distinguishing landmarks of rocks and trees were moved from their usual positions and carried down to the river bank making the danger spots unrecognisable.

John was attempting to negotiate the slippery track in his latest tractor, a Fordson, which he had bought using the profit from the farm and shared with Michael Lawrence. Rose clung onto the side in her brown corduroy breeches, green jersey, bib and brace overalls, boots and mackintosh. Her hair was tied back under a headscarf tied like a turban around her head.

Behind the tractor was a small trailer that seemed to argue with the main machine by refusing to run smoothly on its wheels and sticking stubbornly at an acute angle. They were carrying a ring feeder and hay to feed the sheep on the mountain slopes. The way was treacherous and John's voice was lost in the turbulent wind as he ordered Rose to hold tight.

John screwed up his eyes to defeat the invading raindrops and could see a number of his animals huddling together by a large oak tree, which remained standing. He pointed the way and Rose hopped down to the sodden land, sinking up to her ankles in mud. She attempted to right the trailer, which was obstinately refusing to move in the right direction but the job was too tough for her. Instead, she shouldered a bale of hay and began to struggle in the rain toward the frightened animals.

John tried to shout above the buffeting wind but his words were lost. He could see Rose heading toward a flat jutting out piece of innocent looking reed covered ground but, which he felt sure was bog land, although the familiar markers of the holly tree set by a big white stone that marked its presence were missing. 'Holly trees could almost always be found growing near water,' thought John. Many a time, John had seen water diviners using these as places to look for well water and to dig a borehole. He shook his head what was he thinking about? He needed to get off the tractor and warn Rose.

He applied the brake, leaving the engine running and jumped down, calling out above the cacophony of the wind and driving rain. "Rose! No! Stop!" But she didn't hear and continued on. John ran towards her. She was picking her way through what she thought was muddy ground, not realising the danger she was in. John watched helplessly as she became stuck and unable to move her feet, so great was the suction of the bog. Horrified, John saw that she was sinking.

John ran to the edge of the danger area and shouted, "Don't struggle, you'll make it worse and sink faster." But Rose continued to thrash around in the black ooze. He screamed angrily, "Stop! You must keep still." This time she seemed to hear him; she stopped and turned her head, relieved to see John standing there. He attempted to calm her seeing the acute panic on her face. "Stay put!"

"I'm not going anywhere," she yelled.

"Try not to move. Toss me the hay and then, keep your arms up. I'll get a rope and use the tractor to pull you out, okay?"

"Okay, but hurry."

Rose stood still, stuck fast but did not sink any further. John retrieved the hay bale, and raced back to the tractor. He thrust the bale in the back and removed a stout, chandler type, twisted, heavy rope that he kept for towing and other emergencies. He unhitched his small trailer, and climbed back in the driver's seat and drove the tractor forward before reversing back to the edge of the bog. He securely attached the rope to the tow bar and called above the biting wind. "Rose! I'm going to throw the rope to you. If you can tie it around your waist, do so. If not, hang onto it with all your might and I'll pull you out." John leaned forward over the inky sludge and hurled the rope, which landed with a splat in front of her. Rose stretched forward to grasp it before it began to sink. She tied it as best as she could under her arms and wound it around her wrists and held tight.

"Okay?" called John.

Rose nodded and John put the tractor into gear and began to edge forward slowly. The rain continued to pelt down blinding his eyes as he kept looking back to ensure the girl was all right.

*

Very, very slowly Rose began to feel herself being pulled but the suction was so great she could feel her feet and legs coming out of her boots. She didn't care she just wanted to get out of the stinking ooze.

Her situation reminded her of a story her grandfather had told her when a young soldier fell from the ducking boards covering deep mud in Passchendaele in the First World War. No one could get him out. He was there for days and finally had sunk up to his neck and gone raving mad. Rose shook her head to clear it of such thoughts.

The tractor moved forward again and tugged harder. Rose felt as though her arms were being wrenched out of her sockets. Gradually she began to move and slide through the boggy muck on her stomach and with a strange squelching, sucking sound her body became free from the grip of the gluey bog. She reached out and one of her hands grasped solid grass and ground. She was about to let go but heard John's warning cry. "Hold tight until you're completely free."

Rose did as she was asked and slid along the sodden ground as John continued to inch forward with the tractor until she had totally escaped the evil, clinging, mud. The rain continued to tumble down although it appeared to be easing up a little.

John leapt down from the tractor and helped untie the rope from around her and lifted her onto her feet. "Are you all right?"

"I am now. I'll need some new boots, though."

"I think we can find you a pair at home. We need to get the feed out to the sheep and get you back home. If anyone needs a bath, you do!"

"Thanks, don't think I can bear my own company," laughed Rose. "If it wasn't such God damned awful weather. I'd go for a dip in the river."

"Wouldn't catch me in there. I'm not a good swimmer." John re-hitched the trailer to the tractor. Rose clung onto the side and they trundled onward, heading for the field above the riverbank, where the sheep huddled together in clumps.

John parked the tractor on the slope and Rose took the ring feeder from the trailer and set it out under the ash tree, where some of the animals were sheltering from the testing wind and rain.

John undid a couple of hay bales and roughly spread them out in the feeder before scrambling back down to the machine. He looked up at the murky grey skies. The rain seemed to be slowing, "I just don't know where it all this rain came from. It won't have done the crops any good. We'll need a few days of good sunshine to dry the fields out."

"Can't you harvest them, if it's wet?"

"Heavens, no... the moisture content has to be right or we won't get a good price for the grain. Thank God most of it's in."

"It appears to be stopping now," said Rose. "That was some downpour."

"I've not seen anything like it before," said John. "It makes it all the worse because the ground has been so dry like concrete; the water can't soak away. Where it has been absorbed in the land it can't take anymore. The slopes and banks are really slippery. We need to get back and check everything else is all right at the farm."

"What's that over there?" asked Rose pointing. "And that sound?"

John listened. There was a faint but distressed bleating carried on the wind with an answering deeper alarmed call. John looked where Rose was pointing and could make out a white shape at the edge of the riverbank.

"Duw! Looks like a lamb." He stepped down from the tractor. "Can't leave her," he called.

"Be careful," cried Rose. She watched as he began to slip and slide down the sodden mountainside. "I'm coming with you."

"No. Stay with the tractor. It's not safe."

"And for that reason I'm coming."

Rose jumped down in her socks she chased down after him. The mud oozed and slimed over her feet.

John reached the edge of the swollen Black River that had burst its banks and was gorging on the mountainside before rushing treacherously forward on its given course. So much water flooded the field the other side of the river that it resembled a small lake.

Standing on a flat-topped boulder was a tiny frightened lamb. Water raced either side of the mossy stone. Its mother was knee deep in mud and water, bleating in alarm at her baby's plight.

John edged toward the raging water. He shouted back to Rose, "Stay back it's too dangerous."

"You're not doing this alone," she responded defiantly moving closer to the water's edge.

John stepped off into the surging river and struggled to retain his balance. The force of the storm laden waters almost knocked him off his feet. He grabbed the tiny little scrap of a lamb and fought to stay upright. He shouted at Rose, "Here. Can you take her?"

Rose wobbled toward him and took the squirming frightened creature. She stepped back onto firmer but still saturated ground and set the little one down. The ewe scrambled with difficulty out of the mud toward her lamb and the two hurried away from the turbulent water to the safety of a copse of trees on the mountainside.

Rose turned back and to her horror saw John knocked off his feet by the driving river. He shouted loudly and as the water swept him downstream he floundered on into deeper water. Rose, without a thought for herself, threw herself into the wild river. Carried along by the racing floodwater she kicked out and swam after John, snatching breaths as and when she could.

John's arms were splashing and flapping in the air as he tried to grasp at something, anything to halt his passage through the deadly river. He hit a bank of rocks and tried to hold onto a large mossy boulder several feet from the shingle shore. His fingers scrabbled against the slippery stone. He threw his arms around it as if it were a long lost love about to leave him again and he was terrified of the parting when a sudden surge of water ripped him from it and carted him off down the river once more.

He disappeared under the surface and bobbed up cracking his head on a rock before he floated off becoming tangled in strangling weeds. Rose searched wildly around her and just caught sight of his body pushing into the side of the bank.

Rose took a mouthful of air and dived under the surface. She stretched out urgently with intense focus and sped in John's direction. Every three sweeps she surfaced, snatched another breath, and looked to check on John's movement. He was being tugged by the raging currents, but the reeds were hanging on tightly to his limbs and around his neck, preventing him from travelling on. Rose struck out again and the sheer force of the river helped carry her toward John.

Rose swam powerfully until she reached him. She turned him over, and carried him to the bank pulling off the clinging weeds. Finally, she hauled him out of the water and laid him out face forward muttering to herself; she urgently repeated learned life saving instructions, "Remove foreign matter from his mouth…" There was none. "Bend his elbows, place his hands one on upon the other… okay…. Turn his head slightly to one side and place on hands… Extend his head as far as possible with his chin jutting out." Her voice was cracked and panicked. The fear in her escalated and her hands began to shake. She studied his face, his dark wet unruly hair and strong chin. "What am I doing?" She took a deep breath. Rose knelt at John's head and placed her hands on the flat of his back. She could feel his firm skin and strong sinewy muscles under her fingers. She shook her head vehemently, as if cross with herself, and adjusted her position. She placed the palms of her hands on an imaginary line running across the back from his armpits and rocked forward on her arms until they were vertical. "Allow my upper body weight to exert steady pressure upon my hands. Immediately draw his arms upward toward me until I feel resistance and tension at his shoulders... Come on." She urged herself, "Move it, Rose." Rose continued to work on him trying to expel the water from his lungs. "Come on, John. Damn you, breathe."

Rose counted out aloud beginning to become more hysterical at his lack of movement. Then she was rewarded with a sudden cough as John spewed up river water. He coughed again and began to breathe more regularly. Rose turned him over. He really was quite handsome. She shook him, "John, John? Are you all right?"

His eyes flickered. Rose watched as he opened them slowly trying to focus. Rose's anxious face swam in and out of his vision and he croaked, "Thank you... Diolch."

"Ssh! Don't talk... and don't move."

"I'm not going anywhere," he joked feebly echoing Rose's remarks when she was stuck in the bog.

Rose scrambled up and ran back along the bank, slipping and sliding in the mud until she reached the still running tractor. She checked the trailer before she climbed up to the less than comfortable seat and looked at the gear levers trying to remember what she had learned by watching John drive. She selected the first and began to move forward. The tractor rolled through the mud, cutting deep furrows, and she made her way along the riverside to where John still lay and jumped down. His eyes were closed. She slapped him around his face to rouse him and threw his arm around her neck and tried to lift him up.

Somehow, Rose didn't know how, she was filled with a burst of adrenalin that gave her the power to haul him to his feet and half carried, half dragged him to the trailer and rolled him inside, "Hang on, John. Hang on; please."

John opened his eyes and whispered, "Not so stinky now… That's a hell of a way to get cleaned up."

Rose laughed in relief and delight. "And you thought you'd take a dip just to test out my swimming skills…"

"Something like that…" he closed his eyes again. Rose clambered back in the seat and drove onward. The machine hurried toward the track. The rain had finally stopped.

Carrie stepped out from Mrs Griffiths' house and thanked her for her kindness. She waved at Gerry who was looking very different from the unruly child who had run amok in the church hall.

The sagging grey clouds were starting to lift and cracks of blue were appearing through the dull veneer. The Crescent was awash with water that had diverted from the bottom of the hill down Lewis Road to St. Mary Street and St Margaret's Cemetery. As she cycled down she could see that the houses at the bottom of the Crescent had survived flooding and the excess water had run into the graveyard. She was relieved having never seen a flood like this before and she hurried to look at the stony mountain track where water continued to run and dribble down. The pathway was dangerous and slippery. Carrie decided she would wait a while until the water had stopped coursing and she'd call in on Dr Rees.

Naomi sat at the kitchen table and looked at the meagre offerings she had been given for her tea. Lewis Owen had left promising to call in the next day. The children had had their evening meal. Naomi had helped to cook it and to prepare the children for bed. Jacqueline was bustling around the kitchen clearing up. She turned and smiled unconvincingly at Naomi. "Owen is right. It must be hard for you here amongst strangers. We'll have to put that right." She sighed heavily, "Look we may have got off on the wrong foot. I'd like to start again. Is that all right with you?"

Naomi nodded glumly her eyes still fixed on the slice of

bread spread with dripping and a glass of milk that had been topped up with water.

"Come on, eat up, there's a good girl and I shall give you a treat." Naomi's eyes lifted from her plate and she dared to gaze at Jacqueline. "I picked some fresh fruit today. I've saved an apple for you from the garden. Do you like apples?" Naomi nodded again. "Good, now eat up. I know I have a short fuse and lash out sometimes but that's me. You'll get used to it. I don't mean to be hard."

Naomi picked up the bread and scrape. She began to eat it. It tasted better than she expected. She took another bite when there was a wail from upstairs.

"Oh, what now?" grumbled Jacqueline. "Naomi, go and see who it is and what's troubling them."

Silently Naomi rose and went to the stairwell. She ran lightly up the stairs and opened the first door. Four–year-old Mary was sound asleep. She opened the next one and two and a half year old Ted was sobbing. Naomi went to him, "What is it, Teddy? What's wrong?" The little boy sat up and continued to blubber. "Did you have a bad dream?" Ted shook his head and shamefaced he pushed back his eiderdown and blankets. His pyjama bottoms were soaked and the bed was wet. "Oh no!"

Naomi was filled with compassion for the little one. She helped him out and sat him in the bedroom chair before going to the tall boy to find some fresh clean pyjamas.

Footsteps were heard on the stairs, "What is it?" asked Jacqueline peering in. She groaned, "Oh, no. Not again! You know what I told you after last time," she scolded. Naomi hardly dared to breathe as the woman's manner and apparent good humour had dissolved and vanished. "Get him into dry nightclothes and strip the bed. There are clean sheets in the cupboard on the landing. Go on, move."

Naomi did as she was asked and took some clean jim-jams from the drawer. Jacqueline pulled off the boy's bottoms and smacked him hard on his backside. Naomi winced. She turned and gave the clean clothes to Jacqueline, her eyes downcast.

"Just as well I've put a draw sheet on the mattress. I don't want another one ruined by pee," shouted Jacqueline. "And if you don't stop grizzling I'll give you something to cry about. Now, shut up!"

Jacqueline dragged the toddler from the room, "Change the bed, Naomi, you're sleeping in here tonight. Teddy is having your bed."

Naomi bit her lip. She was horrified but didn't dare say a word. She scurried to the cupboard for fresh bedding in silence as Jacqueline pulled Teddy roughly down the stairs. She heard the child scream and the cellar door opened, slammed and was locked.

Naomi stripped the wet sheets off the mattress and put on the clean ones. She hesitated, was she supposed to change the whole bed including pillowslips? She decided not to and made up the bed as Jacqueline returned to the bedroom.

"I've had a change of heart," she announced coolly. "You are to sleep in here tonight. We'll remove your things in the morning and you can share with Mary. I need the cellar for punishment purposes. It's the only thing the children will respect. Now when you've finished that come downstairs and finish your tea." Jacqueline marched back out of the room leaving Naomi standing trembling. But, although she felt dreadful for the little boy she was also relieved not to be sleeping in the dungeon again. Naomi knew she needed to be on her best and most obedient behaviour so as not to rile Mrs Price in any way.

"I hardly expect anyone at the surgery today with the atrocious weather," said Dr Rees.

"You were lucky you weren't flooded," replied Carrie.

"Yes, it's fortunate the water deviated down Lewis Road and to the cemetery. But, you didn't call about that…"

"No, I wondered if you'd seen Mr Price, yet?"

"Not yet, Carrie. He's first on my list tomorrow. I promise. Along with a couple of other house calls I need to make. Oh, and I have someone I want to add to your list. Hold on…" Dr Rees picked up a piece of paper from his desk. "Mrs Powell needs some more medication. She's not been in recently and I know she must have used up her supply."

"Mrs Powell?" said Carrie more sharply than she intended.

Dr Rees snapped his head around and stared at her, "Yes, Carrie... What do you know?"

"Nothing, but..."

"But...?"

"She's taken two of the evacuees, twin girls. Should I be worried?"

Dr Rees pushed his half spectacles firmly on his nose. "I may be seeming uncharitable but she's not the best choice and not just because of her own problems..."

"Yes?"

Dr Rees sighed, "Edna Powell can be unstable unless she is on her medication. When she is, she is fine, quite charming and very pleasant. But her son, Emrys..."

"What about him?"

" I have no proof but my own assessment of the boy is not good. There is something not right about him."

"How do you mean?"

"He's done some things that I am aware of."

"What kind of things?"

"Cruel things to animals... Now, I only heard this second hand but I was told he'd blinded the little girl next-door's rabbit. No proof mind you, just hearsay and his first puppy, pretty little thing drowned..."

"Drowned?"

"In the bath..." He stopped.

"There's something else isn't there?" prodded Carrie after an uncomfortable pause.

"Mrs Powell had a little girl, just toddling she was..." Carrie remained silent she knew when not to speak. "She died. Put down as a cot death it was but I always had my doubts. I remember the smirk on Emrys' face when the little one was pronounced dead. Edna Powell broke her heart. He just grinned. After that something happened to the woman. She hasn't been right since. Thought it was God's punishment to her and became fanatical about religion. I may be completely wrong but I wouldn't be happy for any children of mine to stay there. She wasn't on our list."

"No, she was one of Christine's. Duw, I wish I'd known this before," murmured Carrie.

"As I said, I may be wrong. It may be perfectly all right…"

"Doctor, I'd take your gut instinct over anything and there was something Ernie said, too…"

"Ah, Ernie! He can be cryptic, so he can."

"He said some children would be fine but others wouldn't fare so well. I must try to see her but sooner rather than later. And I need to track down Jacqueline Price. She's never in when I call round. She was another of Christine's finds."

"Jacqueline Price? She works doesn't she? At the drapers?"

"Yes. And I've crossed swords with her already."

"Yes, I've heard others say she has something of a nettle mouth."

Carrie looked at her watch, "It's stopped raining. I'll go back and see if I can catch Mrs Powell and call back on Mr Price."

Dr Rees just nodded and smiled as she left. He muttered to his wife Millicent as she entered, "Young Carrie Llewellyn is a fine nurse. We are lucky to have her."

The tractor rolled into Hendre's yard, which was still pooling with surface water. Rose shouted out, "Ernie, Jenny? Anyone? I need help." She ran to the door of the glasshouse and hammered loudly.

Jenny hurried to the door wiping her floury hands on her apron. Bethan clung to her mother's skirts as she opened the door. "Yes? Rose? What is it?" But Rose was already running to the tractor-trailer.

"Quickly. It's John," she called back.

Jenny's hand flew to her mouth in horror and she scooped up Bethan and ran to the yard as Ernie emerged from the barn. He hurried to help Rose who was trying to haul John from the trailer.

"What is it? What's happened?" said Jenny tremulously trying not to cry. At that moment there was a break in the cloud. The partially obscured sun dazzled her eyes and she let out a hiccupping sob.

Ernie took John from the trailer holding him under his arms taking the full weight of John's body as Rose tried to guide his form. Their feet splashed in the standing water and Rose went to support John from the other side and they half dragged, half carried him into Hendre and set him down in the parlour.

Jenny put Bethan down and knelt at her husband's side calling frantically, "John, John! Please! Speak to me."

John's eyes fluttered and he murmured, "Rose?"

"No, John. It's me, Jenny."

John coughed and Rose began to relate what had happened.

Ernie set John in a position of recovery and tested his vital signs, before palpating his back. "Jawch! The lad must have swallowed a river. How long was he under?"

"Not long. I swam to him as fast as I could."

"Thank God you did. Jenny, this lass has saved your husband's life." John coughed again and Ernie sat him up as John became more aware. "Duw, Duw, there's a fright you gave us. We must get you to Dr Rees just to be on the safe side."

"How? How can we do that?" asked Jenny. "The track's not safe. All this water has made it treacherous."

"But I got up it with the tractor and trailer," said Rose. "Yes, it was slippery but manageable."

"Going down is bound to be worse," said Jenny.

"Maybe we'll get the doctor to come here. Where's Carrie? She'll know what to do," said Ernie.

"The rain is bound to have delayed her. Can we afford to wait?" said Jenny anxiously.

John's eyes fluttered again and he began to come to, "Don't be bothering the doctor. I'm all right, honest." As if to prove the truth of his words he pushed himself up on his elbows. "Jawch, I could do with a cup of tea and some dry clothes."

Jenny almost laughed hysterically with her nerves so tightly stretched, but she checked herself as Bethan started to cry. "Hush now, Bethan. I need to see to Daddy." With enormous relief and tears cascading down her face she threw her arms around him and attempted to smother him with kisses.

Embarrassed John caught Jenny's hands, "Yerffyn darn, Jenny. I can't breathe. You'll be strangling me more than the weeds in the river."

Ernie grinned and began to laugh. Soon they all chuckled together. "It'll take more than a little water to stop our John."

John sat up and put out his hand to Rose. She moved hesitantly to him. "I must thank you, Rose. If it hadn't been for you ... I'd be dead."

Rose smiled shyly, "I just did what anyone else would have done and remember you saved me, too."

Jenny, wet fronted, looked curiously at them both and turned to Rose, "Thank you, Rose. I don't know what I'd have done without..."

John interrupted, "All is well, but I am indeed indebted to you. Thank you."

Bethan clambered up onto her father, popped her thumb in her mouth, and snuggled in not caring that he was wet through. John clasped his young daughter and took Jenny's hand, "And I don't know what I'd do without you, either of you."

Ernie broke the moment, "Duw, Duw, you'll have us all weeping more than a willow, so you will. Let's have that cup of tea."

Carrie was sitting in Mr Price's kitchen as they shared a warm drink. "I didn't expect to see you so soon," said the old man.

"No, but I needed to speak to you, about your daughter-in-law."

"Jacqueline?"

"Yes. I want you to be honest with me, Howie. Is she to be trusted? With other children?"

"Why do you ask?" the old man's tone was guarded.

"I have a little girl, an evacuee. She's staying with Jacqueline."

Howie sighed, "I don't like to speak ill of the woman. After all she is my son's choice but I wouldn't want a child of mine to stay with her. She can be very harsh. I've seen her in action."

"Hmm, you're merely confirming what I already thought," mused Carrie. She studied Mr Price's face. "There's something else isn't there?"

"I believe she has a male friend..."

"Yes?"

"I know the man…"

"And?"

"Let's say, I don't trust him either."

"What do you mean?"

"I'll say no more but if I were you I'd get her moved." Mr Price closed his mouth firmly signalling the end of the conversation.

Carrie sat silently a moment while she sipped her tea. Eventually, Howie Price spoke again, "And you, Nurse. What's troubling you?"

Carrie was disarmed, "What?"

"There's something worrying you and it's nothing to do with evacuees. What is it? I told you I'm a good listener."

Carrie was stunned; she had been thinking about Matthew and Michael and did not want to admit it.

Howie pressed again, "Tell me. It'll go no further. Honest."

Carrie paused and then volunteered, "I do have a problem and nothing I can talk about at home or to anyone."

"Then try me. I'm not going to blab to anyone else."

Carrie pursed her lips and blew out between them. Her shoulders drooped.

"Come. It can't be that bad, surely? It's about a man, isn't it?"

Carrie glanced up in surprise and nodded. "Yes." She sighed heavily, thinking it may be a good thing to chat to Howie about her problem, after all. Carrie began to tell Howie about the events where her family had lost Hendre and the incredible attraction between her and Michael, which had eventually led to their engagement.

"He sounds like a good man and it sounds like you love him. Your eyes sparkle when you speak of him. I can relate to that so I can. I always had the shine in my eyes for my wife. I don't understand your problem."

"It's not just that. If it were only Michael and me, everything would be perfect."

"But?"

Carrie gulped and launched into her adventures as an SOE and the closeness that had developed between her and the male Special Operation Executive, Matthew.

"But you were in danger. You did what you had to, to survive."

"That's what Michael said."

"You told him."

"Yes, I didn't think it was honest not to."

"But nothing happened?"

"No apart from a kiss."

"And how did that make you feel?'

"Confused. I thought I knew what I wanted but …"

"But?"

"Now, I'm not so sure. You see I've had a letter." Carrie stopped and Howie considered all that she had told him.

"Seems to me, you're in love with two men."

"But I can't be. I can't."

"What does the letter say?"

Carrie put her hand in her uniform pocket and removed the now crumpled, damp letter. She passed it to Howie who turned it over in his gnarled and wizened hands.

"It seems you've shed a few tears over this…"

"What? No… it's just the rain."

Howie put on his newly acquired spectacles, opened the envelope and removed the limp letter. He began to read it. Carrie waited patiently until he'd finished.

Howie sighed, removed his glasses and folded the letter returning it to its envelope and passed it back. "Well, well. The man is certainly carrying a torch. How do you feel about it?"

"I don't know. Everything was fine until I received this and now my whole world is upside down."

"It could be just the adventure you shared," said Howie.

"I know. I should never have agreed for him to write to me and then I remembered Jumbo…"

"Good heavens, who's Jumbo?"

"Oh that's a nick name. Gwynfor, Gwynfor Thomas. He went off to serve in the army wanting me to be his girl. I said, no. But gave him permission to write to me. I'm glad I did because he died."

"Ah yes, Nancy Thomas' boy. I remember…" He tutted, "So young… and you remembered this when young Matthew asked to write?"

"Yes," said Carrie in little more than a whisper.

"Sometimes in the sunshine things get too hot and a storm brews. Thunder claps sound and put an end to the glorious day."

"What does that mean?"

"Thunder in the sun... it happens."

"So, what do I do?"

"That Nurse Carrie is what you need to decide. It has to be your decision. No one can make it but you. Think about it."

"That's what I've been doing. It's driving me daft."

"How do you feel about Michael?"

"I love him. When he's with me it's like there's no one else in the world. If I don't marry him then all the agreements set in place between our families would be ripped asunder. I couldn't stay here. I'd have to move."

"Seems to me, there's two considerations here. Firstly, you must live your life for yourself not for anyone else. Don't stay with someone because it's the right thing to do."

"I'm not. I do care... Oh, we fight sometimes but that keeps it interesting."

"Wise words. If there's no rough, how can you appreciate the smooth?"

Carrie's eyes had begun to smart with tears.

"How do you feel about Matthew?"

"I don't know. He disturbed me. I know I was attracted to him and his kiss turned my stomach inside out... but..."

"But you don't know how you feel now?"

"No."

"Then surely you must meet him. No good spending the whole of your life wondering 'What if?' That way madness lies."

"But, what do I say? Why would I go to Cardiff? I don't like lying. There's been too much of that in the past. I've always been honest."

"Then tell him."

"I don't want to hurt him. He once said what you don't know can't hurt you. And I truly believe my destiny is with Michael Lawrence."

"But one percent of you has a niggling worm of doubt..."

"Yes."

"Meet him, Cariad and then you'll know."

"Thank you."

"That's all right. Talking about things often helps clarify your own thinking. I'm sure you'll do what's best."

"I couldn't have discussed it with anyone else. And you'll keep it just between us?"

Howie Price nodded, "Who have I to tell, eh?"

Carrie patted his hand and drained her cup. It was getting late and she needed to get home. She had a lot more thinking to do.

CHAPTER NINE

Decisions

Carrie rode her bicycle back through the village and as the dreary, drizzly, rain-filled, leaden sky had lifted so had her mood. She was focusing on what she needed to do, her priorities and what she would say to her family and Michael.

She huffed as she pushed her bike back up the slippery stony mountain track toward Hendre. Each step seemed to be more burdensome than the last but still Carrie was optimistic. She knew now what she had to do.

The climb was steep. It was nothing new but the way was more treacherous than usual. Carrie stepped forward and her foot went from under her and she tumbled down with the bike landing on top of her. She pushed herself back to her feet and picked up her bicycle. There was no damage and she stepped out with renewed vigour. Thoughts tumbled through her mind and she knew she would need to be careful around Ernie. He could read her like a book.

Carrie was pleased and more than relieved when she saw the tree by the farm gate where she had often romped with Trix. She choked back a sob wondering where the surge of emotion had come from? There could never be another dog like her Trixie. But home was in sight. She ploughed on and reached the yard. The ducks were quacking and paddling in the now receding surface water. Carrie smiled as Bonnie came running toward her and rushed around her feet, her tail wagging in circles like a propeller.

She hauled her bike up onto the veranda and leaned it against the wall of the house, put a smile on her face and marched into the glasshouse and kitchen. There was no one there. She heard voices in the parlour and went through.

Her smile drained away when she saw the activity around John. She hurried to him, "John, bach. Duw. What's happened?"

John smiled wryly at her, "Nothing I couldn't handle, Cariad. Just went for a dip in the Black River that's all. Don't know what all the fuss is about. Rose was in a stinking state I had to do something to make her wash!" and he winked.

Rose laughed, "Oh yeah! Tried to race me downstream."

Carrie brushed all frivolity aside, "Did he go under? For how long?"

"A few minutes, no more," said Rose more seriously. "I got him out pretty quickly."

"Thank God you did. Was he breathing?"

"No. I used life saving techniques. First time I've done it for real."

"Thank goodness you knew what to do. All the same I think he should be examined by Dr Rees."

"Don't fuss, Cariad. I'm fine, right as rain as they say," said John.

"There was nothing right about that rain. Don't understand that saying," exclaimed Carrie.

"We can't be bothering a busy doctor when all is well," insisted John.

Ernie chipped in, "I should listen to your sister, if I were you, Wuss. You never know. Better safe than sorry."

John rolled his eyes, "Very well, if it will shut you all up. I'll go down in the morning, but I'm sure you could look me over just as well as the doctor, Cariad."

Ernie heaved a sigh of relief in unison with Carrie who didn't reply but made her excuses to get out of her wet clothes and dry off. No one gave her a second glance.

Carrie made her way to her room and stripped off her uniform, put on her robe and flopped on the bed as she had when she was young. She was confused. She was to go to Michael's relatively soon, in just a couple of days' time, and knew she would have to speak to him. She fished out Matthew's letter now limp and damp from the rain and read it again. Her stomach filled with an urgent fluttering almost akin to fear and she rolled over after placing the missive in the bedside table drawer. She said aloud, "How do I feel? Am I in love with two men? No, that's impossible." She tussled with the problem in her head and struggled to think it through logically. She had never questioned being with anyone other than Michael and believed the events with Matthew were just a reaction of the time, situation and place. Now she was being forced to face it again. Of course, she could just not go to Cardiff and her problem would be solved. But then she would always wonder if she had done the right thing. She had arranged to see Michael later in the week and was torn. Should she say something or not? Carrie knew she was not experienced when it came to judging men and relationships, and the battle inside her raged until she closed her eyes and drifted into a fitful sleep.

Michael Lawrence was in the kitchen preparing dinner. He chopped the onion and tossed it in the pan with a knob of butter and a little water. He set it on the range and wiped his eyes, which smarted from the pungent onion juice.

Michael sang a ditty as he opened the pantry door and took a couple of fresh open cap field mushrooms and roughly sliced them adding them to the onions. He sautéed them gently before combining them with some more prepared vegetables.

There was a knock on the door.

Michael took the pan off the range wiped his hands and went to see who was there. The new Land Girl, Sarah, stood there. She smiled and said huskily, "Sorry to disturb you, but…" she sniffed the air, "Oh, are you cooking?"

"Um, yes. Just running up a little something."

"Smells good."

"Thank you… How can I help you?"

"Oh, yes. Sorry." She lowered her eyes, then brought them up and swept them over his face and moistened her lips. "It's just I'm getting a little bored. Oh, not with the work although it does play havoc with my nails. At night… I'm not used to being unoccupied…"

"And?"

"I've read the books I brought with me and I would so love something new and different to read. I thought that maybe you could help me until I can join the town library."

"Um, certainly. Don't know if I'll have anything to appeal to you but you're welcome to take a look."

"Thanks, I will." She smiled dazzlingly at him and swept inside Gelli Galed.

Michael raised an eyebrow as she shimmied past.

"So…" she purred. "Where do I look?"

"Er… Oh, yes," said Michael momentarily disarmed. "Upstairs. My book shelves are in my bedroom."

"Then you'd better lead the way."

Michael took the stairs two at a time, crossed the landing and opened the door to his very masculine room.

"Mmm," her honeyed tones sounded approving. "Lovely room, very you; although, if you were to share it with a woman it would need some softer feminine touches. Oh, yes," she studied the décor and took a deep breath, "I can smell your masculinity."

Michael didn't quite know what to say. He cleared his throat feeling hot and slightly uncomfortable, "The bookcase is over there… I'll leave you to it."

"Oh, please don't go. I could do with some advice, I'm sure," she smiled winningly at him.

"Um, I'm sure the back of book blurb will be more helpful than me and I've got something on the go in the kitchen. I don't want it to burn…" he trailed off.

Sarah smiled cheekily, "Pity, things might have got interesting." She glided across to the bookcase, sat on the bed after removing her jacket, and began studying the novels on the shelves. Michael stood a moment his jaw agape before he came to and returned downstairs.

He glanced at the clock. Carrie wouldn't be long and he couldn't wait to see her. Michael added chopped bacon to the mix before straining a pan of boiled rice and spooning it into the pan. He added some salt and pepper throwing in some fresh parsley and a little more liquid leaving the concoction to simmer gently while he laid the table.

The task completed he returned to the range and checked on his risotto. So absorbed was he in his task he didn't hear Sarah enter the kitchen. She placed three books on the table and sidled up to him. She ran her finger down his back. Disconcerted he turned quickly and she giggled.

"Sorry, did I startle you? Didn't mean to make you jump."

She peered into the simmering pan, "Looks and smells good."

"Did you find what you were looking for?" Michael said abruptly.

"You have an amazing collection of books. I have picked three and when I've read them, I'd like to choose some more if I may?"

"Er… Yes, I expect so," he said hesitantly.

"Well, I'll be off. You must be expecting someone that's far too much for one person and I see you've laid for two."

Michael swallowed hard and replied with emphasis on his words, "Yes, my fiancée. She should be here soon."

"Fiancée? Lucky girl," her voice was filled with amusement and slightly mocking. She twirled around gracefully and picked up her books. "Oh, silly me. I've left my jacket upstairs. Won't be a moment." Sarah left the kitchen and returned to the stairs as the doorknocker clacked. She ran up them as Michael went to answer the door.

He beamed as Carrie entered. He picked her up and swung her around. She giggled, "Duw, let me catch my breath after that hike." She straightened her clothes as he set her down and followed him into the kitchen. He returned to the range to check the risotto.

Carrie nodded approvingly as she saw the table set for two but looked puzzled when she saw the books. She picked them up and turned them over in her hands looking at the titles. "Gone with the Wind, Goodbye Mr Chips, Of Mice and Men… Quite an eclectic mix… Are they for me?" Carrie asked sweetly.

She jumped as a hand reached around her and a sultry voice behind her spoke. "No, they're for me. Michael kindly offered to loan them to me."

Carrie turned to face the owner of the deliberately seductive tones, whose perfume now filled the room almost eclipsing the aroma of the food. Carrie noted the provocative pose of Sarah who lifted the books from Carrie's hands. Speechless she turned and looked questioningly at Michael who spun around and blushed.

Sarah gave one of her expansive smiles and walked to the kitchen door. "I'll see myself out. Thanks for these. I'll definitely be back for more." She called back over her shoulder as she left, "By the way, your bed's comfortable. Very comfortable, indeed."

The front door clicked and Carrie waited for Michael to speak. He seemed stuck for words and stuttered, "It's not what it seems, really."

"Really?" said Carrie an amused twinkle in her eye, "Then please tell me how it is. I'd love to hear."

Michael flustered and blustered in his explanation until Carrie could no longer keep her expression stern and she burst out laughing, "Oh, Michael, you should see your face! Don't worry, I hardly think you'd have a dalliance with another at the exact time you were expecting me to call. Although that man eater does have some questions to answer."

Michael sighed in relief, "I know how that must have looked but it was all perfectly innocent, I assure you."

"And I believe you. But I think I'll need to keep an eye on her, just the same. I believe she's likely to set her cap at any man, just because she feels she can. But we'll see."

Michael pulled a chair out inviting her to sit and the evening sun gambolled in through the window playing on Carrie's freckled face and burnished hair that glittered with golden light.

Michael stopped in awe as he admired the golden aura, which surrounded her and whispered, "You're so beautiful, and I'm so very lucky that some other man hasn't snapped you up."

At the mention of another man, Carrie's heart filled with guilt and her expression changed.

"What? What is it?"

Carrie smiled nervously uncertain how to approach the subject of Matthew. "Let's eat first, and talk later. It smells delicious." Carrie forced a smile, unprepared and unwilling to discuss her dilemma just then.

Michael as perceptive as ever to her moods merely nodded, "As you wish." He took two plates from the warming oven and began to dish up their meal. Carrie studied his broad back and the way his hair fell at the nape of his neck and sighed softly, thinking how right it was that they should be together.

The more she was in Michael's company the more she seemed to know that he was indeed the right man for her. So why had she experienced all this confusion? Thoughts rambled through her mind like ivy scaling and intertwining over the wall of a cottage garden. So deep in thought was she that she missed what Michael said next.

"Sorry, what did you say?"

Michael placed the dish in front of her, "Carrie Llewellyn, you haven't heard a word I've said. Whatever is the matter?"

Carrie looked into Michael's eyes with his long curling lashes and blinked. "Um… Don't know. I was miles away. Sorry." She smiled again, "Come on, let's eat. Plenty of time to talk later."

Michael was accepting of this and they both tucked into their meal and the kitchen was filled with inconsequential chatter and laughter as the evening progressed.

The evening sun had dropped low in the sky daubing the heavens as if with an artist's brush loaded with a deep coral tint. Carrie and Michael sat on the veranda in a double swing seat and watched the changing colours and amorphous clouds that strived to make pictures in the sky. It was hard to believe they had suffered such atrocious weather only a few days before.

Carrie stretched, "I must soon be making my way back down the track."

"Do you have to?"

"I must." She sighed, "That meal was wonderful, so different and delicious."

"Something I learned in Africa. You can do a lot with rice."

Carrie stood, "I must just use your bathroom."

"Of course." He rose politely and followed her with his eyes as she went indoors.

Carrie ran lightly up the stairs to the landing and into the toilet. As she lifted her skirt something crinkled in her pocket. It was Matthew's letter. Carrie started. She had yet to speak to Michael, but knew she must. As she finished up in the bathroom she stepped out onto the landing and something pressed her to move toward Michael's bedroom.

Carrie stepped tentatively to his door, which was ajar, pushed it with her fingertips and stepped inside. His bed was rumpled as if someone had lain on it. Carrie instinctively went across to straighten it and Sarah's heady perfume wafted up her nose. She frowned and as she plumped the pillow something protruded from underneath, which she tugged out. It was a scarf. Carrie removed it and returned downstairs. She stepped outside holding the scarf between her thumb and forefinger, "Looks like the femme fatale left a little present for you, drowned in her perfume, in your bed."

Michael looked surprised, "You went into my bedroom?"

"I was curious. Is your bed really that comfortable?"

Michael laughed, "Well, now you know. I think I should be flattered."

"Maybe, you should." Carrie sat back down in the swing chair. No one spoke as they swung gently back and fore and enjoyed the closeness of sitting together in the summer warmth.

Carrie gazed up at the sky where a flock of starlings dived and swooped in nature's ballet before dropping down the valley to their favourite roosting places in Crynant. A buzzard swept past with its eerie call and vanished into the trees. It was if the bird was prompting Carrie to speak. She stopped the swing abruptly with her feet, "Michael?"

He turned to look at her and their eyes met, irresistibly drawn together. He bowed his head and his lips met hers in a tender show of deep love and affection. Carrie relinquished herself to his kiss before she broke it off, sat back, opened her eyes and held his gaze.

Michael looked puzzled, "What is it? What aren't you telling me? There is something isn't there? I know you too well..."

Carrie nodded and whispered barely perceptibly, "Yes."

Michael looked at her expectantly.

"Duw, this is hard for me. I don't know what to say or how to say it."

Michael raised his hand and stroked the curve of her cheek, "What? You know you can tell me anything."

Carrie shook her spangled curls, which flew wildly in a cloud around her head, "You remember the time I spent in France as an S.O.E.?"

"Yes?"

"I had to pose as a wife to one of the resistance, Matthew?"

"I remember," his tone was measured almost guarded.

"Do you remember Jumbo?'

Michael frowned at the switch in conversation, "Yes, Megan's brother, Gwynfor."

"He died."

"I know…" Michael was more than puzzled.

"I gave a promise to him that he could write to me. He wanted a glimmer of hope to see him through the war. I told him I didn't feel the same but that of course he could write… and then he died."

"So…?"

"I was glad I did that."

"You gave the same promise to me."

"I know."

"Carrie, you're alarming me… what is it?"

"I've had a letter from Matthew. It was filled with loving remarks…"

"Yes?"

"He's to go on a mission through France and into the heart of Germany. He may not come out alive. In fact, he doesn't think he will come out alive."

"I don't understand…"

"Oh, Michael, sometimes you can be so twp!"

"Thank you very much."

"You know what I mean." Carrie swallowed hard, "Matthew is coming to Cardiff on recruitment before he leaves. He wants to see me one last time."

"What have you said?"

"Nothing yet. I haven't replied. He wants to meet me. I have been tussling with the whole thing."

"But, why? It should be an easy decision. Go and see him before he leaves again for war. Make him happy. He will go into his mission feeling positive and will be more likely to survive. What's the problem?"

Carrie said nothing. Her jewel green eyes brimmed with tears as recognition and hurt dawned in Michael's eyes, "You don't know how you feel about him, do you?"

Carrie dropped her head, "I'm sorry."

Michael blew long and hard between his teeth and stood up, which sent the swing seat wild. He paced to the end of the veranda and looked out across the valley in the fading light and spoke into the gentle breeze that had sprung up. "Are you saying you don't love me?"

"No!" Carrie shook her spangled curls fiercely. "I love you. I know I love you, but…"

"But?" he turned to face her.

"I didn't want to lie or deceive…"

"This incredible honesty you have whilst admirable in one respect is also hurtful and threatening."

"I know."

"Are you going to meet him?"

"I think so, yes."

"You could have done so without telling me and I would have been none the wiser. What I didn't know wouldn't have hurt me."

"But I'd have known… I'd have known," she whispered.

There was a silence between them that screamed like a thunderclap in the still of the night.

Eventually Michael spoke, "Do you have feelings for him, feelings for Matthew?"

"Michael, I had to pretend to be his wife. We were in grave danger, of course I feel something…"

"Are you saying you might be in love with him?"

"No… I don't know, I'm confused… I don't want to hurt anyone."

Michael turned away, "Then I think you had better leave. You need to sort your emotions out. You know where I am."

Carrie rose and wiped away the tears that tumbled down her cheek. She walked toward him and placed her hand on his back. Michael turned to her and crushed her to him, kissing her fiercely before pushing her away. "Remember that when you see him."

Carrie feeling ripped apart stumbled off the veranda and headed down the path to the gate and the mountain track. She didn't look back and she didn't see Michael's face set grimly toward the wind with tears rushing to escape his eyes.

CHAPTER TEN

Back to basics

Carrie stumbled along the mountain track her tears blinding her in the wind as she half ran and half skidded down the wet stony trail. The sun had done its best to dry up the sodden mountainside but it was still slippery and therefore a perilous place.

The sun had finally slipped out of sight and clouds chased the waning light as the moon began to cast its silver sheen to the ground. Carrie stepped through frosted creamy pools of moonshine and as she walked she tried to recover her equilibrium. She was relieved when she saw the shadows of the barns and the roundhouse looming larger before her.

Bonnie looked up from her slumbers by the water butt and shook her coat gently and padded toward Carrie who was in need of consolation and Bonnie was not one to disappoint. Carrie leaned against the slatted roundhouse door and fussed the lovable Border collie, "Oh, Bonnie. What have I done? I wanted to be truthful and now I have hurt the one man who has stood by me through everything. I'm wondering if there will be any going back?"

Bonnie whined softly in her throat and put her head on one side and gazed at Carrie before pushing her head into her hands to be petted. Carrie continued to sob and she slid down onto the damp ground where Bonnie fussed and jumped around her, licking her salt tears before finally nestling into her.

The door to the barn opened and Ernie appeared scratching his wiry, tufted head, minus his beret, in shirtsleeves and waistcoat. He looked around him and caught sight of Bonnie by the roundhouse with Carrie. He shuffled through the yard and out to where they sat.

"Jawch, whatever are you doing out by here?"

Carrie looked up at her wise friend, "Oh, Ernie. I've done something so stupid…"

"There, there, no more stupid than a pig eating a pork pie, or a sheep knitting."

"What?" Carrie stopped crying immediately. "Ernie, you do say the strangest things."

"Well, if it stops the tears it's worth it. Whatever's wrong? Not had a tiff with Michael, have you?"

"How did you know?"

"Well, when a young girl comes home from seeing her young man in a state like this what else could it be? Come on, up you get." He extended his hand to Carrie and helped her up. "I'm too old to be sitting on stony ground in the night. Why don't you come with me to the barn and you can tell me all about it."

Carrie gratefully leaned on Ernie and followed by Bonnie they trooped across to the barn. Ernie's oil lamp burned brightly and they sat on straw bales as Carrie began to tell him what had happened. All the time she kept her eyes fixed on the ground.

Ernie listened and Carrie finally was able to lift her eyes and look at Ernie. "Oh, Ernie. Tell me what to do."

"Now, Cariad, you know I'm never one to do that. You must make your own decisions. You are mistress of your own destiny. We all have a free will and can make our own choices. Sometimes those choices are difficult. But they have to be decisions that we can live with. Look inside your heart and ask yourself, how would you feel if you were never to see Michael again? How would you feel if he took another woman as his wife and companion?"

"I'd hate it. I'd always regret what I'd done."

"And if you never saw Matthew again?"

"I don't know. I hadn't thought of him or hankered after him until I got his letter. And, now I'm confused."

"It seems to me that if you'd never had the letter you wouldn't even be thinking of him."

"It's just…"

"I know… you are thinking about Gwynfor."

"Yes. I'd have regretted it for ever if I hadn't set him straight but I still allowed him to write."

"Then maybe you need to do the same again. Michael will come round. In his heart he knows you love him. But you'll have a lot of making up to do to smooth out the roly-poly of hurt you've caused."

"I know. Thanks, Ernie."

"Aw, Cariad. I love you like a daughter. Now, get yourself off to bed. You'll have a tough enough day tomorrow."

Carrie rose. She stooped over and gave the old man a kiss on his cheek. He blushed like a ripening apple and turned his attention to Bonnie to disguise his pleasure.

Carrie smiled whispering her thanks and left the barn. She saw the lights were still on in Old Tom's Cottage and wondered what tales Sarah would be telling Laura and Rose. She shrugged off her feelings of foreboding and crossed the yard to Hendre.

As she entered the glasshouse Jenny came out to meet her, "Thank God you're here."

"Why? What's happened?"

"It's John. He's in bed with some sort of fever. I don't know what to do."

Carrie pulled open the pine door to the stairs and ran up to John and Jenny's room. She dashed to her brother's side. Jenny followed anxiously.

Carrie felt his brow it was burning hot. "Get some cold compresses, we need to get his temperature down. Pull the eiderdown off the bed just let him be covered with a sheet."

Jenny did as she was asked and raced from the room.

John's eyes fluttered and rolled. He saw Carrie's sweet face and noted she'd been crying, "Come on, Cariad. No need for tears. I've got a touch of flu that's all. I keep going hot and cold."

"What else?" asked Carrie taking her brother's pulse.

"My muscles ache, burning and sore. And I have one hell of a head."

"Shouldn't drink so much," joked Carrie.

"I wouldn't mind if it was self inflicted," coughed John.

"I think we need Dr Rees to take a look at you, it could be flu or even pneumonia. I don't like it."

John coughed again and the spittle dribbled down his chin.

"Let's get you propped up. It will be easier to breathe. Jenny!"

Jenny came in carrying a bowl of cold water, which she set on the bedside table, a towel and some clean flannels.

"We need to get some more pillows behind him and prop him up then start the cold compresses. I'll get mine from my room."

Carrie dashed to her own room and removed two pillows, while Jenny found a couple more. Together they lifted John up and pushed him forward stacking the pillows behind him and leaned him back.

"My two best girls," murmured John. "Not forgetting little Bethan. And she's coming on so well with her speech, now. I expect that's because you never stop talking!" he joked.

"Quiet, John." Carrie showed Jenny what to do, "Soak the flannels in cold water, ring them out and place on his forehead and mop his face. Use a towel to stop the drips. As soon as they start to feel warm, rinse them out and repeat. Can you do this?" Jenny nodded. "What about Bethan?"

"She's asleep."

"Good, I'm going for Dr Rees."

"But it's getting late."

"No matter, for this to happen after the flooding there may be a connection. He swallowed a lot of river water. I'll also look in on Rose. See if she has any symptoms."

Jenny nodded and Carrie ran back down the stairs.

Outside the moon was full and on another evening Carrie would have been tempted to run barefoot in glee through the meadow even though the grass was sodden. The millions of stars twinkled in the velvet sky. It was a glorious night. Carrie hurried across the yard and down the path to Old Tom's Cottage and urgently knocked at the door. Sarah opened it and raised one eyebrow, "Problems?" she sniffed imperiously.

"Rose, I need to see Rose."

Sarah called back and her usual honeyed tones became more strident as she lifted her voice. "Rose!"

Rose appeared and looked surprised to see Carrie. "Yes?"

"Are you okay? Do you feel all right?"

"I'm fine," said Rose puzzled, "Why?"

"You're sure? No headaches, sore muscles?"

"No."

"Good. I just needed to check." Carrie turned to leave. "Sorry to disturb you."

"Wait! What's wrong?"

"It's John. He's not well. I think it may have something to do with the river."

"I'm fine but then I didn't swallow any water."

"Thanks." Carrie didn't wait for any more comments. She ran to the barn and led out Senator. Her bike was no use on this occasion. She and Dr Rees could hardly ride up the track on her bike. She quickly harnessed a surprised Senator to the cart. She lit and secured the lamps on the side of the wagon, as Ernie emerged complete with beret and jacket from his quarters.

"Here, let me help you with that."

"Aren't you going to ask me what I'm doing?"

"Well, I take it you're not off on a social call and you're in no fit state to be haring off somewhere on your own so I'm coming with you."

Carrie didn't argue. She was relieved and brushed her lips across the old man's weather beaten wrinkled cheek. "Thank you."

Ernie blushed, "Iechy dwriaeth." He scratched at his face where her lips had touched. "Lips like a butterfly's wing, you've got. Tickling me like a thousand money spiders running over my skin. What a way to get my attention."

"Go on with you," chided Carrie gently.

"Where are we off, then? Doctor Rees?"

Carrie nodded and climbed up into the cart. Ernie sat alongside and took the rein spurring Senator to move down the track.

"It's John," explained Carrie.

Ernie nodded, "I did wonder. What's happened?"

Carrie explained his symptoms and Ernie frowned. "You say Rose is all right?"

"She seemed fine."

"Thing is, this time of the year with the run off from the fields into the river it could be Field Fever."

"Whatever's that?"

"Not very pleasant and if not treated properly can develop

into something much worse. Best get onto the doctor." Ernie shook the reins again and Senator dutifully responded.

Although it was late and past her bedtime Naomi sat at the kitchen table playing cards with Lewis Owen, while Jacqueline checked on the children upstairs. They were playing Snap and Naomi was trying not to get excited and shout out. She didn't want to disturb Jacqueline.

Naomi slapped her card, the Ace of Spades down on Lewis' Ace of Clubs and squealed, "Snap!" and giggled happily.

Lewis covered her hand as she tried to remove the pile of playing cards. He looked deeply into her eyes. "You and I are getting on a treat, so we are Naomi, fach. You have fun with your Uncle Lewis now, don't you?"

Naomi nodded, sweetly. Lewis patted her hand, "That's good. I thought tomorrow, you and I might go out for the day before you start school. What do you think?"

"I don't know if Mrs Price will let me," said Naomi quietly.

"Don't worry about her. I'll see if I can sort something out. If you're a willing, of course." He smiled at her and his eyes seemed to look right through her and her clothes.

Naomi nodded, "If she'll let me."

"She will; especially if I bag her a couple of rabbits and a pheasant or two. Now give me a hug," and he smiled a long slow smile.

Dr Rees had completed his examination of John as Jenny, Ernie and Carrie watched anxiously.

"What is it, then, Doctor?" asked Jenny the worry apparent in her voice.

"I'll need to take a sample of blood, just to be sure, but I'm pretty certain Ernie is right in his estimation, especially after John's ordeal in the Black River. This isn't flu but Field or Harvest Fever and river water was responsible."

"But what is it? What causes it?" asked Jenny.

"Its correct name is Leptospirosis and it's transmitted by both wild and domesticated animals but the usual culprits are rodents."

"Rodents?"

"Rats. Their urine or the urine of infected animals comes into contact with water and then enters the body through cuts or breaks in the skin, through the eyes, mouth or other orifices. He must have swallowed contaminated water. You say sheep were grazing near the bank?"

"Aye," replied Ernie.

"Then you may have some infected animals or more than likely the flood water brought out the rats."

"What do we do?"

"Do as you're doing. I'll get his blood tested and see if the bacteria are present. In the meanwhile he must take some penicillin. That will counteract the bugs. Keep a watchful eye on him. If his skin turns yellow or he starts bleeding, fetch me immediately. That is a sign it could worsen into something far more serious."

Jenny and Carrie exchanged a glance.

"I believe he'll be lucky. It's one of the more common dangers to farmers and vets; I've seen it before. I'll also look over the young lady who saved his life. Rose? Isn't it?"

"Is it catching?" asked Jenny.

"Fortunately, no. He will be very tired, make sure he has plenty of rest and is kept hydrated. As long as he's not vomiting get some hearty food inside him."

Dr Rees donned his outdoor coat again and turned to Ernie, "Can you take me to Rose? From what I know the bacteria can live in mud and from what I've heard she was waist deep in it."

Dr Rees, slim and tall, stooped to exit the room and followed Ernie.

Carrie tried to reassure Jenny, "John will be fine. As long as we do as the doctor says. I'll be on hand to help when I'm home."

"Thanks. We're lucky to have you. Can you keep an eye on Bethan? I'm sure she'll be fine but I want to sit with John."

"Of course." Carrie left her to it and opened the toddler's door. Bethan was sleeping peacefully, her sweet face in repose and her thumb firmly in her mouth. Carrie closed the door quietly. She leaned against it. Her head was spinning. So much was happening and she still hadn't made a decision. Should she go to Cardiff with John home ill or not? That was the question. She hadn't much time to make up her mind and if she went she knew she had to contact the hotel.

The sun beamed down on Katy and Sally playing outside in the garden with Prince. The dog was loving and affectionate and eager to fetch the ball when they threw it. They giggled as they ran around Mrs Powell's large grounds.

Katy lobbed the ball as hard as she could and it landed in the bushes by the garden shed. Prince stopped, his hackles rose and he appeared to be staring intently into the shrubs. A low growl rumbled in his throat. The two girls looked at each other and Sally called the dog, "Prince, here boy. Come." But the dog remained rigid and focused.

Sally walked forward tentatively and stretched out her hand to touch Prince. Suddenly, there was a squirt of water that sprayed the dog in the face. He yelped and ran back to Katy, leaving Sally to get drenched.

Emrys came out from the shrubbery giggling inanely. He stared distastefully at the twins. "I don't want you here. Why don't you go back where you came from?" He shot a stream of water at Sally soaking her front.

Sally began to cry and Mrs Powell hammered on the window. "Play nicely!" she ordered. "Emrys! Give me that water gun, now." Emrys reluctantly ambled to the kitchen door and passed the weapon to his mother. "Now apologise. I want to see you playing properly. Go on, I'm watching and listening."

The twins glanced at each other uncertain what to do. Emrys walked up, "Sorry. Don't take no notice of me. Friends?"

The sudden change in attitude confused the girls. Emrys just seemed to have switched personalities. They stood uncertainly unable to fathom out whether he was sincere or not.

"Let's play hide and seek. You go first and I'll count."

The twins looked at each other and then back at Mrs Powell at the door who nodded approvingly and encouraged them. "Go on. Just be careful by the pond."

Emrys began to count. Sally and Katy darted away followed by Prince.

Mrs Powell called, "And make sure you're back for tea, there's good children."

Emrys hurriedly finished counting to a hundred and shouted, "Coming! Ready or not."

Katy had scrambled up a tree and Prince sat at the base of the trunk, looking up. She hissed at the dog. "Shoo, Prince. Go! You'll give me away." Prince didn't move.

Emrys screamed aloud, "Gottcha!" Prince padded off and returned to the kitchen door where he sat and waited. Katy shinned down the tree skinning her knee. She stifled a squeal and looked at Emrys.

"You'd better get Mam to look at that or she'll think I did it. Then you can come out and help me find your sister."

Katy limped off to the house and Emrys crashed through the grounds looking for Sally.

Sally had run to the end of the garden, past the pond and rockery, through another patch of bushes and she crept into a dilapidated, dusty wooden shed. She crawled into an old trunk inside the hut and stayed as quiet as a mouse. She heard Emrys calling down the garden, "Coming to get you!" Sally didn't move. She heard the door of the shed open and someone step inside. Sally hardly dared to breathe. She heard something being dragged across the floor. Then there was a thumping thud as whatever it was landed on the lid of the chest. Sally froze. She heard footsteps again, the shed door slammed shut and a key turned in the lock.

Sally waited a moment longer. Hearing no more sound she whispered, "Emrys? Katy?"

There was no response. Sally shifted her cramped position in the chest and tried to push up the lid. Nothing. She could hardly move it and it stayed firmly closed. Sally began to feel frightened. She hammered on the lid with her fists and called out, "Help! Please, help!" But no one could hear.

Naomi Clarke sat at the breakfast table giggling. Lewis Owen covered her small hand with his huge fist, "There's lovely to hear you laugh, Naomi. It's like the song on a summer breeze. And you have the smile of an angel." Naomi flushed with pleasure. Lewis patted her hand again. "Seeing as how we're on our own. Would you like to play a little game with me?" Naomi nodded shyly. "Then that's settled. Now, what shall we play?"

"We can play 'Snap'. I like Snap," said Naomi.

"I wasn't thinking of cards," said Lewis carefully. "Something a bit more physical and fun."

"Physical?" asked Naomi.

"Yes, a bit livelier."

"What like hide and seek or Tig?"

"Hide and seek. Perfect. Tell you what, you run and hide. I'll count to fifty and try to find you. If I find you quickly I'll get a reward. If I don't, you'll get one."

"How will I know how long to hide for?"

"If I give up I'll shout, 'come out, come out wherever you are'. Okay?" Naomi nodded happily. "Good, then let's play."

Lewis covered his eyes, put his head down on the table and began to count. Naomi scrambled off her seat and looked about her wildly she ran out of the room and Lewis counted steadily.

Naomi scuttled to the bottom of the stairs. She ran up to the landing and dived into the bathroom where she crouched down behind an ottoman. Her heart beat wildly and she struggled not to laugh.

She heard Lewis call out, "Coming! Ready or not." She lay very still and listened eagerly for any sign of his approach.

She heard doors opening and closing downstairs and the sound of footfalls on the stairs. She waited quietly as the footsteps reached the landing. Again doors opened and shut. Naomi listened as Lewis moved around the room, opening wardrobe doors. She imagined him searching under the beds and tried not to giggle. Doors closed and eventually the door of the bathroom inched open and Lewis stepped inside. Naomi could hear him breathing.

He peered in the bathtub and looked behind the door. He raised the corner of a towel in a pile on the floor before peeking over the ottoman and spotting Naomi who squealed loudly at being discovered. Lewis scooped her up as she wriggled and laughed so he set her down on the floor and tickled her. She twisted and rolled laughing in glee until her sides hurt. Lewis lifted her up and stood her back on her feet announcing, "I claim my prize." He gave her a big kiss on her cheek and Naomi giggled again.

"This is a grand game, isn't it just?" he said.

Naomi nodded, "Let's do it again. Your turn to hide now."

Lewis scrambled up as Naomi began to count and Lewis darted out through the door. He ran down the stairs and opened the cupboard under the stairs and crept inside to wait.

Naomi, now flushed with colour, finished her count and called out that she was coming. She dashed out of the bathroom and quickly looked in each bedroom before running down the stairs. She raced into the kitchen and then the parlour, which she searched thoroughly. Puzzled she stepped back into the hall and examined the space behind the coat stand. It was then she spotted the door to the cupboard under the stairs. She giggled and threw it open. She stooped and stepped inside. Lewis caught her wrist and pulled her to him. "Got me!" he shouted. "Now claim your reward." Naomi laughed shyly and kissed him on his cheek.

Lewis grinned, "Oh, I think we can do better than that, can't we?" He wrapped his arms around Naomi, "I'd like a big hug."

The key to the front door turned and Jacqueline stepped inside talking officiously and was followed by Carrie Llewellyn. "As I said, she's perfectly safe. She starts school next week until then I have a friend keeping an eye on her and my mother has offered to take her with my children to her house, but she often prefers to stay here and help out." Jacqueline took her coat off and hung it on the coat stand. "Come through to the kitchen and I'll give her a call."

Carrie followed Jacqueline through the hall. Lewis stepped out from the cupboard with Naomi but before he exited he put his fingers to his lips, "Not a word now. We'll play again another time." Naomi smiled and nodded her agreement.

Jacqueline frowned and said in her pinched tones, "What are you doing in there?"

"Playing hide and seek we were, weren't we, Naomi?"

Naomi beamed, "Yes. It was fun. He tried to hide in there but I found him, didn't I?"

"You certainly did."

"And you are?" asked Carrie cautiously.

"Owen, Lewis Owen.... Nurse...?"

"Llewellyn, Carrie Llewellyn." Carrie stiffened as old Howie Price's words returned to her. "Um... I'd like to see her room, now, if I may?"

"Certainly," replied Jacqueline tartly. "Naomi, show the nurse where you are sleeping."

Naomi smiled and started for the cupboard in the kitchen. Jacqueline interrupted, "No, upstairs; where you are now," she said grimacing.

Naomi trotted to the stairs and smiled at Carrie, "This way." She bounded up the stairs and entered the room she shared with Mary. Carrie followed.

"So this is where you sleep?"

"It is now," said Naomi.

"What do you mean, now?"

"To begin with I was in the dungeon but after Ted wet the bed. She brought me out of there, needed the cellar for punishment she said."

Carrie frowned. She didn't like what she was hearing. "And what about Mr Owen?"

"He's been ever so kind, plays games with me."

"Yes?"

"Snap, Hide and Seek. For rewards."

"Rewards?"

"Yes, like a hug or a kiss."

Carrie liked this answer even less, and her face showed it. "Naomi, are you happy here?"

"I wasn't. But it's better now. They've registered for me at school where I'll see the others."

"I see. Do you have enough to eat?"

Naomi hesitated, "... Yes. Some of the grub's a bit strange but it's okay."

"Listen, Naomi, I will be coming to see you again and visiting you in school. You will tell me if anything is amiss?"

Naomi nodded, her eyes wide and curious. "I need to go down now and help with tea."

"Do you help with much?"

"Yes, with chores and the children. I don't mind."

Carrie smiled and followed Naomi out of the room and back down the stairs. "Thank you, Mrs Price. I'll be off now. But I'll return soon to visit."

Jacqueline sniffed, "As you wish. Now, if you'll excuse me I have a meal to prepare before the others are home and Naomi usually helps me."

Carrie nodded tersely. She had strong misgivings about this placement and almost said as much, but bit her tongue. Carrie resolved to move the child at the first opportunity, but now she had to get home. She would call in on the Powell family on the way.

Carrie's mind was working overtime as she had much to think about. She left Jacqueline Price's house with a strange nervous fluttering in her tummy. She had a mixture of emotions bubbling under her cool professionalism. She thought back to Lewis Owen and his expression as he engaged with little Naomi Clarke and something in his eyes reminded her of Jacky Ebron and she shivered.

Carrie left and called in at the Post Office, now run by Glenda Pearson who was chatting on the phone at the small exchange behind the counter. Carrie waited as Mrs Pearson curtailed her call. Fortunately, it was quiet and she was able to send a telegram to Matthew Reynolds at The Angel Hotel, Cardiff without any questions or prying glances. It just read, 'I will arrive Sat. after 12. Carrie.' She hastened out of the place her cheeks were now tinged with the hues of embarrassment.

Carrie mounted her bike and cycled down Neath Road toward The Crescent. Her spangled curls flew out from under her felt hat and streamed behind her in the breeze. She grabbed onto it with one hand and steered with the other until she felt she was safe from losing it and caught hold of the handlebars again. Too late, her head covering took flight and bowled behind her, back down the hill. She skidded to a halt and propped her bike up against a garden wall and fled after the escaping item. Carrie rounded a corner and stopped abruptly as a man bent down to retrieve the frolicking titfer. He rose to his full height and Carrie gasped.

"I believe this is yours," he stretched out his hand offering the runaway hat to her.

Carrie stepped forward and grasped the offending item. Their fingers touched and Carrie felt a pleasant tingle run up her arm. She gulped, "Thank you."

Michael Lawrence and Carrie stood silently gazing at each other before she turned quite pink and lowered her eyes.

"Carrie…?" She looked up and engaged him with her eyes. "I need to know…"

Her mouth opened and she nervously moistened her parted lips. She tried to speak but no words would come.

"I need to know if…"

She suddenly found her voice, "If?"

"Do you still love me?"

"Oh, Michael," the pain and passion in her voice was apparent. "I do, I truly do but…"

He stopped her, "Then that's enough for me. Go to Cardiff. Give this operative his hope as you did for Gwynfor and come back to me."

Carrie took her hat and re-pinned it onto her head. "I will."

"And may I accompany you back to Hendre?"

Carrie frowned, "That would be lovely but I have one more call to make."

Michael Lawrence nodded and touched his cap, "As you wish. Or I could wait for you?"

Carrie beamed up at him, "Yes, please."

Michael smiled, "Then let's go."

They walked back along the road. Carrie picked up her bike. They made their way thoughtfully in silence as they turned into the lane where the twins were lodging.

They stopped by the garden wall with an elaborate wrought iron gate set in an arch that led to the Powell's garden. Carrie propped up her bicycle, turned her face up to Michael. "I'll be as quick as I can. Will you watch my bike for me?"

"With pleasure and while you're gone I'll think pleasant thoughts."

"And not of Sarah," quipped Carrie cheekily.

"Now, there's an idea," grinned Michael.

Carrie laughed and walked up the paved drive to Edna Powell's house and knocked. The door opened and Carrie prepared herself with an engaging smile.

"Ah, Nurse Llewellyn, please come in." Carrie entered and the door closed firmly behind her. "You'll be wanting to see the children, of course."

"Yes, and where they sleep. And I've brought your medication from Dr Rees. He asked me to pop it in to you."

"Medication? And why would I need that?" Mrs Powell spoke abruptly and then tempered her words, her tone softened, "Thank you. It's very kind of the good doctor but I don't think I'll be needing it anymore. Still, I'll take it anyway. How much?"

"The doctor will send his bill."

Edna nodded and stopped at the foot of the stairs. "Why don't you see the girls' room first?" Edna Powell took the offered medicine and set it on the hall table and started up the stairs, "This way."

Carrie followed and was shown the twins' very acceptable room. Carrie was impressed with the cleanliness and light airy feel. "This is grand."

"It should be, cleanliness is next to Godliness so they say."

Carrie noticed a spark of something entering Edna Powell's eyes and voice, which made her shiver. "I'd like to see the girls now, please."

"Of course. They've been playing hide and seek in the garden with my Emrys. I have just called them in for Bible study. Katy has washed her hands and is learning the books of the Bible. I'll test her later. Sally has yet to return. Still hiding, I think. I'll give her a call in a moment."

Carrie frowned, hide and seek seemed to be a popular game and in her view a cover for something more sinister, certainly it was in Jacqueline Price's house.

Carrie forced a smile and followed Mrs Powell out and down the stairs to the kitchen. Emrys sat chewing the end of a pencil glowering at a list of questions on a passage of Scripture he had to read.

Katy was looking warily about her. She attempted a smile as Carrie came in and raised her hand shyly.

"Yes?" asked Carrie gently.

"Please... I can't read these words and I can't say them."

Edna Powell jumped in, "What do you mean? Can't say them?" she snapped tartly. "Come on. Genesis, Exodus, Leviticus, Numbers, Deuteronomy..." She glanced around, "And where is your sister? Which one is she?"

Katy shrugged, "It's Sally. I don't know. She hasn't come in yet."

Edna Powell threw open the back door and shouted, "Sally! You can stop hiding now. It's time to come in. There's someone to see you."

Edna closed the door, "Would you like a cup of tea, Nurse Llewellyn?"

"Thank you, but someone is waiting for me. I really just want to see the twins."

Edna looked suspiciously at Emrys, "Do you know where she is? You haven't locked her in anywhere have you?"

"No, Mam," said Emrys in an aggrieved tone. "Why is it always my fault when something goes wrong?"

"Because it usually is! But, I'm being ungracious... Maybe it is, maybe it isn't..."

The look in flint–eyed Edna Powell's face was distracted as if something was bubbling up inside her that she needed to expunge from her system.

Emrys threw down his pen and sighed heavily, "I'll go and look for her."

He went to the kitchen door and Carrie added, "I think we all should go. We'll have a better chance of finding her. After all it is a big garden."

Emrys shrugged, "If you like," and he flounced out of the back door.

Katy scrambled up, "I'll find her." She ran out after Emrys chased by Prince.

Edna Powell followed reluctantly calling out Sally's name and Carrie stepped out into the acre-sized grounds and looked around, "You check the top of the garden by the shrubbery. Do you have any sheds or greenhouses?"

"Yes, right the way down the bottom into the wild part of the garden past the ponds."

"Ponds?" said Carrie with alarm.

Edna Powell looked at her, "Oh my, you don't think...?"

Carrie didn't wait, she ran and shouted to Michael waiting outside, "Michael! Come into the garden through the gate in the wall. Quickly! A child is missing."

Michael heard the commotion and leaving Carrie's bike he crashed through the wrought iron gate and joined them to help hunt for Sally as Carrie quickly explained.

Sally sat miserably in the trunk, looking pale. Her breathing was ragged and she had no more strength to hammer on the lid. She was becoming weaker and more lethargic with lack of oxygen.

Somewhere within the mists of her mind she heard a faint noise outside but feeling disorientated and confused she couldn't work out what it was and she hadn't the energy to call out or bang on the lid and her eyes closed as she fell into a welcome, enveloping cloak of darkness.

She stirred slightly as something scraped across the lid and there was a click but ignoring it all she continued to fade into unconsciousness.

The garden outside was alive with those calling Sally's name. Emrys flew past Carrie who was scanning the large pond and fountain. He yelled, "She's not in the greenhouse."

Edna Powell came puffing up followed by Katy. "She's not in the shrubbery or arboretum. Have you checked the potting shed? Or the garden shed?"

"No," said Emrys now red-faced. "I'll look in the wild part by the rockery."

"I'll take the potting shed. Come on Katy, you call your sister." She turned to Carrie, "I don't know why he didn't check the garden shed; it's right next door to the greenhouse."

Prince bounded ahead of Carrie and Michael who followed Mrs Powell to the far end where the shacks were situated. He stopped outside the dilapidated old wooden shed and pawed at the door. The door vibrated and the old key fell from the lock onto the grass. Prince whined softly in his throat and barked as the others came running. Michael pushed open the door and stepped inside. Dust motes floated like a gathering swarm of midges and he looked around. Prince padded past, sat by the chest and barked.

Michael's keen eye saw the scratch marks through the dirt-encrusted floor. He spotted a heavy earthenware pot now on its side next to the chest and the terracotta scuff –like marks on the top of the old trunk.

He marched quickly to the box and opened the lid, which squealed on its rusty hinges revealing the small pale child inside and scooped her out. Her head lolled back in his arms and her eyes rolled in her head.

"Oh, no!" Edna Powell's hand flew to her neck and throat in distress. Katy stood silently with tears beginning to stream down her cheeks.

"Quickly, let's get her indoors," urged Carrie.

Michael ran up the path with Carrie and the others chasing after him. Emrys hung behind after his mother and Katy, and walked slowly after them.

Carrie pushed open the door as Michael looked around, "Where shall I take her?"

"Into the parlour, if that's all right, Mrs Powell?" said Carrie.

"Of course, through here, into the hallway and it's the second door on the left."

Michael dashed into the room and lay the little girl down on the settee. He stepped back allowing Carrie to come to the girl's side. She checked her pulse. "It's there but very faint. She's been starved of oxygen. Do you have any smelling salts?"

Mrs Powell dithered, "I think so. In the bathroom. Or are they…?

Carrie patted the small child's hands and face, "Sally, come on, Sally wake up!"

Katy stood miserably and pleaded, "Sally, please don't leave me."

Prince padded up to the small child and licked her hand. Mrs Powell was about to remonstrate with the dog but Carrie stopped her, "No leave him." Mrs Powell left the room.

The dog then began to wash Sally's face and he snuggled into the side of the couch. Sally's hand now rested on his back. Prince whined softly again and resumed his licking of her face and Sally stirred. She turned her face away and brushed her hand along the dog's coat. Her eyes fluttered open, then closed and she coughed.

Carrie helped Sally to sit up and checked her pulse again, "Sally, open your eyes. Can you see me?" The six-year-old did as she was asked and nodded. "How many fingers am I holding up?"

"Three," came the feeble response.

"Good. Good. Now watch my fingers as I move them." Carrie moved her hands from side to side and up and down. The child followed the movement with her eyes.

"Good. Now, can you tell me what happened?"

The little girl shook her head and spoke in a tiny voice, "No..."

Mrs Powell entered with the smelling salts. Her face flushed with relief as she saw Sally sitting up, "Is she okay?"

"I think so, but we'll take her to see the doctor just to be sure. Michael, can you carry her?"

Michael lifted Sally up into his arms. Carrie turned to Mrs Powell and said almost threateningly, "Look after Katy I'll be back later."

They left quickly and Carrie jumped on her bike. I'll meet you at the doctor's. Michael nodded and headed quickly for The Crescent.

Dr Rees peered over his half spectacles at Carrie and Michael as he removed the stethoscope from his ears, "Well, it seems the little one is all right now." He turned to young Sally lying on his consultation couch, "So, young lady, how do you feel?"

"As dizzy as a top but otherwise I'm feeling better."

Carrie smiled and said gently, "Sally, can you tell me what happened?"

"We were playing hide and seek..."

"Yes?"

"I went to hide in the garden and..."

"And?"

Sally hesitated and frowned, "I can't remember…" Her eyes filled up and she began to cry. "I don't know…"

"It's all right, Sally fach. Honestly. Don't you worry, now. You might not remember at the moment, but you will later, you'll see," said Carrie.

"What do we do, Dr Rees?" asked Michael taking the doctor to one side and speaking in hushed tones.

"She needs to be kept an eye on through the night. It's best she stays here for now."

"Can you manage?" asked Carrie quietly.

"We've had worse," smiled the doctor. "Remember the Diphtheria outbreak? Millicent will be glad to help, I'm sure."

"In that case, I'll let Mrs Powell know."

Doctor Rees dropped his voice still further and frowned, "She's one of the ones with Edna Powell?"

"Yes, and I passed on the medication as you asked. She said she didn't need it."

"In that case, I think you should find somewhere else for the child to stay. One of twins you said?"

"Yes, Doctor."

"Then I would try an find alternative accommodation if I were you, for both of them."

Carrie pursed her lips and shot a worried glance at Michael. She turned back to Sally, "Sally, you are to stay here for the moment with Dr Rees and his wife. I'll go and see your sister and Mrs Powell. You'll be fine."

"Do I have to go back there?" asked Sally quietly.

"We'll have to see, why?"

"I don't like it there. She's strange. Sometimes she's nice but…"

"But?" questioned Carrie.

"She can be kind one minute and nasty the next and I don't like Emrys."

"Why is that?"

"He hurts us, twists our arms and he's mean to the poor dog."

Carrie kept her face impassive and forced a smile. "Don't you worry none. We'll see what we can do."

"Call in on the way back if you can," urged Dr Rees.

Carrie nodded. She bent down and smoothed the little one's forehead and hair. "I'll be back later. You be good for Dr Rees, now, won't you?"

Sally forced a smile and turned her head away as Carrie and Michael left.

They stood outside the doctor's house while Carrie thought what to do.

"You may as well leave your bike here and pick it up on the way back," suggested Michael.

"Good idea and I just may need your help. I have a plan."

"And I need to tell you what I saw."

"What do you mean?" asked Carrie curiously as they started back up The Crescent to the main road.

"The shed, where we found Sally."

"What about it?"

"No one had been in there for a long time. It was covered with dust."

"So?"

"I could see Sally's foot prints leading to the trunk, and another set slightly larger."

"I didn't notice," said Carrie honestly.

"And another thing. Something had been dragged across the floor to the chest. There were scuffmarks in the dust and red scratches from one of those large terracotta pots on the wooden lid. I think someone shifted a pot and put it on the trunk so the child couldn't get out."

"And you think...?"

"From what I've heard..."

"Emrys," finished Carrie. Michael nodded.

They rounded the top of the hill and walked to Edna Powell's house where screams and shouts assailed their ears. They ran to the door and knocked loudly.

A man was swearing in Welsh and the sound of smashing crockery could be heard. Michael didn't hesitate. He opened the door and ran in. He was forced to duck as a saucepan whistled past his ear and Carrie just moved out of the way in time. It crashed to the floor amidst the fragments of broken dishes.

Carrie looked up the stairs and could see Emrys peering through the banister rail. Katy stood by the kitchen door hanging onto Prince. Edna Powell had another missile in her hands and was about to throw it at her husband, Alwyn, who had his hands up and was trying to reason with her.

"Duw, Duw, Edna. Let's talk about this…" he stopped and turned to see Michael and Carrie standing there. "Who the hell are you? What do you want?"

Edna Powell stopped screaming and tried to regain her composure, "Nurse Llewellyn?"

Carrie swallowed hard, "I came to say that Sally is staying at the doctor's house tonight, just to be on the safe side."

Michael's eyes flicked up to the boy, Emrys, who appeared to have a grin spreading on his face.

"I've also come to collect Katy as the twins are not to be separated."

Michael raised his eyebrows and looked at Carrie.

"When will they be back?" asked Edna a feral glint gleaming in her eyes.

"I'm not sure," said Carrie. She spoke to Katy at the kitchen door. "Can you run upstairs and fetch a few things for yourself and your sister?"

Katy didn't need to be told twice. She dashed from the kitchen and ran upstairs to her room.

Alwyn stood looking embarrassed. "Just a bit of a spat, Nurse, nothing serious. Me and Edna, we were having a difference of opinion. Got out of hand that's all," he stumbled over his words and tried to shuffle next to his wife, who glared at him.

"Mrs Powell. I think you need to start taking your medication, now," advised Carrie.

"That's what the row's about," stuttered Alwyn. "She's not right without it. Flies into a storming paddy, she does, at the least little thing. When she's on her tablets, she's a different person."

"I'm sure she is," said Carrie coolly. "But, I can't leave children in her care when she's like this."

"No, no. Of course, not."

Edna Powell's eyes glittered dangerously. She was about to

speak, when Katy emerged with a bag of things and ran down to Carrie's side.

"Right then, we'll be off. I'll come and check on you next week. Once you start taking your medicine again."

Katy tugged at Carrie's coat and looked up soulfully at her. Her eyes brimmed with tears.

"What is it?"

"What about Prince? What about the dog?"

Carrie was stuck for words and apologised to the child when she found her voice, "I'm sorry, Katy. We can't take him with us."

"But he'll be hurt," pleaded Katy.

Alwyn stepped forward, "Take the dog. The child's right. Here." He picked up a lead from the hall table and called Prince who padded over. Alwyn attached the lead and gave it to Michael. He stooped down and made a fuss of the dog, "You be a good boy now. Look after the girls and go with this lady and gent. I'll see you when I can."

Carrie could see this was hard for the man as his eyes became moist with tears. It was clear he loved the white Alsatian. Michael glanced up again and could see that Emrys' grin had changed to a thunderous glowering.

"You can't do that, dad. He's mine!"

Mrs Powell spoke up, "No, the dog stays."

Michael opened the door and the dog almost trotted out with him, but Mrs Powell pulled him back. Carrie held Katy's hand, followed Michael outside into the fresh air and the door closed firmly behind them. Immediately the door closed voices were raised once more.

Michael looked at Carrie, "Are you mad? Two children and we nearly had a dog? Now what?"

"I've got an idea. Follow me."

"Where are we going?"

"You'll see. I've got a plan. Can you lift Katy onto your shoulders? We've got a bit of a walk."

Michael hoisted Katy up. She held onto his head. He took the bag from Carrie, and while one hand secured the child's legs he held Katy's bag in the other. They made an odd picture as they hurried along Main Road to the far end of the village.

Carrie took a deep breath as she stood outside Four Winds, the mansion house belonging to Mrs Gregory.

"This is it? Your idea?" asked Michael as he lifted Katy down from his shoulders. "You owe me a good shoulder rub for this."

"Just wait and see," smiled Carrie as she dropped Katy's bag and crossed her fingers tightly behind her back. Carrie rang the bell.

Children's voices and laughter could be heard running into the hall. The door opened and Basil greeted them as Timmy darted around Basil's legs chased by Marion. They stopped when they saw Carrie and little Katy.

"Cor, ain't you the girl from the train?"

Katy smiled and nodded, "Sounds like you still do crow impressions."

"Ha, ha forgot about that. Caw, caw, caw," he shouted cheekily flapping his arms and running around.

He stopped as he heard the tap, tap of a stick and Mrs Gregory came into view, "Why, Nurse Llewellyn, and Mr...?"

"Lawrence, Michael Lawrence."

"Well, both... what is it?"

Carrie took a deep breath and launched into an explanation of why she was there and concluded, "So you see, the twins are in a difficult and unhappy situation and I really would appreciate your help."

"Really? But, I don't see what I can do. I already have two children and they are more than enough for me to manage."

Katy stepped forward and pleaded, "Please, Mrs Gregory, we ain't got nowhere else to go. We can't go back to that place."

Basil and the children looked expectantly at Mrs Gregory who shook her head, "I'm sorry, no. It's out of the question. Besides I haven't the room."

"Coo, you've got a huge house, we could share..."

"I'm sorry, no. It's not a good idea for boys and girls to share bedrooms."

Carrie flushed guiltily as she remembered her own experience at home after her mother died when she would bunk in with John and all her persuasive tactics vanished.

Timmy tugged on Mrs Gregory's skirt, "They won't have to share with me. If Marion won't have them you've got that other room."

Basil stiffened and frowned. He took a sharp intake of breath and lowered his eyes.

"What other room?" asked Mrs Gregory puzzled.

"The room off the playroom. The one that's kept locked. They could sleep there."

The colour drained from Mrs Gregory's face, "And what do you know about that?" A tinge of severity had entered her manner.

"Basil said…" Timmy stopped as his sister dug him in the ribs.

"You're not supposed to say nothing," chided Marion vehemently.

"And just what did Basil say?" asked Mrs Gregory coolly.

Basil coloured up and began to stutter but Timmy ploughed on again. "I asked him what was in there and he said to never mind it. It was to be kept locked and that you might tell us about it one day," said Timmy honestly.

"Is that so?"

"Madame, I never meant anything by it," Basil apologised.

Mrs Gregory stepped back from the door and began to walk down the hallway, "You had better come in."

Michael and Carrie exchanged a glance and entered the magnificent house. They followed Mrs Gregory along to one of the reception rooms. Mrs Gregory stopped and turned, "Marion, Timmy take… it's Katy isn't it?" Katy nodded. "Take Katy into the kitchen or out to play, will you?"

Marion took the little girl's hand and led her away toward the kitchen.

Carrie and Michael followed Phyllis Gregory into the drawing room, where she indicated they should sit. They did so and Mrs Gregory walked toward the large picture window that overlooked the garden and stared out. "I suppose you think it wrong of me to refuse the child, so you do, if indeed I do have a room?"

"Mrs Gregory, you have been more than generous and I can

see that Timmy and Marion are extremely happy with you. Believe me, I know I am asking a lot. Four children are more than enough for anyone. Indeed, Timmy is enough for anyone."

Mrs Gregory turned from the window to face them, "Timmy is a good boy. Oh, he's a little boisterous at times and can be rowdy but he has a heart, a good heart." Mrs Gregory fell silent.

Michael rose, "Sorry, I can see that it was the wrong thing to ask. We will collect Katy and leave you to it."

"Sit down, Mr Lawrence, I haven't finished, yet."

Carrie tugged on his coat and he resumed his seat. They both looked up at Mrs Gregory who looked imposing framed in the white light surrounding her as it flooded through the window in sharp contrast to her widow weed black.

Phyllis Gregory sat sedately, leaned forward on her walking stick, and faced them. "Timmy is right, I do have another room, which indeed, does lead off the playroom. Maybe it's time." She swallowed hard; clearly the subject was difficult for her and brought her emotions close to the surface. "I expect it will be better if you see for yourselves." Phyllis Gregory rose and straightened her skirt; "Follow me, if you will."

Mrs Gregory swept out of the room. Michael and Carrie scrambled up uncertainly and hurried out after the old lady whose cane tip tapped as she went.

They walked in silence through to the hall and to the foot of the impressive staircase. There was a majesty about the old lady as she glided up the stairs with one hand on the banister rail and the other on her stick. They reached the landing and walked to a heavy oak door with metal studs and wrought iron hinges. Mrs Gregory reached up to the top of the doorframe where there was a small ledge decorated with a few china mugs and pots. She selected one depicting the face of Queen Victoria and drew out a key. She inserted the key into the lock and swayed slightly as she turned it. There was a resounding click and she pushed open the door and stepped inside. A small sound escaped her lips and as if to fortify herself she took a deep intake of breath and moved toward one window and pulled back the heavy drapes allowing light to filter into the room and illuminate the child's bedroom.

The place was delightful, a large bed with a pink coverlet and a draped canopy stood centre. A small cabinet filled with knickknacks and photographs stared out at them. The pictures ranged from a bonnie, smiling baby held in a much younger woman's arms, through the infant and junior years to a confident pretty girl of about twelve.

There was one of a little girl with blonde ringlets standing between a man and a woman who looked into the camera smiling. Ballet shoes hung by their ribbons on a wardrobe door as did a petite tutu. Fresh flowers sat in a crystal vase on the vanity dressing table and numerous certificates adorned the wall. The later photographs showed the girl had her blonde hair swept up into a bun. She was holding a trophy, a chalice type cup.

Carrie walked across and read the wording on the certificates aloud quietly, almost reverently. Her voice echoed in the space and as Carrie repeated the child's name Mrs Gregory struggled unsuccessfully to blink back a tear.

"Angelica Victoria Gregory Royal Academy of Dance, Grade 8 passed with distinction…"

"What happened?" asked Michael softly as he gazed around at the obvious shrine to this young girl.

Phyllis Gregory tip tapped to the bed and sat down. She inhaled deeply, in an attempt to control her emotions. "Angelica or Angie as I called her, she was my little angel, so she was … So talented, she was heading for London, the Royal School of Ballet." Mrs Gregory paused. Michael and Carrie said nothing and waited for her to continue.

The old lady hesitated and then slowly continued her story, "Her brother, twin brother, Geraint, had gone off to boarding school. He was lucky. He escaped. Angie went down with what we thought was a bad cold but was something much more serious…"

Carrie could feel her own emotions bubbling up as Mrs Gregory struggled to continue. "My poor little one had been struck down with infantile paralysis."

"Polio…" whispered Carrie.

"Yes," affirmed Mrs Gregory. "They put her in an iron lung when she could no longer breathe for herself, but she was paralysed. Her dream of dancing was cruelly snatched from her. She seemed to give up and... and... she couldn't breathe on her own, so... so..."

Carrie crossed to the old lady and wrapped her arms around her, "You don't have to say anymore... it was a terrible thing to happen, cruel beyond belief."

Mrs Gregory's tears flooded out at Carrie's warm, compassionate touch. Michael was quite moved as he listened to Carrie's tender, understanding murmurings of comfort. Mrs Gregory was just wiping her eyes. Her tears had stopped and the room was in a deep hush.

She jumped suddenly as Timmy came hurtling in chased by Marion, Katy and last of all Basil.

"I'm sorry, Milady," her butler apologised. "I couldn't stop them."

"Cor, what's up, Mrs Gregory? Nurse Llewellyn didn't snip your tongue with her scissors did she?" Timmy scrambled across to the old lady and hugged her tightly as she tried to compose herself.

"It's all right, Basil. I'll deal with this. Leave them here."

Marion and Katy looked in awe around the room at the ballet memorabilia and photographs. Timmy stood up, "Are you all right?" Mrs Gregory nodded and replaced her hankie up her sleeve muttering her thanks. "This is where we're not allowed, ain't it? Cor! It's lovely, it is." He ran to the pictures, "This your daughter? She's ever so pretty and a dancer... our Marion would love to dance but our mum can't afford it. What's her name?" Timmy asked peering at the photos.

"Angelica."

"Posh name sounds like an angel. Is she?"

Carrie tried to stop the boy's infectious enthusiasm but Mrs Gregory, interrupted her, "No, it's all right, Nurse. Let me explain. It's about time I spoke her name again."

"Why? What's happened?" asked Timmy curiously.

Carrie rose and stood by Michael and their hands found each other as they listened to Mrs Gregory explaining what had happened to her daughter. Her voice grew stronger as she

134

talked about her Angie. The children listened spellbound until she finished.

Eventually, Marion stepped forward, "It's all right, Mrs Gregory. We won't mess about in here, honest."

"No… no you won't." She stood up. "Katy, you and your sister Sally will mess about in by here. This will be your room."

"You mean…" Katy stopped.

"Yes, Nurse Llewellyn, do the paperwork. I'll take the twins."

Carrie beamed and hugged Michael. She turned to Mrs Gregory, "Thank you so much. You won't regret it; I know you won't. It's a wonderful thing you're doing."

"I hope so, Nurse Llewellyn. I hope so."

Carrie stepped forward, "I'll fill in all the necessary forms. Her bag is downstairs in the hall. Thank you so much. Can you register her at school?"

Mrs Gregory nodded, "Marion, take Katy down to the kitchen and tell Milly we have another for dinner."

The children rushed out, but Timmy came dashing back. He flung his arms around Mrs Gregory's legs and shouted, "I do love you. And your stick. You're the best."

Then, he chased after the others. Mrs Gregory laughed and shook her head in amusement. "I've kept things bottled up for too long. This is the right thing to do."

Carrie gave her thanks and she and Michael left the room as Mrs Gregory ensured all the curtains and blinds allowed the maximum light to invade the room of shadows and ghosts. The gloom had lifted and as Carrie walked back down the stairs Michael said, "You never cease to amaze me, Carrie Llewellyn."

CHAPTER ELEVEN

At sea and beyond

Malta had suffered heavy bombing from March throughout the year and up to August. HMS Welshman had continued to protect Malta bringing essential supplies and food to the Maltese people. The heavy shelling of Valetta had not stopped HMS Welshman from supporting the escorts to the tanker Ohio, which was carrying much needed fuel to the port.

Thomas was taking a break on deck. The ship still flew the French Flag as part of its disguise. His compatriots were busy unloading more supplies in Valetta harbour. He took out his latest letter from Megan and his heart almost burst with pride as he read that he was going to be a father. He looked up at the clear blue skies overhead and swore an oath, "By all that's Holy I will come through this infernal war and be with my Megan again. This is enough to determine me to come out of this hell in one piece."

He brushed his lips on the missive and thrust the letter into his pocket. The cloud of depression that had surrounded him appeared to lift, so much so, he hardly noticed the strange rumbling in the sky.

The droning noise grew louder. Thomas shaded his eyes against the glare of the sun and could just make out the form of a fighter-bomber. He shouted in alarm to others around him, "German attack! Above!"

Sailors ran for cover as the fighter plane dropped its payload before flying off in a celebratory loop the loop. Mariners manned the guns and fired shots at the departing aircraft whose bombs whistled down with that distinctive noise that they had. The Abdiel minelayer suffered a near fatal miss, which damaged her prop shafts, putting one of her three engines out of service.

Thomas recoiled from the blast, slipped on the deck and tumbled off into the sea.

The cry went up, "Man overboard," and seamen scrambled around to throw him a life preserver. The explosion and fall had rendered Thomas unconscious and he rose to the surface water in the harbour floating face down as Malta natives struggled to get near enough to bring the young sailor to safety.

A dashing young man, one of the many heroes from the siege of Malta, Ivan Scicluna, threw caution to the wind and without a thought for his own safety, plunged into the water avoiding floating debris and swam toward Thomas, turning him over and bringing him safely to the harbour side, where others waited eager to help pull the young man out.

Ivan clambered onto the quay and turned Thomas over. He checked his pulse and smiled in relief. He was breathing. Thomas' eyes fluttered open and he coughed up a mouthful of seawater beginning to come to wakefulness. As Ivan looked him over he noticed the rip in Thomas' bellbottoms and blood seeping through it. He tore a strip from off the bottom of his own shirt and tied it around the injured thigh.

The Captain, William Friedburger, disembarked and stooped down by young Thomas, "How is he?"

"He'll be fine, apart from his leg. It's badly gashed. I've tied a tourniquet," said Ivan who spoke perfect English. "Just give him a moment or two and he'll be fully awake. His leg needs attending to by a professional."

"Good. I'll see to it. Because of the damage sustained we have to limp back to Devonport for repairs and he is a fine engineer. We will need his expertise to get us home, before we can attempt another mission. It'll be slow going, I can see."

The Captain helped a dazed Thomas to sit up. "Come on, Able Seaman. Let's get you back on board and into the infirmary. We need you."

Thomas leaned on the Captain, who aided him to his feet. He swung Thomas' arm around his shoulder and they gingerly stepped to the boarding plank. He called back his thanks to Ivan. Then, Thomas hopped forward and together they returned to the ship.

Carrie stood facing Mrs Powell and her husband, with

Michael at her side. Emrys sat on the floor playing with a toy cork popgun. She had finished explaining what had happened to the girls.

"You mean they're not coming back?" said Mrs Powell in disappointment. Carrie glanced at Emrys, who was finding it hard to contain his glee.

"No, they are with some other evacuated children and we hope to have them reunited with another family member. It will be better for them."

"Oh," Mrs Powell was clearly upset.

Her husband tried to comfort her, "Come on, Edna. You did your best. P'raps if you take the medication the nurse has brought you may get them back, mightn't she, Nurse?"

"I don't know about that," said Carrie gently.

"But, never say never, eh, Nurse?" said Mr Powell.

"Er... no. Well, I think that will be all." Carrie walked crisply to the door when there was a loud yelp. She spun around and saw Emrys popping the cork into Prince's eye and prodding the dog. Her hackles rose and she walked to the white Alsatian, smoothed him down and looked at his eye. "He's lucky he's not blinded. But he needs proper attention." She snatched the offending weapon from Emrys' hands and thrust it at his father. "I suggest you lock this away and get the dog to a vet."

"We can't afford that," blustered Mrs Powell.

"No? Then I'll take him. He can come with me."

Emrys began wailing and complaining about losing his toy. When he heard what Carrie said, he glared viciously and gave the dog a kick.

"That settles it!" stormed Carrie. "Prince!" The gentle dog padded toward her.

Emrys screamed, "She can't have him. He's mine."

Mr Powell stepped forward, "Take the animal, Nurse Llewellyn. Emrys isn't fit to keep him." He retrieved the dog's lead from the hallstand and put it on Prince's collar. Mrs Powell was about to interrupt but her husband turned on her, "No, Edna. Prince should have gone before. The dog's better off out of here. And you know it."

Mrs Powell bit her lip. Carrie took the dog and led him

away and out of the house. The door slammed behind them and voices inside were raised yet again.

Michael looked at Carrie in admiration, "For a minute I thought you were going to clout someone."

"Believe you me, I would have liked to. You know me when I get my gander up."

"Indeed I do, Nurse Llewellyn, indeed I do. So what are you going to do with the dog?"

"There's nothing for it. He'll have to come home with me."

Naomi sat shivering at the kitchen table wrapped in a thin towel. She didn't like the way she was feeling and she didn't like what Lewis Owen had made her do. He said it would be fun and their secret, a sign of love he'd told her. But she didn't enjoy it, didn't like what he had done to her and what he'd asked her to do to him. Now her tummy hurt and she felt sick. She looked down at her hands, they were trembling uncontrollably and she stared hard at them willing them to stop.

Lewis walked into the room, smiling and drying his hands. He beamed at Naomi, "We had fun today, didn't we?" Naomi didn't lift her head. "Come on, Nims. Smile. You must have enjoyed the feelings it gave you." He glanced at the clock, "Now you're nice and clean I should run upstairs and get dressed. We can have a game of cards then, while we wait for Jacqueline to come home."

Naomi rose unsteadily and pushed back her chair. She ran to the door as a small trickle of blood seeped down the inside of her thighs. Lewis began to whistle cheerily as he filled the big black iron kettle and set it on the range. He took a couple of cups from the cupboard and laid them out and swilled out the teapot saving the old tea leaves sitting in the strainer ready to make another brew.

The latch on the front door went and Jacqueline bustled in with her shopping. She entered the kitchen and smiled, "Ah, tea. Just what I need, so it is. I'm parched. Mam not back with the children yet?"

"No, not yet. Come by here while we've got the chance and let me give you a kiss."

"Hush up, Naomi might hear. Where is she?"

"Upstairs, I think."

Jacqueline went into the hall and called, "Naomi! Come on down now. The children will be back soon." Jacqueline looked down and noticed the droplets of blood on the floor and leading up the stairs.

"Oh, no." Jacqueline ran up the stairs and into the bedroom where Naomi slept. The child was now fully clothed and looking distraught. "Oh dear. Is this blood you?" she asked. Naomi nodded silently. "Do you know what it is?" Naomi shook her head. "Looks to me like you've got the curse." Naomi said nothing. "Have you had this before?" Again Naomi shook her head. "It's nothing to worry about. It's perfectly normal." Naomi looked up at Jacqueline, in surprise, as she was being unusually kind. "Wait here."

Jacqueline disappeared fractionally and returned with a wad of cotton rags, "Here, put these inside your kickers. It will stop the blood. I'm going down for a cup of tea. You come down when you're ready. All right?" Again Naomi nodded silently.

Jacqueline pursed her lips and returned downstairs to the kitchen where Lewis was now pouring them both a cup of tea.

"Is she all right?" asked Lewis carefully.

"What? Oh yes." She lowered her voice, "I think she's started her periods, poor kid. Doesn't know what she's in for."

"Oh, that explains it. I thought she was a bit off colour. Here, drink your tea. You've had a hard day at work."

"Thank you, bach. I must say I'm finally getting used to weak tea, now. How many times have these leaves been used?"

"This is the third," said Lewis.

"Ah well, best chuck them after this," and Jacqueline smiled at her illicit lover as the door opened again and her mother came in with little Mary and Ted.

Mrs James frowned when she saw Lewis and looked around, "Where's Naomi."

"She's upstairs. She'll be down when she's ready. Why?"

"Oh, no reason. Thought she'd like to come with the children tomorrow instead of being cooped up here. After all, she starts school the next day. She should have some fun before she begins. Must be hard for her, on her own away from her mam."

Jacqueline was in a surprisingly good mood and beamed at her mother, "Yes, why not? A little fun won't hurt her at all."

Carrie and Michael reached Hendre's yard and Prince padded alongside them. "I think Bonnie will have something to say about your new arrival," said Michael passing Carrie her bike that he had pushed for her. "She won't like it."

"She'll learn. She's Trixie's daughter. Trix would have welcomed anyone."

Carrie opened the gate and the willing dog followed. Michael caught the saddle of the bicycle stopping Carrie and he gazed deep into her eyes, "When will I see you again?"

Carrie smiled, "I'm not sure, what with John being ill. I have to check on the evacuees when they start school. Although, why the authorities drag them in just before the weekend is beyond me; much better to start on a Monday and do the whole week, I would think."

"Think of it as acclimatising, a gentle initiation for the new students. What about the weekend?" Carrie hesitated. "Sorry, I didn't mean to ask. I know you're going to Cardiff."

"It's all right." She paused, "You know I have to go… but I will hike up and see you on Sunday, I promise." Carrie went in through the gate and closed it. Michael followed her with his eyes as she wheeled her bike across the yard. He watched with amusement as Bonnie scampered toward her but stopped when she saw the huge white Alsatian.

Bonnie approached cautiously and snuffed the air. Prince sat down and looked at Carrie who waited to see what the dogs would do. Eventually, Bonnie approached and nose-to-nose they greeted each other. Prince stood, his tail wagged low, a sign of friendliness and submission. Bonnie's tail wagged high, upright and challenging. She then moved around to the rear of the dog and suitably encouraged Prince did the same. Once each dog had verified each other's credentials, Bonnie bowed down on her front legs and gave a little excited woof to instigate a game of chase. Before long both animals were charging around the yard, through the chickens and ducks in a delirium of delight. Carrie clapped her hands in pleasure and turned back to Michael, "You see. Trix's daughter to a T."

Michael grinned and gave her a wave. He started up the steep track to Gelli Galed. As he passed the path to Old Tom's cottage Sarah emerged in her working overalls and turban styled headscarf and as she saw Michael, she hurried to catch up with him.

She said something to Michael that made him laugh and patted him possessively on his arm. Carrie frowned, feeling another annoying twinge of jealousy ripple through her before she placed her bike in the barn and walked back to the house. Carrie ran up the steps to the veranda and refused to look back again.

*

At suppertime Carrie sat looking thoughtful as the others chattered animatedly around the kitchen table. Their words zoomed in and out of her consciousness and she missed much of what was being said.

Eventually, Ernie took her to task for it, "It's no good, Cariad. The wind has obviously blown and your face is stuck. It won't be the best expression to wear before your patients, now, will it? Or are you intending to put on a mask? Carrie? CARRIE?"

Carrie jumped, slopping a spoonful of the Welsh stew known as cawl down her front, "What? What's the matter?"

"Got your attention now have we?" exclaimed Ernie.

"Sorry, I was thinking."

"Thank goodness for that. I thought for a minute the ratchets had come loose from my grinding wheel."

"What?"

"That scraping screech of the metal of your thoughts bumping together. Loud it was…" he chortled. "I'm surprised it didn't wake Bethan."

"Go on with you," chided Carrie amiably.

"We were just saying that John seems to be doing well. With a bit of luck as long as we all pull together he'll be back on his feet in no time."

"Good," murmured Carrie.

"Jawch, here we go again. What ever is causing you to be absent from your head?"

"I was just wondering, were you serious about transforming the loft into another room?"

"Well, we've talked about it, why?" asked Jenny.

"I'm not sure, yet, but I think it's a good idea. What needs to be done?"

"Well, it's already boarded out so it's safe to walk around. We'd need to get some sort of permanent ladder or stairway to go up there," said Jenny.

"And you'd need to put some sort of skylight in, else it would be very dark up there," added Ernie.

"Yes, there is that. It needs natural light. We couldn't fix anything more permanent up there, could we?" asked Carrie.

"Don't think we'd get gas light up there, if that's what you mean. It'd be too expensive."

"Nothing wrong with oil lamps," mused Jenny, "As long as you don't knock them over."

"No, burn the place down you would," said Ernie. "Anyway, what's all this about?"

"I'm not sure yet," answered Carrie. "Just thinking aloud, really. It would be useful. I thought that now the harvest will soon be in that we could devote some time to it."

There was a bang on the ceiling, "John's woken up. I'll take him some tea and give him his medicine." Jenny turned to Carrie, "Do you want to go up and see him?"

"Not now, I'll pop up later. I need a word with Ernie."

Jenny nodded and took a bowl from the rack filling it with some nourishing stew. She grabbed a hunk of bread, a spoon and set it all on a tray before disappearing through the pine door and up the winding oak stairs.

Ernie studied Carrie's face, "I don't like the sound of this. What am I letting myself in for?"

"I just think we ought to work at getting the extra space, sooner rather than later. That's all."

"You're not trying to tempt me into the house, now, are you?"

"No. I gave that up long ago."

"Well, what is it?" And Carrie began to tell him all about

143

the events of the day and her major concerns, especially for Naomi.

Ernie listened carefully and the more he heard the more thoughtful he became.

A silence followed and Carrie prompted, "Well? Ernie, what do you think?"

Ernie cleared his throat and looked into Carrie's questioning eyes. "You are right, Cariad. You need to get that child out of the house and as soon as possible."

CHAPTER TWELVE

Naomi

Naomi was excited and smiling broadly as she waited for Jacqueline's mother to arrive. Ted and Mary were sitting quietly playing with a wooden puzzle. Jacqueline Price had already gone to work.

Naomi heard the key in the lock and Lewis Owen breezed into the kitchen. Naomi fell silent. "Hello, everyone! Thought I'd stop by before you set off with Mrs James." Naomi cast her eyes down. "Naomi? Don't you have a nice smile for your Uncle Lewis?" Naomi didn't speak. "I thought I'd pick you up earlier from Mrs James and take you to the park being the last day of the holidays." Naomi still said nothing.

Another key was heard in the latch. Ted and Mary beamed as their grandmother came into the kitchen, "Mam-gu!" they chorused.

"Well, are you ready?" The children jumped up and hugged their grandma. "Lewis," she said curtly.

"Mrs James…"

"Naomi? Are you ready?" Naomi nodded and went to collect her coat. As she put it on in the hallway she could hear muffled voices in the kitchen. She waited quietly, her heart racing. Mrs James emerged with the two youngsters and they left the house. Naomi heaved a sigh of relief as they set off down the road. She shivered as she heard Lewis Owen's voice calling after her, "Don't forget, Naomi I'll pick you up at two."

Mrs James glanced down at Naomi's distressed face, "Is that all right, Naomi?"

Naomi hesitated and then spoke up in a tiny voice, "No. I'd rather not. I want to stay with you all."

Margaret James smiled at the child and reassured her, "You don't have to go if you don't want to."

Naomi immediately brightened up and smiled, "Thank

you." She ran on ahead, a lightness in her step and gazed up at the innocent promise filled sky. The warmth of the sun washed over her face and the day seemed kinder and more benign. She ignored the shriek of an alarmed bird as it flew up from the bushes, which fluttered up and circled before soaring away and out of sight, and she ran up the road ahead whooping happily.

Mrs James smiled at the infectious exuberance of the young girl as the little unit made their way to her house.

Once inside the children dashed to the parlour where they had been allowed to make a den with blankets and chairs. Naomi was more than happy to sit with them and indulge in a game of make believe, which set their imaginations bubbling and laughter frothed from them. Here Naomi felt safe.

The children had just finished their lunch and were washing their hands before continuing with their games. Naomi glanced up at the clock and her face became crestfallen as she noted the time. It was ten-to-two. She shivered but tried to put on a brave face, as Mary wanted to play a game of 'I spy'.

"I spy with my little eye something beginning with 'F'."

Naomi looked around the room and looked at the fringed velveteen cover on the table. "Fringe!"

"No." Mary shook her head vehemently.

Naomi tried to find something else beginning with 'F'. There wasn't much in the room. "Um…" Her eyes lit on the doorframe and pictures on the wall and she said, "Frame."

"No."

There were some goldfish swimming in a bowl on the side and she yelled, "Fish!"

"No."

Naomi couldn't see anything else beginning with 'F' and said so.

"Do you give up?"

"Yes."

Mary announced delightedly, "Photos"

"But…. That begins with 'P' – oh, never mind," she said good-humouredly. Just then the bell rang and Naomi froze.

Mrs James went to the front door. Naomi looked worried as

she heard Lewis Owen's voice. He appeared to be arguing with Mrs James but Naomi couldn't hear what was being said. Eventually footsteps approached the kitchen and Mrs James looked at Naomi, "Naomi, Mr Owen has come to collect you to take you to the playground."

Naomi sat silently and Lewis Owen appeared behind Mrs James.

"Come on, Nims. Get your coat. I promised you a ride on the swings. Remember."

"But…"

"But, what? It's what we arranged," prodded Lewis Owen. "Come on, fy merch 'i. I'll buy you an ice cream at Segadellis."

Naomi turned her huge soulful eyes, eyes that had seen so much pain, on Mrs James and looked pleadingly.

"If the child doesn't want to go, I don't see how you can make her," said Mrs James critically.

"But, Nims, it will be fun," pressed Lewis.

"I'd like to go," said Mary. "Uncle Lewis is fun. Teddy?"

Teddy grinned toothily, "Fun!" he exclaimed.

Mrs James pursed her lips, "Why don't we all go?" Teddy and Mary clapped their hands.

Lewis tried to hide the scowl that manifested on his face. He forced a smile, "Excellent idea. The more the merrier."

Naomi murmured, "And safety in numbers…"

"Pardon, what did you say?" asked Mrs James.

"Nothing," whispered Naomi.

"And where did 'Nims' come from? Is that what you like to be called?"

Naomi shrugged, "Ain't never been called it before."

"No, it's my pet name for her, so it is," said Lewis. "Come on then, get your coats. It'll be grand all of us together."

Mary and Ted cheered and went for their coats. Naomi reluctantly moved forward and took her jacket. Mrs James gathered them together and Lewis stood smiling and waiting calmly. As they left the house, he took Naomi's hand and they walked back down the road to the playground.

This was Naomi's opportunity to run free and jump on the roundabout. She whizzed around scooting her foot on the ground to send it spinning. When Lewis approached to spin it faster Naomi was more relaxed and chuckled. Ted and Mary dived on the seesaw but their discrepancy in weight and size meant that Ted was up in the air and Mary stuck on the ground.

Lewis called the children, "Mary and Ted, you get on one end and Naomi the other. It'll be more balanced and I'll help."

All the while Mrs James watched.

Ted and Mary clambered on one end and Naomi sat opposite. It was more balanced but Lewis came along and put his hands on Naomi's end and pushed the seat up and down. His hands pressed close to the little girl's bottom and she visibly flinched. Mrs James walked across and offered, "I can do that if you like?"

She took over from Lewis and pushed the seesaw up and down much to the delight of the squealing children. Lewis stood back. It was now his turn to watch and he licked his lips.

"Swings, now. Swings," called Mary her face alight with happiness. Mrs James stopped the seesaw and the children dismounted and ran to the swings. Mrs James lifted Ted into the baby swing with its safety cage and pushed him carefully.

Naomi and Mary grabbed a swing each and Mary cried out to be pushed, which Lewis did gently. Naomi swung and swung higher a look of joy on her face as the wind blew in her face.

"I want to go high like Naomi," shouted Mary.

"We can do that," said Lewis to the four year old. Come and sit on my lap and hold tight. We'll try and match Naomi."

Naomi continued to swing harder and harder as if her very life depended on it. "Careful you don't fall," warned Mrs James.

It was as if Naomi was deaf to everything and everyone around her. She careered up and down and back and fore, swinging as if it was all that mattered to her. She was lost in another world.

"Slow down, Naomi, please!" called Mrs James. But Naomi kept swinging until the chain began to flex and twist. She was almost level with the horizontal bar holding the swings and it looked as if she would go all the way around.

"NAOMI!"

Mrs James' voice pierced her thoughts and Naomi came to with a jolt. Realisation dawned that she was sailing dangerously high and she stopped pushing her legs out and allowed the swing to slow of its own accord until it reached a point where she could safely jump off and she ran for the slide. Impervious to the cries of other children she clambered up the steps and slid down the polished metal slope then ran around to do it again.

Naomi seemed to be driven by something else. It was hard to explain but she knew she just had to keep going, to keep playing on the equipment.

A loud bang came from the woods and reverberated through the valley, followed by a succession of shots. Naomi's head snapped up, her eyes looked wild and as she flew down the slide instead of bracing herself for her landing she swept off the end and tumbled down into the gravel grazing her legs and hands.

Naomi sat there in a bundle blinking disconcertedly. Lewis and Mrs James came running to her side, followed by Mary and Ted.

"Are you all right? Whatever happened to you?" questioned Mrs James.

"The noise... what was it?" asked Naomi trembling.

"They're just shooting on one of the farms. Probably after a fox or something," said Lewis.

"Or it could be poachers," said Mrs James.

"I thought it was the Germans," said Naomi beginning to cry.

Mrs James helped her up and brushed her down, "You're not in London now. You're safe. That's why your mammy let you come here. There are no bombs or warfare here. Come on," and she held Naomi tightly to her. "Why, you're trembling. How thoughtless of us... it must have been hard in London." Naomi remained rigid and motionless. Silent tears streamed down her face.

Lewis eventually spoke, "Think I'd better take her home, and get her cleaned up, wash the gravel out of her cuts."

Mrs James nodded, "Yes, I think that's best. I'll take Mary

and Ted for an ice cream and I'll call in on the way back."

Lewis took Naomi's hand and led the shocked child away from the playground. Mrs James followed them with her eyes, shaking her head in dismay. There was clearly something very wrong and she hoped the young girl would be better when she dropped by later.

"What's the matter with her?" asked Mary.

"I think the gunshots frightened her. Reminded her of the war... in London."

Lewis tried to comfort Naomi as they walked back to Main Road and Jacqueline Price's house. Naomi struggled to keep up. Her limbs didn't seem to work properly. She maintained her 'out of world' expression as Lewis half dragged her back to the house. He opened the door and ushered her in. The door banged shut behind them it was like the knell of tolling doom. Lewis removed Naomi's coat and talked soothingly to her, "There, there, Naomi. We'll clean up your cuts and abrasions and you'll soon feel better. There's a fright you've had. It'll be better now you're safely back, so it will." He hung her coat up but Naomi continued to stand there solemn faced as if in a dream.

Lewis led the child into the kitchen and sat her at the table. He fetched a bowl of warm water and some rags and after propping her legs up on another chair, gently bathed her grazes and scratches, firstly her hands. Naomi obediently allowed him to turn her hands over and clean out the grit. She didn't flinch even when he applied some of the new Ibcol disinfectant, which he'd found under the sink.

Lewis progressed to Naomi's legs and dabbed at the congealing blood, mopping away the playground dirt and small bits of gravel from the cuts. Again, he used the stinging disinfectant and Naomi remained still.

Lewis studied her face hard, she appeared to be in some sort of fugue state. He returned the things to their place under the sink and swilled out the bowl. Taking a small hand towel he returned to her and dried her cuts.

Feeling emboldened by Naomi's passive state he returned to her side and caressed the child's legs allowing his hands to drift up the inside of her thighs where they lingered. Naomi was wooden and still, neither speaking nor moving. Lewis talked soothingly to the child but gained no response.

Eventually, Lewis, shouted, "For God's sake, Naomi, say something, anything. This is no fun at all."

Naomi didn't stir.

The day was closing and the twilight hours vaporising into the all-enveloping darkness of the night. Blackout of streetlights and homes allowed the stars and moon to be clearly visible in the normally light polluted sky. Martha had been working late at the shop; her friend and co-worker, June, had left hours ago.

Martha finished her inventory and tidy up of the shop. Unsold papers were tied and bound ready to return. She had taken some samples of sweets and carefully wrapped them in a small empty chocolate box. The box was now covered in brown paper and sealed with string and red wax. She carefully addressed it to Marion and Timmy at Four Winds and sighed.

It was time to pull down the blackout blinds and extinguish the few lights in the shop. She didn't want to attract the attention of any rogue German Bombers or the local Air Raid Protection Warden. She secured the blinds, turned off the lights and picked up a small no. 8 torch. She used it sparingly as batteries were hard to come by and had to place tissue paper over the top to dim the beam and ensure the shaft of light played downward.

Martha sighed, she couldn't face going home to her lonely house and eating her meagre rations. She knew she would only brood about David and the children. She missed Marion and Timmy desperately and then smiled; she was going to go and see them this weekend so a detour via the Railway Station was in order. That thought alone lifted her spirits and she stepped out of the shop and locked up in a brighter frame of mind.

The streets were deserted and no chinks of light showed from any of the surrounding properties. She quickened her step toward the direction of Hackney Downs Station where she hoped to pick up a timetable and purchase a ticket.

To her horror the piercing wail of the air raid siren howled its warning into the sky. Martha could just hear the rumbling, drone of German warplanes coming to fill the East End with terror as it had through the last three years. As she approached the corner of Bodney Road with its recognisable landmark of a tall block of flats, the sound of the German Luftwaffe plane grew louder. Martha stopped, transfixed in fright as the plane droned nearer and dumped its payload of bombs, which rained down demolishing the apartment building.

Martha threw up her hands to protect herself as masonry came crashing down around her. A brick struck her on her head and she fell to the pavement without crying out. Blood trickled from her temple. Screams were heard as walls reduced to rubble collapsed and scattered around her. Wooden frames splintered and cracked as wicked glass shards showered her body until she was completely buried in fallen debris.

Shrill bells sounded as the emergency services came to put out the spreading fire and rescue those that were trapped. A woman hung precariously, on a ledge, still in her bed with the rest of her bedroom blown away.

From Martha there was no sound. All that could be seen was her grazed and bleeding hand still holding tightly to the small packet addressed to Timmy and Marion Noble.

Horrified neighbours emerged from their homes to survey the damage and help as they could. Bodies, battered by bricks were hauled out of the ravaged timber and stones. Fourteen people were declared dead and removed to the local mortuary. An elderly woman picked at the rubble around Martha's hand. She removed the small parcel and began to dig. Others joined in until enough of Martha could be revealed. Strong arms joined those of the old lady as they hauled her out from her stone tomb but it was too late. Martha's eyes were glazed with cataracts of death.

The stranger turned over the small package, looked at the address, and whispered, "It must have been important. I'll see that this gets sent for you, I promise," and she shambled away sadly toward her own home leaving the burning site of misery oblivious to the shouts of the firemen and local residents who were still frantically trying to rescue those lucky enough to be alive but who were still trapped in the carnage behind her.

Mrs James arrived as usual the next morning to collect Mary and Ted. She let herself inside and went into the kitchen. Naomi sat woodenly at the table her eyes emanating immense sadness.

"Come on, Naomi. You have school today. It's your first day. You should be happy about that." Naomi said nothing.

On the scrubbed pine table was a note scrawled in Jacqueline's hand. Mrs James picked it up and read.

'Mam,

There's something wrong with Naomi. Neither Lewis nor I could get one word out of her last night or this morning. She wouldn't talk to the children. It's creepy, like she's mesmerised or something. She is of no use to me like this. When you take her to school you must tell the teacher to contact that nurse and take her away. Find somewhere else for her to stay. I can't be doing with it.

I'll see you later.

Love,

Jacqueline.'

Mrs James frowned and sighed heavily. She crumpled the note up in her hand, which made a satisfying crunch as the paper rustled and she shoved it in her pocket.

"Well, there... are you all ready?" Mary and Ted nodded brightly. "Get your coats and we'll be off. Naomi?" Naomi turned her eyes on Mrs James, "Ready for your first day at school?" Naomi, too, nodded. Mrs James was surprised. Her daughter had made it sound like Naomi was in some sort of catatonic state. "Er... Good. Up you get then, or we'll be late."

Naomi rose and went to the door. She put on her coat and waited with the others for Mrs James. They set off down the road together. The children chattered away to their grandmother as they walked to the small Village Primary School. Naomi stayed at Mrs James' side but said nothing.

They strolled up to the school gates where the youngsters

of the community were running around, playing hopscotch, and with balls and skipping ropes. The new arrivals stood warily in a corner of the playground watching the others play. Gerry beamed when he saw Naomi and rushed up to her taking her hands and running her up to the others in a whoop of glee. Naomi ran along with her brother but said not a word.

Mrs James watched and waited. The other children were excitedly chattering to Naomi who seemed to listen but offered nothing herself. Mrs James continued to watch as Miss Bevan came out with Mrs Tobin and rang the school bell. The clanging sound immediately silenced the students. The children stopped shrieking and laughing and lined up in their respective forms and on instruction trooped into the small school after Mrs Tobin.

Miss Bevan crossed to the new children and spoke to them quietly. It was then Margaret James crossed to the teacher. "Miss Bevan, a word please." The teacher stopped and instructed the children to wait at the school steps and turned to Mrs James who had coloured up with embarrassment.

"Yes? Can I help you?"

"I'm Margaret James and I have brought Naomi Clarke..." Mrs James stuttered out her words, uncomfortable with what she had to say.

"Yes?"

"Um..." She took a deep breath. "There seems to be something wrong with the child. She was outgoing and friendly when she arrived but now appears to have withdrawn inside herself. My daughter, Jacqueline Price had taken her on but it appears that now she doesn't want her. Can't deal with her, she says and asks that the District Nurse be contacted so she can be placed elsewhere." The last few words came out in a sudden rush.

"I see..." Miss Bevan's eagle eye roamed over Mrs James kindly face. "I don't see what I can do about this now... The District Nurse is due to visit later this morning. I shall mention it to her. But it is extremely short notice to re-home the girl. Is there anyone else who can help? Fetch her from school?"

"If all else fails, I can collect her and take her back with me. It's not ideal as my husband is laid up. But I suppose I could manage in the short term until other arrangements can be made."

Miss Bevan pursed her lips and said primly, "Good. I'll see you here after school, then. Now, if you'll excuse me." She turned and walked back to the children and ushered them inside the heavy oak door.

Mrs James could feel the heat in her cheeks as she gathered Mary and Ted and made her way back to her house. Something was wrong, very wrong and she knew it. Ted and Mary seemed to sense their grandmother's discomfort and travelled at her side quietly and unnaturally subdued. Margaret James tussled with the vagaries and concerns that groped through her mind whilst putting on a falsely bright smile for the sake of the children as she made her way back to her house.

CHAPTER THIRTEEN

What next?

School playtime had just begun and the pupils were racing around in the warm sunshine enjoying the good weather and the joy of being back with friends. The playground was alive with the music of laughter and children's voices.

Marion and Timmy Noble appeared to have fitted in easily with the other children as had Gerry Clarke whose twin sisters were a little more unsure of themselves but Naomi was most obviously not settling comfortably. She had set herself apart by the school railings and stood forlornly watching the other children with an abandoned expression on her face.

Carrie pedalled up to the school gates. She clambered off her bike and wheeled it into the school grounds and looked around at the happy smiling faces immediately identifying the evacuees who for the most part seemed to be having fun and then she saw Naomi.

Her heart swelled with compassion and she was about to walk across to her when the teacher, Miss Bevan came running down the school steps. "Nurse Llewellyn! Nurse Llewellyn..." Carrie stopped and looked back as Miss Bevan puffed up to her. "I need to speak with you on a most urgent matter. Can you accompany me to the headmistresses' office?" Without waiting for an answer she stalked back inside the building and Carrie followed curiously.

An older, bigger boy helped her with her bicycle up the steps and opened the door for her. Carrie wheeled the bike inside and left it in the visitors' cloakroom before she scooted after the teacher.

Carrie felt a little like a naughty schoolgirl; being in the building reminded her of her own schooldays, not that she was ever carpeted by Mrs Tobin unlike some of her other friends.

Miss Bevan knocked politely on the door and waited for the instruction to 'Enter'. She opened the door and ushered

Carrie inside. Mrs Tobin turned and smiled, "Well, well, Carrie Llewellyn, how lovely to see you. I can see that you have done all right for yourself, so you have. But, there I haven't asked you to see me to discuss your welfare. Please take a seat."

Carrie sat and studied Mrs Tobin's face as she walked around her desk and leaned against it. "Naomi Clarke."

"Yes?"

"Was lodging with Mrs Price, Jacqueline Price."

"Was lodging?"

"Sadly, the woman claims she cannot deal with her anymore."

Carrie stiffened, "I see."

"No, I don't think you do. Apparently, to begin with things appeared to be going reasonably smoothly, at least, as smoothly as could be expected. But yesterday, something changed."

"Oh?"

"Naomi has become silent and withdrawn. Mrs James, Jacqueline's mother, brought Naomi to school today with strict instructions that her daughter couldn't cope with her anymore. I don't like this any more than you do. It seems to me to be shabby treatment of the child and a rushed decision. After all, things were all right to start with..." The headmistress paused to take a breath. "Now, Mrs James has offered to collect her and take her in as a temporary measure until a suitable placement can be found. Mrs James is a sympathetic, pleasant woman and the child could do a lot worse. However, Mrs James has her own difficulties and family responsibilities with an invalid husband to look after and what with caring for her grandchildren, too, it could be difficult..."

"I see," Carrie paused. "Is it possible to speak with Naomi?"

"You can try and good luck with that. I have not heard her utter one single word." Mrs Tobin turned to the teacher. "Miss Bevan?" Miss Bevan nodded. "Bring Naomi to meet Nurse Llewellyn." Miss Bevan nodded again and scooted out.

Carrie sat and waited; listening politely to Mrs Tobin and exchanged pleasantries until there was a timid knock on the door and Mrs Tobin's voice boomed out, "Enter."

Miss Bevan brought Naomi into the office and sat her on a seat next to Carrie. The little girl sat quietly and stared blankly ahead.

"Hello, Naomi," said Carrie gently touching the girl's arm. The child turned to look at Carrie's sweet face. Carrie took this a good sign and continued, "How are you? Are you happy with Mrs Price?"

Naomi didn't speak. She turned away and a single tear dropped from her eye. Carrie continued to talk soothingly to her but the child refused to answer. Miss Bevan and Mrs Tobin exchanged worried glances.

Mrs Bevan spoke timidly, "She hears what we say. She seems to listen in class and does her work, but won't say a word, not even to her siblings. It's all very strange."

"Even more worrying," said Mrs Tobin, "As I have said, is the fact that Mrs Price no longer wants her. I know her mother, Mrs James, has said she would have her temporarily but it's not ideal."

Carrie thought for a few seconds and made a decision. "I'll take her home with me. If you can tell Mrs James and ask her to pack Naomi's things and bring them to the school later and I'll take them back with me when I pick her up. Is there anyone who can remain with her after school until I get her?"

"I'll wait. And I'll see Mrs Price at lunchtime. I don't have anything to race home for… but shouldn't she see a doctor or something?" asked Miss Bevan.

"Don't worry, she will. Thanks, Miss Bevan." Carrie rose and stooped before the little girl. "Naomi, you are to wait for me. I'll be back after school and you can come home with me. All right?" Naomi looked at Carrie's earnest face and blinked. "That's good enough for me. I'll take that as agreement."

Carrie left the site, straddled her bike and pedalled away. Her thoughts were racing. There had been a huge change in the little girl since she had last seen her. Carrie had suspicions but that's all they were, suspicions. She needed to complete her rounds and then she decided she would call in on Mrs Price at the drapers and visit Margaret James. From what she had seen she was in no mood to temper her remarks. But, as she told herself, first things first, she needed to visit Howie Price.

Carrie breezed into the old man's kitchen and wore a cheerful expression and friendly smile. Howie beamed as he saw the young nurse. He was sitting comfortably in his chair by the fire reading Jock of the Bushveld.

"Not finished your book yet, then?" asked Carrie.

"No, not yet. I was just wondering about some of these illustrations. I think the artist has got some things wrong."

"Whatever do you mean?"

"Why, look." Howie leafed through the fine pages of the novel until he found what he was searching for. "See, here. This horse is supposed to get out but looking at this picture it's impossible. How can he pull himself out of something as sheer and vertical as that there? There's nowhere to get a foothold."

Carrie studied the pen and ink sketch and had to agree that there was no way the horse could rescue itself. "Maybe you ought to write to the publisher and point it out."

"Aye, I might just do that."

"More importantly are you enjoying it?"

"Oh, yes. It's an excellent yarn."

"Good. And the glasses?"

"Work an absolute treat."

"That's grand. Now, let's have a look at your leg."

"It's feeling a lot better, Nurse. Not so sore. Whatever you've done it seems to be working. I can even bear weight on it and get upstairs."

"That's what we want." Carrie carefully unwrapped the dressing and inspected the wound. "It certainly is looking better. Do you know, I think I can clean this up and just cover it lightly with some gauze? Let the air get to it."

"And some more of that jollop. That's good stuff so it is."

"Ah, yes, the colloidal silver. Yes, it is good stuff." Carrie carefully cleaned around the lesion and was pleased to see it wasn't any bigger, the edges were cleaner and new skin was forming. She treated his leg and as promised let the air get to it while she made a cup of tea.

"You're certainly looking better, Howie. Looks like Gwyneth is really looking after you."

"Oh, she's a treasure that one, a jewel, so she is. I've never had better meals no, not in a long time. I'll soon be bouncing around like a new flea. Then, I'll be able to look after myself and do something to thank her, so I will. And none too soon."

Carrie smiled at the old boy while she poured them both a cup of tea. "I'll get Dr Rees to sign you off, soon, if you continue to improve like this."

"Oh, don't do that, Nurse. I won't be seeing you then and I look forward to your visits, so I do."

"Well, we'll see," said Carrie stuck for something to say.

"What about your problem, Nurse? What are you going to do about your young men?"

Carrie blushed, "I'm going to Cardiff tomorrow and I've told Michael. He's been more than understanding. At one point I thought it was over for us."

"Aye, honesty can have that effect. You must tell me all about it."

"That I will. And now I must be off. I have more visits to make."

"Do you have to go?" said Howie looking miserable.

"Yes, I do," laughed Carrie rising and washing out her cup.

"What about that girl? The one lodging with my daughter-in-law?"

"She's coming home with me."

"Good, I'm glad. I don't like to speak ill of others, but Jacqueline... well, she's not quite right. Not since my lad went to war." Carrie turned a sympathetic eye on the old man. "He used to be a bit free with his fists, knocked her about a bit and the last time he was home on leave was so bad she ended up in hospital. Changed her. Addled her brain like... Think that's why she took her anger out on me. Don't get me wrong, I love my son, but war changed him... Seeing your chums blown up...." Howie fell silent.

Carrie nodded sympathetically and crossed to him. She laid a layer of gauze on his leg and taped it. "We'll leave it like that for the moment. I'll see you, Monday. Don't get it wet."

"Aye, all right."

Carrie left quickly and cycled onto the draper's shop. Even with this new information about Jacqueline Price she couldn't reconcile herself with the woman's cruel treatment of Naomi.

Carrie propped her bike against the wall and marched into the shop. The bell tinkled behind her. Jacqueline Price stood ramrod straight behind the counter in her shop assistant dark uniform.

"Yes?"

Carrie noted the heavy sigh and inward groan, and attempted to ignore it. "I just came to say that Naomi will be coming back with me after school."

Jacqueline sniffed, "I'm sorry it didn't work out. But, I can't be doing with a child that's mentally ill. I have too much on my plate."

Carrie could feel her temper rising but managed to bite back her angry retort. "Your mother has collected her things. If, perchance anything is left you can drop it off at the school for her."

"And when am I supposed to find time to do that?" she grumbled. "Still, I suppose I could always get Mr Owen to do that for me. He would have taken her in, you know."

"I'm sure he would," she said cynically. Carrie turned to go, "A word of advice. I don't think Mr Owen is all he seems."

"What's that supposed to mean?" snapped Jacqueline.

"It means watch out and watch your children." Carrie left swiftly avoiding further confrontation although her hands were shaking and her face had coloured up. She had wanted to say a lot more but hearing what old Mr Price had to say she had tempered her remarks and not flown into a full tirade, which she had intended prior to visiting the old man.

Carrie hopped on her bike and pedalled back down toward Margaret James' house. Time was getting on. With a bit of luck she would get there before the woman left for the school and save her a trip. As she cycled she caught sight of Mrs James stepping out onto the pavement. Carrie pedalled harder and skidded to a stop next to her on the road. "Mrs James. I'll take that. Save you walking all the way to school."

Mrs James looked relieved, "Thank you, Nurse." She handed over Naomi's battered bag. "Don't think ill of Jacqueline. She wasn't always like this."

161

"No, I have heard. But it doesn't excuse her treatment of the child." Mrs James became silent and nodded.

Carrie wanted to say so much more but didn't. She took Naomi's bag and placed it in her basket and made her way back to the school where mothers were collecting their children and Mrs Gregory's cook, Milly waited. Carrie smiled at the woman who was gathering Mrs Gregory's brood together who all chattered excitedly about their first day at school. The evacuees looked contented and happy, which made Carrie feel much better. The children clustered around Milly who was laughing along with them as they walked away.

Carrie left her bike leaning against the wall, ran up the stone steps and entered the foyer. Miss Bevan was standing there waiting with Naomi whose face was no longer blank and her eyes no longer unseeing but she was still silent.

Carrie beamed, "Hello, Naomi. How was your first day at school?"

The child said nothing and looked down. Miss Bevan said quietly, "She's been fine, except she hasn't said a word. She seems to be quite bright and did all the tasks asked of her but wouldn't read aloud or answer questions. I kept her in with me at playtime to do some jobs, as she didn't want to go outside or speak to the other children. I hope come Monday she will be back to normal."

Carrie nodded, "We'll call in on Dr Rees on the way up. Thanks, Miss Bevan."

Miss Bevan pursed her lips and watched anxiously as Carrie took the little girl's hand and led her outside.

The afternoon sun played on the metal handlebars of her bicycle and her bell shone. Naomi seemed to be fascinated by this and gently fingered the bell. "You can ring it if you want," said Carrie. "Just a few times, not continually otherwise no one will take any notice of me when I want to cycle past. Like the little boy who cried wolf." Naomi looked curiously at Carrie. "You know the story?" But Naomi showed no recognition in her eyes.

Carrie placed the child's hand on the bell and encouraged her to ring it, which she did. A fleeting expression of delight came and went. She rang it again and then stopped.

"Now, let me see. How are we going to do this? Why don't we put you on the saddle and I'll push you along. Your bag is safely in the basket but when we get to the mountain track you'll have to walk with me. The way is steep and rough. But first we must get to The Crescent."

Naomi allowed Carrie to lift her onto the bike and with a struggle she managed to control the bike with the child sitting on it who stared numbly ahead of her. "So, you don't know the story of the boy who cried wolf?"

Naomi continued to gaze straight ahead and Carrie began to relate the old Aesop's fable. Carrie didn't know if Naomi was taking it in but she finished the tale and chattered on brightly.

They soon reached The Crescent and Carrie asked her to dismount as travelling down the hill would make the bike too difficult to control. Naomi slid off the saddle.

Carrie encouraged Naomi to walk alongside her, which she did still not saying a word. They soon reached Dr Rees' house and Carrie left her bike against the gate and took Naomi's hand. The child didn't resist. She took small steps and waited as Carrie knocked on the surgery door.

Petite Mrs Rees opened the door wide with a welcoming smile and Carrie stepped into the hallway with Naomi and took her into the waiting room. "Ieuan is free now, if you want to see him?"

"Please. Naomi, can you sit here a moment, please?" The little girl settled herself in a seat. Carrie found a comic, The Beano, and gave it to Naomi to browse through. Naomi looked at the cover, opened it up and began to read. Carrie tapped on the doctor's door.

Dr Rees opened the door and peered over his half spectacles, smiling, "Carrie, come in, come in. Sit down." He was clearly delighted to see her.

Carrie closed the door quietly behind her, and sat, "Doctor, I don't know what to do. I have a little girl out there, one of the evacuees," and Carrie explained as best she could what had happened. "I think you should look her over. She doesn't seem to be in the catatonic state anymore that Mrs James described. She appears to have done her work in school, taken everything in and listened but she hasn't uttered a word."

Dr Rees rubbed his furrowed brow, "I'll take a look, but before you bring her in, what about the twin girls with Mrs Powell?"

"Safely, with Mrs Gregory. She has a houseful! And lovely it is there, too."

Dr Rees nodded and managed one of his rare smiles as Carrie detailed everything that had happened. "That all sounds good... And now for Naomi; bring her in."

Carrie jumped up and went back into the waiting room. She stooped down by the little girl now engrossed in her comic. Carrie brushed the child's hair away from her eyes and whispered, "Naomi?" The little girl didn't stir. She was fixated on the Beano. "Naomi...?" This time the child looked up and Carrie saw deep into her eyes. She saw the pain etched there and something else... something that reminded her of herself. "Naomi, I want you to come and meet Dr Rees." Naomi obediently folded up the comic and placed it on the seat next to her and stood up. Carrie held out her hand, which Naomi took and together they entered the doctor's consulting room.

Naomi gazed wide-eyed in awe at Dr Rees' imposing figure. Dr Rees patted the seat opposite his desk and said kindly, "Sit yourself down here, Naomi. I've been hearing a lot about you and Nurse Llewellyn wants me to check you over just to make sure things are all right. Is that okay with you?" Naomi said nothing.

Dr Rees took the child's pulse and tested her reflexes. He shone a light into her ears and examined them with an auroscope before he made her follow the movement of a pen with her eyes. "All seems perfectly normal there. I'll just listen to her chest. Can you take off your jacket, Naomi, please?" Naomi removed her outer clothes and the doctor put on his stethoscope. He went to lift up Naomi's blouse and the child flinched and froze. Dr Rees glanced at Carrie.

"It's all right, Naomi," said Carrie reassuringly. "The doctor just wants to listen to your heart and your breathing. Carrie held out her hand for the stethoscope, "Let me show you what he wants to do, is that okay?"

Naomi still looked frightened but Carrie gave the little girl the doctor's stethoscope and told her to put it around her neck.

"There really is nothing to be afraid of... Now, if you place the ear pieces in your ears you will be able to listen to what is going on inside me." Carrie undid the top buttons of her uniform and placed the chest piece against her sternum. "We use the bigger side of the diaphragm to listen to me. When we listen to you we'll use the smaller side. Go ahead." Carrie pressed the diaphragm to various positions on her chest. She breathed heavily in and out and coughed. The little girl looked less afraid and even managed a smile when she located the beat of Carrie's heart. "There you see, nothing to be scared of, now is there?" Naomi shook her head slowly. "Now, will you let the doctor listen to your heart and chest? I'll be right here, holding your hand."

Reluctantly, Naomi nodded and Carrie returned the stethoscope to Dr Rees. As soon as the doctor touched her Naomi's heart thundered away, but she did as she was asked and breathed deeply and coughed on instruction. "Very good," murmured the doctor taking the stethoscope from out of his ears. "All seems perfectly normal except when I listened to her vitals her heart was racing away... Okay, Naomi, pop your jacket back on and you can finish reading your comic, in fact if you like you can take it with you when you go. I just want a quick word with Nurse Llewellyn."

Naomi skipped off her chair and returned to the waiting room her face no longer filled with anxiety. Dr Rees turned to Carrie, "Something has happened to traumatise the girl. I don't know what; although I know you could hazard a guess. I think we have a case of elective mutism."

"Elective mutism? What's that?"

"There are various forms and I came across it just once... Put simply, a child who has experienced some form of trauma or abuse simply stops talking, refusing to speak even though they can. It is usually an attempt to regain some control in their life, when it manifests itself in this manner."

"Do they talk again?"

"You will have to be very patient; sometimes it doesn't take long but in the most extreme cases it can take years. I suspect in this instance, as she is so alert that once Naomi feels safe she will talk again."

"I see… is there anything else I can do?"

"Just be you. Don't get angry around her. There's not much known about the condition. It is very rare. Try and include her in family things, often you will have to issue specific instructions to her rather than anything general. Sorry, I can't be of more help. Bring her back to see me in a month. You say she was lodging with Jacqueline Price?"

"Yes."

"Not the most pleasant of women."

"I believe she had a punishment room in the cellar…"

"That may have done it, if the child is afraid of the dark. Often it is a result of a deep shock or abuse…"

"It's not a happy household and Jacqueline's man friend is someone I wouldn't trust."

"Who's that?"

"Lewis Owen."

Dr Rees frowned, "Hmm. I have heard rumours about that man but he comes across as harmless enough."

"Maybe." Carrie stared thoughtfully ahead, "Looks like I'll have my work cut out."

"That you will, Carrie fach. That you will."

Carrie said her goodbyes and left the surgery with Naomi. The Beano comic went into Carrie's basket and they walked together to the mountain track. Carrie chatted away to the little girl, realising what hard work it was to monologue and not have any response or interaction. Carrie explained about her family and the animals and hoped that Naomi was at least taking some of it in. The time passed quickly and they soon reached the gate to the yard and Hendre.

The little girl's face brightened when she saw the chickens and ducks and she beamed in delight when Bonnie bounded across and licked her face and hands. However, she was more wary of the large white Alsatian, Prince. But Carrie made a point of introducing her to the big dog. She took Naomi's hand and ran it down Prince's back and when the dog wagged his tail, rolled over and offered his tummy for a belly rub, Naomi looked much more at ease.

"Okay, Naomi. Let's get you indoors. You can share my room, we'll take your things up and I'll introduce you to everyone." Naomi looked a little afraid at the suggestion but Carrie continued, "They're all lovely people as you will see. And I will have to explain about tomorrow, as I am not going to be here. I have to go to Cardiff but there will be plenty of friendly people who will be on hand to help you settle in, you'll see."

The little girl's face looked disappointed and Carrie tried to cheer her up. "This way, Naomi. You take your comic. I'll bring your bag."

Naomi dutifully followed Carrie up the steps, onto the veranda and into the glasshouse. There she stopped, looking overwhelmed. She gazed at her surroundings. The sound of a piano playing filtered through and a glorious soprano voice could be heard singing a traditional folk song.

"That's my sister-in-law, Jenny. She has a wonderful voice. She's singing a very famous Welsh song, Myfanwy." Naomi looked curiously at her. Carrie continued, "It's a love song, from a poet who lost his true love's heart and doesn't know why."

Carrie ventured into the kitchen, through the door and into the parlour where Jenny played the piano. Naomi followed.

Bethan sat quietly on the floor listening to her mother sing. Carrie and Naomi both stood there to listen, too, as Jenny sang her heart out before she became aware of being watched. She stopped.

"Oh, don't stop!" said Carrie. "You have the voice of an angel."

Jenny laughed, "You flatter me, Carrie fach." She looked curiously at Naomi, "And who is this?"

"This is Naomi, she will be staying with us for a while."

"One of the evacuees?" Carrie nodded. "Well, hello, Naomi. I am Jenny and this is my daughter, Bethan." Bethan looked up at the mention of her name and smiled. Naomi smiled back at the two and a half year old toddler. "You like children?" Naomi nodded. "Good, you'll be able to play with her. Bethan will love that." Naomi cast her eyes down. Jenny glanced at Carrie, "Shy, is she? She doesn't say much…"

"No… How is John?"

"Oh, he's getting there. The fever's gone and it's all I can do to make him stay in bed. Terrible patients men; I don't know how you cope."

"Oh, I don't know. I've always preferred nursing men to women. Women can be dreadful complainers."

"Maybe. He just needs a bit more rest to fully recover and get his lungs stronger. He's still wheezing and gets breathless but the worst is over. I think."

"I'll pop in and see him, once Naomi is comfortable. She'll be sharing my room., for security… Is that all right?"

"It'll have to be. I'd better get on; I have supper to prepare. Good job you came when you did, else we'd all be eating late tonight."

Carrie nodded and led Naomi out of the parlour to the pine door that led to the stairs, while Jenny looked after them thoughtfully before closing the piano lid, scooping up her daughter and retreating to the kitchen.

Carrie walked across the landing to her room and opened the latch, "This here is my room. There's plenty of space for you to sleep with me until we sort something else out. You unpack your things. Take the bottom drawer of the tallboy." Carrie opened the drawer and removed a handful of items and shoved them in another, which she struggled then to close. "Duw, Duw. Think I need a clear out so I do." Naomi sat on the bed. "Take your time and when you're ready give me a call and I'll show you the rest of the house." Naomi's face filled with horror and Carrie almost bit her tongue in reproaching herself, "Sorry, Naomi. Tell you what, you put your clothes away and I'll pop back in say ten minutes." She smiled reassuringly at the child placing Naomi's bag on the bed next to her.

Carrie left her and knocked on John's door. She heard him wheeze an instruction to come in and entered. "Jenny tells me you're improving. That's quick, I thought you'd be laid up longer."

"I feel a fraud, being waited on hand and foot. I am a lot better."

"But you've still got respiratory problems. You can't go back too soon or you'll set yourself back."

"But there's the harvest to finish…"

"You let us worry about that. Just take your medicine and get well."

Carrie stopped and John studied her freckled face that he loved so much, "What is it, Cariad? What's wrong?" So, Carrie told him all about Naomi using hushed tones. "Poor child, what can we do?"

Carrie shrugged, "Be supportive, make her feel safe and hope she recovers from this trauma. The problem is, I have to go to Cardiff tomorrow and I don't know whether to take her with me or leave her here. She doesn't really know anyone and she's already frightened enough."

John looked concentrated in thought, "Well, this means I can get up and even if I'm not going out in the fields I can make a start on converting the attic. It was always going to be a playroom for Bethan. It may as well be a bedroom for Naomi. The spare room still needs decorating and is sparse of furniture, only has a bed."

"Don't you go overstretching yourself. The girl will be fine with me for a while."

"Why are you going to Cardiff?"

"I have to meet someone."

"That sounds secretive."

"I don't mean it to be. I'll tell you all about it when I get back but in the meantime what about Naomi?"

"I have an idea. You know who'd be perfect to spend time with her?" Carrie looked at her brother curiously, "Ernie. Remember how good he was with us? If there was a falling out he always had a trick up his sleeve."

"Or under his beret," laughed Carrie. "Remember Bandit?"

John grinned, his endearing lopsided smile, "Aye! That I do." They both sat quietly a moment enjoying the memory of the little duckling that had stolen their hearts and had become something of a family pet.

"You know, I think you're right. If Ernie can work his magic... where is he?"

"They're working in the steep field, gathering the hay in for winter feed. He'll be there along with Laura and Rose."

"Great. I'll go and see him. Thanks, John." Carrie slipped out of her brother's bedroom, thankful that things were so much easier between them now. She returned to her room and Naomi who was sitting on the bed reading her comic. "Naomi, I have to go out a moment. Will you be all right here? Of course you will. You have the Beano, what better company, eh?" Naomi looked up at Carrie but said nothing. "Okay, when I come back, I'll come and get you, okay?" Naomi nodded and her eyes returned to her comic.

Carrie skipped back down the stairs stopping to explain to Jenny about Naomi. Jenny's face filled with compassion, "Poor child. Torn from her home, separated from her brothers and sisters and then left with some insensitive soul. I'll do all I can to help, I promise." Carrie impulsively hugged Jenny who blushed, "Good heavens, what was that for?"

"Just for being you."

Carrie stepped out into the yard and Bonnie came running up. She gambolled alongside her together with Prince. The two dogs played chase and then tore after Carrie as she made her way to the steep field.

Ernie was manually tying the bales with two baling wires as they were made. The baler was a stationary implement, driven with the tractor using a belt on a belt pulley. Laura and Daisy were bringing the hay to the baler and feeding it in by hand. Sarah didn't seem to be doing anything very much and worked more slowly than the others. She stopped to chat to Sam Jefferies who was holding the formed bales for Ernie to tie.

Carrie tried to make herself heard above the sound of tractor engine. "Ernie! Ernie!" Sam heard her and alerted Ernie. Sam took over from Ernie and Sarah was forced to hold the bales for him to tie.

Ernie came across to her and the dogs danced around him begging for a fuss. He stooped and ruffled both dogs behind their ears. Content with that they hared through the golden stubble in a frenzy of delight. "Sorry, Ernie. I need your help and your advice."

"Then it must be urgent, if you've come all the way out by here. What is it, Cariad?"

"Can we go somewhere to talk? Away from this din?"

Ernie nodded and crossed back to Sam and said something.

Sam appeared to nod agreement and the little man strutted back to Carrie with his uneven gait. "I'm all yours, Carrie fach. Sam can do without me. Besides it's time the princess got her hands dirty," he chortled.

They walked out of the field and trekked back to the yard. All the while Carrie explained as best she could about little Naomi. "Thing is, Ernie, if anyone can help her, you can. And..." she paused, "Tomorrow I have to go to Cardiff." Ernie raised an eyebrow. "Don't look at me like that. You know why... Can I leave her in your care? John is still not better and Jenny will have Bethan to mind. Naomi needs someone to feel confident with, someone to trust... Ernie?"

Ernie scratched his bristly chin, removed his beret and rubbed his wiry tufts as he thought. "Elective mutism? I've not heard of that."

"Nor had I."

"Seems the little one is trying to get some control on her runaway life just as the doctor said. She needs to feel loved and confident."

"That's what I thought. That's why she's sharing my room. Ernie, can you spend time with her this weekend? Tomorrow when I'm away?"

"Cariad, you know I will do what I can. Let me meet her tonight at supper. See if she takes to me. From what you've told me she may be afraid of men."

"She was all right with Dr Rees."

"He's a medical man. He inspires trust."

"And so do you. Ernie?"

"As I said, I'll do what I can. Come on let's meet her."

CHAPTER FOURTEEN

Rolling Stones

Chatter at the supper table was tempered. No one wanted to pressure Naomi. Brave attempts were made to include her in the conversation although she couldn't be persuaded to speak and didn't offer any comments or opinions. She picked at the food on her plate moving it around from one side to the other.

Ernie tapped his fork on his plate and Naomi's eyes flicked up at his face, "Ah, Naomi, just the one I want to listen. I know you like animals; you do don't you? And I have a treat in store for you. Tomorrow when Nurse Llewellyn is away, I'm going to take you on a wonderful walk and show you things, you'd never dream of. There's a family of otters in the riverbank, if we're lucky we might see them. They've got young. Pups, they're called, playful little critters. I bet you've never seen an otter."

"Don't think I've ever seen one either," said Jenny.

"Nor me," chorused Carrie and John.

"Well, well, you'll be telling me next you've never seen a badger either."

"I haven't," said Jenny.

"I have," smiled Carrie as she remembered. "When I was about six years old, Dadcu…"

"That means Grandfather," interjected Ernie.

"Yes, well my granddad took me out at twilight to watch at a set in the woods. We waited hours, Dad was with us, too."

"Where was I?" asked John.

"You were off playing with Thomas, somewhere. I'd been told to be as quiet as the breeze and not to make a sound. We lay down in the ground and waited and waited, and as dusk faded into dark and the moon came up, old Mr and Mrs Brock came out from their burrow with three little cubs that played and tumbled and ran. And what did I do? I oohed and aahed with a big giggle and the little creatures fled back to their den.

And that was that. All that waiting and I scared them off with a silly sound."

"Aye, but Naomi won't do that, will you?" said Ernie and he ploughed on, "If we're lucky we may even see some fox cubs. I know where to look."

"Not the ones that's been after our hens, I hope," grumbled John.

"No, I don't think so. I've seen the tracks. They belong to a vixen and her babies. The one that got old Korky was a big dog fox, not the same family. There're some birds of prey, up the mountain, too. You never know what we might see."

"I'm sure Naomi will like that, won't you?" Naomi turned her huge eyes on Carrie and blinked. "Excellent, I'll hear all about your adventure when I come home and who knows, perhaps we can invite your sisters and brother to tea, sometime, as well."

Naomi seemed to absorb all this information and instead of picking at her food she began to tuck into her meal. Carrie and Ernie exchanged a look as if to say, so far so good. Normal chatter resumed and the rest of the meal passed pleasantly without any undue focus on the child.

Surprisingly as the last bit of pie was mopped up with a piece of bread and the plates pushed away, Naomi rose. She picked up her plate and that of John's and carried them out to the sink. The rest of the family watched in astonishment as the young girl proceeded to clear all the dishes from the table. Jenny said, gently, "Why, thank you, Naomi, but you don't have to do that."

Naomi appeared to take no notice and Jenny was about to speak again but Carrie stopped her. "Thanks, Naomi. Your help is gratefully appreciated."

Naomi gave a half smile and went to the glasshouse and filled the sink with water from the kettle on the range. Jenny went to stop her but Ernie insisted in a whisper, "No, let her be…"

They watched as the little girl began to scrub the plates. Carrie rose and grabbed a tea towel, "We can't let you do all the work. Here, I'll dry up."

"And I'll put away," said Jenny.

The three of them worked until everything was shining and clean. Jenny sang happily and they all laughed when Ernie attempted to join in. Even Naomi managed a full smile. Ernie took it as a good sign.

That evening, Carrie went up the stairs with Naomi to her room. She showed her the bathroom first so that the little girl could clean her teeth and wash. Carrie sat her on the bed and took her mother's much-loved silver hairbrush and vanity mirror. She gave the silvered looking glass to the child to hold and brushed her hair for her. "See these, they belonged to my mam. Very proud of them she was and I keep them polished up in her memory, she was a wonderful woman. You can use them while you're here. You have lovely hair. Reminds me of my friend Megan, her hair shines like yours. I expect your mam brushed your hair for you at night. She must miss you and I'm sure you must miss her. We must write to her this weekend and tell her you've moved and give her this address. She may want to come and see you, you never know." Carrie finished brushing Naomi's tresses. "Now get changed for bed, there's a good girl. Here let me help you. You can fold your clothes and put them on that chair. You can sleep on the window side. I hope you don't wriggle. I know I did at your age." Carrie went to the bottom drawer and saw the meagre amount of clothes that had seen better days and was flooded with compassion. The child had been fine until she'd lodged with that abominable woman. Carrie inwardly cursed herself for allowing her to go with Jacqueline Price.

Carrie passed Naomi her nightdress and smiled. The girl began to undress slowly. When she reached her vest and knickers she hesitated and stopped. Carrie folded her other garments and placed them on the chair. "What's the matter? Do you want a hand?" Carrie stretched out her hands and helped to lift the vest over her head. She frowned when she saw bruises on the girl's body, imprints as if someone had squeezed her too hard and had left fingerprints on the girl's torso and it looked as if her early budding breasts had been pinched.

Carrie bit her tongue, she didn't want to alienate the child and impulsively she clutched the little one to her and held her. To begin with Naomi was stiff and wooden in her grasp and then she relaxed and sank into the hug, wrapping her own arms around Carrie and holding onto her.

Carrie swallowed hard, and released the girl from her grip. She raised the nightdress and dropped it over Naomi's head. Naomi looked so young and vulnerable standing there in her nightie. "You slip your knickers off now and pop them on the chair."

Naomi removed her pants and tossed them on the chair. Carrie's eyes fixed on the dark brown bloodstain in the gusset and said lightly; "Think we'll put a clean pair out for tomorrow. I'll take these away to wash them, all right?"

Naomi blinked.

Carrie's thoughts were racing away. Was the child old enough to have begun menstruation? She didn't think so. Where had the bruises come from? And what had happened to her? Was there truth in the suspicions that Howie Price had voiced? None of these questions could be answered until Naomi was prepared to speak and how long that would take she didn't know.

Carrie tucked the little girl in and smoothed her hair away from her forehead. She leaned over and kissed her, and as she did so a single tear escaped from her eye. Carrie pretended not to notice and spoke soothingly, "There, there. You rest now. I shall be up soon and we can cwtch up together. That means cuddle. We'll have you knowing a few Welsh words very soon." She dropped another kiss on Naomi's forehead before leaning across to draw the heavy curtains that would eclipse the evening sunshine. Carrie walked back to the door and her eyes lingered on the little girl's face, which was frozen in uncertainty. She whispered, "Don't you worry none, Naomi. As God is good the angels will look after you and we will keep you safe." With that she closed the door and retreated back down the stairs.

Ernie sat by the fire in the family rocker. "It will be a hill to climb, Cariad. Not easy like ABC but together with patience, love and determination we can help the little one. I'm sure."

"I hope so, Ernie. And if she starts to communicate again…"

"Not if, Cariad, when…"

"All right, when… then I will get to the bottom of what happened in that house."

"And it looks like I'll be volunteered for building work as she's staying."

Carrie laughed, "Come on, Ernie… what do you feel about the girl."

"Cariad, she's been hurt, physically and mentally. This not talking is her defence to protect herself. Who knows how long it will take but I can tell that you two will plait yourselves together and I think our Jenny will have a profound effect on her, too."

Carrie crossed to the old man and gave him a swift peck on the cheek, "Ernie, you are an inspiration, honest."

"Jawch!" he spluttered, for once lost for words.

That night Carrie ascended the stairs and after her ablutions she crept quietly into her bedroom and changed trying not to disturb the sleeping child. Carrie snuck into her bed and wriggled into position. To her surprise Naomi cuddled up to her and placed her arm around her waist. Carrie encased the child's hand in hers and drifted off into a fitful sleep filled with vivid dreams where Michael's face melded with Matthew's.

She was walking down a long, dark, dismal tunnel and strands of foliage dangled menacingly before her. Fibrous roots twisted and writhed trying to grasp her in its python grip. Carrie evaded the serpentine coils that reared and struck at her face and body. As she hurried through the ever-continuing channel filled with grasping, noxious weeds an opaque, milky light began to glow in the distance. In front of her was a tall male figure beckoning her but no matter how hard she tried to reach him he was always elusively too far ahead. Suddenly the floor beneath her began to move and slide as if motorized in the opposite direction from where she wanted to go. She struggled to remain upright and balanced precariously; she was compelled to run against the flow of the floor. She ran and ran. The man stopped and turned, stretching out his hands toward her, it was Michael but then his face rippled and changed becoming that of Matthew. Carrie stopped suddenly and was flung backward and the figure hurtled on toward the light and vanished.

Carrie awoke with a start and shivered, confused by the dream. She felt Naomi's arms tightly around her and assumed they must have been the snake like coils that had tried to entwine her but the rest of the dream she could not fathom.

Finally, she drifted off back to sleep.

The following morning, Carrie woke early. She tiptoed out of bed and vanished into the bathroom. Her nursing days in Wales, Birmingham and London had trained her to be one of the first in the bathroom where there would be a queue of other nurses waiting. Carrie got herself ready and returned to her room. She opened the door and Naomi had slipped out of bed and was in the process of removing her nightdress. She snatched her things to her but again Carrie noted the bruising on the child's budding breasts. The inside of her thighs also showed signs of skin trauma, which she hadn't seen before.

This time, Carrie spoke to Naomi but gently. "Oh, Naomi. How did this happen? Who did this to you?" Of course the little girl said nothing and just lowered her eyes. "Don't you worry, none, my lovely. I think I know." Naomi looked up suddenly in alarm and gazed into Carrie's eyes. "I believe you'll talk about it when you're ready. I'll not press you now." Again the little girl lowered her eyes. "Why don't you take your turn in the bathroom now, before the others are up?" Naomi picked up her things and meekly left for the toilet.

"Oh, Ernie. I hope you can work your magic with this one," murmured Carrie to herself before she tiptoed off down the stairs.

As she was the first one up she let both dogs out and filled the big black kettle before re-stoking and bringing the cinders back to life with strategically placed logs and coal. Taking the bellows she pumped air into the embers and the new fuel caught alight. Carrie set the kettle onto boil.

She heard someone moving around and footfalls on the stairs. To her surprise John appeared through the pine door into the kitchen. "John! Whatever are you doing up?"

"Feeling stronger and better. I can't languish away upstairs. There's work to be done and with Ernie babysitting young Naomi today, the farm needs me."

"You be careful. We can't have you overdoing it, now can we?"

"Don't fuss. I'll be fine. I need good air in my lungs, so I do."

"Maybe so, but you don't want to set yourself back and end up with something worse. You must still take those antibiotics Dr Rees prescribed."

"Aye I am, and I will. Is the kettle on? A man could die of thirst here. Then I must get upstairs and get clean. Bathroom was occupied."

"That's Naomi. She won't be long."

"Taken on something there, so you have. She seems sweet enough, but who knows what's going on in her head."

The door opened and Naomi crept in quietly. "Ah, Naomi," smiled Carrie in welcome. "It would be lovely if you could help lay the breakfast table. Can you do that? Plates, bowls, cups and saucers are in the cupboard next to the range. We need to lay up for five and pull the highchair up, too."

Naomi obediently did as she was asked and Carrie took out the milk and butter from the larder with some of Mam-gu's special raspberry and blackcurrant jam. She picked up the homemade loaf, tucked it under her arm and as her mother had done before her she began to slice the soft bread and placed it on the breadboard in the centre of the table.

Carrie took a plate and laid out bacon and eggs ready to cook along with freshly gathered mushrooms and some lava bread that Jenny had bought from the butchers. It was then that Jenny entered with Bethan on her hip. She looked around bleary eyed, "There's early you all are!" she exclaimed. She popped Bethan in her high chair and gave her a rusk to nibble on while she prepared breakfast. "You'll soon be grown out of that," said Jenny. "Then we'll have trouble."

Carrie glanced at Naomi who looked forlorn and lost. She grabbed the brass toasting fork hanging by the grate and spiked a slice of bread holding it before the now roaring fire. "Here, Naomi. You can do this, see?" Carrie showed her how to brown the bread in front of the fire and Naomi eagerly complied.

"I have to go now, Ernie or I'll miss my train."

"Why don't Naomi and I take you down to the station? We can talk on the way. Yes?"

Carrie smiled gratefully, "That would be grand. I'll get Senator and harness him to the cart and Naomi can finish her toasting." Carrie put on her outdoor coat and ventured out in the now early sunshine and crossed to the barn. Prince and Bonnie came rushing up looking for affection. Carrie laughed and obliged them both with a friendly pat before disappearing inside the stable to get the faithful Senator.

Carrie harnessed the strong shire up to the wagon and waited for Ernie and Naomi to join her. She gazed lovingly at her beloved Hendre that she no longer felt tied to in quite the same way. It was an odd feeling, one she couldn't describe. As a child it had been her strongest desire to run the family farm alongside John but her new found identity and nursing talents were leading her away from Hendre so she daydreamed about what life had in store for her married to Michael Lawrence and working on the hill farm Gelli Galed.

As she stared dreamily ahead Matthew popped into her mind and what could be expected of her if she chose to work again as an SOE. Those thoughts were interrupted by the arrival of Ernie and Naomi.

Ernie instructed the little girl to climb aboard and the child sat frozen faced between Carrie and Ernie who endeavoured to engage in somewhat stilted conversation as they started down the trail.

The cart rumbled down the steep mountain track and after an awkward silence, Ernie began to sing somewhat less than tunefully his favourite, "Sospan Fach."

Carrie winced, "Duw! Stop, Ernie. It's like rusty nails scratched down a blackboard." She covered Naomi's ears, "Don't listen to it, Naomi. It's a famous Welsh song and it's lovely when Jenny sings it. Not so our Ernie. It's an affront to the senses."

Naomi's eyes widened and Carrie thought she could detect a small spark of something. She continued to chat in a lively manner engaging with Ernie, teasing him and laughing. The time passed quickly and they soon arrived at the station.

Naomi was no longer as stiff and rigid and had relaxed somewhat. Carrie gave Ernie a hug before she stepped down and smiled at Naomi. "Ernie will look after you today and I will be back before you know it."

"We'll be here to pick you up this evening," said Ernie agreeably. "Well, you're a big girl now, Carrie fach. We'll be off, we have some otters to see, I hope, haven't we, Naomi?"

Naomi said nothing but managed a small nod. Carrie thought she detected a flicker of a smile.

Carrie's stomach was churning with those writhing, wriggling worms of fear yet tinged with excited anticipation as she walked from the station and made her way to the Angel Hotel.

She could see the damage Hitler's bombs had done to the city and it reminded her of her stint in London and the Blitz. She had read how the nave of Llandaff cathedral and many chapels had been damaged not to mention the three hundred and fifty homes that had been destroyed. The worst hit areas were Grangetown and Riverside and many civilian lives had been lost.

Some of Hitler's bombs had hit closer to home damaging Neath Abbey, Bridgend and Swansea. Merthyr Mawr Church had been hit and the blast blew out many of the windows in the village. All this was around June 30th through to July 4th and Carrie hoped it was the last. It seemed the Germans had lost interest in that part of Wales and Crynant was safer than many places in Britain. More recently news had been heard of mines exploding in the sea near Dunraven. She attempted to put aside these distracting thoughts. She had to compose herself for this crisis meeting.

Her heart was pounding so loudly she could hear it and the rush of her blood surging through her head sounded unbearably loud like the repetitive whooshing of a machine on a factory floor. Was this because of her own memories of being bombed or was it that she was soon to see Matthew? She didn't know.

Carrie could see the hotel sign swinging on its hinges as if pushed by unseen hands. Her throat constricted and her mouth went dry as she neared the worn stone steps, which had felt the tread of so many guests and visitors through the years that they bowed in the middle.

She took a deep breath to still her inward trembling and stepped up to the entrance. The reception desk was inside and off to the right, behind which stood an austere looking woman with her hair tightly pulled back into a bun and dressed in black service attire. Her eagle eyes fixed on Carrie and she said primly, "Yes? Can I help you?"

Carrie hesitated and then stepped forward with more confidence than she felt, "I am here to meet someone. One of your guests who is staying here."

"Name?"

The very physical lump that had manifested in her throat almost prevented her from speaking Matthew's name, which she finally managed to blurt out.

The receptionist opened the large ledger on the desk and looked through the entrants, "Ah yes, you're expected ... If you would like to go through to the hotel lounge I'll have the bellboy alert Mr Reynolds."

"He is in then?"

"Yes, he said he was not to be disturbed until a young lady arrived. I assume that's you?"

Carrie blushed. She felt hot right the way through to her stomach, which was twisting and somersaulting erratically. Carrie left the desk and moved into the spacious guest lounge and sat at a small table, where a mournful looking waiter arrived to take her order.

Carrie declined politely, "I'm waiting for a friend."

She studied the faces of the other staff who were serving guests and decided that The Angel couldn't be the happiest of places to work. The general demeanour was one of sobriety and reticence. Hardly a smile cracked on those 'professional' faces. They all looked miserable, just like the frowsty-faced receptionist. Carrie cast her eyes down and waited nervously. She couldn't seem to stop her left knee from jiggling and trembling. She clasped both knees tightly with her hands and willed them to stop shaking and then felt a tap on her shoulder. She turned and looked up into the face of Matthew Reynolds.

He beamed at her, "Even though I had your message I didn't think you'd come."

"I almost didn't," she said honestly.

Matthew sat opposite her and snapped his fingers at the tall waiter whose expression was best suited to chief mourner at a funeral. He sloped across to them and with a face that expressed disaster wherever he looked he asked glumly, "Can I help you, Sir?"

"Pot of tea for two and a menu, please." He glanced at Carrie, "You will lunch with me won't you?"

The words stuck in Carrie's throat and she managed to croak, "Of course."

The sorrowful waiter bowed obediently and sidled off to the kitchen. Carrie watched him go. "He'd be better suited in a job as an undertaker more than a waiter, don't you think?"

"I'm afraid most of the staff here have that melancholy look. Perhaps they know something we don't. It used to be a very friendly place but all the younger staff seem to have gone off to war."

"The war... breaks hearts and minds. It's dragged on for too long now."

"And what about you, Carrie? Do you break hearts and minds?"

Carrie stopped and hesitated, her mouth was dry, "Matthew..." There was a sigh in her voice.

"No, don't answer, at least not yet. Let's enjoy this time together and our lunch... please."

Carrie brightened and attempted a smile, "Yes, why not?"

The conversation that began was somewhat stilted and a little awkward but the emotion that ran underneath was plain to feel and see. Carrie tried to steer the chat around to their time in France together.

Reliving the memories and the danger, in which they had been immersed, seemed to do the trick and they became more relaxed with each other; so much so that when the waiter arrived with their tea they were convulsed in laughter over their reminisces of the episode in the shoe shop, when Carrie posing as a French woman didn't know the sizing of French shoes, which differed from those at home.

Carrie's uncontrollable, almost hysterical giggles had a profound effect on Mr Dreary, as Carrie had nicknamed him, that he almost dared to crack a smile. Her laughter was so infectious others in the lounge began to laugh although they didn't know why, and even the miserable, gloomy attitude of the waiter began to crumble.

Anyone could see that Matthew was studying Carrie's sparkling eyes, the curve of her lips, the smattering of freckles on her upturned nose and impulsively he placed his hand over hers as she moved it to pour the tea. She didn't withdraw it.

"Carrie, I need to know. Is there any hope for me?"

The confusion was apparent in her eyes and she swallowed hard, "Matthew... I am engaged to another..."

"I know."

"We shared so much in France, the excitement and danger. It was another time and..."

"And?"

"I don't know. I am confused."

"In that case, it proves that you feel something. I know you do. Tell me I can write. Tell me I can come and see you when the war is over. Please. Give me some hope."

Carrie paused and carefully weighed up her words, "Matthew, I have thought long and carefully. I don't deny that I felt something for you... that there was an attraction. But I know I love Michael and he trusted me enough to visit you today. Why, I questioned my sanity; I even wondered if it was possible to love two men. My heart is completely torn and..."

Matthew put his fingers to her lips, "Say no more. That is enough. It is enough to give me hope that you care. It proves to me that I am not wrong to love you and that I may be able to change your mind. That alone will give me the strength to live through this next mission."

"But, Matthew, it will be too hard. I would betray my family and friends. To be with you I would have to leave Wales, everything and everyone I know and love."

"You can't live your life for other people, Carrie. You must be true to yourself."

Carrie smarted at his words, her cheeks burned hot and pink as she flushed with indecision. Matthew picked up the teapot and poured them both a cup of tea. He passed her one of the menus with shaking hands.

Carrie rose, "I must go to the Ladies Cloakroom. Please order for me. You know me well enough to do that."

"Yes, I do. I also know that I want to know *all* of you…"

His words were left hanging in the air as Carrie walked to the Ladies cloakroom.

Carrie stared at herself in the mirror above the washbasin, "What are you doing, girl? This is stupid, stupid, stupid!" she exclaimed.

The door opened and a large woman dressed in a substantial fox fur and off the face hat, entered and smiled at her. "Hello, dear. You and your young man have certainly entertained us with your laughter. You really lifted my spirits."

The woman spotted Carrie's ring, "Your fiancé is it? Going off to war I expect. You mark my words, take advantage of the time you have now. Get a special licence; get married. Enjoy a night of wedded bliss. No one knows what the future holds."

Carrie went to speak but thought better of it and just smiled. The woman disappeared inside a closet and Carrie studied her face in the mirror. Her heart was pounding. Her hands were shaking. She had a feeling of energy spinning the wrong way inside her and a tightness travelling up her chest to her neck. She knew she had to calm down. She stood no chance of sorting out her emotions while she felt like this.

Carrie splashed her face with some cold water and patted it dry with one of the flannels laid out and then tossed it into a wicker basket with other used linens. She took a deep breath and steadied herself before leaving the Ladies Room and walked back into the lounge. Her heart was still thumping so loudly she believed others might hear it and she returned to Matthew.

She sat still feeling flustered and confused, these emotions were now overlaid with anger at herself. Matthew looked at her, "What is it?"

"I came to meet you today to …"

"To?"

"To… say that you could write to me."

"That's good, isn't it?"

"I don't know… Matthew, I want you to come through the war. I want you to live…"

"I'm sensing a but here…"

They were interrupted by the arrival of the waiter, "Mr Reynolds, your table is ready."

Matthew rose and extended his hand to Carrie, which she took. She felt a tingle of electricity pulse up her arm. She stood up, dropped his hand and straightened her coat. He offered her his arm and together they walked to the restaurant.

CHAPTER FIFTEEN

Back to nature

Naomi and Ernie had travelled back to Hendre. He had chattered animatedly to her and the little girl appeared to be listening although she said nothing. Naomi watched as Ernie unhitched Senator and took him to the stable. She followed him meekly and watched as Ernie stuffed the horse's net with hay and put out fresh water and some horse nuts for him.

Naomi walked softly up to the gentle giant of a horse and raised her hand. She glanced at Ernie who encouraged her, "Aye, go on, rub his nose. He likes that and here..." Ernie pulled out an apple from the barrel. "Give him this. Put it on the palm of your hand and hold your hand flat. Like this." Ernie demonstrated and then gave her the apple.

Naomi hesitated but urged on by Ernie she put out her hand with the apple and Senator took it eagerly and crunched loudly as he munched. Naomi stroked the good-tempered shire and rubbed his soft muzzle. A partial smile tugged on the corner of her lips.

Ernie observed. "Now then, let me show you something to make you and Senator friends forever." Ernie walked across to the horse. He fussed over the majestic steed and gently blew into the horse's nostrils. "See, he gets the scent of you forever and there you go, chums for life. Come on." Naomi hung back and stared stonily ahead. "Not to worry," said Ernie. "When you're ready and when Senator's ready, too." Still the little girl didn't move. "Never mind." Ernie smiled reassuringly at her and patted the horse once more, who was now engrossed in devouring some of his fresh hay. Naomi stood silently and watched. Ernie grabbed a rug and threw it over his arm.

"Come on, Naomi, now Senator's settled I'll show you the farm." The little girl followed Ernie out from the stable into the yard. The Land Girls emerged from Old Tom's cottage in their work garb and waved cheerily at Ernie, calling out their greetings.

Naomi stood frozen and silent and moved partially behind Ernie. "Now, Naomi fach. Don't you worry none. They are our Land Girls who work and help on the farms, ours and Gelli Galed at the top of the track. A hard climb it is there. We'll visit one day. But now, now we must set off for the riverbank and see if Mrs Otter and her young pups are out and about."

Solemn-faced Naomi stepped out after Ernie who chattered about the chickens and ducks. Bonnie and Prince trotted after the couple but Ernie ordered them back. "Not today, Bonnie, Prince. I promise I'll take you out later. Now you stay, there's good dogs."

Bonnie's tail drooped and she skulked back to the water butt by the barn and lay down looking sorry for herself. Prince followed and slumped down next to her. They followed Ernie's movements with their eyes, but soon leapt up when they saw John emerge from the house. He whistled, their ears pricked up and they dashed to him, tails wagging, followed him to the tractor and jumped into the trailer.

Naomi had turned her head at John's shrill whistle. She watched the excited dogs race to the tractor before turning back and trotting after Ernie who led her through the gate and the meadow. "This meadow was always a favourite of Carrie's er... Nurse Llewellyn. She used to romp with her collie dog through the grass and roly-poly down the slope. If you stay here long enough I can see you doing the same with Bonnie and Prince. Now watch your feet by here." Ernie indicated a boggy patch and skirted around it. Naomi hopped past it, too.

Two shots rang out and echoed in the air around them. Naomi stopped, her face looked panicked. "There, there, not to worry, Naomi. It'll be someone hunting a rabbit or a farmer after a wily old fox that's been snaffling the hens. Come on, quietly now. Not a sound. We are nearly there. Let's hope the hunter has finished, too or there'll be no sighting today."

They edged toward a small clump of trees. Ernie put his fingers to his lips, not that he needed to tell Naomi to be silent. He spread out the rug in the cover of the small copse with a fine view of the banks on the opposite side of the river. Ernie lay down on his stomach and gestured for Naomi to do the same. She scrambled down. Ernie pointed at the opposite earthen bank. "See, Naomi, over there. Under the overhang of the bracken by the roots of the old Ash tree? There's a hole, a burrow, called a holt. That's where the pups live for the first two months of their lives before they learn to swim. They need a quiet place left undisturbed and clean water. They're very territorial. Generally they can patrol twenty-four to twenty-five miles of riverbank. See the reed beds over there. That's great for them and other wildlife. They eat a lot, about two pounds of grub a day. Not just fish, but small crustaceans, newts, frogs, small animals like mice and even slugs and dragonflies. If we're lucky we'll see the mam or dad come home with a fish. Hush, now." Ernie froze.

A large dog otter came swimming up to the holt with a trout gripped tightly in his jaws. The creature scrambled up the bank and looked warily about him. Ernie almost chuckled as he saw the creature struggle with the large wriggling fish before he disappeared into his den.

"See that! He's taking it to feed his family before going off on another hunt," he whispered. The little girl nodded. "By my reckoning they've been almost two months here now. With a bit of luck the young will be out to play on the bank. We may even see them have their first swimming lesson."

Naomi stayed motionless hardly daring to breathe or so it seemed to Ernie. They waited … and waited. Ernie could feel his feet going numb. He started to turn over to give his legs a rub when there was a movement opposite. Ernie stopped and he, too, held his breath.

Emerging from their den came the father followed by the smaller mother and three little pups. Ernie glanced at Naomi, her eyes were sparkling and she was silent. The little ones romped, rolled and played on the bank, diving and squeaking their unique chattering sounds. Their mother called to them tempting them to the water's edge. The curious babies ventured closer as their mother tried to show them how to slip into the river. One of the pups was slightly larger than the others and he tentatively stepped closer. The mother called again and this time the baby slipped into the water beside her.

He splashed and squeaked seeming to flounder. His mother nipped him on his ear trying to calm him and keep him in order when suddenly the baby began to flip and swim. He dived under the water and burst upward with a stream of bubbles. He frolicked and chased calling excitedly to his siblings. They too edged closer and growing in confidence they eventually slid into the water.

Ernie and Naomi were treated to an amazing spectacle rarely witnessed by man. The little girl was enchanted and she clapped her hands delightedly. Immediately the mother darted out of the river and called to her babies, which scrambled up after her and they vanished back into the holt.

Naomi's bottom lip quivered and silent tears ran down her cheeks. "There, there Naomi. Not to worry. I would have had to move soon anyhow, my legs are sparking like the fizz in a bottle of pop. We can talk now. We are very lucky to have seen this. We can visit again and see how they grow. Unusual to have three pups, though. It's more often only one or two. We've been blessed. Up you get, we must move on. There's lots more to see yet." Ernie held out his hand and Naomi took it and jumped up. Ernie gathered the rug and shook it free of dirt and debris. He threw it over his arm and they moved back from the copse.

Ernie felt he was making progress with the little girl and building a connection. He hoped he was right. They trundled back along the track and this time they climbed higher. The late summer sun was warm and shone brightly bathing everything in its melted butter glow. On they climbed until Ernie reached the notorious Bull Rock where they sat and surveyed the lush green valley before them. Ernie pointed out the sights of the picture perfect landscape with its sturdy oaks and spiralling firs. The verdant green leaves of the broccoli-topped trees were just beginning to turn. The truly beautiful summer heralded a magnificent colourful autumn to come.

Circling above them and crying plaintively was, Ernie explained, a peregrine falcon. They watched as it hovered above them staying in one position its wings fluttering to keep stable on the thermal. The bird suddenly dived and swooped into the undergrowth. "It'll be after a rabbit or mouse or any other small creature it can catch. Then it'll be taking it back to its young I expect."

Ernie sighed as he watched the little girl, clearly mesmerised by all the beauty around her, "Duw, Naomi. I wish you'd talk. Tell us what horrors you've faced to strike you dumb like this. You won't find a better or safer place than Hendre. That's the name of the farm. They're all good people there. They opened their hearts to me like I'm family. I have got family. I've got a daughter and one day when I'm ready I'll visit again but at the moment I'm needed more here."

Ernie didn't know why he was pouring his heart out to her but he knew it felt good to share his feelings with the little one. "Know why this is called Bull Rock? Although some say, Top Rock but Bull Rock it is to us," and he began to relate the story of how it was named.

Carrie was walking back to the train station with Matthew. Their manner was easy together. He made her laugh and she felt more optimistic. She was clearing her head and sorting out her confused emotions. His arm brushed against hers and she felt a pleasurable tingle pulse through her. She stopped, "Matthew…"

He turned and gazed at her, "No, don't say anything. I want to remember this moment." He tapped her nose playfully, "I just adore your freckled nose. In fact, I adore everything about you."

"But…"

"But, nothing…" Matthew swept her into his arms and held her tightly. He seemed unaware of the stiffness in her body. She didn't relinquish herself to him but he didn't care. He leaned forward to kiss her but she turned her cheek and his lips brushed against her milk white velvet skin. "Sorry… I didn't mean to come on so strongly. I know from all you've said that you are torn and that fact alone gives me hope. Please, Carrie… may I kiss you? Please."

Carrie squirmed in his grasp. She felt hot and uncomfortable, "Matthew…"

"Please." He tilted her chin and she lowered her eyes but she didn't move away.

He bowed his head toward her and kissed her tenderly. Carrie pulled away, "You are making this very hard."

"I intend to," said Matthew.

"I'm nothing if not honest. I won't play games with your feelings. You have to know my heart is at home, with Michael. He has always been my one true love."

"But you feel something, I know you do."

"I'm not denying that. I'm just saying…" Carrie stopped stumped for words.

"Then never, say never. I will come back for you, Carrie Llewellyn."

Carrie's shoulders slumped. "But, Matthew… I love Michael. I always have and my future is with him. I know it is. I'm sorry…"

"Don't be," Matthew seemed unusually chirpy and confident. "I have learned enough. You have told me I can write. For the moment that is enough."

Carrie and Matthew continued on their way. Carrie was silent. She was pleased when the railway station came into view. They went inside, "It looks like my train is in. Thank you for lunch. It's been good to see you again."

"Yes, it has," said Matthew less formally and he took her hands. "I won't say goodbye but au revoir."

Carrie nodded and rose up on her tiptoes and pecked him on the cheek. "I must go. Be careful…." With that she escaped his arms and boarded the train. She settled in the window seat in an empty carriage adjacent to the platform. Matthew put his hand up to the window and very tentatively Carrie raised her hand slowly. Their fingertips touched with the glass between them. Carrie blushed as the guard blew his whistle and Matthew blew her a kiss as the train chuffed out of the station.

Carrie sat back in her seat and smiled. She no longer doubted her feelings. She knew. She was pleased she had travelled to Cardiff. She knew that although Matthew was charming and lovely, the attraction was just that; an attraction born from their time in France coupled with the attention he had paid her. It was Michael she loved and she loved him with all her heart. Her heart swelled with joy and she settled back to enjoy the journey home.

Ernie and Naomi sat on Bull Rock. The little girl swung her legs and Ernie chattered about what they'd seen and what other sights he would show her. A cry alerted them and they both looked up to see the return of the beautiful peregrine falcon. This time it brought its mate. The two birds dipped and soared, playing together on the wind. They watched as one of the birds flew up the cliff side to a rocky ledge.

"See there, Naomi. That's their nest. They don't build them like other birds; they scratch out a bowl with their feet, out of the debris on the cliff side. They must have young. They usually lay from two to four eggs. The young should have fledged by now. If we're lucky we may see them learning to hunt. Keep watching."

The mother bird flew up from her nest followed by three young ones. They were not as expert as the adults in their aerial manoeuvres as they ducked and dived in the cobalt sky. Suddenly a shot rang out and one of the youngsters appeared to be hit. It fluttered and tumbled from the sky whilst the others retreated to the safety of their mountainside lair.

Naomi gasped and Ernie swore softly under his breath. "Jawch! Who would do such a thing?" Ernie scoured the ground below and caught the glint of a rifle barrel in the wooded and bracken bank. Whoever it was scrambled back along the bank toward the track and road. "A game keeper or poacher, I'll be bound. Every animal deserves the right to feed, but some selfish humans see these beautiful creatures as rivals to them. I'm going down to see. The bird could be dead or in agony. That's not right."

Ernie clambered off the huge rock and held his arms out to Naomi who willingly sprang into his arms. "Be careful now, Naomi. The way can be slippery. I don't want you to fall. Here, take my hand." Naomi trustingly took Ernie's hand and together they negotiated the steep mountain and picked their way through the thick undergrowth. "Watch your step by here, Naomi. You step where I step we don't want to disturb an adder or such, nasty bite they have but very shy. They'd rather slither away than face people." Naomi's eyes opened wide with fright. "Now, don't you be scared none, will you? We'll be fine just keep close to me."

The two carefully picked their way down to the track and road and faced the rushing water of the Black River. Ernie studied the bank and the depth of water that led to the expanse of stones in the centre and gauged the flow of water and how far it was from the stones to the other side. "Now, then, Naomi, I'm going to cross the river. I believe I'll be safe. I want you to wait here. Understand?" Naomi nodded and sat on a boulder by the water's edge and watched as Ernie took off his boots and socks. He rolled up his trousers above his knees, stuffed his socks inside his boots, tied the laces together and hung them around his neck and stepped into the cool river water. "Iechy dwriaeth! There's cold. He hobbled over the sharp stones until he reached the river silt that squished up through his toes where he could walk more easily. He ooch-ouched over the centre splay of stones and stepped out to wade through the deeper part of the river to the bank. Naomi giggled at Ernie's exaggerated discomfort and watched as Ernie reached the other side where he waved reassuringly before he disappeared into the undergrowth.

The little girl looked warily about her as she heard the snap of a twig behind her toward the roadside. To her horror she heard a familiar voice, "Why, Nims, whatever are you doing out here alone?"

Naomi froze as Lewis Owen, carrying a rifle and with two rabbits slung over his shoulder tied together on twine appeared behind her. The little girl sat rigidly and was silent. Lewis thrust down his rifle and the brace of bloody rabbits and sat beside her. Naomi's eyes were filled with fear and she trembled uncontrollably. "Why, whatever's the matter? Not afraid of your Uncle Louis, are you?"

Naomi said nothing.

"Duw, why so silent? We can play a game if you like? Come with me over there." He picked up his rifle and the dead rabbits. He pointed to the arch of the bridge that crossed the river and pulled Naomi to her feet. Naomi opened her mouth to scream but no matter how hard she tried no sound would come out.

Ernie now re-booted but without his socks was attempting to find where the young falcon had fallen. He saw above him the mother bird circling and made his way to where she was hovering. He heard a thrashing and fluttering and came upon the young bird. The youngster struggled to hop away as Ernie drew nearer. Ernie spoke soothingly to the fledgling. He removed one of his socks from his pocket and stealthily approached the injured bird. Ernie gingerly reached down for the bright-eyed chick and slipped his sock over its head, which immediately calmed it. Ernie was able to scoop it up and seeing its injury he proceeded back the way he had trekked.

Ernie stopped suddenly as a strange feeling thrummed through his body. He had been so focused on rescuing the bird that his heightened sixth sense had been subdued. Now he was on high alert. Ernie carefully placed the young falcon in the roomy inside pocket of his jacket and began to speed back toward the riverbank. He shouted out, "Naomi! Naomi I'm on my way." Huffing and puffing now, Ernie didn't stop to remove his boots but waded into the streaming water and began to cross the river.

Ernie couldn't see the child where he had left her. He hurried to the bank and boulder and saw blood on the ground next to the stone. His heart thumped loudly as he gazed wildly around. He studied the earthen river path and could detect a trail as if something or someone had been dragged toward the tunnel under the bridge. Ernie filled with urgency raced toward the tunnel. He stopped as he saw Naomi standing with her back to the bricks. Her face was devoid of colour and she stood with silent tears flowing down her cheeks. Blood was trickling down her legs.

"Oh, no!" Ernie rushed to her side, "Naomi, fach. What is it? What's happened?" but the little girl stared frozenly ahead with an expression of pain fixed in her eyes. For once Ernie was at a loss at what to do. Movement in his pocket brought his attention to the young bird in his pocket. He retrieved the fledgling, "See, Naomi. I found it. It's alive but injured. We'll get it back to Hendre and you can help me get it fit and well but first we need to see Dr Rees. Can you walk?"

Naomi said nothing but Ernie guided her from the dank tunnel full of dark secrets and foreboding, out into the bright sunshine, which promised hope and recovery. She was slow on her feet as if it hurt her to walk. Ernie wished he had Senator and the cart with them. How was he going to get the little one back in her current state?

Ernie helped the child up the track to the road. Approaching the bend from the hill was a vehicle. Ernie stepped in front of the Hillman Minx waving his arms. The car screeched to a halt.

"Duw, whatever is it?" asked the small moustached man driving toward the village.

"This little girl needs medical attention. She can't walk. Can you help?"

"Hop in. Tell me where you want to go." The man was more than happy to help and pulled on his handbrake and stepped out of the car. He opened the rear passenger door as Ernie lifted Naomi gently into the back.

"Dr Rees ten The Crescent and hurry." The man got behind the wheel as Ernie clambered into the front and checked on his baby peregrine.

"Whatever have you got there?"

"Injured falcon chick, some blackguard shot it. I'm going to try and nurse it back to health."

"Remind me now, where's The Crescent?"

"On the Neath road, Neath end coming into the village."

"I know." The man sped on through the Village Square and past Segadellis, and on again past The Star and Garter before he turned right into The Crescent. The car raced down the hill and slid to a halt outside the doctor's house.

Ernie scrambled out of the car and helped Naomi out from the back, "Thanks, Wuss. You're a life saver."

"No trouble. Hope the young girl will be okay. And the little bird."

Ernie nodded. He opened the gate and walked up to the door carrying Naomi and hammered loudly as the Good Samaritan drove away.

Mrs Rees opened the door, "Yes? Why, Mr Trubshawe, Ernie…."

"We need the doctor, urgently." Ernie moved into the hallway as she opened the door, wider and called to her husband.

"Ieuan! We've got an emergency, hurry." She led the way into the waiting room and surgery. Through there."

Ernie opened the door and entered the consulting room. He lay Naomi on the doctor's couch and paced frantically.

The young chick scrabbled about in his pocket as if the urgency of everything had penetrated through to the young bird. Ernie asked, "Mrs Rees, do you have a cardboard box going spare?"

"Ooh, I don't know. I'll have a look." She disappeared out through the door as Dr Rees entered. He put his half spectacles on the end of his nose.

"Ernie… What's happened here?"

"I don't know. She was doing so well. I thought we were getting through to her and felt it wouldn't be long before she started to talk again. I only left her a short while by the river while I went to rescue a young bird. When I came back she was in the tunnel like this."

Dr Rees frowned as he studied the little girl. He put his hand on her leg and she flinched and drew her legs up protectively, her face was expressionless but her eyes were glazed with the dullness of horror. Slowly, Dr Rees took some muslin and dampened it with some water and antiseptic. Naomi relaxed her legs but her face remained stark and impassive. For a moment the golden light outside the window dimmed and diaphanous shadows chased across the floor.

He gently wiped away the blood from inside her thighs and spoke softly, "Naomi, fach, no one should have hurt you like this. I wish you would speak and tell us who it was that has violated you."

"Violated? Oh, Duw, no," groaned Ernie. "She was doing so well. Who would do this? I'll swing for him."

"We'll only know that when she's ready to talk. If she doesn't block it from her mind altogether."

"How bad is it?"

"It's bad. Pity Carrie isn't here. Ernie, can I ask you to step outside. I'll get Millicent to help me."

Ernie assented and went into the waiting room as Mrs Rees returned with a box. She gave it to Ernie and went back into the surgery as her husband beckoned her. Ernie opened the box and carefully removed the fledgling from his pocket. He left the sock over the bird's head to keep it calm. He examined the wings and could see that fortunately the flight feathers were intact as were the tail feathers so the youngster should still be able to fly. There was a small injury to the young one's foot where a pellet had struck but nothing more. The little bird's heart was beating furiously and Ernie was concerned that the chick might not survive. It would be the shock more than the damage that would be the biggest threat to its life.

Ernie looked about him and picked up an old newspaper from the table. He checked the date and was sure that Dr Rees wouldn't mind him using it. He tore the paper into shreds and when he had a suitable pile he gently removed the bird and made a bed for the fledgling and carefully placed the bird on it. Then he picked up the lid and looked around. On the windowsill stood a potted plant with a stick to support the new growth. Ernie whipped it out and used it to piece holes in the lid before replacing it. He put on the lid with its air holes and sat down to wait.

As he sat, he thought and thought. The baby bird would need time and patience to bring it back to full health and to be able to set it free. Mostly he left baby birds where they fell and the mothers would tend to them but this one was different and would not be able to escape predators. It would be a tasty meal for a fox, stoat, rat or weasel. Ernie did not want that fate for the bird.

His thoughts turned to little Naomi. She was a thin little waif with huge eyes and her eagerness and delight when she watched the otters had touched him. She had absorbed all he had told her and he was certain that she was improving. Now this. His thoughts travelled to Lewis Owen. He'd never met the man but from what Carrie had told him he seemed a likely suspect. But what would he have been doing by the riverbank? Had he been watching them? Ernie didn't think so. Was it an opportunist crime? Whatever it was, the poor child had suffered what no child should. Ernie swore vehemently under his breath using language that he would never normally entertain, "Bastard!"

The surgery door opened and Ernie rose anxiously. The doctor called him over; "I'm keeping Naomi here. To keep an eye on her."

Ernie nodded, "Pity. She was just getting used to us. A bit of security for her. Poor girl pushed from pillar to post. And now this."

"More importantly we need to tell the police."

"Aye, so we should but what do we say?"

"The evidence will speak for itself. The fiend must be found and dealt with. We can't let this happen to another child."

"Carrie had her suspicions…"

"Who? What did she say?"

"Jacqueline Price's fancy man, name of … Owen I think…"

Dr Rees shook his head, "Don't know the man."

"I do," said Millicent. "Lewis Owen. He wasn't a bad lad, very shy. Could be quite charming. Moved to Crynant a couple of years ago. I was surprised when I bumped into him in Neath market."

They turned to look at her, "Hails from Merthyr, Cefn-Coed, same as me. I went to school with him. Vaynor Penderyn. The family had to move."

"I hardly dare ask, Why?" ventured Ernie.

"Lewis' father. He was a bad lot. Petty pilfering, Always in trouble with the law. And he had a thing about little kids. I'm not saying he did anything but there were always rumours. Eventually, it got too much. The family shifted, Swansea, I think."

"The more I hear, the more I don't like it," said Ernie. He pulled off his beret and scratched at his wiry tufts.

"I suggest you come back in the morning. The child needs to rest."

Ernie nodded. He gestured toward the consulting room, "Can I?"

Dr Rees nodded. Ernie went and stood by the couch. He looked down at the little girl and spoke softly. "Naomi, fach.

We'll be waiting for you to get better. We've got a chick to heal and animals to see. I'll be coming to see you regularly till we have you back at the farm." He gently stroked her brow and his eyes misted over. He sniffed hard and wiped his nose on the sleeve of his coat. Ernie thanked the doctor, picked up the box and set off up the mountain track. Even though his sodden feet were uncomfortable he took no notice. His contact with Naomi had disturbed him in more ways than one. He felt her pain, her fear and the trauma she had suffered. He blurted aloud, "Why can't I see the man? Why can't I see the bugger's face?"

CHAPTER SIXTEEN

Opening up

Ernie had picked Carrie up from the station and they were on their way back to Hendre. He had recounted all that had happened.

"So now, you've got a young bird to raise as well as everything else?"

"Aye. But what about you? I sense you've sorted out your feelings, at last?"

"Oh, Ernie. I have. I think a lot of Matthew, it's impossible not to, but Michael has my heart. I truly believe that and it is such a relief."

"I always said your happiness was in your own back yard."

"I remember."

Ernie urged Senator on up the track. The late sun was fading and twilight hues washed the pebble and stone trail, which crunched satisfyingly as the metal rim of the cartwheel rolled along.

"Never been in a motor car before, Cariad. It was quite something."

"Pity you weren't in any position to enjoy the ride. I've been in a couple. It was quite exhilarating. But, Naomi … have the police been informed?"

"I think the good doctor will be speaking to them."

"They'll want to speak to you, too."

"Aye, no doubt."

Ernie shook the reins and Senator continued to plod up the track.

"I'll go first thing to see her. I hope I can bring her home."

"I'll come with you, bring the cart. You can pop your bike in the back and get off to work after."

"Thanks, Ernie. What are you going to do about this fledgling?"

"I thought, I'd work with it, teach it to hunt so it can

manage in the wild when it's better. It's not seriously damaged, so it should be fine, eventually."

"Rather you than me. Won't you need specialist equipment? And how about feeding it?"

"I'll manage... a bit of improvisation is what's needed."

The wagon rumbled on and the sun began to set brushing the powder blue sky with vivid reds and gold.

There was great excitement in the Gregory household after the postman had made his rounds. Timmy and Marion's parcel had arrived containing his teddy, a letter from their mother and sweets for the children just as they were preparing to leave for school.

Marion squealed in excitement, "Mum is coming to see us this weekend."

"Cor!" exclaimed Timmy. "Won't she be surprised when she sees where we are!"

"Can she stay just one night, Mrs Gregory? She can sleep with me," asked Marion tentatively.

Mrs Gregory smiled, "Of course. That's lovely, it is. I will get to meet your mother and tell her just how well you are both behaving. She will be proud, I know."

The twins listened enviously.

Timmy pounced on his bear and hugged it. "Sloppy!" he exclaimed. "Mum remembered!"

"You haven't needed him here," Marion pointed out and then explained to Mrs Gregory. "Timmy could never sleep without him at home. But he's been fine here."

"That's because there are so many lovely toys to play with and I've been taking Patch to bed."

"Who is Patch?" asked Mrs Gregory.

"That's what he calls the cuddly toy dog. He keeps it on his bed."

"Ah, yes. I know," smiled Mrs Gregory. "Now these sweets, I think you should leave them here until you come home and then share them with Katy and Sally."

The twins smiled in pleasure and danced holding hands.

So delighted was Timmy with his teddy he didn't argue as Marion thought he would and just whooped.

"That's fine. I'll put them in the kitchen with Milly and you can have some after tea. Now get your coats, Basil will see you to school."

The children scampered around and got their things. They each had satchels with pens and pencils and happily followed Basil out of the house. "I will be meeting you after school today," added Mrs Gregory and the children grinned in delight.

"Top notch!" shouted Timmy and thrust his bear at Mrs Gregory. "Will you look after him for me?"

"I most certainly will," said Mrs Gregory, "And I may have something in my sewing box to replace Sloppy's missing eye."

"That would be grand," beamed Timmy and hugged the old lady around her legs.

"Careful, you'll have me over," said Mrs Gregory but she smiled and waved goodbye to the youngsters as they left for school. She closed the door with a satisfied sigh.

She studied the threadbare teddy. "I think we can smarten you up a bit; a new eye would make all the difference," and she made her way to the kitchen clutching the sweets and bear. She placed the sweet treats in a dish and ordered Milly, "The children can have some after their tea and not before. Is that understood?"

"Yes, Milady," answered Milly. "It's grand having them here, isn't it? The house hasn't felt so happy in a long time, if you don't mind me saying."

"Not at all, Milly. The children are a delight, an absolute tonic. I will tell their mother when she comes at the weekend. It will be good to meet her. I know I will certainly miss them when they go."

"Ain't that a fact!" exclaimed Milly as she chopped vegetables for the stew pot to make cawl.

The old lady smiled and took a jar of various brightly coloured buttons and beads from a shelf in the larder and her sewing box and retreated to the drawing room where she sat trying to find a suitable alternative eye for the little bear.

Mrs Gregory was so engrossed in poring through her buttons and beads she almost missed the polite knock on her door. Basil entered and held out a handwritten letter postmarked London, "One the postman forgot and this." It was an official looking telegram.

Mrs Gregory took them and perused them with a puzzled expression on her face. She set the bear down as Basil left discretely and walked toward the window overlooking the garden. She opened the telegram and was shocked to read of the death of Timmy and Marion's mother. There were no real details just that she had lost her life during a bombing raid and that the authorities were grateful for her continued care of the children and would be in touch again after the war.

Mrs Gregory's hand shook as she folded the missive. Her first thought was for the children. How on earth could she tell them? What effect would it have? They were expecting to see their mother at the weekend. Phyllis Gregory's eyes smarted with tears. She knew she would have to speak to Nurse Llewellyn.

Phyllis looked at the letter and muttered, "Well, you'll be none the wiser until you open it!" she ripped open the envelope and noted the address in Hackney and turned the page to the author, June Barnes. It was no one she knew and she returned to the beginning and read the letter.

'Dear Mrs Gregory,

It is with regret that I have to inform you of the death of Martha Noble, mother to Timmy and Marion who I believe are lodging with you. Martha was delighted that the children were so happy with you and I know she had hoped to visit at the weekend. Indeed she was on her way to post another parcel to the children and confirm that fact although whether the letter will arrive now, I don't know, as it could have been lost during the bombing. Martha loved her children very much and the last time we spoke the conversation was all about them.

I don't know if there are any other relatives that can be contacted but I will look through her address book and see what I can find and I will keep the shop open for her until her final wishes are known. Maybe Marion might be aware of other members of the family I know Martha never mentioned anyone.

Marion and Timmy's father, David Noble, is believed missing in action, another blow for the kids. Martha doesn't know if he's dead or been made a prisoner of war and there is no way of knowing that until after this lousy war is finished with.

I realise this will be a shock for both you and the children and I promise to write again. Rest assured I will do my utmost to protect their interests. You have a difficult task ahead of you should you wish to share this sad news with them now. Please pass on my love and good wishes to them both along with my sincere sympathy.

Cordially yours,

June Barnes.'

Mrs Gregory sighed heavily; her heart thumped in her chest. If the children hadn't read their mother's letter she could have picked her moment to tell them but they were expecting her to visit this weekend. Mrs Gregory felt she hadn't dealt with anything so crushing since the deaths of her husband and daughter.

There was nothing for it. She would apprise her staff of the situation and visit Dr Rees to see if he could locate District Nurse Caroline Llewellyn. Then, she would decide what to do.

Dr Rees had opened his morning surgery after a visit from Pritchard the Police who was now on his way to interview Ernie at Hendre Farm after learning all he could from the doctor.

Naomi was looking somewhat better but was still uncommunicative and Mrs Rees had taken the child into the kitchen and given her some paper and crayons with which to draw. At the moment, Naomi just sat rigidly at the table. Her eyes seemed blind to everything and her expression was distant as if the little girl was locked up tight.

Mrs Gregory tip tapped her way into the waiting room and looked around at the two people waiting to see the doctor. She nodded at Godfrey Ellis who was coughing profusely. He blew into a handkerchief and nodded at Phyllis.

The other patient was Brenda Floyd who sat rigidly looking pale and shivering slightly. Mrs Gregory pursed her lips, "Mrs Floyd."

Brenda Floyd gave a pinched smile and croaked, "Mrs Gregory."

The door opened and Dr Rees emerged and young Carrie Llewellyn exited the consulting room. She beamed at Phyllis. "Mrs Gregory. I hope all is well?"

The old lady rose and tip tapped toward her, "It's you I've come to see, Nurse. Can we talk somewhere, privately?"

Dr Rees called in his next patient. Godfrey Ellis stood up and went into the surgery. Brenda Floyd looked on curiously. Carrie beckoned Mrs Gregory to follow her. "I'm sure Mrs Rees won't mind if we go into the hall."

They ventured into the hallway. Carrie looked at her curiously and waited for her to speak. Phyllis reached into her bag and took out the letters. "Here. I received these this morning just after the Noble children received a parcel from their mother telling them she was coming this weekend. Read these and you'll see my problem, so you will."

Carrie digested the contents of both messages and sighed, "Oh, no. Poor little things."

"What do I do? They've settled so well. If they hadn't heard from their mam I could have waited for the best time to tell them and what if their dad has gone, too? What then?"

"I can't answer that, Mrs Gregory. I really don't know. But, if they're expecting their mam they'll have to be told. It will be hard, very hard. Do you want me to be there?"

Mrs Gregory thought for a moment and nodded. "Yes, please. I don't know how they will take it."

"Very well, I'll come to the school to pick them up with you; I think that will be best. We can tell them together when we get to your house."

"Very well."

"And now I must be on my rounds after I've seen Naomi."

"Naomi? Why what's happened?"

Carrie went onto explain how the child had been struck

dumb and that they suspected she had been abused by someone. Mrs Gregory sighed, "What a wicked, wicked thing to do. I don't understand the mentality of folks who could hurt a child. Will she recover?"

"We hope so, in time. Meanwhile she will stay at the farm with my family. Hopefully, the police will get to the bottom of it. At least, they may once she is prepared to talk."

"Then it's more important than ever for the children to be accompanied to and from school. You just never know." She paused, "Thank you, Nurse Llewellyn."

"Please, call me Carrie."

"Very well, Carrie. Thank you." Mrs Gregory regally swept out with her stick and Carrie moved into the kitchen to see Millicent Rees and Naomi.

Naomi sat at the table her eyes cast down as if she had totally withdrawn inside herself. Carrie drew up a chair. She took the young girl's hand who flinched but allowed Carrie to hold it. "There, there, Naomi. We will find out who did this to you and the person will be punished. I think you will have to stay home from school for a little while. I'll see Mrs Tobin and Miss Bevan, get some work for you to do at the farm and when you're feeling better we'll get you back to class and lessons. I promise." Naomi said nothing.

"What will you do?" asked Mrs Rees. "I rather think she should stay here today and perhaps you can collect her on your way home, if that's all right."

"That will be fine. I can't take her on my rounds. If you are sure?"

Millicent Rees nodded her assent and Carrie rose from the table, "I'll see myself out. Tell Dr Rees I'll speak to him later."

"And we might start doing some drawing and colouring. I've heard it's very therapeutic, so I have."

Carrie paused at the kitchen door and watched a moment while Millicent laid out paper and colouring pencils before slipping away to go and see Howie Price.

HMS Welshman had limped into Devonport for repairs and a number of sailors had been granted unexpected leave.

Thomas had recovered from his injuries and was busy working with the other engineers. He wiped his oily hands on a rag and rested on the rail on the deck of the ship. His friend Jonno was having a quick smoke.

"Not right, Thomas."

"What isn't?"

"Us stuck here while everyone else if off enjoying themselves. I was hoping to get home, if only for a day. My family don't live that far away."

"Never asked you, Jonno. Where is home?"

"Cornwall."

"Cornwall's a big place. Where exactly?"

"Penare. It's a tiny place of a few farms near Nare Point across the bay from Falmouth. Nearest village is St. Keverne and Helston is a bus ride away. Father farms two hundred and fifty acres and runs a dairy herd there. Me? I couldn't wait to be off and join the war effort, see the world and enjoy adventure."

"And now?"

"And now I wish I'd never left."

Thomas nodded. "I know what you mean. Duw, it would be lovely to see Megan again if only for an hour."

"Where is she?"

"Middle East somewhere, performing for our lads. Then she's heading home. It's her last tour."

"Let's hope you both make it through."

"Let's hope," agreed Thomas.

A shout went up from below, "Able Seaman Davies! We need you below, now!"

Ernie was busy washing and grooming Senator in the yard. He looked up as Sarah came out from Old Tom's Cottage and strode toward the mountain track. She walked in the direction of Gelli Galed, clutching the books she had borrowed from Michael and there was a dogged determination in her very feminine stride. Sam Jefferies emerged from the barn. Ernie watched as he ran to catch up with her. He put his arm around her, which she shook off.

Sam stopped her walking by grabbing hold of her arm.

They appeared to have words. Sam dropped her arm and scowled after her as she picked her way back up the track.

Ernie busied himself with Senator as Sam returned to the yard. Wisely, he said nothing. Sam looked flushed and angry and stamped his foot. He crossed to Ernie and exploded, "I've been a fool an absolute idiot." Ernie offered no comment but stopped brushing the shire to listen. "That little vixen is poison. I've been a complete nincompoop." Ernie still said nothing. "Ernie?"

Ernie looked up and Sam continued, "I've hurt Laura. She didn't deserve that and all because I had my head turned with flattery and vain beauty. What do I do, Ernie?"

"Seems you should be speaking to Laura not me."

Sam sighed, "You're right. That's if she will speak to me."

Ernie glanced across the yard as Rose and Laura came out from the cottage. He indicated her with his head, "Maybe you should take the opportunity to try now, before she starts work."

Sam nodded and ran after the two Land Girls. Ernie resumed grooming Senator and thought. He didn't like the feeling he was getting and brushed more vigorously. Senator whinnied in complaint, "Jawch, sorry, Senator. Bit rough was I? There, there." He smoothed the horse down and nuzzled his neck. "There's sorry, I am. Here…" Ernie took an apple from his pocket and gave it to the gentle horse and patted the great steed.

Ernie glanced across at Laura and Sam who had stopped by the gate. They were deep in conversation and Sam opened his arms to Laura who, reluctant at first, finally fell into them and they held onto each other. Ernie grunted, pleased at their reunion.

"Now, I must take you to the field and then I have a chick to deal with. Come on, Senator." Ernie led the majestic horse out to pasture. He opened the gate and watched as the loyal creature kicked up his heels in delight and ran in the meadow.

Ernie retraced his steps to the barn and placed a stout leather glove on his right hand and opened the cardboard box. "Jawch! You must be hungry. Let's see what we can do." He lifted the chick out of the box and set it on his hand. From his other pocket he took a dead mouse he'd retrieved from a trap and held it firmly between his thumb and first finger. Slowly, he removed the sock that covered the bird's eyes.

The youngster was alarmed and flapped its wings but Ernie had prepared well. Attached to his gloved wrist was a leather thong that was tied to the falcon's good leg to stop it trying to fly away; the other leg he had treated and taped. He talked soothingly to the young bird and coaxed it to eat the mouse. The bird wasn't interested and finally sat quietly on Ernie's arm.

"Come now, Bravura. You must eat. You need to eat to get well. Then I can teach you how to be in the wild so you can have your freedom."

Bravura seemed to like his name and cried out, a plaintive, wild call that set the hairs pricking on the back of Ernie's neck. Ernie wiggled the small rodent and the bird finally became interested, shrouded the dead critter with its wings and began to eat. Ernie was relieved.

Sarah had arrived at Gelli Galed and hammered frantically on Michael's door. Boots began to yap loudly and whine. Footsteps approached the entrance and Michael opened the door. Sarah fell inside. She had been weeping and she tumbled to the floor dropping the books. Michael helped her to her feet and gathered up the novels.

"Sarah? Whatever's wrong?"

"They hate me. They all hate me. I can't live there anymore," and she wept even more. Michael helped her to her feet and led her into the kitchen. He sat her down at the table and put the books on the side.

"Let's get the kettle on." Michael picked up the teapot and prepared it with tea before sitting next to her. "Now, Sarah. Tell me from the beginning what has happened."

Sarah sighed. Her breath came in hiccupping gasps until she seemed to steady herself and turned her huge doe eyes on Michael who waited patiently for her to speak.

Her well-manicured hands flew to her throat and Sarah's eyes locked onto Michael's as her syrupy tones began to explain.

"Oh, Michael. I don't know what to do. It's Sam..."

"Sam Jefferies?"

Sarah nodded, "He's been coming on really strongly to me. At first it was a bit of harmless flirting. I like flirting," she admitted.

Michael nodded encouragingly he already knew this having been on the other end of Sarah's provocative quips. "Yes?"

"It was just a bit of fun, nothing serious and then Sam took it all the wrong way, broke things off with Laura and insisted I be his girl. I didn't want that. I don't want a relationship with him, to be courted by him... Laura was his girl. And now they all hate me. They think I engineered it. I can't live in that cottage anymore. They are being hurtful and nasty to me. I don't know where to go or what to do. Besides it's your farm I'm assigned to not Hendre." She began to sob again.

Michael was flummoxed. He was aware Sam had been paying attention to Sarah. He hadn't thought it was serious. Now he had a weeping woman at his table and was stuck.

Sarah lowered her honeyed tones and looked pleadingly at him, "Please, Michael. Can I stay here? My life is not worth living at the cottage. I won't have to see them and Laura and Sam can sort things out without me being around, please."

Michael stuttered, "Sarah, I don't know if that's wise..."

"Please," she took his hand. "I'm begging you."

Feeling hotly uncomfortable and somewhat confused he finally agreed, "All right. But, only as a temporary measure, you can have the spare room. I'll keep your work schedules tied to Gelli Galed."

"Oh, thank you. Thank you so much." Sarah stopped crying and began to smile. "I've brought your books back..."

"Um, yes. I saw. But you need to know, Sam is my farm manager you will see him again."

"That's okay. I can cope with that. I know I can, especially with you around to diffuse the situation."

Michael rose and paced in the kitchen, "What about your things?"

"Can you get them for me? I can't go back there, yet. I just can't."

Michael came to a decision and nodded reluctantly, "I'll

pick them up for you. Now, why don't you freshen up? I'll show you where you'll sleep." Michael led the way to one of the other bedrooms and opened the door. "Will this do?"

Sarah lowered her eyes and smiled coquettishly, "It's perfect. Thank you. May I use your bathroom?'

"Of course. Towels are in the cupboard on the landing."

Sarah purred again, "Thanks, Michael. You're very kind." She allowed her eyes to roam over Michael's face and body and watched him as he left the room and smiled.

Carrie bustled around Howie Price's kitchen. He was her last call of the day. She was delighted to see that the kitchen was cleaner and tidier and Howie was in much better spirits. He was better nourished and stronger. Carrie had made them both a cup of tea and she was now examining his ulcerated leg. "Duw, Howie. That's so much better. The wound is getting smaller and healing well. That's good news."

"Aye, Carrie, love. I'm able to manage the stairs myself now. Gwyneth has been a star, so she has, as have you."

"Go on with you. I'm just doing my job that's all."

"More than that, Carrie love. You've done more than your job."

Carrie beamed, "And I've enjoyed it, Howie. A few more visits and I'll have the doctor come to check you and sign you off."

"I'll miss you, Nurse. You'll still pop in won't you? I'm always good for a cuppa even in these straightened times."

"Howie, I'll not forget you, rest assured. You're not out of the woods yet and I'm always glad of a friendly face and place to stop for a cuppa."

Carrie treated the old man's leg and they chattered animatedly before she washed her hands and had to move on.

"Home now, is it, Carrie fach?"

"Soon. I've got to visit the school first."

"Oh?"

"It's a sad tale. Something that needs to be done now." Carrie explained to Howie the difficult job ahead of her and Mrs Gregory before bidding him goodbye and setting off for the Primary School.

Carrie pedalled off toward the school passing people along the way and waving cheerily to those she knew. All the while she thought about how best to break the tragic news to the children. The problem was that she had no solutions, no answers, and no words. As she cycled on she caught sight of Mrs Gregory ahead tip tapping her stick and still clothed in her black signatory attire.

Carrie scooted to a halt next to her, hopped off and walked alongside the kindly old lady. "Mrs Gregory!"

"Nurse Llewellyn." Mrs Gregory greeted her but her expression was one of worry. " How on earth am I going to tell them, how?" She shook her head despairingly. "This will be one of the hardest things I've ever had to do."

"I suggest we wait until we reach Four Winds. This isn't something to tell on the way home."

"Agreed. I'll make sure Katy and Sally are both fully occupied. They can go with Milly in the kitchen."

Carrie nodded her agreement. "We don't want to pre-empt anything, either. No use in having them worrying on the way home."

"I suppose not."

They walked on quietly, neither of them feeling the need to talk as they contemplated what was ahead.

It wasn't long before the school gates were in sight and the playground milled with happy children escaping the regimen of school. Mothers waited to collect their children and others in familial groups with an older sibling gathered together before walking home.

Timmy soon spotted Mrs Gregory and whooped in his usual effervescent way as he raced toward her. The twins were calmer and Marion seemed to have taken charge of them holding their hands as they walked to greet Mrs Gregory.

"Where's Milly? Is she all right?" questioned Marion.

"Milly is fine," assured Mrs Gregory. "She's at home and waiting."

"But she usually comes to collect us. Isn't it hard for you with your stick an' all?"

"Don't you worry none. I felt like a walk today. That's all; and I had Nurse Llewellyn to keep me company."

"Has she come to inspect us again?" asked Timmy.

"Not quite. She just wants to see how you are," replied Mrs Gregory evasively.

Seeming happy with the explanation. Timmy whooped again and ran on ahead whilst the others followed in a more sedate fashion.

"I was thinking," said Marion solemnly. "I'm old enough to see us to school and back. It will save you and Milly a trip."

"That's very thoughtful and kind," said Mrs Gregory.

"I used to walk us to school in Hackney cos Mum had the shop to open. I can do it, really I can."

"I'm sure you can," agreed Mrs Gregory. "But, I wanted to walk today, for a change."

"Suit yourself," said Marion brightly. "But the offer's there. I'm just saying."

"And I'm sure there will be times that we will take advantage of that. Maybe in a few weeks; I know you can be trusted and you're responsible enough."

Marion smiled then spoke again. "Naomi wasn't in school today. The twins and Gerry missed her."

"No," said Carrie carefully. "Naomi isn't too well at the moment so she's staying with me. As soon as she's better she'll be back."

Sally looked up, "She was acting strange the last time we saw her, wouldn't talk or nothing."

"No, I know. Hopefully, it won't be too long and she'll be back to normal."

Satisfied with the answer, Sally let go of Marion's hand and ran on ahead with Timmy. They were quickly followed by Katy and happily skipped in front. Timmy had taken a six-inch ruler from his pocket and dragged it along the metal railings on some garden walls. It made a satisfying rattle, which he clearly enjoyed and he whooped again.

Carrie found it hard not to smile at the little boy's cheerful exuberance. And as Marion decided to chase after her brother Carrie whispered, "This is going to be tough. Do you think we just tell Marion?"

"No. They must both know. We can't expect Marion to keep a secret from her brother. It's not wise or fair."

"Yes, I believe you're right."

They continued in silence until they reached the gates of Four Winds and walked up the path. In the hallway, Mrs Gregory turned to the twins. "Off to the kitchen. Milly is expecting you. I think she has some milk and biscuits ready."

"Coo, I want some, too!" complained Timmy.

"And so you shall but not just yet. I need to speak to you and Marion. Come into the drawing room."

Mrs Gregory tapped her way through the hall to the elegant room.

"Never understand why it's called a drawing room," said Timmy. "Don't do no drawing or colouring in there."

The children bounded into the room and Mrs Gregory firmly closed the door. "Please sit down."

Timmy and Marion looked at each other. This was most unusual and a flicker of alarm flashed across Marion's face. She became subdued and her demeanour affected Timmy who at once became more serious.

Mrs Gregory's voice took on a grave tone, "Marion, Timmy I want you to listen carefully."

"Cor! Are we in trouble? I ain't done nothing, honest You're not sending us away?"

"No, you are not in trouble and I know you haven't done anything. I most definitely am not sending anyone away…"

"Then what is it?" asked Marion her face filled with consternation.

"Well, you see," began Mrs Gregory. She looked wildly at Carrie.

"It's about your mother," said Carrie gently rescuing Mrs Gregory.

"She's not coming, is she?" said Marion crestfallen. "She can't leave the shop, I bet."

Carrie exchanged a look with the old lady, "No, you're right. Your mother can't make it. We heard from your Aunty June who was going to look after things."

"Huh! Bet she let mum down," said Timmy in complaint.

"No…" said Mrs Gregory. "She didn't let your mother down, on the contrary…" She stopped and looked at Carrie, "Oh dear, this is much harder than I thought."

Marion's eyes searched those of Mrs Gregory and Carrie and said quietly, "Something's happened to mum, hasn't it?"

"I'm afraid so," confirmed Carrie.

"What? What's happened? Is she going to be all right?" said Timmy beginning to breathe heavily.

Carrie looked at him in concern. He was beginning to gasp for air and started wheezing. Mrs Gregory looked on in alarm. Carrie explained, "He's asthmatic. It was in his notes."

"What do we do?"

"We must get him outside in the fresh air and keep him calm. They say it's a psychiatric condition. It's often interpreted as a cry for mother. But, I don't believe that. The symptoms are entirely physical. I think it is a respiratory illness, some sort of inflammation sometimes brought on by stress or trauma."

Immediately Mrs Gregory rang for Basil who took one look at Timmy's face and lifted him up. He carried him outside to the garden and sat him on a bench seat. Carrie attended to him and spoke soothingly, trying to calm him. "It's all right, Timmy. There is nothing to be afraid of. Everything is fine, you'll see."

Marion hung on to Mrs Gregory's hand, "Will he be all right?"

"Yes, yes. As you can see the nurse is looking after him."

Carrie encouraged the little boy to take deep breaths and gradually the wheezing slowed and Timmy began to breathe more easily. "I suggest, Timmy goes to lie down until tea time or until he feels better. Marion, go and join the others in the kitchen. I need to speak to Mrs Gregory."

Marion dutifully returned to the house as Basil carried Timmy back inside and up to his room. Mrs Gregory faced Carrie, "Now what?"

"We can't tell them, not yet. Not if it provokes that sort of reaction in the child."

"They'll have to know sometime."

"Better to let them think their mother can't make it this weekend. We'll have a rethink."

"I don't like it, Nurse," said Mrs Gregory shaking her head.

"Neither do I but it's all we can do for the time being."

"Very well."

Mrs Gregory returned to the house and Carrie picked up her bike. "I'll be back to see you to work out how to proceed, I promise." Mrs Gregory assented with a nod of her head and disappeared inside. Carrie was left to try and make sense of this new problem. "Why is nothing straight forward?" she remonstrated with herself as she cycled toward the doctor's surgery.

Carrie collected Naomi from the doctor's house. Pritchard the police had been summoned and a report had been made but as the child didn't speak there was no way of knowing who could be the perpetrator of this heinous crime. It was agreed that whoever was responsible was a monster and enquiries would be made as well as warnings given to the general public.

Carrie struggled to talk to the little girl on the way back to Hendre. At first she didn't know what to say and then she believed that maybe if she opened up and shared her terrible experience with Jacky Ebron that maybe Naomi wouldn't feel so alone. And so, Carrie began to relate events she had not spoken about since her Aunty Netta's trial. She found that after her hesitant beginning that the more she talked the easier it became. How much Naomi took in was uncertain but Carrie had to admit this sharing had in some strange way helped her, too.

Once in Hendre's yard both dogs came to welcome Carrie and the little girl who showed some recognition of the animals. She allowed herself to be licked and eventually stooped down and patted both of them. Carrie thought this was a good omen.

Ernie tramped across the meadow with John who was now up and about and looking better. John went into the farmhouse muttering about making a start on the loft and Ernie greeted Naomi. "Well, well, there's good to have you back, fy merch 'i. Come and see our chick. He's doing well, so he is. When you are up to it you can help me train him, ready to be set free in the wild."

Naomi looked up at Ernie and it was clear there was an element of trust present. She followed Ernie willingly into the barn. Carrie sighed, this would give her a chance to explain to the others what had happened. She was hoping to enlist Jenny's help in nurturing Naomi back to health and speech. She bounded up the steps and indoors where Jenny was laying the table.

"Where's John?"

"Gone upstairs with a measure. I think he's going to make a start on the new room."

"Good. I need to talk to you."

Jenny detected the serious note in Carrie's voice and listened carefully to all she had to say. "That's champion, so it is. I can teach Naomi. She's a bright little button. I know she'll help with Bethan and when Bethan has her sleep I can do her school work with her and even teach her to play the piano since she's shown an interest in it."

"That will be grand. I can't imagine what she must be suffering. I'm sure with all our help something will break through that barrier."

"Let's hope."

In the barn, Naomi was studying the young bright-eyed bird. She noted the leather glove that Ernie wore when he handled her and the perch Ernie had made for the chick. She looked with distaste at the dead mice Ernie had collected, but appeared easier when he explained that the bird needed fresh meat to live and to repair his injury. "I promise you, Naomi that tomorrow you can come with me to the field and see me feed him. We need to get him used to the space and as soon as his leg is better we can teach him to fly, safely of course. We don't want anything else to happen to him."

The little girl listened and Ernie was convinced she was connecting with him, again. "There you are, then. That's what we'll do. But now we must get indoors, my stomach's rumbling like a storm. It's setting up a growl that will make Bonnie bark, so it is."

Ernie walked to the barn door but Naomi stood transfixed staring at the bird. She tentatively began to raise her hand but Ernie called out, "No, Naomi! Don't touch, not yet. Let him get used to you first. He could give you a nasty nip."

217

The little girl dropped her hand and turned to the barn door. Ernie was pleased; she was indeed connecting with him. This proved it. He began to whistle as he held open the door for her and she followed him out into the yard and the house.

Once inside she was greeted warmly by Jenny, who hugged the little girl to her but Naomi remained stiff in her arms. As if she didn't notice Jenny continued to include the child in a bubble of chatter and encouraged Naomi to help her finish laying the table. Like a little lamb, Naomi did as she was asked and then sat on the floor to play with Bethan.

Jenny smiled, "This is what she needs, love and a proper home." She called down to Naomi as John entered the kitchen and disappeared outside only to re-emerge struggling with a stepladder. "After supper and Bethan's in bed I'll show you how to play some scales on the piano. You'll like that, won't you?" Although Naomi said nothing it was clear from the expression in her eyes that she would.

John battled through the door and up the winding stairs with the wooden steps and could be heard crashing about. Carrie emerged; she had changed into her dungarees and a gingham top, "Duw, there's a racket. It sounds like John's demolishing the house."

"I hope not," said Jenny, he's supposed to be making it into a happy home not wrecking it." She eyed Carrie's clothes, "You working on the farm, now?"

"I'm glad to get out of my uniform. I'll be off to Michael's after tea but thought I'd take the dogs for a walk first. This garb is much better suited to that."

"Fine. Come and sit up and we'll get started. Then you can walk your four legged friends."

CHAPTER SEVENTEEN

Breaking hearts

Michael went to pick up Sarah's things. Rose had emptied Sarah's wardrobe and drawers and tipped them into her bags. She brushed her hands together as if dusting them off, as she passed them across to Michael. "Good riddance that's what I say. She's hurt Laura too much. What woman moves in on someone already spoken for?"

"I wouldn't know," replied Michael. "But there are two sides to every story."

Rose threw her arms up in the air, "Don't say she has you fooled, too. Huh! Men!" She closed the door leaving Michael standing there feeling awkward and nonplussed. He took the bags and tossed them in his trailer and started back up the track passing the postman on the way. He didn't see Carrie leaving the house and running to the meadow with Bonnie and Prince on her tail. His face was fixed front and he didn't hear Carrie call to him and wave when she caught sight of the tractor driving on up the track.

Carrie shrugged. She believed that he clearly hadn't heard her above the din of the engine. No matter she would be seeing him soon anyway. She ran into the meadow and gambolled with the dogs, rolling and tumbling like a young child. She stopped and lay flat out on the grass. Bonnie stood over her licking her face until she cried out, giggling, "No, Bonnie, no tongues," as the over enthusiastic dog proceeded to wash every inch of her face and had just caught her lips.

Carrie sat up laughing and ruffled Bonnie's fur, "Duw! As long as you live, Trix will live on in you." She turned her attention to Prince who stood watching their antics, his tail wagging slowly and low and she called him over. "And don't you go getting any ideas, Mr Prince. We don't want you disgracing the household with Bonnie and bringing lots of babies to the door like Suzy Evans in the village, now do we?" she said waggling her finger in a joking manner. Prince put his head on one side, bowed his front legs and woofed before chasing Bonnie down the hillside in a wonderful game. Carrie laughed and watched the joy of the two dogs as they pranced through the grass and she sighed. Life was so uncomplicated for them and she announced, "Next time, I'm coming back as a dog! But only to a loving happy home."

She stood up and gazed across the valley. The harvest was safely in. Farmers had helped each other, as always, as they travelled around the neighbouring farms all for the price of a good fry up and a pint of cider. Usually it was a family affair but now with her job, her input into the farm was minimal. She didn't quite know how she felt about that and she allowed her mind to wander to her brave friends still nursing in London and her lovely pal, Gilly, who had died so tragically and for a moment a lump manifested in her throat. "Whatever's the matter with me?" She reprimanded herself but it didn't stop her thoughts, which moved onto Hawtry and the heroic way she had died. Her hand went to her throat and she fingered the St. Christopher medal that had been given her by Hawtry's mother. It had certainly kept her safe and brought her luck. At that moment she felt an inexplicable feeling of warmth spread through her and she smiled. She felt the presence of her friends around her and for some reason Gilly's beau from Ireland, Patrick popped into her head and the dashing Peter Gilbert who had wanted to take Gilly out in Aberystwyth when she had been seeing Lloyd.

Carrie sighed, why was she feeling these things now? Was there a reason? She was interrupted with the arrival of Laura who ran down the slope and sat on the grass as she watched the dogs.

Carrie dropped down again beside her. Laura picked a daisy and twirled it between her fingers and pointed at the sea of poppies running through the meadow. "So delicate. Yet, they survive the battering of the wind. They're flexible and bend their stems, but do not break…"

Carrie nodded, "Their wills are strong although they look frail in spite of their beauty."

"Do you think there is such a thing as destiny?" asked Laura.

Carrie pursed her lips, "That's an odd question. I believe what will be will be and everything happens for a reason."

Laura nodded, "Me, too… Is that why I've had this hard lesson that men aren't to be trusted?"

"Whatever do you mean?" quizzed Carrie who was unaware of the problems that had faced Laura.

"I don't know… I thought Sam was dependable and strong…"

"Well, he is isn't he?"

"In a way. But he still managed to get his head turned by a Jezebel."

"Whatever do you mean?" asked Carrie curiously and Laura began to relate her heartache over the flirting between Sam and Sarah.

"I mean to say, there's flirting and flirting…" Carrie looked at her but said nothing. "The harmless kind that is just a bit of friendly banter and teasing, and the dangerous kind."

"Dangerous?"

"When there's an undercurrent of something implied that could go further. Believe me, you'll recognise it when you see it. And no man is safe with that minx. She collects men's scalps and hearts as a squirrel gathers nuts for the winter."

"I must say I'm surprised she applied to be a Land Girl. I'd have thought she'd be better suited to something where she didn't have to get her hands dirty."

"Huh! She doesn't. Always manages to wheedle her way out of it. I tell you, no man is safe from that predatory witch, not even Ernie.'

Carrie laughed, the thought of Ernie having his head turned amused her.

"You can laugh… but no one is safe. No one."

"But you and Sam, you're all right now, aren't you?"

"In a way. But it will never be the same. I can forgive him but I can't forget and when trust takes a beating it's hard to get back on track. I think I'll swear off relationships for a while. I've had my fill. What with Arthur…"

"Arthur?"

"Grainger Mason or whatever he called himself... and now this."

Carrie impulsively put her arms around Laura. She wasn't used to engaging in this type of soul searching with someone who wasn't very close. Laura nestled into Carrie and the warmth of human contact was too much and she began to cry. The dogs gambolled back and sat with them and watched. They, too, felt Laura's sadness.

Time passed. The warmth of the evening sun began to fade and the two sat there looking across the valley as the sun dipped lower in the sky. They sat like that for some time without a word. None was needed. There was a mutual understanding and a new bond of friendship was born.

Michael put away the tractor and removed Sarah's bags. Lost in thought, his face was grim as he passed the letterbox on the gate and didn't notice the edge of an envelope protruding. He carried the bags up the veranda steps and set them down outside. Boots followed him looking curiously at his master and lay at his feet. Michael sat in the swing seat he had purchased for just such a beautiful evening and swung back and fore, his expression inscrutable before rising and finally entering Gelli Galed.

There was no sign of Sarah downstairs so he left the cases in the hall by the door and retreated to the kitchen and busied himself preparing a snack. Soon the smell of toast filled the air and Michael munched contentedly. He wiped the crumbs from his face and returned to the hall picked up the luggage and mounted the stairs. He put them outside the room Sarah was to use and returned to the kitchen, but he couldn't settle.

Michael went back outside and calling Boots to him he walked along the upper track to the top of the incline and sat astride a boulder enjoying the clear mountain air. He breathed deeply and steadily to clear his head when a movement further down the track caught his eye. His heart skipped a beat as he recognised the red-gold spangled curls of Carrie and a smile tugged at the corner of his lips. He jumped down and began to walk back to the farm when Sam Jefferies appeared on the path having come from the steep field. He stopped Michael and although Michael was eager to get away he found it impossible as Sam wanted to talk and talk he did.

Carrie stepped out on the track. She puffed a little as she reached the toughest part of the climb. It was getting better. She wasn't as out of breath as usual. This trek would certainly keep her fit, she mused with a smile.

Carrie hopped onto the veranda and knocked on the door. There was no answer so she hammered again. Eventually she heard a soft footfall. The door opened and Sarah stood there looking fragrant and fresh swathed in a large bath towel with her hair damp and falling in tiny curls. Carrie gasped.

"Yes?" queried Sarah a mischievous element entering her voice and an impish spark in her eyes.

"Um... is Michael there?"

"Michael? Er... No, he just stepped out leaving me to languish here alone. I had hoped he was going to dry my hair for me. So much better when someone else does it for you, don't you think?" She smiled languidly as her honeyed tones slid over Carrie's ears.

Carrie was momentarily dumbstruck as she looked on Sarah's obvious vampish charms. The towel was draped just low enough to reveal an ample cleavage with pert breasts and it hung in folds accentuating her small waist and full hips. It was short enough to expose her lengthy, shapely smooth legs with skin like satin and Carrie gulped.

"Would you like to come in and wait?" she purred. "I don't know how long he's going to be or I can give him a message, if you like?"

Eventually Carrie stuttered, "What are you doing here?"

Sarah smiled expansively, "Oh? Didn't he tell you? The naughty boy," she simpered ... "He invited me... asked me to move in."

Carrie's cheeks flamed with acute embarrassment, which almost matched her hair. She stood a moment uncertain of what to say or do.

Sarah asked again, "Any message?"

"No, no message," she turned and walked away and began to retrace her steps back down the mountainside. Her heart was thumping fit to fly out from her chest and her thoughts were as confused as her tangled curls.

As she opened the small wooden gate she blinked hard trying to stop the tears from rushing down her cheeks, all reason had fled and she was filled with heart breaking hurt. She began to run, her tears blinding her. She slipped on the stone track and grazed her knees, grit dug into her hands. She stayed on her knees and sobbed. But then her eyes filled with chips of ice and she rose and told herself, "No. Something's not right. I won't believe it," and she began to slowly walk back to Gelli Galed.

Michael finally concluded his conversation with Sam and hurried back to the farmhouse. He burst in hoping to find Carrie waiting for him. She wasn't. Puzzled, he called out at the bottom of the stairs, "Sarah!" before marching into the kitchen, where he picked up Boots' dish to feed the little Jack Russell. There was no reply but Sarah still wrapped in a towel looking damply fragrant began to slink down the stairs silently and she oozed with sensuality.

Michael fussed his little dog and presented him with his bowl of dog meat and stood up. He was still deep in thought and didn't hear Sarah enter. She bottom swayed silkily to him and as he rose he felt her finger trace down his spine. She reached up and quickly covered his eyes with her hands and he laughed.

At that exact same moment Carrie arrived back at Gelli Galed. She peered in through the kitchen window and saw Sarah's slinky, sexy walk across to Michael who stood there as if waiting for her. When she saw Sarah's finger drawing down his spine, her arched back and seductive smile Carrie bristled and as Sarah's hands went over Michael's eyes and Carrie saw him laugh she did not want to see anymore and hurried away.

Michael turned beaming and saying in pleasure, "Carrie..." He opened his eyes and saw scantily clad Sarah before him and exclaimed in surprise, "Sarah!"

"Yes, Sarah. Who did you expect? After all, you called me. I thought it was important or I would have dressed." Her manner had changed to one of modesty compounded with apparent embarrassment as she clutched her towel to her.

"Um, I thought I saw Carrie coming. I…"

"Oh, you did. But, she left without leaving a message."

"What?"

Sarah was now the epitome of innocence, "She hammered on the door so hard I thought the door would break so I ran down to open it. She seemed surprised to see me…"

"I bet she did…"

"So, I explained that you were very kindly helping me out… in letting me stay… I didn't want her jumping to conclusions. I asked if she wanted to wait but she didn't." She smiled sweetly and continued, "I need to get dressed, can't have you getting the wrong idea, can I?" With that she minced out of the kitchen and back up the stairs. Michael's jaw was agape as he followed her with his eyes. He was now very confused and sat with a thump at the kitchen table remaining there, hardly blinking, for a good ten minutes.

He suddenly took a huge intake of breath, seeming to come to. He bent down and smoothed Boots' fur as he contemplated what to do next. The little dog had now finished his supper and was ecstatic with the attention; he enthusiastically jumped up into Michael's arms and licked him. Michael murmured, "There's nothing for it, Boots. I need to get down to Hendre. You can keep me company."

He rose and started for the front door when there was a rumbling crunch. Michael rushed out to see Sarah, now fully clothed, tumbling down the last few stairs on her bottom. She squealed loudly.

Michael hurried to help her up, "Are you all right?"

"Stupid shoes," she cursed.

Michael glanced down at the fashionable strappy wedge heels she was wearing on her dainty feet, which were smaller than he thought, and surprising in one so tall. "Not the best shoes to wear on a farm."

"No, but I'm not working any more today and I miss wearing things that make me feel like a woman. I should have known better I suppose. I caught my foot in the trouser cuff and tripped. Ouch!" she exclaimed as she tried to put weight on it and looked up appealingly at him. "I hope I haven't broken it."

"I don't think so. It's probably just bruised. Let's get you in the kitchen and take a look. Lean on me."

Sarah nestled into Michael smiling shyly up at him through her dark fringed lashes. Michael seemed to be unaware of her proximity although she was deliberately leaning into him and exaggerated her limping hobble.

He helped her to a seat and examined her ankle. She winced as his thumb palpated one spot, "There. That's where it hurts."

"No need to worry, it's not broken. Nor is it swollen or sprained. You've taken a knock and it's probably just bruised. A cold compress with your foot up should do the trick."

Michael lifted her foot onto an adjacent chair and rinsed a cloth in cold water. He wrapped it around her ankle, rose and started for the door.

"Where are you going?"

"Sorry. I have to see Carrie; she must be wondering what's going on. We have much to discuss."

"Please, don't go..." Michael turned quizzically, "I'm terrified of being alone in a strange place. Please don't leave me."

Michael hesitated and then apologised, "I must. I'm sorry."

"Promise me you'll be back soon, please."

Michael opened the kitchen door to the hall, "I'll be as quick as I can. Boots!" Michael left with Boots scurrying after him and Sarah glowered in the chair.

She waited a few moments once Michael was out through the door then stood up with no visible sign of a limp. She tossed the compress into the sink and ran out of the kitchen and back to her room.

Closing the door firmly, she emptied the contents of her handbag and hunted through her cosmetics. She pulled out a lipstick, some rouge and a blue and green eye shadow and set to work. She carefully rubbed on some rouge and mixed it with a scarlet lipstick so that her ankle looked angry and red. Next she dabbed on some blue and then green eye shadow to give a bruised appearance. Once pleased with the appearance she set the camouflage with a little powder and eyed her ankle critically. It would do perfectly; it looked sufficiently bruised to warrant her staying off work and resting up. She was delighted.

Next, she turned her attention to her face and attempted to make her eyes look as if she had been crying; a slight touch of red under her eyes, perfect.

Sarah trotted back downstairs and into the kitchen. Soon, she would put the next part of her plan into operation.

Carrie had stumbled down the track. She didn't want to return home. She didn't want family questions but needed to clear her head and still her beating heart. She ran out onto the meadow. As soon as Bonnie and Prince caught sight of their beloved mistress they followed her but instead racing around in their usual delinquent fashion they seemed to sense her mood and came and sat close to her as she flopped down despairingly in the grass.

Further down the slope she watched Ernie who was out with Bravura and Naomi. Ernie caught sight of her and waved. She raised her hand in response and focused on how Ernie was training the young bird. It was a long and difficult process. Carrie knew he had been trying to get the bird into the air since the chick's wound had healed sufficiently. He threw the bird up into the air but it repeatedly fluttered and fell to the ground. She heard him say, "Come on now, you're not trying hard enough. You have to fly to survive. If you can do that we can let you go."

Naomi watched anxiously and Carrie perused the little girl's expression. She was stoic in her attitude but there was a keenness present, a look of determination and something she interpreted as resembling strong will and desire. Carrie knew she had been right to bring the little girl home. She was sure they would have a breakthrough soon.

Ernie was continuing to encourage the bird to fly. He took some accoutrements from his bag on the ground. Naomi watched curiously as the fledgling was attached by its leg to a long leash that was fastened onto Ernie's leather gloved wrist. He tied another long cord to which he had secured a morsel of raw meat. He began swinging this around his head in a circular motion and the bird was watching it move.

Ernie dropped his voice and although Carrie could hear the sound of his voice on the wind she couldn't discern what he was actually saying. Naomi was observing intently almost mesmerised by the swirling lead. Suddenly, Bravura took off and circled as much as the leash would allow, flying above its supposed prey. Ernie hooted with joy, this was exactly what he wanted and Naomi clapped her hands and even though Carrie was upset she became engrossed in their world and she, too, grinned in delight. Their success was infectious.

Bravura continued to circle, now he had found his wings and was flying he called his distinctive cry before folding his wings and dived, pouncing on the food with his talons, grabbing it before he dropped to the ground, shrouding his 'kill' with his wings as he proceeded to eat the titbit.

Carrie could see Ernie explaining something to the little girl who nodded and Carrie continued to observe marvelling at the immense progress Ernie appeared to have made, both with the child and the bird. The man continually surprised her. Was there nothing he couldn't do?

Carrie looked up as Laura came to join her and flopped down beside her. "Watching Ernie?" Carrie nodded. "He's amazing. His patience knows no bounds. I like to observe from the window when I can. He really seems to know what he's doing." Carrie said nothing. Laura studied Carrie's face and remarked, "You've been crying? Whatever has happened?"

Carrie hunched her shoulders and murmured softly, "I don't want to talk about it."

"Come on, Carrie. That's not like you. And talking to you certainly made me feel better, please, tell me."

Carrie sniffed hard and feeling comforted by Laura's presence began to relate what had happened. Laura listened sympathetically, "The woman's a witch. Casts a spell or curse wherever she walks." She paused, "I know it all looks bad but are you sure Mr Lawrence is complicit in this seduction?"

"I know what I saw," said Carrie vehemently.

"Even so, as he rightly said to me, there are two sides to

every story. Maybe you saw what she wanted you to see."

"But, she's moved into Gelli Galed," protested Carrie.

"Not exactly," said Laura. "She had to get out. She couldn't share with Rose and me anymore and I reckon she played on his sympathies. He didn't seem entirely happy about it when he collected her things. I can't believe things have galloped apace as quickly as that. Not in one afternoon. You need to speak to him. Give him a chance to explain. Like he said, "There are two sides to every story.""

They both stopped their discussion as they watched Bravura take off again and circle before accepting Ernie's arm as a place to perch. "That is amazing. I have never seen anything like it, have you?" Carrie had to agree. Laura rose, "Go and see Mr Lawrence. Speak to him, not her. Sorry, I have to dash. I've got a couple of orphan lambs to feed. That's one of the nicest parts of this job." Laura retraced her steps back to the yard and barn leaving Carrie to think on what she said.

John was feeling much better and considerably stronger after his bout of Field Fever. He had recovered more quickly than expected and was now sitting in the loft with his legs dangling through the entrance space. An old worn ladder, which had seen better days, lay against the wood of the hatch and John was viewing the roof space using the light from a paraffin lamp. He set it inside, swung his legs up and stood. All the ceiling joists had been boarded over so now it was safe to move around on the newly laid wooden floor. There was more than enough height for him to stand in the centre and he wondered where he could place a window or skylight. He didn't like the idea of relying on oil lamps and the like, because of the danger of fire. He took some measurements, scribbling them down in a little notebook and worked out that he could either open up part of the eaves to allow a narrow spillage of light into the area or possibly it would be better to be bolder and cut a proper skylight in the roof.

John decided he would take advice. Although he could do all the basic work himself he didn't feel his expertise included making windows. As soon as he was able he would contact

Prew the builder and plumber who had fitted their bathroom. This would be a job for a professional.

John sat back at the entrance and swung his legs over the gap but remembering Ernie's words about breaking legs and ladders he shouted to Jenny who was singing joyfully below, "Jen…! Jenny!"

Jenny stopped her song, popped her head around the pine door and shouted up, "Yes?"

"Come and hold the ladder for me. I don't fancy it slipping after what Ernie said."

"Hang on, let me put Bethan where she can't get into mischief."

A wail went up as Bethan was obviously placed out of harm's way in her playpen, although, now she was getting too big for it. For the moment it would do, a miniature prison to keep her safe. The grizzling stopped as Jenny had obviously given her something to play with or to eat, something that at least would keep her quiet for the moment.

There was a knocking at the door and although John couldn't hear what was said he heard a man's voice, as it opened, followed by Jenny's softer tones. The door closed and whoever it was had gone away. John surmised it might have been Sam or even Ernie. He shrugged and whistled through his teeth as he waited.

Jenny came trundling up, rested her hands on the sides and lower rungs of the ladder and steadied it. John slid out of the roof void and turned to clamber down, closing the hatch. The wood creaked as he began to step on each rung. Much to his horror one of the splintered rungs cracked, his foot slipped and the ladder began to fall backward. Fortunately, with Jenny holding it firmly she was able to rest it securely against the hatch and John continued safely down.

"Duw, there's a fright I had," blustered John. "If you hadn't been holding it…" He didn't complete the sentence.

Jenny pursed her lips, "As if we didn't know. But that will teach us to listen to Ernie."

"Always," agreed John and as he reached the bottom he took his wife in his arms and held her close.

Jenny gazed up at her husband and he kissed her tenderly

when there was a blubbering wail from downstairs. "Jawch! It's time's like this I wish she had a longer afternoon nap."

"Go on with you," laughed Jenny and added impishly, "There's always tonight," and she scurried back down the twisting pine stairs to attend to her crying daughter.

John put the ladder back and followed his wife downstairs. Naomi and Ernie were indoors and Naomi began to help Jenny with the table getting it ready for the morning.

"It's funny. I thought Carrie would be back by now," said John.

"Oh, didn't I say?" replied Jenny. "Michael came looking for her but I had no idea where she had got to. I thought she went up to Gelli Galed."

"So she did," chortled Ernie. "And back again. She was in the field watching Naomi and me with Bravura. Get quite an audience we do. Laura came out as well. But, I thought Carrie'd come in."

"No," said Jenny frowning. "That's strange."

Carrie was on her way back to Gelli Galed this time with Bonnie and Prince in tow. She had taken Laura's words to heart and the more she thought about it the more it didn't make sense. If, as Laura said, Michael had been forced to take in Sarah and if the woman was as manipulative as she had been led to believe. It was possible she had engineered the situation to look like something else. Michael didn't strike her as being the fickle type or the sort of man who would have defective trouser flies!

She muttered to herself as she walked, arguing with the devil and angel sitting on opposing shoulders until finally the small wooden gate of the farmhouse came into view. The adjacent letterbox had something protruding from it and Carrie pulled out an official looking letter with a royal crown and military insignia embossed on the envelope saying OHMS. She frowned. Touching it had given her a bad feeling.

Carrie walked toward the wooden veranda and the swing seat. She sat on it a moment and swung gently to and fro. As she sat she became aware of raised voices and stood up. Carrie glanced in through the kitchen window seeing Sarah sitting red-faced with her foot up on a chair. Michael was looking cross. Carrie tapped on the window and when he saw her Michael's glum face turned to one of pure joy. Sarah, however, looked most displeased at her arrival.

Michael dashed onto the veranda and picked Carrie up in his arms and swung her around, much to the delight of the dogs who ran around the yard with Boots. "I wondered where you were. I saw you coming up the track but got delayed by Sam and when I got in you'd gone without leaving a message."

Carrie weighed up her words carefully, "I sort of had the impression that you were otherwise engaged."

"What?"

"With Sarah."

"God, no. She's only staying here because she had nowhere else to go. Not an arrangement I'm happy with either."

"You seemed to be happy when she put her hands over your eyes in the kitchen."

"What? I don't understand." Michael looked puzzled.

"I saw you," said Carrie. "Together."

"Only because I thought it was you, as soon as I realised it wasn't... What's that?" he asked pointing at the envelope the now smiling Carrie was holding.

Carrie thrust her hand out, "It was in your mailbox. Looks official."

Michael took it from her and stared at the OHMS stamp. "Good thing you are here. Sarah has damaged her ankle. I've had a cold compress on it and there's no swelling but it does look bruised."

"I seem to remember you deal very efficiently with those type of injuries," said Carrie playfully, recalling his treatment of her when she had twisted her own ankle. "Aren't you going to open it?"

Michael slapped the letter in his hand, "In a moment. Come on in." Carrie followed him into the kitchen coming face to face with Sarah. "Look, Sarah. Just the thing, we have a real nurse to tend to you."

Sarah stiffened and withdrew her leg from the chair with a pretence of grimacing and picked up her walking stick. "No, really. It's no bother, just a bit bruised. As you said, nothing is broken."

"While I'm here I may as well check it over," said Carrie in nurse mode.

Sarah protested still further, "I'd rather not. I'm such a baby and it hurts to touch it."

"I promise I'll be gentle, insisted Carrie.

Sarah reluctantly began to lift her foot back onto the cushioned seat as Michael tore open the letter, "Oh, no!"

Carrie stopped, "What is it?"

"I'm being called to fly again."

"But, I thought that was it for now?"

"So did I. Seems they want me for one more mission."

Sarah retracted her leg and stood up. She leant on her cane and hobbled to the door, "It's clear you both need to talk. I'll get myself upstairs and rest my ankle. It's sure to be better by morning."

Carrie didn't object as she studied Michael's concerned face. They only seemed to have eyes for each other. "What are you going to do?"

"I don't know. I truly believed that was it after I was wounded. Looks like I was mistaken. What about you? What have you got to tell me?"

Carrie sat down and patted the seat next to her and began to relate the weekend's events. Michael listened with a grave expression. "Sounds like Matthew has set his cap at you…"

"Maybe he has, but I am only interested in one person, you," assured Carrie.

The couple continued to talk at depth late into the evening until Carrie rose. "I really should be getting back. I'll see you tomorrow. Let me know what you decide."

"That's if I have a choice," whispered Michael before he embraced her, kissing her tenderly. He nuzzled his face in her hair, "You must remember, you are my girl. There is no one else."

"I know." She broke away and glanced down. Something caught her eye. She picked up the cushion on which Sarah had rested her foot and brushed it. A suspicious gleam entered her eyes. "Next time you see Sarah insist on her having another cold compress... and give her ankle a good rub with it."

"Why?"

"Because I think her bruise is cosmetic; a dab of lipstick, a smudge of eye shadow. Oh yes, I think your house guest has been faking it!"

CHAPTER EIGHTEEN

Truth will out

Lewis Owen sat at Jacqueline Price's kitchen table enjoying a cup of tea. His eyes roamed over the little girl, Mary. She wasn't ripe yet like Naomi but she soon would be. His eyes glittered with unhealthy desire.

Jacqueline set some food on the table, "What are we going to do, Lewis?"

His eyes narrowed, "What do you mean?"

"When Emlyn's home from war. We can't carry on like this…"

"That's if he comes home."

"Yes, well… we all hope he does, of course. But, if he doesn't…?"

"We'll cross that bridge when we come to it. For the moment, we're all right as we are, aren't we?"

"Aye, of course." Jacqueline sighed, "Well, we'll leave it for now there are little ears listening. But we will have to talk about it sometime."

Lewis nodded, "Well, of course, fach." He took a slurp of his tea. "Thought I'd go out after work tomorrow and see if I can bag us a couple more rabbits. That's if those falcons haven't taken too many."

"Falcons? Huh, poachers more like," laughed Jacqueline.

"Hush! That needs to be kept quiet," laughed Lewis winking. "But, seriously though, these falcons are a plague and drain on the wildlife for our dinner table. We need to be rid of them. I intend to finish the job… And now, let me help to get the little ones to bed. It will give us more time for us this evening and we can have that talk."

Jacqueline smiled, "That will be grand. If you can take them upstairs, I'll clear up. Read them a story and I'll be up to say goodnight."

Lewis grinned. This was exactly what he wanted and he

coaxed the two little ones out of their chairs, "Come on then, Mary, Ted; I'll race you upstairs. You can have a head start. I'll count to ten first."

Ted and Mary giggled and wriggled off their chairs and chased out of the room as Lewis began to count.

Naomi followed Ernie out into the field; "This is our last training session today. Tomorrow we take him back to where we found him and let him free to fly with his parents and live the life he was meant to have.

Naomi's face crumpled and Ernie reassured her, "There, there, Naomi fach. This is nature. He is a wild bird and meant to be free not cooped up in a barn. And although to have trained falcons is considered the sport of kings, I would much rather see these magnificent creatures soaring in the sky, flying free in the wild like our otters, badgers and foxes. Don't you see? It's wrong to keep them a prisoner?"

Who knows what went through Naomi's mind as Ernie said this? Maybe she was remembering her time locked in the dungeon basement at Jacqueline Price's house or perhaps some other horror or memory. Either way she appeared to reconcile herself with his words and she nodded soulfully. She looked up at Ernie, as if for permission, as her hand tentatively moved up to the magnificent bird. Ernie smiled and indicated his agreement. He brought his arm down and Naomi's hand stretched across to the majestic creature, which although hooded, allowed her to gently stroke its breast feathers. Her expression was one of pure joy.

"I expect you're bursting with questions that I would be only too happy to answer, if only you'd speak."

But, Naomi clearly was not ready. She continued to stroke the creature's breast as if locked in a protective bubble. It was only as Ernie's back began to ache, stooped over, as he was that he was forced to rise and stand upright. "Sorry, fach. I can't bend in one position like I used to. Let's fly him again and this time I'll let you swing the lure." He handed Naomi the cord with the meat attached. "Now we don't want to make it too easy for him. Swing it around your head like a lasso. You've seen me do it. Now you have a go."

Naomi's face shone with light and love as she took the lure from Ernie and tried to swing it above her head. "Stand further away from me and lift your arm as high as you can. Really swing it; don't be afraid you'll do it too fast. Pretend you're playing with a skipping rope and you're going to do doublers. Go on. When I think you're ready I'll take Bravura's head cover off.

Naomi appeared to gather her strength and the twine whizzed through the air as she focused on following Ernie's instructions. Ernie removed the homemade hood from the bird and Bravura watched as the meat circled in the air. Then he took off with a flurry of his wings and soared crying plaintively into the balmy smooth early autumn air. He swooped and dived catching the meat and dropped to the ground for his prize. Ernie was gratified to see that Naomi's face was creased with smiling joy.

Ernie stayed out with the bird and Naomi until his supply of meat had all been devoured. He retrieved Bravura and hooded him and they walked back to the barn, all the while Ernie chattered to the young girl. "Duw, I shall be glad when this one is back with his parents. I'm sure I'll be running out of mice and rats and we don't want Bravura getting a taste for our meat, now do we?" Naomi shook her head. "Now when I've set him back on his perch it's into the house with you and you must wash your hands thoroughly we don't want you to pick up anything nasty from the meat or the bird."

Naomi watched silently as Ernie set the bird on the perch he had made for him before following him out across the yard to the house. On route they passed a bantam with a brood of chicks. Naomi beamed in delight and stopped to watch them scurrying after their mother who called to them making a low gulping sound in her throat to draw the chicks to the tasty treats she had raked up for them.

Ernie watched the girl, scratching his head. He hoped her love of animals would be key in helping her get back to normal. This was like nothing he had ever experienced and he vowed in his heart to devote his time to her until she recovered.

"Come on then, Naomi. Time to go in."

Naomi followed Ernie up the steps into the house. Jenny

was in the glasshouse. She had just finished preparing vegetables from the patch. She looked up and smiled at the little girl. "Ah, it's good you're in. Time for you to do your lessons; I've had strict instructions from Carrie and the school to keep you up to date with your schoolwork until you go back. Then, I thought that if you wanted, you could sit with me at the piano and I could help you learn?" Naomi smiled brightly in agreement. "Good, I'll take that as yes. Come into the parlour I have your books ready. We must start with arithmetic. You don't want to get sharked when you're grown up. You need to be able to do simple arithmetic and tables. I thought we'd have a little test first." Naomi's face dropped and a glimmer of anxiety showed in her eyes. "Oh, it's nothing to worry about. I just need to know where you are with your studies. Come on. And you, Ernie can have your weekly bath, while there's no one else here. Go on. You'll enjoy it more if you don't have to rush."

The two went into the parlour and Ernie did as he was told, plodded up the twisting staircase to the bathroom. He didn't know why but he felt the need not just to get clean, as a bath was much better than topping and tailing in a wash down, but something was urging him to write to his daughter. He decided that once his ablutions were over, he would write that long overdue letter, while Naomi finished her lessons.

Mrs Gregory sat with Carrie in the kitchen as Milly prepared the evening meal. Milly had made them a pot of tea and she listened without comment as the two talked.

"I don't think it's right to leave it any longer. The children deserve to know. In fact, they need to know," said Mrs Gregory.

"I agree. It is just so hard especially with Timmy's asthma. We don't want to trigger another attack."

"That we don't," agreed Mrs Gregory and she paused. Carrie studied the old lady's face curiously. She had no idea of the boundaries of kindness of the lady but was relieved that she had opened her home to the children. Phyllis Gregory had welcomed the children into her heart and Carrie was delighted with the placement.

"Nurse Llewellyn?"

"Yes?"

"What happens to them if their father doesn't return from war. After all he is deemed to be missing in action?"

"I don't know. I don't think we should alarm them with that information yet. Best to be sure. It'll be enough that they've lost their mam."

"I agree, but supposing they have?"

"What are you thinking?" asked Carrie.

"Well, I know I am considered old but if needs be I'm thinking maybe I would like to offer them a home, a permanent home with me. Although, I haven't fully decided I just wanted to see what the possibilities were. Marion is showing great interest in dancing and they are both coming on so well..."

"Mrs Gregory, while what you suggest is admirable we don't know if there are any other family members to take them on and if their father comes home..."

"And if he doesn't?" she reiterated. "It worries me. And I'm not certain about taking them on, you understand, but I am considering what options they have."

"Let me see what I can discover. If it is something you want to proceed with I'll speak to the authorities on your behalf... but first we need to tell the children. What time are they expected home?"

"Basil has gone to collect them. They should be in any time now, so they should."

At that moment they heard the front door open and the children piled into the kitchen where Milly fussed over them giving them a glass of milk each and a Welsh cake.

Timmy eyed Carrie, "What are you doing here? Are we in trouble?"

"Not at all," smiled Carrie. "Drink your milk and then I want you and Marion to come into the parlour where we'll be waiting. Katy? Sally? You can stay in the kitchen with Milly, if that's all right?" Katy and Sally nodded, their mouths full with the cake. Timmy and Marion exchanged a nervous look.

Carrie rose and Mrs Gregory got to her feet and using her stick she tip-tapped out of the kitchen to the parlour.

Michael Lawrence was trying to reconcile himself with the news that his new houseguest was likely to be staying a while. Sam Jefferies had decided to move from Gelli Galed and take Sarah's old room at Tom's Cottage feeling that he needed to build bridges with Laura and make amends. Sarah, however, was doing her darnedest to play on Michael's sympathies but Michael was lacking in trust. He remembered Carrie's words, and suggested, "Let's be safe and put another cold compress on your ankle. It should help the bruising."

Sarah played coy to begin with but edged closer to him and murmured, "It's lovely to know you care." Michael side stepped away and pulled out a chair, to which Sarah limped. He took another chair and placed a cushion on it and gently lifted her foot onto it. "Oh, you are so gentle. You should have been a doctor," she purred.

Michael moved smartly to the sink and ran the cold water; coming from a well on the property it was always ice cold. He rung out a knitted dishcloth and soaked it before squeezing out the excess water and crossing back. He gingerly lifted her foot and Sarah winced slightly as he placed the wet cloth on her ankle making a big show of wrapping it around tightly.

"Oh, not too tight. It still hurts," she simpered.

"Sorry," said Michael dragging the cloth off. He looked at her ankle and examined the cloth now covered in a light purplish stain. Her ankle, too, looked cleaner and smudged. "I think you need to put a bit more rouge on your skin. It certainly helps to bring the bruise out, all over the cloth," he said accusingly.

Sarah didn't know what to say. She jumped up with no suggestion of a limp and flounced out of the kitchen and back up the stairs. Michael watched in amusement and muttered, "Now, get out of that one if you can!"

Timmy and Marion Noble sat frozen. Mrs Gregory held Timmy's hand as a tear rolled down his cheek. Carrie passed the boy his bear, Sloppy, which he clutched tightly to him.

Marion said one word, "Why?" and turned her eyes, pooling with tears ready to spill over, on Carrie.

Carrie spoke gently, "Why does anyone know why anything bad happens? I lost my mam when I was your age. It always hurts when I think about it. But the pain gets easier in time. No one will pretend it's not tough. I lost my da, too, a few years later so I understand how you're feeling."

Mrs Gregory continued, "What you need to remember is that your mam did the very best for you. She wanted to keep you safe from the bombs in London knowing that trying to keep the family business going and your home that it would be better for you to be out of the war zone. The good nurse here knows what the blitz was like. Indeed, she got bombed herself."

Timmy stared wide-eyed at her, "Did you? Did you get bombed?"

"Yes, with six other nurses. We were lucky to get out alive."

"How did you?"

Carrie went on to explain what had happened knowing that in times of trauma and pain it is often good to share experiences and also to listen as it helped those affected to know that they were not alone. Timmy took in everything she said and much to Carrie's relief he didn't fly into a panic and have an asthma attack.

But after a moment's silence Marion flooded with tears and moved to Mrs Gregory. She put her arms around the old lady and sobbed. Phyllis Gregory hugged the distraught child and her own eyes filled with sorrow and tears at their distress. "Oh, Marion fach. What can I say? I know what loss is and it is always hard. But whatever happens you and Timmy will always have a home with me if you want or need one."

Carrie raised her eyebrows in surprise and as Mrs Gregory nodded to her she realised that it had been an impromptu comment but one that was sincerely meant and the old lady had made up her mind. Carrie suspected the decision had surprised Mrs Gregory as much as her.

"But what about Daddy?" questioned Timmy.

Carrie and Mrs Gregory exchanged a look. "Your daddy will be welcome as your mother would have been and your Aunty June promises to keep in touch. She will run the family shop and let us know when he's back home."

Timmy appeared satisfied with the response and in an extraordinary act of maturity he snuck across to his sister to comfort her. "We'll be all right, Sis. Mrs Gregory will look after us until daddy comes home. We don't have no one else, do we, Marion?"

Marion shook her head, "No, Gran and Gramps are gone."

"Both of them. No aunties or uncles. There's only dad and us, now."

Phyllis Gregory embraced both children choking back her own tears, "There, there, my loves, Mrs Gregory is a bit too formal now. Why don't you call me Aunty Phil?"

The children snuggled into her. Timmy popped his thumb in his mouth and Marion stopped crying. There was no need for any words. Carrie rose quietly and left them, closing the door gently behind her, determining that she would, indeed, speak to the necessary authorities on Mrs Gregory's behalf.

Michael had packed a small bag, which rested on the kitchen table. He looked up at Sarah who had sidled in. She slipped closer to him and murmured, "I'm sorry."

"Why? Because you lied or because you were found out?"

"It's not like that," she protested.

"It is from where I'm looking."

"You don't understand…"

"Then perhaps you'd like to explain."

Sarah sighed, and lithely like a panther, sensually crossed to his side. "Please, don't think the worst of me. I am not what everyone believes."

"And what is that?"

"They think I'm a spoilt brat and a man eater."

"Sounds like a pretty good description to me."

"You don't know why I came to help out in this war."

"Then tell me," said Michael coolly.

Sarah sat at the table studying her nails with an ardent voracity suggestive of desperation. Michael waited. She dropped the examination of her hands and took a deep breath, "I come from a good family, a wealthy family." Michael nodded, as this was what everyone assumed. "I have a twin sister, an identical twin." Michael raised an eyebrow questioningly the thought of two like Sarah was hard to imagine. "We did everything together. We attended university and both got a degree in Science. We never intended to use them. Our passion was fashion. Our parents sent us off to finishing school once we had qualified, a long way round I know, and we both intended to go into fashion design and modelling." Sarah stopped and swallowed hard.

"Go on."

"We were very close until I fell in love with a wonderful man, who swept me off my feet. He was the son of a well-respected family friend. He inherited a large department store in Oxford, where we lived and promised to include, and have made up, my sister's and my designs, to sell in his elite boutique section. Stephen and I began to court. We walked out regularly and both families expected that we would marry eventually. What I didn't know was my sister, Therese, had also fallen for him. She set her cap at him with her constant flirting and before I knew it she had stolen his heart and had won him away from me, deliberately, my own sister. Therese ended up with the ring on her finger and I was lost. I stopped eating. The pain ripped into me and my weight plummeted dramatically. I couldn't eat, couldn't bear to see them together. That's why I left Oxford and applied to be a Land Girl somewhere far away from them both."

"Then you of all people should understand what it is like to lose your love to another. You deliberately played with Sam Jefferies and Laura."

Sarah lowered her eyes in a semblance of remorse, "I know. I don't know why but I somehow felt a need to prove myself. I needed to know that I was attractive and desirable. I wanted to see if I could possess another man, any man. I needed to be loved and admired. It seemed I had declared war on all happy couples and wanted to destroy their happiness as Therese had mine. I didn't realise that was what I was doing. Really I didn't. It just happened and once I started I couldn't stop. I loved the power it gave me. It was so easy, so blissfully easy. So I did it just because I could. And you... you seemed something pretty special and I realised that you were more worthy of my attention."

"You hardly know me," interrupted Michael. "And you know I'm engaged."

"Yes, but I couldn't help myself. I'm sorry." Sarah rose from her seat and placed her hand on Michael's arm. "Don't send me away please. I couldn't bear it." Saying that she began to sway and tumbled to the floor. Michael hesitated believing it to be another ploy but when she didn't stir he knelt beside her, checked her pulse and lifted her up. She was as light as air. He carried her to the parlour and laid her onto the sofa. He tapped her face trying to bring her round. Her eyes fluttered open and she moistened her lips, "What happened?"

"You fainted, I think. When did you last eat?"

Sarah shook her head, "I'm not sure."

"Hell, woman. You need to eat."

"Food makes me sick."

"You must try. That's part of your problem. Let me make you something. Wait here." Michael returned to the kitchen and rustled up a fried egg sandwich. He took it into her together with a glass of milk.

"I don't want it."

"You'll eat it or I'll be taking you to the hospital."

Sarah took the sandwich reluctantly and bit into it. She struggled to stop herself from retching and regurgitating the first mouthful.

"I'm not moving until you eat the whole thing."

It was hard for Sarah to swallow. She managed another two mouthfuls before putting it down. "I can't eat anymore. I'll be sick. Please..."

Unwilling to let her out of his sight he took the plate and remains of the sandwich from her and gave her the milk, which she slowly drank.

Michael was now faced with a dilemma. Should he let her stay without medical supervision? Could she remain here when he was planning on returning to war and what would Carrie say about any of it?

CHAPTER NINETEEN

Breakthroughs and setbacks

Word had spread through the village. A number of the young men who had enlisted and gone to war would never return. Mothers and wives dreaded the arrival of official mail or in some instances a telegram. Amongst the many notifications to arrive in Crynant, Jacqueline Price had learned that her husband Emlyn had been one of many men killed in action. She received the news with a mixture of relief and despair. Sad that her husband had lost his life and left her children without their father but pleased that an awful decision had been taken from her. She was now free to welcome Lewis into the family without fear of reprimand and gossiping tongues. Her cover story of how Lewis had been kind enough to help her in her time of need was accepted and it was only one step further to understand how they could become close. But Jacqueline's mother had strong reservations that continued to cause friction between them.

Jacqueline called into her mother's to collect her children after being released from work early. Mrs James looked up in surprise as her daughter came into the house. She marched to the sitting room where the children played happily. "Why are you here so early? You know I would have brought them back as usual," said Mrs James.

"I know. I needed to show you something and I was sent home in sympathy." Jacqueline reached into her handbag and took out the official notification. Her face was pinched and worry was etched on her face.

"Oh, no! Is that what I think it is?" Jacqueline passed it to her mother to read.

"Oh, Jacqueline. I am so sorry…"

Jacqueline stopped her mother from saying anymore, putting her fingers to her lips, "There's no reason for them to know yet."

"No, I don't suppose there is. What are you going to do?"

"I'll manage. I still have you and Lewis."

"Lewis, you be careful now. You know I don't trust him."

"Mam, Lewis has been a boon. He's helped me and he's wonderful with the children."

"I bet he is!"

Jacqueline bridled at this, "Why are you so against him? He's been very good to me."

"I'm sure," said Margaret James tartly. "Just be careful that's all. I've heard rumours."

"Aye, gossips putting two and two together and making eight!"

"Jacqueline, take heed of my words. I don't want to deprive you of friendship but just watch him with the children."

"Mam, Lewis had a horrible childhood. He told me all about it. Folks that know his background like to make mischief; he would never hurt my kids after what he's been through. Never."

Mrs James snorted, "Don't say I didn't warn you. And I'm not sure he didn't have something to do with that little girl's silence."

"That's nonsense."

"Is it? She was fine before we went to the swings."

"I'm not listening to this." Jacqueline called her children to her and gathered their things. She set off for her own home and Mrs James looked concerned. She placed the letter she was still holding on the mantelpiece and sat reflectively in her chair.

Carrie was on her way out from Mr Price. She picked up her bike and was surprised to see Michael striding toward her. Her face flushed with pleasure. "Well, well, there's lovely. Come to meet me have, you? Couldn't wait…"

"Carrie we have to talk. You were right about Sarah…"

"I knew it. The strumpet…"

"But there's more to it than that," and he began to recount the story he'd been told.

"That doesn't excuse her actions," said Carrie hotly.

"No, but it explains them. And there's more. I believe she

is deliberately starving herself. I don't understand why but it's come that she can't face food without wanting to vomit. I've told her she can stay until she decides what to do."

"Oh?" said Carrie with her hackles rising.

"Carrie… You know I've been called back to serve. Now my injury is better. They want me back to fly again."

Carrie's face turned white, "No, you can't. Michael… what if you don't come back?"

"Don't be such a pessimist. There's no reason why I shouldn't and I really have no option. My country needs me and my expertise. I have to go. But you know I will come back to you. I promise."

"Then I suppose you must," said Carrie quietly.

"The thing is that I want you to take over at Gelli Galed. Keep an eye on Sarah. Help her."

"I can't do that. I have my own job."

"I know. Look, Sam will do the every day running of the place. It is purely to keep Sarah out of Sam's hair so to speak. He'll report to you unless you can find an alternative. Will you do it?"

Carrie was flummoxed she felt pushed into a corner but finally nodded her head. "When do you go?"

"Tonight. I'm sorry, Carrie."

The shock was evident in Carrie's face. "I came back, left London and took this job to be near you."

"I know." Michael looked at the apprehension in her face, with her eyes wide with concern, her lips slightly parted and unable to resist he crushed her to him. She melted into his arms feeling a pleasurable tingling flutter in the pit of her stomach that made her quiver and shiver with desire.

As they broke apart she moistened her lips, "What time? What time do you go?" Without waiting for an answer she swore, "Damn this war. Damn, damn, damn." And her shoulders began to heave. The ache in her heart of longing and loss brought tears to her eyes, which she brushed away angrily. Michael continued to hold her tight until her shuddering sobs subsided.

Michael brushed her hair tenderly away from her weeping eyes. "We have a few hours. I intend to spend them with you."

Ernie and Naomi retraced their steps to the Black River with Bravura hooded and secured to Ernie's glove. As they reached the path to the bank she looked fearfully at the tunnel. Ernie reassured her, "Naomi fach, you are safe with me. There is no one here to harm you. Believe me." Her face was wooden and expressionless. "Come. We'll cross the bridge, go over the tunnel and find our way through the bracken on the other side."

They crossed over and slipped down to the other side and began to work their way through to where Ernie had originally found the bird. Naomi gazed about her in wonder until they came to a small clearing in the woods. The cliff face stretched up and she could see one of the parent birds flying above, calling to its mate.

"That's good. With a bit of luck, when I untie the strap Bravura will fly off unrestrained and join his parents. Let's hope they accept him after all this time especially as he has the scent of man on him." Naomi looked at Ernie curiously not fully understanding his meaning. Ernie continued, "It should be all right. Jawch, he's been kept in a barn, more likely to get the smell of the chickens on him than us. I've been very careful, only handled him to help him fly, but we'll see. I'll wait till both birds are in the air and then we'll see."

Naomi looked less worried but, as Ernie busied himself with the bird, something caught her eye in the thicket ahead. She saw a movement and a glint of metal and edged closer to get a better look. To her horror she saw Lewis Owen with a brace of pheasants strung over his shoulder and a dead rabbit. He put his fingers to his lips as he caught sight of her and stepped back into the undergrowth raising his gun. She froze.

Ernie was oblivious to this as he removed the falcon's hood. He glanced around for Naomi who was standing with her back toward him. "Come on, Naomi fach. You don't want to miss this. See here, the parents are on the cliff. When they take to the air I'll release the strap holding him to me and we can pray that ... Naomi?"

Naomi began to walk backward but Ernie was searching the sky. He saw one parent bird and then the other as they took off from nest and began to circle with their mewling cry.

Naomi was still watching Lewis Owen who had his gun following one of the adult birds. He adjusted his aim and trained it on one majestic critter as Ernie was releasing Bravura from his ties.

Lewis' finger was on the trigger and he gently began to squeeze it, holding off, it seemed, until he was certain of a hit. Naomi's mouth was open as she fought with herself, whether to stay silent or even if she had the capability to cry out. The sound was bubbling up inside her as she battled to form the words. It was as if a hand had reached down into her stomach and was wrenching them out. Could she speak? Could she? Naomi honestly didn't know if she was capable of making any noise, or allowing any words to spill from her. The phobic war and conflicting arguments raged inside her all in the matter of a split second but seeming like hours. In her head time had slowed to treacle.

Bravura sat majestically on Ernie's gloved hand and as Lewis was about to pull back the trigger and let it go, Naomi flew into the thicket at Lewis and screamed, "NOOOOOOO!"

She caught the man off guard pummelling him in his middle, winding him and bending him double. The rifle dipped as the bullet was released, travelling forward instead of in the direction of its intended target high in the sky. As Bravura flew up with joyous answering cries to his parents, Ernie dropped to his knees and Lewis pushed Naomi roughly, sending her sprawling, before he hastened away crawling through the undergrowth and out of sight.

Naomi raced to Ernie's side, her eyes streaming with tears, uncertain what to do. She looked wildly around her knowing she had to get help. She glanced up and was gratified to see the birds diving and swooping in pure joy at being reunited when Bravura flew off at an angle and dived his talons outstretched crying shrilly.

She heard Lewis shriek as he crashed off and then saw the bird soar.

Naomi knelt down at Ernie's side. His eyes fluttered open, "You'll have to get help, Naomi love," he managed to rasp. The little girl could see blood seeping from Ernie's chest and she rose quickly and began to run.

She ran through the bracken and thick tangled weeds, which threatened to snatch at her and hold her back. Her clothes tore as she scrambled up the bank to the bridge where she stopped abruptly and stiffened. Taking a deep breath she spurred herself forward hurried across onto the deserted road and ran as if her life depended on it.

Her feet clattered on the hard concrete surface as she ran and ran. She raced on, tears streaming down her face, gasping for breath. She had to get help for Ernie. Naomi was now frantic and making small sounds of distress as she sprinted toward the village square and Segadelli's.

Naomi burst in through the door much to the shock of the people in there. Seeing the distraught child whose hands and legs were scratched and eyes wide with fear. Mr Segadelli's daughter, who was not in school that day, came from behind the counter.

"It's one of the evacuees, Naomi, the one who stopped talking. She's in my class."

Mr Segaadelli came into the café and knelt down, "Naomi? What is it? What ails you child?"

Naomi took a deep breath and as if her tongue had been blessed by angels the words streamed from her, "It's Ernie. Ernie from Hendre. He's down by the Black River. He's been shot!"

"What?"

"Hurry; you must hurry. He needs help." Naomi dashed to the door and looked back anxiously.

"Of course." Mr Segadelli called out to his wife, "Mind the café, mi amore." He glanced around and gestured to two men enjoying a cup of tea, playing cards, "Jonas, Hugh, come quickly I'll need help. Stella, run for Dr Rees, get him here as quickly as you can, there's a good girl. Run now. Come on, boys. Mrs Chapel, see if you can raise Colin Isaac. Tell him to get his car and drive to the bridge. And now, Naomi show us where he is."

Naomi sped back the way she came followed by the three men who chased after her. They crossed the bridge and scrawled through the undergrowth where Ernie was lying. He was semi conscious and still bleeding. Mr Segadelli snatched out his hankie and stuffed it over the wound in Ernie's chest, packing it under Ernie's waistcoat. Jonas and Hugh lifted Ernie to his feet and half dragged; half carried him along the difficult and overgrown path. Mr Segadelli kept his hand tight on Ernie's chest to stem the flow of blood. They helped him over the bridge and continued along the road back to the village.

Colin Isaac was driving toward them and with a squeal of brakes stopped next to them. They loaded Ernie into the car. Naomi clambered into the front whilst Mr Segadelli stayed in the back still compressing the injury, until they arrived at the sweetshop and café.

They ferried Ernie through the shop and out the back into the parlour and laid him on the settee. Dr Rees arrived simultaneously he was ushered through to them and hastened to Ernie's side. He undid the waistcoat and shirt, pulling it back to reveal the wound, "Duw, Duw, however did this happen?"

"Can you help him?" whispered Jonas, a burly minor from Cefn-Coed Colliery, whose mellifluous voice belied his bulk.

"Get me some hot water, quickly please. Ernie! Ernie! Can you hear me?" Ernie's eyes opened fractionally, "Good, now stay awake." Dr Rees opened his bag and removed some cotton wool and ether. He swabbed the area and muttered, "If this had been an inch more to the left. He'd be dead. You're a lucky man, Ernie."

Something of what the doctor said got through and he coughed, "Not so lucky from where I am... Naomi, what about Naomi?" he asked trying to sit up.

"Cwat lawr," warned the doctor, "Save your strength... Has anyone seen Nurse Llewellyn?" The assembled shook their heads. "Can one of you get across to Howie Price? She may be there."

"I'll take the car, drive around, see if I can find her in the village," offered Colin Isaac.

"Good man. When you find her, bring her here." Colin nodded and rushed from the room as Dr Rees prepared to clean up the wound. "I've only dealt with a gunshot wound once before. I have to get the bullet out and that won't be easy."

"Good job it wasn't filled with pellets," said Mr Segadelli. "If it had been. He'd be dead. This is a rifle shot."

Naomi was being comforted by the local villagers in the shop, where she had been taken to sit, out of the way of the doctor as he treated Ernie. Previously, silent she had now found her voice and was describing what had happened.

A flurry of people had entered the café and stopped to listen in shocked horror as she described the events. The locked up words spewed from her; once she had started, it seemed there was no stopping her.

The door opened and Naomi ceased her chatter and stared in fiery anger at the man who walked into the crowded shop. The side of his face bore deep scratches.

Something snapped inside Naomi. She raised a finger and pointed accusingly at Lewis Owen who had strode to the counter for a pouch of baccy. He was oblivious to the child, as she had been hidden by the crowd around her.

Her clear and unfaltering voice rang out, "That's him, Lewis Owen. He's the one who shot Ernie."

Lewis spun around on his heel in surprise. The ready smile, always present faded and he turned white as Naomi hesitated and then cried out, "And the one who did dirty things to me."

There was a gasp from some of the women. Lewis Owen staggered backward and stuttered, "Now, Nims that's not nice...."

"My name is not Nims, it's Naomi and what you did to me was not nice," she shouted.

Lewis Owen shoved his money back in his pocket and headed for the door just as Carrie entered with Colin Isaac and Pritchard the Police, who all stood in his way.

He shouted, "Let me through!"

But, Carrie, quickly grasped the situation and pronounced, "I think not. Constable Pritchard, I believe this is your man."

The other customers barred his way and Pritchard lurched forward, driven by everyone and took hold of Lewis Owen. "I'll need statements." Pritchard nodded at Naomi.

"I'll bring her to the station later, but now I have to see Ernie."

Pritchard propelled Owen who continued to shout and protest his innocence out of the door.

Carrie pushed through the onlookers and spoke to the now seemingly fearless young girl, "Wait here, there's a good girl. I'll be out as soon as I can."

Naomi nodded and sat, happy to be given a drink of pop and some sweets. She sat kicking her legs happily on the chair. Carrie disappeared out back and the rest of the occupants fell to a fervid, discussion on what they had just witnessed.

Carrie hurried through the back of the shop. Ernie was stretched out on the dining table in the parlour resting on a coverlet and covered with a blanket. Dr Rees looked relieved when he saw Carrie enter, "Thank God you've come. I need you to assist me. Quickly, now; his temperature is fluctuating with shivering fits and rigor then he's sweating in a fever. Mrs Segadelli has got some hot water and I've cleaned the wound. We need to get the bullet out."

Carrie looked at her beloved Ernie. She refused to allow her emotions to get in the way and immediately adopted a no nonsense professional approach. "I'll try and keep his temperature regulated. How deep is the bullet?"

"I can feel it under the dermis. It's hit a rib. Good job, too. It could have hit his lung or an inch to the right and it would have been curtains… right in his heart… This isn't ideal but we don't have time to get him to hospital. You better get scrubbed up."

Ernie's leaden eyes opened as if constrained by sleep, his gaze lit on Carrie's sweet face. He managed a smile and forced out, "I'll be all right now, with you and Doctor Rees."

"Hush! Don't talk. You need to save your strength," reassured Carrie.

"And… Naomi?" he faltered.

"Naomi will be fine, she's talking again. I knew you'd do the trick. Bit drastic though, getting shot to do it!" Ernie nodded with a smile on his lips and closed his eyes, as Dr Rees prepared a syringe.

"Right, Nurse Llewellyn are you ready?"

CHAPTER TWENTY

Life goes on

Colin Isaac had kindly driven up the bumpy rough mountain track to Hendre transporting Carrie, Naomi and Ernie, who refused to go to hospital and was now in Carrie's care. Ernie was ensconced in the spare bedroom despite his continued protestations. Carrie would have no arguments and despite Ernie's insistence that he would be better off in the barn she would have none of it.

"But, I haven't slept in a proper bed for years."

"Then it's time you did. You are not getting any younger."

"Thanks for reminding me!"

"And your bones will thank you."

"But my head won't."

"Go on with you. You need to rest where we can keep an eye on you. You've lost a lot of blood. There will always be someone by here. No more arguments."

"You can be a feisty little piece when you want to be," said Ernie resignedly. "More orders than a sergeant major and twice as tough."

"Then maybe you'll do as you're told," laughed Carrie.

"I suppose. But more like you'll soften me up."

Carrie laughed at the banter between them and continued, "Now, is there anything you want? Let's get you propped up a bit. Duw, we'll need to be buying more pillows. I'll have to see if I can get a job lot at the market."

"Pen and paper and something to lean on would be good. I wrote to my daughter earlier and said I hoped to visit soon. I'd best tell her what happened and that I'll see her when I'm fitter."

"That would be wise. I'll see what I can do, and get you a jug of water and a glass."

"I'd prefer a drop of cider."

"I'm sure you would. But we need to keep you hydrated

and Adam's wine is the thing for you." Ernie sighed in that long-suffering way he had forcing Carrie to smile. "If you behave, and I'm not promising mind, I'll see if you can have a glass with supper."

"Duw, you're a hard taskmaster should have been the boss on a galley slaver not a nurse," he joked as she turned to leave the room.

"Well, you thank the Lord I'm not or I'd be whipping you back to health to the beat of a drum, not cosseting you in comfort."

Ernie smiled and his eyes twinkled as Carrie went to do his bidding. He was lucky to be alive and he knew it. He had little Naomi to thank for that.

Downstairs Naomi had certainly found her voice, after a trying interview with Constable Pritchard and Dr Rees' and with Carrie's support she had it seemed faced her demons and was now full of questions. It was deemed that she would remain at the farm for a while and Jenny would home tutor her for the time being.

Naomi sat at the piano with Jenny and had begun to learn some scales. Jenny was extremely patient as she showed Naomi the correct fingers to use on the keys and Naomi was finding she had a capacity to learn and was eager to do so. Jenny smiled at the torrent of questions, which she answered as best she could just managing to satisfy her young charge.

Carrie breezed into the room, "I won't interrupt your studies but I thought Naomi might like to explore the farm with me and see it through my eyes."

"Certainly! We'll be finished in about ten minutes. If Naomi wants to go?" said Jenny.

Naomi nodded shyly, "I'd love to. I've never seen such an amazing place."

"Well, with Ernie laid up and John not back to full strength, I thought I'd show you some of the things I used to do on the farm. Things that were my job when I was a girl."

"That would be lovely," smiled Jenny. "It will give me more time with Bethan, although I expect she will still want to help with collecting the eggs."

Carrie nodded, "I'll be in the kitchen when you're ready. Going to take a cuppa to Ernie."

Megan Thomas, now Davies, and Carrie's best friend from school was on her way home. Finally, she had finished her last tour of duty and her baby bump was becoming more apparent. She rubbed her belly as she felt movement inside her. She didn't know how she felt about becoming a mother.

Megan eyed the other people in the train carriage; a young mother and her baby, a gentleman with his nose buried in a newspaper. Headlines blared, 'Close encounters at sea. Naval ship evades German and Italian scrutiny on Malta run.'

Megan's heart began to thud and that awful gnawing, griping ache that manifests when fear is present began to take hold. Megan began to shake and tremble uncontrollably. She attempted to still her quivering hands and snatched a breath, which culminated in a strangled sob.

"Are you all right?" asked the young lady, a look of kind concern on her face.

"I don't know," gasped Megan. "I feel, I feel... Excuse me." Megan rushed from the carriage to the corridor and struggled with the window, securing it with its leather strap. She pushed her head out of the window and vomited violently. She wiped her mouth with her gloved hand and pulled her head back inside. She wasn't sure if she felt better or not but her legs felt as if they didn't belong to her and wobbled like jelly.

Her mind wouldn't settle and her dangerously overactive imagination took charge. She walked back to the carriage bumping unsteadily each side of the corridor and retook her seat. The young woman asked again, "Are you feeling any better?"

Megan rubbed her stomach as a sharp pain knifed through her belly. She groaned, "I don't know... I..."

"You're pregnant," said the young woman. "First time?"

Megan nodded weakly, "My husband's in the navy. I saw the headline in the gentleman's paper and panicked." She heaved a shuddering sigh, "I'm petrified of losing him before we've had chance to have a life together... I'm sorry," she added realising she was divulging far too much about herself.

"Don't apologise. This rotten war has destroyed numerous lives, not least mine. My husband's in a military hospital just outside London... Shell shock," she added quietly. He saw his friends blown up before his eyes. He's lucky to be alive. He was peppered by shrapnel and badly burned. I wonder how he'll come through it?"

Megan nodded in understanding, tears had started to pool in her eyes threatening to spill over and cascade down her cheeks. "We've had so little time together, so much was wasted and now I wonder if I'll ever see him again or if this little one will ever know his or her father."

The woman smiled sympathetically, "You must be positive. You have to believe the best. It's the only thing that gets me through the day."

"She's right," added the man. "Worrying won't help you or your baby." He shook his paper closed and folded it. "How far are you going?"

"Neath," said Megan. "And you?"

"Cardiff."

The sway of the carriage and the rumble of the wheels on the track lulled them all into silence. They sat quietly a few moments longer as the train chuffed on into the late afternoon.

Megan gazed out of the window at the passing countryside. She huddled into her seat, snuggling up with her thoughts and drifted off into a light sleep.

CHAPTER TWENTY-ONE

All Change

Constable Pritchard sat in his office with his feet up and a cup of tea. He was waiting for prison officials to come and remove Lewis Owen from the cells and put him on remand in Swansea Prison. The door to the police station opened and two prison officers entered. Pritchard sprang up and took the men out to the back to take Owen away.

As the trio and Pritchard returned to the outer office Jacqueline Price sailed in. She flew at Lewis Owen; her hands and nails raised like the paws and claws of an attacking grizzly bear. She shrieked at him as she cursed and tried to batter his already scratched bloody cheeks.

"You bastard! I trusted you!"

Pritchard tried to restrain her but she threw him off as she attacked Owen again. "If you've so much as touched my Mary or Teddy I swear I'll kill you." Lewis attempted to protest his innocence but she would have none of it. "I've heard all about you and your sordid little secrets. You dirty bastard!"

Pritchard picked himself up from the floor and this time managed to drag the screaming woman back. Hot tears of anger coursed down her cheeks as she yelled, "I'll swing for you, so I will. You're filth. That's what you are. No better than dog shit on the streets."

Jacqueline Price was in a frenzy. The officials hurried the prisoner out and she collapsed in a heap on the station floor whimpering like a beaten puppy.

Pritchard helped her to her feet and sat her down. She continued to tremble and shake. "Why didn't I listen? Why was I taken in? God forgive me."

Constable Pritchard did his best to console her before offering to accompany her to her mother's house and she allowed herself to be led outside. It seemed as if all the bravado had deserted her and she was now an emotional, blubbering wreck. She leaned on Constable Pritchard's arm for support as they walked along Neath Road to number 44.

Carrie and Michael were wrapped in a tender embrace as they said their goodbyes on the station platform. She had taken the train to Neath with him and they had shared a last meal together at the Castle before his departure to London and who knew where.

"It feels like the last supper," she quipped as she looked up at him. "Promise me you'll stay safe. Promise me you'll come back."

Michael's eyes burned into hers, his lips were parted, his buttocks clenched as his heart filled with needy wanton desire. "No war will keep me from you. I will be back. I promise. You and I have unfinished business, Carrie Llewellyn."

Carrie sighed, "If there ever were any doubts of where my heart was meant to be they fled a long, long time ago. I know I only want to be with you."

Michael kissed her again as the train getting ready to depart blew its whistle and pillows of steam clouded up into the evening sky. "I must go. I'll be in touch as soon as I can. Pray for me."

Carrie nestled into his strong chest and drank in the aroma of his masculinity. "This is too, too cruel."

Michael released her from his passionate clasp and tipped her face up to him, "Farewell, Caroline Llewellyn. Wait for me."

She nodded trying to stop the tears that insisted in falling from her eyes and stepped back as he boarded the train. He opened the window and seized her hand as she placed her hands on the glass, "I love you, Caroline Llewellyn. Remember that."

The guard blew his whistle and the train began to steam out of the station as Carrie fingered the butterfly brooch, which had belonged to his mother Isobel, and watched as the train chugged on and out of sight.

Carrie seemed transfixed to the spot but when she could no longer see the tail of the train she moved back and flopped into one of the seats on the platform. Her heart was heaving. She was emotionally wrung out and confused. How could this have happened? The words of the woman from the Ladies Room in the Angel Hotel came rushing back to her. "...You mark my words, take advantage of the time you have now. Get a special licence; get married. Enjoy a night of wedded bliss. No one knows what the future holds." And Carrie wondered if she and Michael should have taken that advice.

Carrie sat there and sat there. She didn't know for how long. Another two trains had arrived and idled on the tracks as she waited and now there was yet another one steaming into view. She chided herself, "Dera nawr! Time to move, you'll miss the bus back." She rose from her seat as the train rumbled into the station. Doors opened and people spilled out from the carriages. She began to walk to the station entrance when a shout stopped her, "Carrie! Carrie! Caroline Llewellyn!"

Carrie stopped and turned. She was amazed to see her friend Megan chasing up the platform after her. They fell into each other's arms and hugged each other tightly. "Megan? Is it really you?"

"It is, it is. Oh, we have so much to talk about but you, why are you here? You couldn't have known I was coming, could you?"

The two friends fell into step with one another and full of chatter began to share their news. They walked out of the station and Megan said, "Forget the bus. We'll get a cab to Crynant."

"Oh.. but..."

"I'll pay. We can talk on the way. We've so much to catch up on."

Naomi sat and read to Jenny. Bethan was tucked up safely in bed and Jenny was using the time to get to know the girl better. "You're doing well, so you are. Very good."

"I like reading. It takes me into another world. I would like to write."

"And I'm sure if you put your mind to it you will," encouraged Jenny.

"Do you think so?" asked Naomi earnestly searching Jenny's face.

"But of course. With a good education and belief in yourself you can do anything."

"You make it all sound so easy."

"Tell you what, you can make a start tomorrow. After your essential lessons let's write a story. Little steps first. What do you say?"

Naomi beamed, "I'd like that. Can I go and see Ernie, now?

"Yes, and then bed. It's past your bedtime now, so it is."

Naomi's face fell, "Oh, I wanted to see Nurse Llewellyn, too."

"You'll see her in the morning. I don't know when she'll be back." Jenny glanced at the big grandfather clock, "Duw, it's later than I thought. Come on, up the stairs now, clean your teeth, say goodnight to Ernie and then bed." Jenny's tone was firm and serious.

A partial smile played on Naomi's lips, she rose shyly clutching her book, stooped forward and kissed Jenny lightly on her cheek before darting out of the door and up the stairs. Jenny touched her cheek and a increasing glow of pleasure trickled through her.

Naomi bounded up the twisting pine stairs her heart felt wild and free; feelings, which were new to her, now she'd risen from a very dark place. She crossed the landing and knocked gently on Ernie's door, "Yes? Come in."

Naomi lifted the latch and popped her head around the door. "I just wanted to say goodnight. How are you feeling?"

"Sore and tired, fy merch 'i."

"What does that mean?"

"Fy merch 'i?"

"Yes."

"Little lady. You are a little lady. It's a term of endearment Naomi, fach."

"Oh... Ernie?"

"Yes?"

"Thank you for what you did."

"Jawch, I have to be thanking you. Saved my life, you did."

Naomi fiddled with her fingers, examining them closely before speaking, "But you saved me, too." Naomi pushed open

261

the door and scooted to Ernie's bedside. She whispered, "Will you still show me things and take me to see the animals when you're better?"

"Of course, I will. We've got badgers and foxes to see and we want to check up on Bravura. That is of course when I'm well and you've finished your chores." His eyes drooped.

"You're tired. I can see."

"That I am, little one." He allowed his eyes to close and Naomi left him quietly blowing him a kiss from the door.

Carrie struggled up the steep hill. It was a glorious night. The sky had turned from its dusky twilight hues to midnight blue and to black. The myriad of stars freckled the magical ceiling. She stopped to catch her breath and gazed up at the moon, which was almost full; another two nights and it would be. Carrie stared at the shadows on the moon with its map-like surface, which appeared to shift and move. It was a magical sight; its opalescent sheen gleamed enchantingly lighting the stony track. Crickets thrummed and hummed and a tawny owl's melancholy hoot sounded somewhere in the distance.

She was glad of the time spent in walking despite the climb. So many thoughts raged in her head as others withered away. So much had happened, it was difficult to fathom. Now, with Michael gone she had to make good on her promise to reside at Gelli Galed and help with the running of the farm. Perhaps her childhood wishes were coming true after all. Then again, was that what she really wanted?

Carrie sighed and began her ascent again, if she was to reside at Michael's for the duration of his mission, how could she engage fully with Naomi and bring her back to full mental health? Or ensure John and Ernie were completely better? It was as if a cloud had descended robbing her of her peace of mind and shrouding her in uncertainty. Why had she got these rumbling feelings of misgiving and why did they continue to bubble to the surface seemingly knocking all sense of reason from her? And why now? She had started the climb in good temper and in contentment but now... now that had changed and all in the space of a few minutes.

Carrie stopped and stamped her foot. She was thinking like

a crazy woman but these indefinable niggling fears seemed to loom larger with every step, plaguing her with doubt, leaching positivity and hope from her. She felt doom was hanging in the air and knew she needed to speak to Ernie who would understand. She trusted this man more than any other. Ernie would be able to explain why she had these inexplicable concerns that had no name.

Carrie plodded on up the incline and filled with relief at the sight of Hendre and its welcoming, twinkling lights. She ran up the steps and into the house. Bonnie and Prince roused themselves from slumber on the multi-coloured rag mat by the range and came to meet her. Their delight in seeing her was apparent and Carrie was instantly soothed by their gentle unconditional and all enveloping love.

She bent down and ruffled the fur of both dogs. Bonnie was most persistent in demanding her attention pushing her head into Carrie's hand and licking her. Carrie chuckled in spite of her feelings of despondency and set about brewing a much-needed cup of tea.

Jenny slipped quietly into the kitchen making her jump, "Jawch, you almost frightened me out of my knickers!"

Jenny laughed, "That's not like you. Why so skittish?"

"I don't know and that's part of the problem. You know, when something niggles at you and you can't explain why you're feeling a particular way."

"Hormones," said Jenny matter of factly. "That's usually at the back of it."

"Aye, maybe you're right," agreed Carrie.

"Whatever's bothering you... it will all seem different in the morning, you'll see."

"I hope so. So much has happened in so short a time," and Carrie began to explain all that had transpired that evening with Michael and concluded, "And Megan's back."

"Megan? Never."

"Yes, and she's pregnant, with Thomas' baby. I can't believe it... Thomas a father."

"And Megan a mother..."

The two gossiped together like the old friends they were before the conversation became more serious.

"Will you manage at Gelli Galed?"

"I'll have to. I promised Michael. But I'm not looking forward to sharing with Sarah. According to Laura even Ernie wouldn't be safe around her."

Jenny laughed, "I can't see that happening. I'm so glad he's out of harm's way… He had me worried for a while. He will be all right, won't he?"

"He'll have to be. We couldn't do without him now, part of the family he is."

"I know, and I dread the day…"

"Don't say it. That day is a long way off," said Carrie as she drained her teacup. "I must get to bed. I've a lot to do tomorrow."

"You get to bed. I'll see to these," said Jenny indicating their cups.

"I won't argue," said Carrie yawning. "I'm bushed," and overcome with exhaustion she made her way up the crooked pine stairs.

The sun probed its fingers of gold through the chink in the curtains and caressed Carrie's face. She awoke with a start and stretched tensing every part of her body. Naomi lay next to her and disturbed by the movement slowly opened her eyes. She saw Carrie and beamed, "Nurse Llewellyn!"

"Please, call me Carrie. Can't share a bed and be so formal now, can we?"

"I suppose not," said Naomi shyly.

"The sun is telling me it's time to rise although I'd much rather linger here and snatch another hour's sleep."

"I expect you could if you wanted to," murmured Naomi studying the ceiling above her.

"No, mustn't be a lay-a-bed, as my Auntie Annie would say. She'd pull off the bedclothes and drag me out."

"Would she, really?"

Carrie chuckled, "No, not really. She's kindness itself. I do miss her."

"Why? Is she dead?"

"Heavens, no. She's in Australia with her family."

Carrie sighed and swung her legs out of bed. Today was

going to be bursting with too many things to do. "I'll get into the bathroom, now. See you later."

An hour later the Llewellyn household had breakfasted. Naomi and Jenny were clearing away and Bethan was upstairs with her father who was dressed and ready to progress with the attic room that was waiting for the window to be fitted by the builders. John was enjoying some special time with his young daughter and Carrie was sitting at Ernie's bedside holding his hand. He was propped up on a mound of pillows still looking pale but better than he had the last time she saw him.

"It's a hell of a way to skive off," she playfully admonished.

"Duw, Cariad. That bullet felled me. It's the Universe's way of telling me to slow down and take stock."

"Well, it's got you into the house and a proper bed at long last where we can keep an eye on you."

"Aye. It will make me soft, it will. But I know you, Cariad. That's not why you're here. You are troubled."

Carrie whistled low between her teeth, "I am, Ernie. I am. It's as if I've got this weight pressing on my chest, and a tight band around my head. My head is bursting with the pressure but I don't know why."

"Sounds like you need a doctor," joked Ernie.

"No, it's not physical… How can I explain it? I have this feeling of awful trepidation…"

"Like a premonition?"

"I don't know. I just know I'm scared. Things seem out of control."

"Well, they are in war. Trust your instincts."

"What does that mean?"

"Anything that pops into your gut that you feel… Trust it. First instincts are almost always right." Ernie took her hand, which was trembling. "My, my; you are feeling agitated and…" Ernie stopped and a shadow crossed his face. "I can feel your fear." Ernie sighed, "Cariad, what will be will be and no amount of worrying will change anything."

"That's what Aunty Annie used to say. It was her motto; worry about it when it happens."

"And she's right. Rest assured some things are meant to be and some we are not meant to know."

Carrie nodded silently but it didn't calm her thudding heart nor fill her with peace. Something was gnawing inside her. She just felt something terrible was going to happen but she didn't know what or why and said so concluding, "Do you sense anything, Ernie? Do you know what is to come?"

The old man shook his head. "I know now why I needed to write at length to my daughter. I didn't see this coming," he indicated his chest wound. "But that's a good thing. Anything else is lost to me, for the moment, while my body and senses labour to mending me. And you, Cariad you need to work. You need to focus on your job. That will help take your mind off these uncertain rumblings."

Carrie smiled and stood up. She knew Ernie was right. Whatever it was wasn't going to disappear or manifest in a blinding flash. She had to put it aside and get on with things but also she knew this damned feeling of foreboding would be hard to shake off."

CHAPTER TWENTY- TWO

Dangerous times

Michael rubbed at his collar chafing his neck. He had not worn his uniform in a while. He was attending a briefing at Martlesham Heath Air Base where the P-47 Thunderbolts of the US 8th Air Force resided. His pencil poised he made notes. They were receiving orders to continue with a combined bombing mission to rain terror on German cities. He marvelled at the canny plans where the silence of eastern England's picturesque counties was shattered by the dull rumble of piston engines. All day, every day, these surrounding quiet farming communities were alive with the sound of war as British and American heavy bombers took off to wreak havoc on targets in continental Europe. Michael knew that many of these missions had already taken place and not everyone had returned, many lives had been lost.

He listened more closely. It was to be a big raid. The plan was to bomb northern Germany, eighty-three British Lancaster bombers were to attack Wismar, twenty-eight Halifax bombers were to drop its payload on Flensburg and twenty-four Stirling bombers were to attack Vegesack. The raid was imminent and set for the night of 23rd September.

He listened as the Marshal of the Royal Air Force (MRAF) continued with briefing and a warning. On the 19th September just a couple of days before, one hundred and eighteen British bombers comprising of seventy-two Wellington, forty-one Halifax, and five Stirling had set off and attacked Saarbrücken, Germany. The report from those on the ground revealed that they had generally missed military targets and instead destroyed thirteen houses and killed one civilian; five bombers had been lost on this mission.

Michael wondered if Matthew was one of the SOEs on the ground reporting back on this activity. He almost missed what the MRAF said next as his thoughts drifted to Carrie, Hendre and the Dulais Valley. He pulled himself up short and stopped doodling on his notepad, as the Marshal announced, "Sixty-eight Lancaster bombers and twenty-one Stirling bombers attacked München - Munich, last night and six bombers have been lost on this assault. Gentlemen, this is dangerous mission and why we need the best. Our aim is to cripple Germany as they have tried to cripple us. There will be a further briefing before take off. For now, that is all."

The men sat there a moment in subdued silence as they contemplated their fate, before those sitting scraped back their chairs and filed out of the room. Michael retreated to his office, he had a short time to write a letter home to Carrie and he knew there was something he had to set straight.

Back at Hendre the upstairs was in chaos as Prew the builders were cutting out a section of the roof to insert a window in the attic that would let light in and negate the need for artificial light in the daytime.

Dust and debris billowed from the hatch although John did his best to clear up as they went along. Ernie kept his door shut firmly and had poked his head under a pillow to drown out the sound of sawing and hammering.

Jenny flinched at the clattering above as she tried to listen to Naomi read. Bethan was being grumpy, as she demanded attention. Eventually, Jenny set down her book. "It's no use I can't listen to this racket. It feels like the roof is about to cave in. Naomi, why don't you feed the chickens and collect the eggs?"

Naomi stood up as Bethan tugged on Naomi's skirt, "I want to come. Please." Naomi looked across at Jenny questioningly.

"It's all right, you can take her. But, Bethan, listen to Naomi and don't go running off and getting into trouble."

"I won't, Mammy."

Naomi picked up the basket and off they went together.

"It would be lovely to have five minutes peace," she murmured. She closed her eyes, "I'll just rest for five minutes," she told herself.

Her peace was short-lived as another crash reverberated

around the room. "Duw, this is no good." Jenny rose and ventured up the pine stairs to see how work was progressing. She saw John emerging from the hatch covered in dust. "How is it?"

"Almost done. Although, how do we get a bed up here?"

"In bits," said Jenny. The bedstead won't be a problem but the mattress? That won't be easy. It'll be tough getting anything up there."

"I know. I'm wondering whether we put some stairs, permanent ones from the landing up."

"Won't that take a lot of room?"

"Better than a rickety ladder, though."

"True, true," smiled Jenny. "We'll have to get a new one."

John looked at his wife and overwhelmed with a feeling of love, pulled her into his arms and kissed her. "Oh, Jen, I do love you."

"And I you," she replied returning his kiss.

"It's about time we thought of a little brother or sister for Bethan. The time's right, don't you think?"

Jenny beamed, "Yes, I think you're right. It's about time."

John grinned in that lopsided endearing way he had and announced, "Ah well, back to work!"

Jenny laughed and retreated downstairs humming gently. Her heart was filled with love and she felt better than she had in a long time and her humming turned into a song as she began to sing. There was another crash from upstairs and Jenny grimaced. She picked up the trug from the glasshouse and stepped out into the yard.

Bethan giggled as she chased the chickens. They fluttered and squawked out of her way. "Mammy!" the little girl shouted and went running after her mother.

Naomi looked up as Jenny waved to her, "It's all right, Naomi. Finish collecting the eggs and then you can practice your scales at the piano. I'll be back up in a minute."

Naomi grinned and began to walk to the house carrying her precious basket of eggs as Jenny and Bethan headed for the meadow.

Michael sat at his office desk; his face was grim. He didn't doubt the importance of the mission or the danger he and his men would be in. He had a plain piece of paper in front of him and took his fountain pen from his pocket. How to begin his letter that was always the hardest and to write it in such a way that it would remain without being censored. He began:

'My darling, Carrie,

The time has come and I will be off later doing what I have been trained and ordered to do. As you know I cannot divulge anything to you but I know it's going to be tough and it's thoughts of you that will help to carry me through.

My darling, I am compelled to write because as you know I will do everything in my power to come home to you. I fully intend to keep my promise but if, God forbid, anything does happen to me I want you to know that you have been my light and my beacon in this difficult world.

Saying that – although it is hard for me ever to imagine you with another, I want you to promise me that should the worse happen that you will not languish and spend your life alone. My love, you are not meant to be alone and know that I only wish for you to be happy in your life.

Don't shut yourself away throwing yourself into your work. Make time for you, your friends and if, perchance, you do meet someone who lifts your spirits or indeed, if Matthew comes back to find you, don't reject him. I don't want you to be alone.

Saying all that please remember I love you and if it is meant to be I will find my way back to you and we will spend the rest of our lives together. I want to grow old with you and have a family. Let's give little Bethan a cousin. I'm sure John would like that.

But that's enough doom and gloom. I am counting the days until I am back and you are in my arms. Give my love to everyone at home.

Look after Gelli Galed. As you know if the worst happens I have left everything to you, including Boots. No more mistakes over property…

Pray for me. Know that I love you.

Your loving fiancé,

Michael.'

He read it through, folded it up and sealed it in an official envelope and addressed it. He was sure he hadn't given any important information away. It was purely personal and although he didn't relish another reading his outpouring of love it was more important that it reach Carrie intact.

With steel-eyed determination he took the letter and made his way to the Flight Sergeant's office. As he walked he made a vow to himself that he wouldn't fail his country and he wouldn't fail Carrie.

Bethan was chuckling as she ran after her mother. She had managed to clamber over the five bar gate without any help and jumped down into the field. She raced onto the trees where her mother had set down the trug to look for mushrooms. She selected some apples that were not bruised or wasp nibbled and set them together.

Bethan was already climbing up her favourite tree and swinging on the lower branches. She brought her feet up to hang on the branch with her hands like a sloth and then pulled her self up on top.

She giggled deliciously as she crawled higher and higher in the tree.

"Bethan, you be careful. You'll get stuck!"

Bethan glanced down and went rigid. Her bottom lip began to quiver, "Mammy!"

Jenny looked up at Bethan's precarious perch, "I should come down now, Bethan. Take it slowly. Come on."

Bethan inched down the old tree at Jenny's encouragement, scratching her chubby little legs on the bark. "Ow! Mammy!" She called again, "I'll jump."

"No, not from there. It's too high. I can't catch you from there."

But Bethan was already rising and launched herself at her mother. Jenny hurried forward in a brave attempt to catch her as Bethan flew through the air with her feet outstretched she caught Jenny in the neck. There was a horrible crunching snap. Jenny fell to the ground with Bethan on top of her. Bethan scrambled off her unscathed, "That was fun! Let's do it again." But Jenny lay very, very still. She didn't move.

"Mammy?" Bethan shook her mother whose head lolled to one side. "Come on, Mammy, wake up!" The little girl sat down on the grass beside her and popped her thumb in her mouth. She sat there quietly waiting for her mother to stir.

Ernie sat bolt upright in bed. His face filled with panic and he rose from his bed. The crashing and banging had finished. Mr Prew was packing away his tools. John shook hands with the builder, "Good job, Mr Prew. Thank you." Mr Prew beamed and made his way back down the twisting stairs. John put his hands on his hips and grinned delightedly as Ernie poked his head around the door.

"John? John, where's Jenny?" His voice was filled with urgency.

"Jenny? Downstairs I expect with Bethan. Why?" John saw the consternation in Ernie's face and his demeanour changed. "What? What is it? Ernie?"

Ernie's face paled, "You need to find her. Now." Ernie swayed. John stepped forward to steady him. "Don't worry about me. Find her, please."

John sprinted down the stairs, calling Jenny's name. There was nothing. He ran out of the house and careered wildly around the yard, shouting in panic at the top of his voice. The ducks and chickens scattered at his feet.

Naomi was playing in the yard with Bonnie and Prince. She looked up at John's anxious cries.

"Naomi, where's Jenny? Have you seen her?"

"She went to the meadow for mushrooms?" said Naomi. The anxiety communicated itself and Naomi followed John to the gate.

John leapt over and ran down the incline toward the trees. He could see Jenny's fiery tresses sparkling like tinsel in the sunlight. Naomi hesitated and stayed put as John raced, his breathing rough and laboured, as he stumbled down the slope. He fell down on the grass beside her and a bellow like that of a raging bull erupted from his lungs and sent birds flying up from the field.

He hugged the lifeless body of his wife to him and rocked back and fore on his heels mewling like a stricken animal.

Tears streamed down his face as he sobbed her name and cried his denials, "Nooo! Jenny, my Jenny, no!"

At this pitiful cry Mr Prew who had been packing up his tools moved slowly toward the gate and Ernie in striped pyjamas and coarse woollen dressing gown staggered miserably toward the meadow. His face was solemn, his eyes filled with sadness and he murmured quietly, "Why, God? Why? Why take such a good life?"

Naomi bit her lip and Ernie slipped his arm around the child. They stood silently drawing comfort from each other at this tragic time.

CHAPTER TWENTY-THREE

Aftermath

Almost the whole village attended the funeral. Jenny had been a very popular young woman. Her parents were full of grief as was John and the rest of the family. They gathered together in Hendre where Carrie, Rose and Laura had helped prepare refreshments after the service. The wake didn't subside into a celebration of Jenny's life with laughter and song but remained a sombre, solemn affair.

Carrie was reminded of her own mother's funeral and her father's decline into seeking solace in a bottle before he, too, lost his life most tragically. Naomi seemed to meld into the shadows with Ernie close to her side. The little girl was shocked and saddened that someone she was beginning to love had been ripped from her and worst of all no one knew exactly what had happened. Little Bethan had remained silent when questioned, as she had not got the words to explain. She only said that her mammy had fallen over and wouldn't get up and because she was missing her mother so dreadfully no one pressed her further.

Villagers spoke in hushed tones as they sampled Welsh cakes and sandwiches. They supped tea in between whispers of pity for John's sad plight.

Jenny's mother touched John on his shoulder as he sat silently lost inside himself, "John?" He didn't move. His expression remained morose. He appeared to block out the voices of those around him. She tapped him again. This time he raised his eyes to his mother-in-law's face but couldn't speak. "John, I wanted to say that if ever you need any help with Bethan or indeed, anything we will be more than happy to help." John managed a nod before suppressing a hiccupping sob. He rose, left the funeral party and walked out of the house. He walked and walked mindlessly until he found himself at Bull Rock where he sat quietly in his anguish and pain.

The service in the chapel had been a blur. Nothing could console him. His heart pounded like a pile driver almost leaping out of his chest. He was lost and bereft and believed he would never again be happy. In his mind's eye he saw her lovely face with her milky, fair, fine porcelain skin and her cheeky upturned nose, her cloud of magnificent wayward curls and rosebud lips, her glorious voice and his body descended into shuddering sobs. The abundant tears streamed down his face as his outpouring of sorrow finally fully manifested with no one to see and no one to hear. John cried. He cried as he needed to and dabbed his eyes on his sleeve until he seemed filled with an unnatural calm and stared across the beautiful land he called home.

John found it hard to reconcile his sadness with the beauty of the day in the warm autumn sunshine. How could nature continue to thrive and lives go on as before when he felt as if his heart had been slashed out?

In the distance he could see folks dressed in black leaving the house, some trekking back down the mountain and others climbing into a trailer on a horse driven cart to return to the village. He was relieved to see them leave. Life would be unimaginably hard without Jenny who had been his rock. Now, he was a widower and Bethan was motherless. He wondered how he would manage to raise a child alone?

John shaded his eyes and looked down at the track where he could see someone walking with Bonnie and Prince. They were headed his way. John sighed heavily in an attempt to quell his bubbling emotions. The light caught the hair and John could see it was his sister Carrie and he heaved a sigh of relief. He really couldn't face talking to anyone else.

The dogs reached him first and fussed around him trying to infuse him with love. Bonnie's persistence even managed to raise a half smile from John. Carrie soon appeared and climbed up beside him. She embraced her brother who fell weeping into her arms and they remained like that for some time until his tears finally stopped. Not a word had been said but now Carrie jumped down and turned back to her brother, "I expect everyone has gone now. Come on, John it's time to go home. Your daughter needs you."

John got up and plodded after her with weariness in his stride and as he walked he became stronger as if he had been encompassed by love, "Jawch, Carrie. I can feel her. I can feel Jenny..."

"And so you will, replied Carrie. "Talk to her and keep the link... I do. I talk to mam and dad all the time. It will help, you'll see."

"I don't know, I'll try. But I know there are things I can't face. What about all her clothes, bits and pieces, her piano? I can't bear to think about it."

Carrie smiled ruefully, "I'll help and do what I can I promise."

They walked on in silence down the rest of the track. Bonnie and Prince stayed close as if they were fully aware of the upset. They didn't race on ahead as they would have normally done.

John reluctantly stepped up onto the veranda and entered the glasshouse as he walked into the kitchen he froze. Someone was playing the piano. He roared from the pit of his belly, "Shut up! Stop! No one is to play that piano again. No one! Do you understand?" His face was thunderous with rage and he marched into the parlour where Bethan was sitting on the piano stool tinkling a simple tune. "Stop! Do you hear? Bethan?"

Bethan's face crumpled and she scrambled down in tears, toddling across to Carrie and diving behind her skirts. Carrie winced at John's angry tones and sheltered the little girl. She whispered softly to her little niece, "Don't worry, fy merch 'i. Daddy's not quite himself. He doesn't mean it." Then she spoke more sharply to John, "John, a word. Now!"

John was shaking with emotion. He turned, opened the stair door and ran up. Carrie followed. John dashed into his bedroom and like an adolescent threw himself on the bed. Carrie sat next to him. His shoulders were heaving She hesitated in touching him but succumbed and rested her hand on his back. He turned toward her and clasped her tightly sobbing anew.

Carrie waited until his heart breaking cries diminished and then said gently but firmly, "John you cannot stop Bethan or

276

anyone playing the piano. Jenny would not have wanted it to be kept silent. She loved her music as she loved you, and Bethan, and that music lives on in your daughter. It must be nurtured. Jenny would wish that."

"But, why, Carrie? Why did she have to die? We don't even know what happened... how..." He stopped lost for words. "You can't go up to Gelli Galed now, Cariad. We need you here. What with, Ernie laid up, and Bethan and Naomi. Duw, what am I to do?"

Carrie took a deep breath, "Ernie will mend and I'm sure one of the Land Girls will help with Bethan and Naomi. I can't move Naomi anywhere else. She has had enough trauma and insecurity in her life. We'll manage somehow. There is a lesson here, John bach."

"I don't want lessons. I want my Jenny back."

Carrie sighed sadly. She hated seeing her brother in this wretched state. "Listen to me."

John continued to wail and Carrie said more firmly, "We don't want you going the same way as Dad. Remember that? Remember how we felt when Mam went? He carried on like some gin sodden workhouse renegade. The bottle became his way of coping and look what happened to us." At those words John stopped his piteous whimpering and stared back at her. "You have to be strong. Strong for Bethan; for all of us. I know you can do it."

John wiped his eyes with a damp rag of a hankie and muttered, "I know. I know."

Carrie extricated herself from his grasp and stood up. "I have a lot to do. It's not going to be easy and I need my strong dependable John back on track."

John nodded at his sister knowing she was right and he watched her leave the room. He sat in uncomfortable silence; his body was rigid. The gentle notes of piano music filtered up the stairs and he clenched and unclenched his fists. John didn't want to come out of his room. He didn't want to face his future, not for Bethan not even for Carrie and he suddenly understood all that his father, Bryn had suffered.

Carrie had a brainwave. Clarity had struck her like a

lightning strike. She had a plan and believed it was a good plan, but first she needed to hike up to Gelli Galed and see Sarah. It would need her agreement. Carrie smiled in the face of all the sadness; she felt she had some solutions.

Carrie changed out of her funeral black and dour clothes donning something more comfortably casual. She looked in on Ernie who was sitting in the kitchen drinking a cup of tea. His face lit up when he saw her. "Cariad! I know that look. What are you thinking?"

"John isn't fit for anything at the moment and with me working and you not completely well how can he look after Bethan and school Naomi?"

"Jawch, I'll soon be up and about. I can teach little Naomi. We understand each other."

"Yes, but you can't do it yet. Look I have to see Laura and Rose and Sarah. I have an idea." Carrie proceeded to tell Ernie what she believed was an inspired idea. Ernie listened carefully. "Well?" she asked him impatiently when he said nothing.

"I think you have a grand blueprint, a proposal that could work very well. But what about you on the District?"

"I'm sure I'll manage and when you're better you can take over from me."

Ernie nodded sagely, "Very well, Cariad. Give it a go. What about John?"

"He's still in his room. I reckon he'll be there awhile. It'll help him out until he can get back in the saddle. And now, I'm off to Gelli Galed. Rose and Laura have gone back to the fields. There are still bales to bind. Work doesn't stop for them or anyone."

"Don't you worry none. I'll see John. We'll have a chat. He'll listen to me. But you, Cariad... I'm worried about you."

"Me?"

"Yes, I can see ..." Ernie stopped.

"See? See what?" prompted Carrie.

"No, best I say nothing. I don't understand it anyhow."

"What?"

"All I'll say is that you will be tested. Emotionally. And don't ask me why. My visions are somewhat shaky at the moment. Not up to full speed so to speak. I can just see you with your head in your hands tussling with some problem."

"When it becomes clearer, you will tell me won't you?"

"I'll tell you, Cariad. But you have to let me figure it out first."

Carrie knew not to press him and she picked up an apple from the bowl and bit into it. It crunched crisply and Carrie went into the yard. She called the dogs and they set off up the track. The dogs danced ahead of her and Carrie worked out what she was going to say.

Carrie's heart was saddened. She had thought a lot of Jenny. She had certainly 'saved' her brother John and she worried that his former obsession with her might return, but then dismissed the idea as ridiculous. He had been married with a family and they had been so right for each other. Other black thoughts crowded into her head; she was frightened that he might follow the path of her father when her mother, Miri died. Bryn had found it all too easy to sink into depression and drink himself into oblivion. This had badly impaired his judgement and led to a catalogue of disasters for the family.

Carrie remonstrated with herself; no that was not going to happen. Surely, John was man enough now to remember how they had suffered with their father's drinking? She brushed these thoughts aside as she continued the climb to Gelli Galed, which well deserved its name. It had been 'hard living', indeed when she and John had relocated to the derelict property after Hendre had been swindled from the family by the villain, Jacky Ebron.

Carrie shuddered. These thoughts and memories would not help her mood. She knew she had to be more positive for John, Bethan and her own sanity and indeed, to sell her idea to Sarah.

Bonnie barked joyously as they approached the small gate, which led to the path and the house. Prince wagged his tail as Boots came tearing across the yard yapping little growly barks of welcome. Carrie opened the gate and Boots jumped on his hind legs, his little feet pawing the air like a prancing horse. He would not stop until Carrie stooped down to pat him. Once the common courtesies had been observed the three dogs proceeded to charge around in doggy delight and Carrie ran up the steps onto the veranda and knocked on the door, which opened almost immediately.

Sarah stood there in her work garb and frowned when she saw Carrie, who walked past her, "May I come in?"

"Looks like I have no choice," said Sarah following her visitor into the kitchen.

Carrie turned and stared at Sarah framed in the doorway. "I wasn't sure if you'd be here."

"I'm not exactly looking forward to working with the others," said Sarah tartly.

"That's what I thought," continued Carrie. "I may have a solution. Let's sit and discuss it, please."

Carrie sat at the scrubbed pine table and Sarah dragged out a chair. She sat albeit reluctantly and studied her fingernails as Carrie spoke. "Look, I know that things are difficult for you with Laura and Rose…"

"And Sam."

"And Sam," agreed Carrie. "And you haven't exactly endeared yourself to me either." Sarah had the good grace to look suitably shame-faced and lowered her eyes. "Sarah, how are you with children?"

"All right. Why?"

"You know that Jenny has died?"

"Yes. I'm sorry I couldn't face the funeral with everyone there. I thought it best if I stayed away."

"Never mind that now." She wanted to add that no one had minded or even noticed but she checked herself. "You are an intelligent woman with a science degree and gifted in art and design."

"Yes?" said Sarah curiously.

"You say you are good with children?"

"Not bad. I had thought of teaching once but then my sister…" She changed tack, "I was thinking of going into teaching."

"Good. Because I have a proposition," Carrie took a deep breath. There was nothing for it but to say it outright, as she thought, with no circumnavigating the issue. "We have a young evacuee, Naomi, staying with us. She has been heavily traumatised and is being home schooled. Jenny was her teacher."

"You want me to teach Naomi?"

"And look after Bethan."

"Like a Nanny come Nursery teacher?" she said in her smoked tones.

"You would teach them, play with them. You're more than qualified and…" she paused, "You'd be responsible for getting their meals… and that may help you," she said carefully.

Sarah bristled, "He told you, didn't he? Michael told you about my problem?"

Carrie nodded, "A good job, too. It helped explain your wayward behaviour."

Sarah coloured up and grudgingly answered, "I suppose…"

"Think about it. It's perfect. You could look after the children. They would benefit from all your knowledge. You'd be helping us, especially John and you wouldn't have to have daily contact with Sam or the girls."

Sarah pursed her lips, "I'd be able to stay here?"

"Stay, sleep here, yes. But, look after the children at Hendre… What do you say?"

Sarah was silent as she mulled over Carrie's proposal. Carrie waited expectantly. Finally, she nodded. "All right. I'll give it a go. I'll try."

"Excellent. I'm sure you'll do a grand job."

"When do you want me to start?"

"How about now? Come down with me now and meet the girls properly. No point in wasting time."

Sarah nodded, "In at the deep end, so to speak."

"It's often the best way," said Carrie who had nose dived into many an unfamiliar situation when she decided to nurse, first in Aberystwyth at the Maternity Unit and then in Birmingham followed by London during the Blitz. She stood up and extended her hand to Sarah, "We'll call a truce, shall we?"

Sarah took her hand and shook it. "Wait a moment, let me fetch some of my art materials. I'm sure the girls will enjoy drawing and colouring."

"I'm sure they will," agreed Carrie and waited while Sarah

ran up the stairs to her room. She emerged with a cloth bag with drawing pads, a bulging pencil case and colouring pencils.

"This will help to break the ice," said Sarah feeling a little more confident.

"Have you eaten?" asked Carrie as they stepped through the door.

"Um... no..." she replied honestly.

"Better start as we mean to go on. We can have some toast together when we get in. We'll need it after this hike."

Carrie noticed that Sarah swallowed nervously at this but she was determined to keep her promise to Michael. They continued down the slope and the dogs bounded along with them, including Boots. No more was said and Carrie trusted her instincts as Ernie had told her to do. She hoped that John would see the sense in this arrangement.

Naomi sat quietly and resolutely at the kitchen table reading a book. Screams came from upstairs. Bethan was grizzling as John tried to dress her. Unused to the tiny buttons his strong practical fingers had difficulty doing them up.

Naomi glanced up as she heard Bethan wail, "I want mammy." Naomi bit her lip as she knew Jenny would not be coming back. She could hear John's voice but could not make out what he was saying to the snivelling child. The door opened and Naomi looked up. A smile creased across her face when she saw Carrie, a smile that drained away when Sarah appeared behind her.

"It's okay, Naomi. This is Sarah. Sarah is going to help teach you until you're well enough to return to school. Naomi eyed the glamorous Land Girl inquisitively.

Sarah put a broad smile on her face and sat next to Naomi at the table. "What are you reading?" Naomi turned the book over for Sarah to see. "Heidi!" exclaimed Sarah. "That is one of my all time favourites. I would love to read it again with you."

"I got it from the bookshelf on the landing. I hope that's all right?" said Naomi.

"Of course," said Carrie. "It's one of mine. I loved that story, too."

"I haven't got very far," Naomi apologised.

There was another wail from upstairs. Carrie said, "I'd better go and see." She left the two of them together and ran up the pine stairs to John's room and knocked on the door, "John? Do you need a helping hand?" She could see that John was struggling to dress Bethan who was now red in the face and bawling loudly.

John sighed and removed Bethan from his lap and sat her on the bed, "Here, you try."

Carrie walked across and helped Bethan to finish dressing while John sat woodenly on the vanity stool. Bethan soon stopped crying and once dressed she clambered off the bed and popped her thumb in her mouth. She toddled toward John holding her arms out and he embraced his little girl mouthing his thanks at Carrie.

"I'll take her downstairs to meet Sarah. Sarah is going to teach Naomi and look after Bethan for us."

John's face flooded with relief, "That will be grand. I'm not good at child minding. Jenny always did it."

"You'll learn," said Carrie. "You need to get fully healed and keep an eye on our Ernie."

"I'm fine, Cariad. I'm back on my feet now and it's back to work for me. I need something to occupy my mind."

Carrie nodded, "I think it's best if Ernie stays in the house until he's stronger."

"I agree. I believe he should stay in the house with us, too, full time. Be better for him."

"Good luck with persuading him," grinned Carrie. "Come on Bethan. I need you to come with me." Carrie prised the toddler away from her father and led her from the room.

They trooped downstairs and into the kitchen where Naomi was reading aloud to Sarah. Carrie stopped to listen not wanting to interrupt them.

"That's excellent," praised Sarah in her silky tones. "Now if you can try and write a short précis of what you have read."

"Précis?"

"Um... a summary. A shortened version of what you have read in as few sentences as possible. Have a go, Naomi. Will you?" The little girl nodded and opened her exercise book. She took a pencil and began to chew on the end of it while she thought. Sarah turned her attention to Bethan and welcomed the little girl. "Hello, Bethan. I'm Sarah, a friend of your Aunty Carrie." Bethan looked solemnly from one to the other. "Would you like to come and do some drawing? Sketch a picture of anything you want…"

Bethan peered up at Carrie for reassurance and seeing Carrie nod agreeably she toddled to the table and climbed up on a chair. Carrie looked gratified. It seemed her plan just might work.

CHAPTER TWENTY-FOUR

Trouble in the skies and beyond

Michael had taken off from Martlesham with his 617 squadron. The fighter-bombers had hummed across the Channel and although carrying exhaust shrouds to mask the flames from their exhausts from enemy fighters they didn't entirely work sometimes scarring the night skies with a wispy vapour trail. The different contingents veered off toward their targets to attack Wismar, Flensberg and Vegesack.

The sortie seemed to be on track but Michael was knotted up with nerves, outwardly cool and calm but inside his belly was churning. He couldn't help but remember his last mission when he had ended up in hospital but had fortunately come into Carrie's care in London.

He agreed with the drive to knock out military targets such as the U Boat Yard at Flensberg and the aircraft factory at Wismar. He also understood the reasoning behind the raids on Dresden and Berlin leading to the intended demoralisation of the spirit of the German citizens but he didn't agree with targeting famous landmarks and historical sites. He knew the Luftwaffe had done the same to Britain, all over the country, Coventry Cathedral had been bombed, historic Plymouth, notable palaces and other famous historical buildings precious to the state had been damaged and destroyed but it didn't make it any easier to reconcile his feelings. He knew he had to focus. He had his orders, but at least his target was a military one, not a valued landmark and for that he was grateful. Other bombers were working toward a final push to blitz Berlin in the same way as London had been blitzed.

Hitler's intention was to break the morale of the British people so that they would pressure Churchill into negotiating. However, the bombings and mass destruction had the opposite effect, bringing the English people together to face the common enemy. Encouraged by Churchill's frequent public appearances and radio speeches, the British people became determined to hold out indefinitely against the Nazi onslaught. "Business as usual," could be seen everywhere written in chalk on boarded-up shop windows. Michael tried to hold on to that fact as they flew on toward their targets.

Michael knew that with the increasing number of British raids the German Ack-ack guns would be ready and waiting. He flew steadily on at the head of the droning convoy.

They crossed the coastal border flying through France and into Germany. The German ground forces were ready and waiting. The midnight sky was lit up in a blaze of gunfire, which exploded in the heavens like a gigantic pyrotechnic display. Sounds of the bombs and shots shattered the night. The Lancaster bombers flew dropping their payload on their strategic objectives. A bomber on Michael's right received a direct hit from the ground and exploded in mid air. The blast buffeted those in flight. Pilots struggled to maintain control.

Another adjacent bomber was hit and one of its engines burst into flames, then the other; the plane took a nosedive whining in its death throes as it fell to the ground. Michael kept his course steady barely managing to avoid a direct strike. He tried not to think of the men and planes that had gone down.

He made a pass over the Dornier aircraft factory in the coastal Baltic town of Wismar, opened his bomb bay and dropped his 'Blockbuster' a shell supplemented with smaller bombs and incendiary devices.

The bombardment was it seemed successful as flames roared up from the earth. Michael made a low pass to check the hit had been made and that the factory was alight. He was gratified to see that the fire below was growing in strength.

Michael began to turn back as others in his squadron bombarded the surrounding factory buildings. A shout erupted from the wireless operator and flight engineer; another of their squadron had gone down. That made three. Before Michael could complete his turn anti aircraft gunfire disabled a propeller, which began to splutter. The plane faltered in the air and then the second propeller was damaged and the Lancaster began its groaning descent to the ground. Michael gave instructions to bale and he ejected along with other crewmembers. The wireless operator clutched his box of carrier pigeons and managed to release the birds, which flew up and away unscathed.

Michael's last thoughts as he descended were of Carrie. German ground shots took out two of the crew whose bodies hung limply as their parachutes took them to ground. Michael, his radio operator and gunner drifted down to earth, unhurt but on enemy soil and facing certain capture.

Thomas was on his way home. HMS Welshman had sailed on without him after its damaged parts had been replaced and the Abdiel class minelayer was fully repaired. It continued masquerading as a French ship and was well on its way to beginning another mission protecting the waters around Malta and ferrying in much needed supplies.

He thought back to Devonport where the ship had limped back for repairs. The events played like a film reel in his head and he couldn't shake off the images. He glanced down at his left hand badly damaged and burned and relived the accident yet again.

The ship had been preparing to sail. Young sailors were returning from their unexpected gift of leave on shore. Supplies were being loaded. The boilers had been stoked ready for departure and highly pressurised steam lines were present in many parts of the engine room.

Thomas was working alongside his mate Jonno checking the boiler mounting valves. Thomas wiped his oily hand across his face and stood up. His expert eye just glanced around the pipe work close by and he noticed a small crack in one of the steam joints. He stepped nearer to take a closer look, "Hey, Jonno. Is this a crack or just the paint flaking? What do you think?"

Jonno moved closer to Thomas to see where he was looking, "Bugger. It's a crack. We'll have to shut down and reseal." As Jonno turned away the joint split and Thomas pushed Jonno clear raising his arm to shield his face. A jet of steam caught his hand and knocked him over. He fell in screaming agony.

Thomas shivered as he recalled the incident for the umpteenth time. Was there anything he could have done differently? Certainly he had saved the life of his friend but at what cost? He studied his scalded hand and arm. He had suffered severe burns and the tendons in his hand had been damaged. Even though he was right handed he was no longer able to do the intricate maintenance work required on board and had been honourably discharged from duty.

Thomas glanced out of the window on the train. He hoped the journey would go quickly. He knew he had to change at Exeter but pressing on his mind was what Megan would say. He couldn't wait to see her but she had no idea that he was on his way home. A telegram had been sent but if Megan was still in transit she wouldn't have received it. More worryingly, he hoped he would be able to return without any problems to his farm duties. His damaged hand shouldn't affect his ability to run a farm. With Gwynfor gone Megan's mother expected her daughter and son-in-law to take over the reins.

Thomas sighed. They were all coming home. Friends would be reunited and for the first time in weeks a gentle smile of anticipation played on his lips.

Back in Crynant, things were moving along better than had been expected. Carrie's common sense approach to life had done her proud. She enjoyed her job on the district but missed Michael. She longed for him to return and hugged his letter to her. It accompanied her everywhere tucked safely in her apron pocket. She had read it so many times she knew it off by heart.

Carrie hummed as she cycled to Howie Price's house. There had been such a change in the man. He was brighter, fitter and more mobile and Carrie was delighted that his ulcer had shrunk and healed due to her skill.

She propped her bike up outside and called out as she opened the door, "Oo oo! Howie! It's Carrie."

"Out by here, Carrie fach."

Carrie walked through the passageway and into the kitchen. Howie was on his feet and already making a pot of tea. She beamed at him. It did her heart proud to see him so much more active than when she had first met him, when he was hunched in a chair, immobile, under nourished and smelly.

"Well, Howie I could do with a cuppa. I left you till next to last so we could have a chat."

"There's lovely. You know I look forward to seeing you."

Carrie sat at the table and waited while Howie had served them both a cup of tea. The tremor always present in his hands had subsided. The old man looked and sounded stronger.

"I'll be closing the book on you after today, signing you off."

"No, never... What'll I do?"

"Don't worry, I'll still pop in but socially this time not professionally."

Howard Price's face crinkled into a deep smile of pleasure, "Then that's grand."

Carrie stayed and chatted before taking a final look at his leg. "You'll be jitterbugging with the best of them now, Howie. Ought to get yourself along to the sixpenny hop when you can."

"Only if you will partner me," he grinned.

"Don't know if I could keep up with you," she quipped with a wink. "Dance me off my feet, you would."

"In my youth maybe. I could trip a good step, I could."

She stayed chatting happily with the old man before glancing at her fob watch on her uniform. "Duw, is that the time? I must get on. I've one more house call to make."

"Very well, not that I want to see you go. But you come back soon. Promise?"

"I promise." Carrie stood up and swilled out her cup. She turned to the old man and kissed him lightly on his forehead. "See you next week. You take care."

"I'm all right. Safe enough by here. You are the one who needs to take care."

Carrie smiled and left him as he searched amongst his books for something new to read and Carrie resolved to see if she had any reading material at home that he might like. She waved goodbye and feeling more contented than she had for a long time mounted her bike and set off for Four Winds.

The ride was exhilarating. She enjoyed the feel of the wind

in her face and although not as warm as it had been there was still enough sunshine in the day to enjoy. Carrie dismounted and walked through the impressive entrance gates. She wheeled her bicycle up the path leaned it against wall and rang the bell. She knew the children had an unexpected day off school as Mrs Tobin and Miss Bevan had both gone down with some awful tummy bug and there was no one to take their place.

Children's voices could be heard laughing together and little footsteps trotted to the door, which Timmy opened, "Cor! It's the nurse." Timmy flung the door open to admit her, "Do you want us?"

Carrie smiled, "Not today. It's Mrs Gregory I've come to see."

"Whee!" he whooped, dashed down the passage and thumped on the drawing room door, "Aunty Phil! That nurse is here to see you," and then he raced past Carrie to re-join the others, who all tore off down the passageway toward the back door and raced outside.

Carrie laughed to herself at their natural liveliness. She knocked politely on the door and opened it. Mrs Gregory was sitting in a large wing back chair facing the doors looking out into the garden. She was watching the children as they all played happily together.

She turned in relief when she saw Carrie. "Ah, Nurse Llewellyn. I'm glad you've come. Please sit down."

"Is everything all right? Are the children causing problems?"

"No, not directly, the children are fine. They bring me more joy every day. I often wonder what I did before they came to stay. I can't imagine life without them." Mrs Gregory stopped, her eyes filled with tears and she sniffed. "I've received another letter from Timmy and Marion's Aunty June."

Carrie raised an eyebrow and came right into the room after shutting the door behind her. She sat opposite the old lady, "Tell me."

Phyllis stood up and tip tapped to her bureau. She unlocked it and removed a letter. She passed it to Carrie. "It came this morning. I've said nothing to the children, yet."

Carrie opened the letter and read:

'Dear Mrs Gregory,

I am delighted the children are doing so well. They are certainly in a better place although I did hear that you'd had bombs in Swansea and Neath but there again, so much safer than here. Families who have insisted on keeping their children with them are now regretting it. But, there that's not what I am writing about.

I'm afraid I have some very sad news. After a particularly heavy night of bombing, the children's home and surrounding three houses were hit. I believe Marion and Timmy have had a lucky escape.

However, the shop is up and still running and I will keep it going as long as I can. I have had all the family mail diverted to the shop address and this is how I have learned the most devastating news. A letter arrived from the military declaring the children's father is dead. His dog tags were returned with the enclosed official letter. So, I believe their father is no longer thought to be a Prisoner of War, which I know Martha was hoping for.

I have searched through Martha's private diary and address book. I have made some phone calls but her immediate family have passed. There is one cousin in Hertfordshire, Maisie Wilkins but she has children herself and has had no contact with Martha since they were growing up. She was apologetic but not prepared to take them in.

I am sorry to have to tell you this. Please advise me what you want to do about the shop. It is rented. The lease is up for renewal. I am prepared to take this on if everyone is agreeable.

Yours cordially,

June Barnes'

Carrie didn't bother with the enclosed brown envelope notification. She stared at Mrs Gregory who was wringing her hankie in distress. Carrie took a deep breath, "Do you know what I would do?"

"I'm hoping you have some good advice."

"I will take this letter with me. I suggest that you say nothing to the children, yet. Let them think their father is alive. Time enough for the truth when the war is ended. Let them enjoy their life here with you. It's bad enough they've lost their mother."

"And the authorities?"

"It's all in hand. This letter will help our case. I'm seeing someone tomorrow."

"Do you need me to come?"

"Not yet, although if everything goes through, you will have to be interviewed at a later date."

"I'll be ready."

Carrie sat waiting in front of scrawny looking woman with mousey hair rolled back fashionably edging her face. She wore heavy framed spectacles. The nameplate on her desk read: Mrs Ethel Maguire. She had an unfortunate habit of clearing her throat as if she had a lump in her oesophagus. ' Hmm. Globus Hystericus,' thought Carrie.

The light peeking through the window played on Mrs Maguire's face mottling her skin with golden speckles. She finished reading the letters, sighed heavily and looked up. "Ahem!" She tried to free her constricted throat again. "What you're suggesting is not impossible but it will take time to go through official channels. You say she wants to adopt them?"

"Yes. She has a wonderful home, the children love her and will have an excellent life."

"So you've said." Mrs Maguire was dismissive and off hand with her comments. "It's her age. She's rather old to adopt two young children. If something happens to her what then?"

"I am assured Mrs Gregory has made provision for them in any eventuality. It seems a marvellous solution. If they return to London with no home and no family they'll be sent to some institution not conducive to their growth and happiness," pressed Carrie.

"Nurse Llewellyn, you have argued your case very well." The throat clearing continued, "Aargh!" She took a deep breath and a sip of water from a glass on her desk. "We have been through all the relevant information but everything comes down to the woman's age."

"But…" interrupted Carrie eager to fight for Mrs Gregory and the children.

"I haven't finished, yet. I didn't say it was impossible. They may be another way of looking at this. Contrary to what you are thinking I am not an ogre and I, too, want the best for these children." Carrie looked up hopefully. "Firstly, I will draw up the papers to put the children into official foster care with Mrs Gregory as the foster mother. In these difficult times there should be no dissension. There will of course be reviews but I see no reason why she shouldn't then apply to be their legal guardian and adopt. I will do my best to see this is looked on favourably and with your evidence, as well, I don't foresee any major problems. Will the children agree to this?" There came another cough after her mammoth speech.

Carrie beamed, "Of course. They adore her."

"Then leave it with me. I will be in touch. Where do I address the correspondence?"

"That better be me." Carrie gave her personal contact information and rose smiling. She shook the lady's thin hand. Her grip was surprisingly firm not like the limp fish she expected.

Carrie left light of step and felt buoyed up at the result of the meeting she had been dreading. In fact, she felt so positive and hopeful that she decided to take a quick look around the market before returning home.

Carrie enjoyed her stroll around the market. She determined that she would bring Naomi with her one weekend and treat the child to the mouth-watering faggots and peas that was always on offer. Carrie browsed the stalls and not having seen any toys in Naomi's possession she stopped at a second hand toy stall where there were an assortment of dolls from simple hand made rag dolls to a couple of more beautiful porcelain faced ones. Carrie picked one up with tawny brown hair dressed in a bonnet and Victorian style clothes with button up boots. "How much?"

The stall holder looked at her recognising her Nurse's uniform and said, "For you, fy merch 'i, I'll take fifteen bob. Dolls are hard to get, I was lucky with this lot. Came from a bombed building in Swansea."

Carrie frowned, "Sorry, I don't have that much money. It's for a little girl, an evacuee."

"Well, I didn't think it was for you."

"She's got nothing." Carrie replaced the elegant dolly and picked up a simpler cloth one. "And this?"

"You can have that for half a crown."

Carrie fished in her purse and pulled out the coin, "I'll take it. Thank you."

The stallholder packed it in a brown paper bag. He looked thoughtfully at Carrie, "Tell you what. If you really want that doll I'll put it by for you and you can pay a bit each week. You should have paid for it ready for Christmas and I'll knock another two and six off. How's that?"

Carrie smiled, "That would be grand. Thank you."

"There you go, I'll pop it in a bag with your name on."

"It's Carrie. Carrie Llewellyn."

She thanked him again and left clutching her purchase and made her way to the station. She trundled onto the platform and looked around her, there were not many passengers waiting for the local train to Crynant but one person caught her attention; a young man in a Navy uniform. She moved up the platform for a closer look as he had his back to her. His stance was familiar, the way he held his head on one side as he scrutinised the adverts on the billboards.

He turned and she exclaimed, "Thomas! Oh my goodness!"

His face creased in pleasure and he picked her up and swung her around, "Carrie! Little Carrie. I hardly recognise you in your uniform."

"Don't tell me, my hair gave me away."

"Well, it is pretty distinctive. Yours and Jenny's."

At the mention of Jenny's name she stopped, "There's something you should know," and she proceeded to tell him about the terrible tragedy.

He stood in silence, shocked at the news. "How's John taking it?"

"Not well. It'll be a tonic for him to see you. But what are you doing home?"

Thomas lifted his hand, "Not much use as an engineer with this," and Thomas related the details of his accident to her. Carrie nodded in sympathy and wondered if there was anything she could do to help but Thomas seemed very accepting of his injury. "I shall be glad to see Megan. Is she home yet?"

That moment their train chuffed in and they climbed aboard remaining deep in conversation for the rest of the journey back. As the engine rolled into Crynant, Carrie asked, "Are you coming to Hendre?"

"No. I'll be making my way up to Megan and her mother's... Did you know, we got wed?"

"I did and it's congratulations all round. We must have a celebration so we should. It will help John to take his mind off things."

"I will, I promise. Tell John I'll be up to see him tomorrow and Ernie."

The cousins hugged and said goodbye. Carrie retrieved her bicycle, popped the doll in her basket and pedalled off to the village thinking what a glorious day it had been. Everything seemed to be going very well.

CHAPTER TWENTY-FIVE

More upset

"Nooo!" cried Carrie, her face crinkling up in anguish. "It can't be."

John gazed at his beloved sister and understood her grief, "I'm sorry, Cariad. The letter came today." He put his arms around her and whispered, "It's just us again, Cariad. You, me, Bethan and Ernie."

Carrie blanched at his words so afraid was she to a return of his unhealthy love of her that she pushed him away and ran up the stairs.

Sarah came out of the parlour with Naomi. "Is everything all right?"

"It's her fiancé, Michael. His plane went down across enemy lines. He's missing presumed dead," said John stone faced.

"Oh, no. How terrible." Sarah sauntered into the kitchen. "I'm making some tea to take a cup to Ernie. Do you want one?" she purred.

"No thanks. I must get out. Things to do." John left abruptly. Sarah's liquid tones were wasted on him.

Sarah set out a tray. Naomi sat and watched her. "I'm hungry."

"I'll see what there is in the larder." Sarah stepped to the food cupboard and searched around. She found a cake tin and opened it breaking a nail, "Oh, shalutta!" She nibbled at the offending tear before removing four Welsh Cakes. She gave Naomi one and a drink, "I won't be a minute. Just taking this to Ernie." She returned to the parlour where Ernie sat now up and dressed.

"Here." She passed him a cup and two Welsh Cakes.

"Are you going to join me?" asked Ernie with a twinkle in his eye.

"Um, we have ours in the kitchen," she flustered.

"Come back in the parlour. Keep me company and you can tell me how Carrie is."

"Miserable. She ran upstairs crying."

"Understandable," muttered Ernie. "She could probably do with a drink, too. Nothing like a cuppa for making you feel better."

Sarah nodded and ushered Naomi back into the parlour and prepared a tray for Carrie. She hesitated at the pine door uncertain if it was the right thing to do but spurred on by Ernie eventually took the tray upstairs and knocked on Carrie's door and pushed it open.

She tentatively stepped into the room, "I brought you this. You look as if you could do with it."

Carrie sat up and sniffed loudly, "Thank you," she managed to say and gratefully accepted the offering.

"I'll leave you to it... I couldn't help overhearing... you must believe he... Michael could be all right. You never know."

"I know you're trying to help, to be a comfort, but it seems pretty final to me."

"Never say never," said Sarah and forced a smile before leaving quietly.

Carrie sat and thought awhile sipping her tea, "Ernie would know. Surely to goodness he would have had some warning. He always had before. She drained her tea but ignored the cake determining to speak to Ernie as soon as she'd calmed down. She was surprised at Sarah's thoughtfulness. Maybe, the woman had turned a corner. Maybe, she was realising the cost of all her actions... maybe.

Michael was dazed and raised his hands in surrender. He and his men had landed close to the area they had bombed and had tried to flee. They had run to an abandoned warehouse, tried to hide and formulate some sort of plan to escape. German soldiers had been quick to track them down and the place had been surrounded. They were ordered to submit or face certain death.

The battered wooden door was kicked in and troopers with rifles raised entered and trained their guns on the three survivors. From the other three downed planes there was no sign of anyone.

The German commandant, a tall thin man with a crescent shaped scar on his cheek, perused the airmen and snorted in derision. He sneered at them and in broken English addressed them as he paraded in front of them. "So, you think you can escape us by hiding in here, English swines?" Michael stood tall and said nothing. The Commandant stopped in front of him and stared into Michael's face. He did not flinch. "So you are the Squadron Leader, eh?" Still Michael did not respond. The German spat in his face and cracked him hard on his back, with his swagger stick, felling him to his knees. The Commandant screeched, "Get up! Get up! Get up, NOW!"

Michael had buckled under the assault but stood up, his manner resolute, his expression determined. This only seemed to anger the man even more. He scoffed again, "Think you can't be broken. Think again." He snatched at Michael's dog tags around his neck and ripped them from him before ordering his men. "Take them away."

The three men were forced at gunpoint to leave the warehouse. They were roughly ordered into an army jeep. One German soldier sat in the back; his gun trained on them. Michael sat silently, his gunner, Frank Marshall, glanced up at Michael. "What do you think is going to happen to us, Sir?"

"I don't know. If they adhere to the Geneva Convention we should be housed in a POW camp until the end of the war. "

The wireless operator, George Field, glanced at the German watching them, "Hey Fritz, what's the drill?"

The German soldier turned his eyes on Field and in faultless English replied, "My name's not Fritz."

"No? Gerry, then."

"Nor Gerry."

Michael warned, "Careful what you say. He understands and speaks English perfectly. That's why he's sitting with us."

Marshall and Field stared at the young German Landser, the equivalent of a Private. Field spoke again, "So if it's not Fritz or Gerry, what's your name and what can you tell us about where we're going?"

The blonde blue-eyed soldier stared at them as if he was

making up his mind to speak. He eventually responded, "Landser Manfred Klein."

Michael studied the young man and believed him to be about twenty-one. "How come you speak such good English? You have hardly a hint of an accent."

"I studied languages at Cologne University."

Michael nodded, "And may I ask where we are headed?

Landser Klein hesitated uncertain how much he was permitted to tell them but with the throaty rumbling of the jeep engine and the bounce of the vehicle on the road he dared to speak, "As captured prisoners of war you have to pass through a Dulag, a German Durchgangslager. These are transit camps where your details will be processed and then you will be interrogated."

Field rolled his eyes, "And then?"

Klein continued, "From there you will be escorted to a Prisoner of War Camp, and travel by train."

The Commandant swung around, "Enough! No more talk."

Suitably chastened Klein fell silent. The jeep continued to bump along the road to who knew where.

Michael studied his men. There was an unspoken understanding between them. None of them knew what to expect or what lay ahead.

They journeyed in the jeep for some hours, mainly in silence. They didn't want to risk giving anything away. The red blush of dawn was tinting the skies with its crimson hues but gunmetal clouds rolled ominously in the distance becoming more visible as the sun grew higher in the sky spreading its rays on the long road ahead. The morning dew glistened like diamonds on surrounding grassland and hedgerows, a beautiful and benign picture that contrasted sharply with their plight.

The military vehicle rumbled onward. Michael leaned forward in his seat and peered through the blue-grey canvas. Ahead on top of a hill he could see guard control towers positioned at regular intervals sealing in a camp surrounded by a high metal fence with rolls of barbed wire at the very top. A sentry box with a wooden barrier lay ahead standing before the huge metal gates.

The buzz of the engine altered as the driver changed into a lower gear to mount the approaching incline. Michael sat back as the vehicle slowed. A German voice screamed, "Halt!"

The German soldier on duty stepped forward his rifle at the ready. German words were exchanged. The sentry peered into the back before raising the barrier and waving them through to the gates, which were dutifully opened with a grinding clang.

The Commandant jumped out from the jeep and rapped on the canvas instructing his soldiers to move the prisoners. Michael and his men alighted squinting in the patchy sunlight. They tried to stretch and move their cramped limbs but were not afforded that luxury and were shoved roughly in the back along a dirt road to a wooden hut.

The door creaked open and they were marched inside. The door slammed shut behind them. They looked at their sparse surroundings. "What now?" asked Field.

"We just give them our name, rank and number, nothing more. Understood?"

Marshall shivered, "Do you think we'll come out of this alive?"

"They signed up to the Geneva Convention. Let's hope they abide by it."

The three fell silent as they contemplated their fate. They didn't have long to wait as two German soldiers burst into the hut and dragged Marshall out leaving Michael and Field alone. The door crashed shut once more leaving Michael and Field staring at each other. Michael walked to the window with its grimy cracked panes and stared outside. The rain laden, black bubbling clouds were bowling closer and the sky was growing darker. Nature seemed to be reflecting the dire mood of the airmen.

Megan lay on her bed in Bronallt. Her mother was at her side and Thomas was pacing in agitation. "Shouldn't we get help? Surely this isn't right?" he said.

Megan squealed in pain again, "Mammy, I feel like my guts are being raked out.... I want to push... Argh." Her face contorted in agony as she groaned out the words.

"Hush now, Megan fach." Nancy held her daughter's hand.

"There's no time to fetch anyone. The baby is coming and there's nothing we can do to stop it."

"But it won't survive. It'll be too small," said Thomas wretchedly. Megan screamed again. "I can't listen to her crying like this. I've got to do something. I'm going for the doctor."

Thomas hurried out of the door as another shriek of agony reverberated around the room.

Megan gripped her mother's hand, "Why, Mam? Why is this happening?" She squealed again.

"Megan, fach. I don't know. It's too early, it is. I can only think there's something wrong. Nature's way of dealing with it. Ours is not to reason why."

"But it hurts like hell. Mammy, I don't want to lose it," and she dissolved into tears of pain and anguish.

"I know, fach. I know." Nancy held her daughter's hand tightly and looked lovingly at her daughter. "But we must look to saving you. Breathe through the next contraction. It may help. I'll do it with you. Squeeze my hand when you feel the next one coming." Nancy sighed, "Be prepared, Cariad. We could be here for hours."

Two hours passed, Megan was exhausted. Thomas had returned with Carrie who had put aside her personal tragedy and with her no nonsense attitude had assessed the situation.

"Where's Doctor Rees?" asked Megan's mother.

"Cilfrew, on a home delivery with Christine Figgis. Duw, Duw. This shouldn't be happening. I'll need plenty of towels, hot water and a spare sheet. Roll it up and string it through the bedstead. She'll need to hang onto it. Thomas you go downstairs make us all some tea."

Thomas fled seemingly happy to be away from this dramatic scene. Nancy gathered some fresh linen and did as Carrie asked.

Carrie scrubbed her hands and arms using the jug and basin, "I'll need more water." Nancy hurried from the room. Carrie tuned to her friend and spoke softly. "I'm going to examine you, Megan. Hold tight."

Carrie palpitated her friend's abdomen. She opened her bag

removing a pair of forceps and surgical scissors and laid them out on a clean cloth. "I need to open your legs. Can you part them?" Megan moaned softly as she complied and Carrie made a quick inspection. "All right, Megan. Let's put you on your side, far more comfy for you."

Carrie spoke quietly to Megan's mother who had just returned. "The baby's stuck in the birth canal but its passage is impeded. We have to get it out or we'll lose her."

"What can we do?"

"I'll need your help. Just do as I say."

The next thirty minutes were fraught with tension as Carrie tried to help the passage of the tiny baby down the birth canal. Finally with the use of forceps she helped the little one into the world. The child was tiny, blue and stillborn. Carrie swallowed trying to oust the lump that had risen in her throat. She wrapped the baby up and cut the cord. "You need to push again, Megan fach, to dispel the placenta. Go on, just one more. I know it's tough." Megan gave an almighty grunt and strained hard.

The blood flowed in a rush and the afterbirth came away. Megan flopped back exhausted. Carrie heaved a sigh of relief. She cleaned her friend up as much as she could and removed the stained towels from under her. She checked her over and struggled to hold back her own tears.

"Megan, I'm so sorry. The little one didn't make it."

"Is it a boy?" Carrie nodded. "Can I see him?" Carrie passed her the swathed bundle with its tiny face peeping out. Megan kissed her son's forehead. "He would have been perfect. Why, Carrie? Why?"

"I don't know. I don't know." She exchanged a concerned look with Megan's mother and whispered, "She needs to rest she's lost a lot of blood. I'll get Dr Rees to see her."

"What about the baby?"

"Let her hold him a bit longer. When she's ready I'll take him. Where's Thomas with that tea? Tell him to come up."

Thomas came into the bedroom and hesitantly approached the bed. He took the baby from her and kissed it before handing him to Carrie. Thomas hugged his wife to him and Carrie and Nancy left the room.

"Thank you, Carrie. I don't know what we'd have done without you."

"I'll be back tomorrow. Make sure she has plenty of fluids and keep an eye on her."

Mrs Thomas nodded, "Bless you, Carrie fach. Bless you."

Megan called out, "Where are you taking him?"

"To the doctor first. Then you will have to make your own choices about burial once we have the death certificate. Is that all right?"

Nancy nodded, "It'll be fine. Do what you have to do."

Carrie slipped out quietly. Her heart was full and sad. In times of tragedy she had often questioned her faith. She grieved for Megan's lost baby; she grieved for Jenny and most of all she grieved for Michael. She swallowed a sob. How could life be so cruel? Why did these terrible things happen? What had that tiny soul done to be forced into the world before his time? Carrie leaned against the stout wooden door of the farmhouse and wept. Her body convulsed with heaving sobs as she took her bike and began the journey back into the village with the tiny body strapped into her basket.

The funeral was a quiet affair attended by Megan, her mother, Thomas, Dr Rees and Carrie. Megan sobbed as the tiny wooden coffin was lowered into the small grave. As the minister, the Reverend Richards, said the final prayers Carrie could feel her own emotions rising. She struggled to be strong for her friend but could not help the hot salt tears that spilled over.

Dr Rees gave his condolences to the family and spoke quietly to Thomas, "May I have a word?"

Megan was so caught up in her own emotion that as she leaned on her mother for support, she hardly noticed the hushed conversation between her husband and the doctor. Carrie, however, did and was not sure what to think after what she heard. She approached the doctor and they walked together from St. Margaret's.

"Why did you say that? It seems so hard."

"Carrie love, in my experience, when a woman has lost a child the best thing for her to fill the void and soothe her raging hormones is to have another child as quickly as possible. Obviously she has to heal first but as soon as they can they should try otherwise…"

"Otherwise?"

"I have seen women change to never wanting a child again. It can destroy what were loving relationships. Believe me, it is the best thing."

They walked on in silence. Carrie ruminated over the doctor's words and thought again how cruel this would be.

Michael and his men had spent three weeks at the interim camp being interrogated and sleep deprived. They chanted their name, rank and number automatically at every question asked until they recited them in their sleep, "Michael Lawrence, Squadron Leader, one, six, one, seven, four, six."

Michael had requested the return of his dog tags but was told these had been either lost or sent to Central Command. When the identification discs turned up they would be then forwarded to him. The Commandant grinned sadistically and added that there was a small possibility of them being returned to his base as evidence of him being lost in action.

Fear gripped Michael's core for he knew the heartache that it would cause Carrie. Silently he prayed that they would turn up.

Rain had fallen steadily off and on for the duration of their time in the camp. The battering of bullet drops on the metal roofs had served to keep them awake night after night, preventing them from having a decent night's sleep. They had developed strategies to keep them occupied with card games. Field had even taught himself to juggle with stones. Marshall it appeared was quite a good artist and spent his time sketching and drawing on any paper that came to hand.

The dirt roads outside the hut had been reduced to mud, which made exercise difficult. Close to the trench-dug latrines the smell of human sewage permeated the air. The rain did nothing to dampen the smell, which wafted on the wind. They strived to keep themselves clean as possible but it was no easy matter and they had learned to be silent around the enemy determined not to give anything away.

Eventually, at the beginning of their fourth week according to the pencil strikes on the wall they received notification that they had been ordered to move onto Silesia. It was a bleak and dismal day. The sun was unable to break through the bulging lead grey sky and heavy clouds emptied their load on the Germans and prisoners alike. There was no distinction as far as nature was concerned.

They lined up with two other airmen, boarded a military jeep and left the camp. The wipers squeaked as they struggled to remove the continual wash of water, which streamed unrelentingly over the windscreen. The sound and movement became almost hypnotic and no one said a word.

The journey seemed endless such was the drab dreary surrounds in the drizzly half-light. They must have been on the road for over sixty minutes and the airmen had nodded off with the soporific rumble of the engine and the warmth of each other's bodies as they pressed against each other drawing comfort from human contact in their plight.

A sudden lurching stop woke the prisoners who were herded out and marched to the platform of a railway station where a goods train of sorts waited to transport them to a Prisoner of War Camp for Officers and Airmen. Although, weak from not having had enough to eat they were in agreement that they had been treated reasonably well.

The military jeep drove to the station where other airmen from different camps were waiting to board the train but there were no faces that Michael recognised. They had learned to be guarded in their conversations with each other in the presence of any of the German soldiers after their experience with Landser Klein.

The prisoners knew nothing of their final destination except that it was a POW camp for officers and airmen. Once they were all loaded onto the carriages the train blew its whistle and began to steam out of the station. The transport was by no means comfortable more like cattle trucks with slatted wood sides that revealed little of the countryside they were passing through. They sat silently trying to make the best of it but some brave souls ventured into song. *"We're going to hang out our washing on the Siegfried line...."*

Often the train would be shunted into a siding to make way for a passing troop train. Prisoners were of secondary and lesser importance, as the officers in charge had been keen to point out. This made the trip longer and more of a trial.

At regular intervals the train would stop and all the prisoners would be expected to get out of the train to either relieve themselves or empty their bowels by the side of the track. There was no dignity here and morale was not improved by squatting down under the predatory eyes of the guards who were waiting for someone to make a fuss or step out of line. Neither Michael nor his men were going to give the Germans that satisfaction. □

At first the train seemed to be travelling close to the coast as seabirds could be heard mewling in the air when the engines rumbled to a stop and the smell of salt was noticeable but this changed as the train with their closed smelly cattle wagons took a different direction and journeyed inland flashing through desolate countryside driving further and further into occupied Poland. The weather was becoming colder and green gave way to white as the snow drifted down.

They were tired and hungry having travelled for over two days but refused to let themselves be cowed by their captors and in the presence of other airmen, for outside appearances, they determined to keep their spirits high.

The train squealed on its tracks as it ground to a halt and the men were roughly herded off like cattle and forced to board military trucks amidst guttural shouts and yells from German soldiers, who pushed them in their backs, prodding them forward like animals in the circus. Once on board they were sardined together and driven along the icy snow covered roads to the notorious Stalag Luft 111 camp. The road was long, treacherous and frozen with compressed ice. The vehicles had studded chains on the wheels for grip and to stop them sliding. Michael took the dire conditions as an omen.

Michael knew from previous intelligence and talking to other captors that individual camp layouts varied from camp to camp, but they all were enclosed with barbed wire and contained guard towers, which were manned by armed German soldiers ready to shoot anyone trying to escape.

Prisoners were reputedly housed in one-storey wooden barracks, which contained bunk beds, which were two or three high, and a charcoal burning stove in the middle of the room. In the freezing conditions this was essential although it didn't give out that much heat.

After they had been counted and registered they were taken to their huts, no more than wooden shacks. Michael took a lower bunk, while Marshall and Field bagged the upper ones. Field, who was known for his excessive flatulence, let rip with an explosion of wind. The smell was appalling, as they had been fed mainly on root vegetables in a thin broth. Michael immediately regretted taking the lower bunk and said so, "If you're to be above me and if you don't burn the mattress out first, try and keep your vegetarian pong to the outside, please."

"I can't help it. When it comes, it comes," apologised Field as he let another one rip. This time the others in the barrack chided him, too.

"Hey, Field!" called Marshall. "We could use you as a source of heat, bottle the gas and use it to keep warm."

"Yeah, light them why don't you? At least the blue flame will kill the stink," shouted another.

More jibes and good-humoured banter followed as the men tried to settle in to their life at the camp. The regime was monotonously the same. They were generally given two meals a day consisting of thin soup and black bread. No one was going to get fat on that. Needless to say hunger was a feature of most of their lives.

They quickly learned that the Red Cross sometimes made deliveries, which all the men looked forward to especially the food parcels, which contained 'luxury' items such as butter, biscuits, chocolate and condensed milk as well as dried fruits and vegetables. The men quickly learned to improvise making their own brick stoves and cooking their food in empty milk tins.

It seemed from discussions that daily routines varied from camp to camp but all prisoners were expected to parade at least once daily for a roll call. Every man was always on the lookout for a breach in security or a way of escape, considering it their duty. But this camp seemed locked up tight with little hope of any escape although that was their goal as prisoners of war to make life as difficult as possible for the enemy. Some men were put to work either around the camp or in the locality. They were for the most part compensated for the work they did although officers were not required to take on any job. Most of them dreaded being sent to the mines. Marshall was one of the unlucky ones. He was a thickset man with considerable brawn and singled out for the backbreaking work underground. How long he and the others would have to endure this purgatory was unclear.

Some of the longer-term residents at the camp tried to cheer the others up with tales of what they could expect when the weather turned warmer. Shaffer an airman from the Stirling Bomber command told them that when the weather was fine they were allowed to play a range of sports and in the evenings there were sometimes concerts.

However, for most, the overriding features of life in this prisoner of war camp were boredom, hunger and dreams of a better life once the war was over. Michael's thoughts were of Carrie and he prayed that if he could survive his time here that he would get back home to Wales, Gelli Galed and Carrie.

CHAPTER TWENTY-SIX

Looking ahead

Weeks passed and Carrie threw herself into her work. She needed her job now more than ever. It gave her a focus and a reason to rise every morning. Christmas was fast approaching and so much had changed. The war had damaged them all.

The evacuees billeted in Crynant seemed to be faring better than others in the county. Checking on each family took up a large proportion of her calls. She still had her regular visits on the district and had made time to see her friend Megan who was now making good progress in dealing with her loss. She had thrown herself into training horses with her mother and Thomas was running the family farm.

At home, Naomi was flourishing under the tutorage of a changed Sarah, who enjoyed the role of teacher and seemed to have undergone something of a transformation. She had filled out looking even more alluring than she had before but she didn't flaunt it or flirt with every man with whom she had contact. Both Naomi and Bethan were learning the piano under her guidance. John had finished the attic room. Naomi and Bethan had been allowed to share and Naomi was to return to proper school after Christmas.

Farming activities at Hendre and Gelli Galed appeared to be carrying on as normal and most surprisingly Ernie had been persuaded despite his protestations to live in the house. He was getting back to his old self and had even found time to visit his daughter, albeit briefly.

But John worried her. He continued working in his solid reliable way but his manner was distant even with young Bethan. It was as if he had shut down his emotions and built an impenetrable force field around him and turned his back on love, any type of love, even his fatherly love. His conversation at the dinner table was lack lustre and monosyllabic no matter how hard she tried to involve him in anything.

Crynant, through the years, was fast gaining a reputation for its Christmas plays and pageants that attracted audiences from the surrounding villages. It was a beacon of light in the dim and tragic times. Carrie tried to persuade her brother to become involved, "It will do you good," she said at supper that night. "Megan is taking part and Thomas has agreed to help build the scenery. You should do so, too. Come on, John. Join us... me."

John shrugged. He had resisted any attempts to drag him out of his indifference and misery. Carrie found herself more and more behaving like her Aunty Annie in coaxing, cajoling and speaking home truths as Annie had to her brother Bryn, their father. when he was wallowing in drink and melancholy.

Carrie waited until the meal was finished. She helped Sarah clear away and John retreated to the parlour as was his habit of late. Ernie watched him go, "Something needs to be done. If he doesn't change it will make life impossible for you again, Cariad." He stared meaningfully at her and she bowed her head, finding it hard to face the possibility of a resurgence of her brother's suffocating love. Ernie continued, "Not only that Bethan needs a proper father not an occasional visitor. Jawch, the tragedy suffered should have brought them closer together not built a wall between them."

Carrie and Naomi helped Sarah with the dishes and while they settled at the kitchen table to read together Carrie tilted her chin, held her head aloft and marched into the parlour. John looked up and could see she meant business.

"Esgyrn Dafydd! What now? Are you coming to lecture me again?"

Carrie sat opposite him and leaned forward. "Not to lecture, to talk."

"Talking always seems to end in you telling me what to do."

"Maybe. But, you remember dad?"

"Of course I do."

"And how we felt, how we hurt, and how he ruined himself and us?"

John glowered, his dark unruly hair falling across and shading his eyes. Reluctantly, he replied, "Yes, so?"

310

"Well, you are behaving in the same obstinate, difficult way he did. If you're not careful, you'll lose your daughter and that's all you have left of Jenny and...." She took a deep breath, "You'll lose me. I can't be doing with your sullenness, and melancholy. I have my own demons to face. It's not easy for me either but you neglect to see that so you do. I suggest you start looking forward, John Llewellyn, start being a father and a man." And with that she stood up and marched to the door with her head held in her signature style. As she reached the door he stopped her.

"Cariad, wait, please." She stopped and turned in the doorway. "Please sit down."

Carrie crossed to the chair and sat again facing her brother, "There's a lot you don't understand..."

"Then tell me..."

"Look, I know you're right. I know what I'm doing and I can't seem to help myself. But..." he sighed heavily. "I loved Jenny, oh not at first, I was fixated on her because..." he hesitated, "because of you." Carrie blushed knowing the truth of his words. "But, I came to love her, love her deeply and I am finding it hard to go on knowing my suspicions."

He had Carrie's full attention now, "What do you mean? Suspicions?"

"There's nothing for me to do but say it... It was Bethan that caused Jenny's death."

"What?"

"I should have remembered, Jenny would tell me how Bethan would scramble up the apple tree and jump out. Jenny would catch her. It was all a big game."

"And so?" Carrie's heart was pounding.

"I think she went up too high and when she jumped she hit Jenny and broke her neck."

"What makes you think that?"

"I talked to Bethan... she said..." He stopped and swallowed hard, "Look, I know it was an accident but every time I look at her I see Jenny's sweet face and my heart rips in two."

"What did Bethan say?"

"She said she climbed higher that day, higher than before

311

and she still jumped. I can see it all in my mind's eye." John stopped to catch his breath he was becoming choked with emotion.

"But you don't know… not really… and even if that were the case it was an accident. How do you think Bethan will grow up if she feels you blame her for her mother's death? John, you must stop thinking like this."

John rubbed his hand over his brow, "I know, I know. I know you're right."

"Don't you see? Getting out and doing something with others will help you, so it will. At least try. Jenny wouldn't want you to be like this. She wouldn't want you to blame Bethan. She loved her."

John looked up with his misery filled and defeated eyes, "All right. All right. I'll try. For you, I'll try."

"Not for me," corrected Carrie, "For yourself." John nodded. "And there's no time like the present. There's a meeting in the village hall this evening for all interested parties and a read through for casting the pantomime. Let's go. Thomas and Megan will be there. Sarah will look after the girls. Rose and Laura are going. Come on, go and get changed. It will be fun. The cart leaves at six-thirty. You've got half an hour."

John sighed and wearily stood. He nodded and crossed to the door. "Give me a minute."

"You've got fifteen. Chip-chop."

The village hall was packed with people. Carrie recognised most of them. The room was filled with chatter as Mrs Tobin the headmistress of the small village school strutted around with a clipboard. She placed herself at the front of the hall and called everyone to order, "Well, well, it's lovely to see such a grand turn out. Other villages in the locality are looking forward to our Christmas entertainment. We are gaining quite a reputation so we are and a good one at that."

The villagers chattered brightly. There was an air of expectancy and optimism in the hall. One chap called out, "What are we doing this year, then?"

Mrs Tobin cleared her throat, "I'm coming to that. Miss

Bevan and I have written the script for Aladdin. There are plenty of good parts for everyone and I'm happy to say that we have a professional in our midst as Megan Thomas…"

"Megan Davies, now," called another.

"Yes, well, Megan as most of you know was in ENSA and so we have our own star. I thought we'd begin with sorting out the actors from back stage staff, costume and scenery. We can thank Mr Bevan, Miss Bevan's father, who, as usual, is helping to provide material for some of our costumes and I have a team of ladies prepared to make what we need. Firstly, let's see what we've got. Those who wish to be involved in making scenery, working back stage, and on costumes line up on my left. Sort yourselves out in distinct groups. On my right those who wish to act."

There was a lot of shuffling and people seemed to organise themselves into the respective groups. Mrs Tobin studied them all appreciatively, "Very well, now I have the scripts we need to audition for the main parts. But first, Thomas you'll be in charge of scenery. John what are you interested in doing?"

"I'm not sure," murmured John sheepishly.

"Go and join the actors, we don't seem to have enough men and from what I remember at school, you had quite a good singing voice."

But…"

"No buts. Over on the other side. You…" She pointed at Laura, "You can do props. Who will help her?" Sam Jefferies put up his hand. "That's grand, but I may need you for a smaller male part. You can do both." She then singled out her sewing bees for the costumes. "Now, who's left?" She looked at Carrie, "You can be my stage manager." The rest of you, take a script, have a look through and see what you want to try out for. Come on, hurry up."

People seemed to be beetling all over the hall while the 'would be' actors sat in a clump looking through the script. Land Girl, Rose found herself sitting next to John and smiled shyly at him. "Didn't know you could sing?"

"Neither did I. It was a long time ago."

"You must be better than Ernie, voice like a rusty nail he's got."

They pored over their scripts looking at the roles and Mrs Tobin went around them all asking what they wanted to play. Megan offered herself up for the role of Aladdin, while Rose suggested she try for Princess Baldroubadour. Pritchard the police offered to read for the Grand Vizier, whilst others vied for some of the smaller parts.

John scratched his head in confusion and Mrs Tobin pronounced, "I think you should try out for Wishy Washy, John. And you," she pointed at Mr Segadelli, "Can try Widow Twanky. You made a wonderful dame last year in Mother Goose. Now let me see…" She looked around and soon had others lined up for the King, the Genie and the two comic policemen, Hong and Pong. "The rest of you can be in the chorus and take minor roles and whoever doesn't get the part they tried for will be in the general company. Right, now let's get started."

Carrie, John and all from Hendre Farm travelled back in the cart. The excited bubble of chatter as they left the hall had diminished as everyone was tired and as John had exclaimed that he didn't know what he was letting himself in for. Senator plodded on and in the last few hundred yards people had stopped talking altogether. Carrie was pleased to see that Sam had his arm around Laura and things seemed to be better between them. Carrie was tired, she yawned loudly, "Oh, goodness me. Sorry… how rude," but no one took any notice. As they reached the yard everyone tumbled off the wagon, said their goodnights clutching their scripts and notes and retreated back to their homes.

"I can't believe I agreed to this," complained John.

"Go on with you," said Carrie. "It will do you good. Remember what you've promised me."

"I know, I know," he muttered. "I must be mad. I mean… me, Wishy Washy. Jenny would have laughed."

"Yes, she would," agreed Carrie. "You've done the right thing. Jenny would be proud of you." Silently Carrie thought John had taken a step forward being able to talk about his wife without falling into a swamp of despair. She hoped it would continue.

Carrie had a meeting the next morning with Mrs Gregory and Mrs Ethel Maguire. The paperwork had been completed and Mrs Gregory sat nervously in front of the big desk. She leaned on her stick and waited hardly daring to breathe.

Mrs Maguire read through her notes and the forms, checking them one more time. She removed her glasses, which made her look far less severe, "Well, I think that is it. These are difficult times otherwise I may not have been able to process this in the way that I have. Nurse Llewellyn will continue to monitor the children. This will put your standing on a more official footing as a bona-fide foster parent." A rare smile tugged at her lips, "Official guardianship will be the next step once we have established there are no living relatives or immediate family. Congratulations!"

Phyllis Gregory sighed in relief and delight, "Thank you. That is wonderful news and thank you, Nurse Llewellyn I know this would never have happened without you."

Mrs Maguire replaced her spectacles, "You're right. Nurse Llewellyn made a very strong case for you and it's thanks to her I rushed the paperwork through. Good luck!" She stood up and shook both of their hands. Carrie beamed with pleasure. "You won't regret it, I know you won't. Thank you." The two left the office. Carrie and Mrs Gregory and her stick tip tapped out of the door.

Carrie tried to throw herself wholeheartedly into her work. She needed to numb the pain from Michael's loss, which had been compounded by the arrival of his dog tags in the post. Michael had no family and he had listed Carrie as next of kin and she was almost wishing that she had indeed taken the advice of the woman in the hotel and made Michael's last night with her one to remember. She recalled the moment when she arrived home and John had passed her the official letter announcing that with the receipt of the identification discs that it was unlikely he had survived the plane crash. Her hope that he was alive and had been taken prisoner had been uppermost in her mind and had at least given her hope.

Hendre was steeped in sadness. The cheerful mealtimes

with Jenny singing and the lively chatter and banter had diminished to civility and over politeness. Sarah was proving to be surprisingly good with the children, who were both flourishing. Naomi was now looking forward to a return to school after Christmas.

The family sat at the tea table where the conversation was muted and quiet. Sarah had put Bethan to bed and was sitting upstairs with Naomi hearing her read before she returned to Gelli Galed. The children had eaten earlier as it was rehearsal night and she wanted to get them settled before Carrie and John went off. Ernie was now back to work but he remained in the house and had not retreated back to the barn unless he needed to tend to a sick lamb or calf and he seemed to be enjoying his newfound luxury.

Ernie scrutinised the faces of those around him and asked, "How is the Christmas play progressing? I'm looking forward to seeing it."

Carrie smiled at the old man, grateful that he was attempting to engage them in conversation, "I never realised back stage work could be so hard. I have to check the props and the scenery as well as prompting the actors. Do you know I have to write down all the places they stand on stage and the furniture has to be marked with tape so it's in the same spot. It's not as glamorous as we are all led to believe. It's hard work especially for us backstage."

Ernie looked at John, "And you, John, bach are you managing with the role of Wishy Washy?"

"Duw, trying to learn lines and get them stuck in my head is like catching bubbles in a gale. Sometimes I remember them and at others I go completely blank and then make something up. It's not easy. And having to sing and dance at the same time is tough."

Ernie was pleased that at least they were talking with a bit more animation as usual. He bravely continued, "You two have to face facts that your loved ones are gone. Jenny would not want you to mope around feeling sorry for yourself. Bethan needs you, needs you more than ever now."

John sighed, "I know you're right, Wuss. But I find myself feeling guilty if I laugh or seem to have a good time. I remember she's not here and wonder how I can be so insensitive. I even wonder why I am still here…"

"Jawch, John. It's good to talk about her, to remember things you did and to laugh together. It's all part of the healing process. Life goes on and that's what Jenny would want. She wouldn't want you shutting yourself away. She would be pressing you to look forward for Bethan's sake. It's a good thing, this play you're doing, a good start." Ernie turned his eyes on Carrie, "And you, Cariad. How is your heart now?"

"Full as a water butt. I still can't believe it. He was so alive, so vibrant; it's hard to believe his light has been snuffed out."

"Aye, I must say. I found it hard to believe, too, still find it difficult, if the truth was known. I had hoped there was some mistake like with you on your stint in France. There we were all thinking the worst and then up you popped taking us all by surprise. And what a wonderful surprise it was."

"I know," said Carrie quietly. "I keep thinking it can't be right but now with his identification discs it confirms the worst… I'm glad of my job and the play, at least it stops me brooding."

Ernie paused and then said carefully, "And what about Matthew?"

"I don't know. I've had one letter. I wrote back."

"Have you told him about Michael?"

"No. That seems to make it all the more final somehow."

"You should, Cariad. You should."

Carrie said nothing at first but then, "I just can't imagine another man in my life other than Michael."

"And would Michael want you to live a lonely life without anyone?"

"You've managed all right."

There was a knock at the door and Rose came in, "It's only me. I've hitched up the wagon to Senator. We're all ready to go." She looked around them expectantly.

"Go on now, you get off to the hall. I'll clear up. I'm not afraid of a bit of housework."

Carrie and John scraped back their chairs glad to leave the conversation that was uncomfortable for them under Ernie's searching eyes. They gathered their scripts and coats as winter had really begun to set in. Carrie wrapped a thick woolly scarf around her neck, one of Aunty Annie's many offerings in the knitwear department and scooted out before anymore could be said.

John nodded perfunctorily at his workmate and trusted friend before making his escape. They stepped outside into the chill night. Their breath clouded the air like smoke. Rose, Laura and Sam were chattering happily in the cart as they waited for the siblings. Carrie climbed into the back and huddled with the others. Their combined body heat making the cold more bearable.

John lit the lamps on the wagon and climbed up taking Senator's reins and clicked his instruction and the gentle shire plodded out of the yard and made his way down the mountain track.

The chatter in the back was quite lively but John remained silent at the front, clearly deep in thought. Carrie watched the back of her brother knowing and feeling his loneliness. She was glad of the distraction of the Christmas play. It was not something she'd been involved in before but in truth she was enjoying it and she was looking forward to seeing Thomas and Megan who seemed to be more optimistic about their future together after their own personal tragedy.

The hall was alive; groups of volunteers sat sewing, making costumes. Others were painting scenery and the smell of fresh paint filled the place. Mrs Tobin strutted around ensuring everyone was almost ready. One of the workers tried to close the curtains on the stage and they stuck on their runners. He tried to draw them forward and back in quick succession to free them but they were well and truly jammed.

Rose grabbed a pair of stepladders, dragged them to the stage to climb and unsnag the drapes from the runners where they had snarled up. John steadied the rickety steps as she climbed up.

Rose stretched up and fiddled with the hangings. She snorted in frustration, as the things were proving fiddly to right. She stopped and relaxed her arms, which were aching from holding them high over her head. "It's no good, I can't see properly. I'm just not tall enough."

"Let me try," said John. He waited for Rose to come back down and their arms touched. Rose turned suddenly and found herself in very close proximity to John. She laughed nervously and stuttered, "S... Sorry."

John returned her smile and tried to move out of her way. What followed was a strange square dance of apologies as they attempted to move out of each other's way. John finally managed to climb the steps and Rose secured them. John freed the offending curtain and climbed down. Rose let go of the steps and stood up her eyes level with his lips. A moment passed as the two stood there uncertainly, neither of them wanting to move.

Mrs Tobin clapped her hands, "Places please." Actors scattered and she signalled to Gwyneth Hughes on the piano who struck up the chords of the overture. Rehearsals had begun.

The Polish winter was bitterly cold. Men huddled around the feeble stove in the hut and exchanged stories of home. Michael's thoughts drifted back to Carrie. It was thoughts of her, her sweet face and wild hair that kept him sane, he thought.

"What are we going to do for Christmas?" asked Field. "We must do something to celebrate."

"A bowl of thin soup is hardly a goose," scoffed Marshall.

"Christmas will be what we make it," said Michael. "Why shouldn't we try and mark it with something special?"

"The Red Cross will send us a food pack we can have our own Christmas," said another.

"And, I have an idea," said Michael. "If it works Christmas could be better than just another day in this purgatory." The other airmen looked interested. Michael continued. "The supply train comes through on Thursday. Those of you who work on the sidings at the station can organise a distraction..."

"Like what?" said Marshall interested.

"Snowball fights, building snowmen anything like that."

"And then?" asked Field.

"The rest of us could raid the supply wagon and help ourselves to potatoes and other foodstuffs and smuggle them back into camp. No one checks us, as long as we aren't too greedy, we could develop quite a stash in time for Christmas Day."

"And where would we put them? Down our pants?" said Field.

"Not me," said Marshall.

"Why?" asked Michael.

"No room…" he grinned impishly and they all laughed.

"Either that or they'd cook down there," said Field meaningfully. They laughed again.

"You know that's not a bad idea," said Dickie Stamford from B company fifth Hampshire regiment. "Croker and King can start that off, Wilkinson and Hicks can lift the extra grub, Lawrence, Field and Marshall can keep a look out. The rest of you can get involved in the snowball fight."

"Why don't we cause them a little more trouble?" said Michael mischievously.

"Yes?" queried Stamford.

"Suppose we uncouple some of the wagons. That could cause the Gerries some distress. Delay their supply train from getting to the front… what do you say?"

The men chortled together pleased with their plan. They huddled around the stove and tightened up the details of how it would work.

"I'll be stuck down the mine at Kazimer," grumbled a brawny chap called Keeping. "But I'm sure we could filch a bit of coal, which would keep our fire burning and be great for baking the potatoes."

"But we must keep it quiet. The guards won't want us to celebrate."

"No, probably make us work all through Christmas," said another. "I'm doing thirteen hour shifts down the mine. The rats are the size of dogs, talk about a hell hole."

"Just don't get caught," said Stamford.

The thought of defeating the guards in some small way filled them with hope. If they were scheming and making plans. They had hope.

Mrs Tobin clapped her hands; "Let's take it again from the top. I just want to run the opening few scenes again and then we'll call it a night. Mrs Hughes, piano please."

The butcher's wife played the chords for the overture. Backstage the chorus were waiting to do the opening number, John as Wishy-Washy was waiting in the wings with Mr Segadelli as the Dame. They waited until the rest of the company had completed their first song and dance number and as they trooped off, John followed Mr Segadelli onstage bemoaning the amount of work he had to do in the palace laundry.

They had an odd routine where Wishy-Washy ended up going through the prop mangle. John did a somersault off stage and landed at Rose's feet. He stood up apologising profusely. They were pressed so close against a flat masking the stage entrance that John could not help being aware of Rose, her feminine proximity and a tingling sensation coursed through him. He stepped back bumping into Megan and apologised again, "Sorry, Megan, Rose... Um," and stuck for words he fled.

Megan shrugged and made her grand entrance into the palace garden and Rose looked after John almost missing her cue.

"Stop! That's it," called Mrs Tobin. "Everyone should be word perfect by now. There will be no prompts in the show. Professionals do not have prompts. We won't have prompts. Carrie has the rest of the rehearsal schedule written out; take note of when you're wanted and what time. Don't be late," she thundered. Her school ma'am authority silenced the amateur cast and crew and they scurried to the board to view the timetable scribbling down the dates and times they were needed.

Rose found herself standing behind John and being jostled by other cast members as they tried to vie for a place to see their timetable. He turned coming face to face with her again. He gulped and pushed his way through the rest of the cast. He blushed and escaped outside to the waiting cart. His hands trembled and he fumbled with the matches as he struggled to light the lamps around the wagon. He stopped to draw breath and leaned over just as Sam exited the hall.

"Are you all right?" he asked with concern.

"Yes. Just a bit wobbly."

"Pre-show nerves. Bound to happen. I'll drive Senator home." Sam climbed up to take charge of the reins before John had a chance to protest and Laura clambered up next to him so that John was forced to get into the cart. He sat there clutching his script and his head was buzzing. He was confused and could not understand why he had these feelings especially so soon after his Jenny's death. His thoughts were charged like a lodestone covered in iron filings, moving whichever way the magnet led.

The doors to the hall opened, light spilled out onto the street and company members emerged nattering excitedly. Rose and Carrie appeared with Megan and Thomas. They stopped and chatted awhile before coming across to the cart.

John forced a smile, "Megan... Thomas, it's good to have you home. Don't forget to come and see us at Hendre."

"We will, we will," said Thomas agreeably.

"I thought," interrupted Carrie, "We could have everyone with us for Christmas and your mam, too, Megan."

"I'll ask her. It will probably do her good."

"That's grand," stuttered John. "Like the old days, of Dad and Aunty Annie."

"It'll do us all good," said Carrie.

"We can play games. I'll make up a few," said Megan.

"Sorry to butt in, but it's freezing hard, can we get moving?" said Sam.

Rose stepped up and sat in the cart. John moved up to make room as Carrie clambered in as well.

"Duw, it's cold enough to freeze a polar bear's bum!" quipped Carrie. "Cwtch up John, Rose. We need to keep warm. Come on. I'm colder than an icicle." Reluctantly John scooted toward his sister. "You, too, Rose. Come on, huddle up."

John found himself with Carrie on one side and Rose on the other. He sighed and put his arms around both of them. Sam shook the reins and Senator began to clip clop along the road through Crynant to the mountain track.

The wagon continued on its way with some friendly chatter about the play and the evening's rehearsal. Their breath streamed like that of a snorting bull in the darkness.

John continued to be disturbed by Rose's presence. To his relief she appeared to be unaware of the effect she was having on him and he relaxed a little. Gradually the conversations halted and both Carrie and Rose began to nod off on John's shoulder. He looked fondly at his sister and turned to study Rose's features. She had thick dark hair with a soft wave; her skin was clear and fresh. He noted how the cold had tinged the end of her nose pink and there was a glow in her heart-shaped face. She wasn't beautiful but strikingly attractive with dark lashes that rested like spider's legs on her cheek. Her cheekbones were pronounced and she had full lips with a pretty cupid bow that pouted provocatively. John tuned his head quickly. He didn't understand why he was looking at her in this way and remonstrated with himself inside his head. He was anxious to be home.

Once at Hendre, Sam unhitched the cart and took Senator into the stable. Laura rushed in promising to make a cup of tea as Carrie and John stepped down. Rose was the last to move. She yawned. John was cross with himself as he found his eyes wandering to her full breasts where the material strained against them as she stretched. He helped her out of the wagon and she stood directly in front of him; so very close. Angry with himself and without a word he turned on his heel and went smartly into the farmhouse. He could feel Carrie's eyes on him, looking after him curiously. He knew she would think he was being rude as it was unlike him not to say goodnight.

John fled inside and banged the door. Ernie was sitting in a chair by the fire, John breezed past him and ran up the stairs. He tiptoed into Bethan's bedroom where his little girl lay fast asleep. His heart swelled with love and emotion. How could he raise her alone? Jenny had been wonderful with her. He didn't have an Auntie Annie to run to now. John bent over and kissed her lightly on her forehead. She stirred slightly and not wanting to disturb her further he crept out quietly. He could hear the rumble of voices downstairs and not wanting to be challenged on his behaviour he went straight to his room and lay on the bed. His eyes were fixed on the ceiling in an unblinking stare. The moonlight intruded through the open curtains, poking its frosty fingers into the corner of the room where Jenny had her dressing table and vanity set. Her hairbrush was still sitting there as if she had just used it, her powder and puff sat proudly on top. John sighed in despair, would there ever be anyone like Jenny again?

He turned over in stubborn defiance unaccepting of the feelings, which had surprised him that evening. How could he be so disloyal and a traitor to his wife? His heart was racing; his mind was raging against him. He knew sleep would come late that night.

Downstairs Carrie had settled in the chair opposite Ernie and told him about the rehearsal and John's odd behaviour. "It's early days, yet, for him, Cariad. He needs to grieve. It must be hard."

"I'm sure he blames Bethan for Jenny's death," admitted Carrie.

"You could be correct but he won't dwell on it."

"I hope you're right," said Carrie uncertainly. "You never know with John."

"No... he's got a personal battle to fight but I have every faith he'll come through... but what about you?"

"Me?"

"Yes, you. You have had that terrible news about... Michael," he hardly dared say his name. "But you seem to have tried to wipe him from your mind, working, rehearsing, doing all sorts but not sharing how you feel."

"Nor will I. Duw, Ernie, I must keep sane. I throw myself into my work and everything else so I won't have to deal with it. Life is too cruel. I can't believe he's gone... all our plans... our future... snuffed out in an instant. It's not fair."

"No, but there, life's like that. The only thing to do when knocked down is to come up fighting and believe the best is yet to come."

"I wish I could..." said Carrie her eyes misting up.

"Cariad, I can't believe Michael has gone either. It was a shock to us all. That I never had an inkling ... but there, I had been shot so I suppose that dulled my senses for a while. I know he would not want you to be alone."

"Yes, he said that." Carrie stifled a sob.

"Cariad, it's all right to cry. And cry you should, cry the rain. It's an old saying but it's true and you will feel so much better. No one wants you to forget him. I know it's early days but you of all people should know how important it is to move on."

"I know… I know but every time I think of him the pain cuts me like a knife. Sorry, Ernie. I know you're only trying to help."

Carrie rose and crossed to the old man and kissed his weather beaten wrinkled forehead. "Night, Ernie."

She slipped out of the kitchen and upstairs to her room where she quietly got ready for bed trying not to disturb the sleeping Naomi. She would be glad when the little girl started back to school and her bed had been put in the attic so she could sorrow in privacy but then again. The body of the little one brought her great comfort on a night like tonight. She snuggled down but like John sleep was long in coming.

CHAPTER TWENTY-SEVEN

Christmas

The final preparations for Christmas were in progress and the company had safely completed the technical rehearsal without too many mishaps. They were getting organised for the dress run. There was much excitement backstage and both John and Carrie found themselves being swept along by the fun of it.

The bubble of excited chatter filled backstage as costumes were fitted, makeup slapped on. John in a kimono top and loose trousers was attaching his hat complete with a long black pigtail, a Chinaman's queue, down his back. He was trying to secure both that and a bootlace for his moustache but not having much success.

Rose laughed, "I should forget the moustache. The last thing you want is for it to fall off in the middle of your song."

"It is a comedy," rebuffed John.

"But that's the wrong sort of comedy," asserted Rose with a rascally look.

Rose looked stunning with her hair tied up and a pair of knitting needles pushed through for effect. She was dressed in a floor length kimono that had been embroidered as richly as possible, in these straightened times, and with her rosebud lips accentuated she really looked the part. John found himself staring at her in admiration. This was the woman who had been instrumental in saving his life. He shook his head to bring himself back to reality. "I expect you're right," he muttered.

"Of course, I'm right," she smiled. "Oh, there's my cue." Rose stepped on stage with her entourage covered by a giant parasol with ribbons streaming down from it hiding her face. John watched admiringly from the wings.

In the camp Michael was assessing their rations for their

Christmas lunch. One of their team, Clemans, had been caught uncoupling a supply wagon from the train. His punishment was to be sent down the mine at Kazimer. Luckily, a Polish mining engineer, had insisted that Clemans work with him in the disaster and rescue squad thus preventing him from working in the extremely dangerous conditions of the mine, which was prone to collapse, rock falls and slides. It was easier to dig miners out than be dug out and Clemans was grateful for this. As they descended in the cage he would keep spirits high by singing, "You are my sunshine", at the top of his voice.

Michael heard the voice and the song as footsteps approached the hut. He hid the secret stash and replaced the loose floorboards covering it with an old rag mat that Hicks had struggled to make out of scrap bits of material and odds and ends. They used to sing or shout to announce their approach with the German guards like an early warning system. The door opened and Clemans hobbled in using a makeshift crutch from a branch off a tree. The guard shoved him inside and slammed the door.

"What happened to you?"

"Damn wooden strut fell on me when I was dragging someone clear. Fell on him, too. He died." The occupants of the hut fell silent. They contemplated their fate, as it could have been anyone of them. "They only good thing is the busted leg has got me out of that hell-hole until it mends, which could be a very long time. Here…" Clemans removed a couple of nubs of coal from inside his trousers.

"How did you get away with that?"

"Easy. They just think I'm a very impressive chap," he winked. "I stuff a bit down there on the outward journey and replace it with coal. They believe I'm a big boy," and he laughed. "Anyway, how we doing for grub?"

"Not bad. We've enough spuds to go round. Hicks managed to steal a cabbage; Wilkinson nabbed a swede and carrots. We've enough for a veritable feast!" said Michael.

"And the meat? Don't suppose you want one of the boys to catch a few rats?"

"Er … No. No matter how hungry we are I don't think we'd

run to that – anyway," Michael smirked, "I was saving the best for last. Marshall has snaffled two chickens. Rumour has it that we are to be given half a horse's head to put in our usual broth."

"Chickens, yes. Horse's head, no. We had horses on the farm at home. They were like friends. No matter how hungry I am I couldn't bring myself to eat them," said a chap called Evans.

"Count me in," said Hicks. "Puts a whole new meaning on the phrase 'I could eat a horse'. If you're starving even rats would be on the menu," he said seriously. "I want to survive this place. Do you know there's a death camp just down the road? Place called Auschwitz the guard said. Only twenty miles away from us. And another called Oswiecim. Those poor buggers would be glad of anything. I intend to try and keep my strength up." He laughed and raised his arm strongman style as if to show off his muscle. "If it's edible I'll eat it."

The others fell quiet, as a few had heard about the notorious death camp where Jews were starved and gassed. It didn't bear thinking about. At least they were faring better than many other POWs.

Michael's thoughts again turned to Carrie. He had to survive or he would never see her again and that didn't bear thinking about.

Matthew had written twice more to Carrie. He had no way of knowing if the letters had got through. He sat on the train he had boarded in Hamburg. He was travelling back on a dangerous and hazardous journey to cross through Germany and into occupied France.

Matthew had been instrumental in enlisting Norwegian Saboteurs to prevent the German nuclear energy project from acquiring heavy water, deuterium oxide, which could be used to produce nuclear weapons.

At Vermork, Norsk Hydro built the first plant capable of producing heavy water a by-product of fertiliser production. Bombing raids were orchestrated to obliterate the power station at the Rjukan waterfall in Telemark, Norway. The

French secretly transported the heavy water firstly to Oslo, and Perth in Scotland and then to France. It was imperative that the Nazi's were prevented in using this water for the production of nuclear weapons. Matthew had been on covert operations with the Norwegian Resistance to destroy the plants. Operation Grouse had been successful, not so Operation Freshman. Operation Gunnerside was scheduled for early 1943.

Miraculously, Matthew had escaped from the Gestapo who had captured the survivors of the gliders, tug and Handley Halifax bomber, which had crashed short of their target before completing their mission.

The vicious Gestapo interrogated captors with no mercy and then executed all survivors. Matthew was now on his way back having been helped by resistance fighters in each country. He was returning to England to oversee Operation Gunnerside and SOE-train Norwegian Commandos for the final push in annihilating the plant. His knowledge and intelligence was vital to the programme, but he needed to stay alive.

Matthew froze as a group of SS officers boarded the train. They walked through the corridors looking in each carriage and asking for papers of anyone they thought of as suspicious.

Matthew pulled his hat down over his eyes feigning sleep. He pretended to drool with a few snorts and some gentle snoring. The carriage door opened. A man with a wolfish face, and mercenary features kicked Matthew's foot with his jackboot. Matthew snorted as he acted awaking.

"Wacht auf! Wake up. Papiere bitte."

Matthew pretended to be groggy and fumbled around in his coat for his papers and passed them to the officer who eyed him disdainfully. He gave them a cursory look and thrust them back at Matthew.

Matthew said nothing and put them away. The officer made as if to go and then turned sharply and demanded where Matthew was going, "Wo gehst du hin?"

Matthew looked up, "Mein Endziel oder die nächste Station?" he queried in perfect German asking if the officer meant his final destination or the next station where he would stop and change train.

The SS officer sneered, "Versuchen Sie nicht, schlau zu sein. Endziel, bitte." He accused Matthew of trying to be clever and demanded the final destination.

Matthew's heart was now almost leaping out of his chest, yet his demeanour was calm and collected, "Es gibt keine Notwendigkeit, unhöflich zu sein." He coolly commented that there was no need for the man to be rude. He knew he was risking a lot but he needed time to think.

The German bellowed for him to answer the question, "Beantworte die Fragen!"

Matthew raised his eyebrow and responded curtly, "Dusseldorf."

The officer didn't respond and strutted up the corridor, his face a picture of distaste.

Matthew breathed a sigh of relief but his heart didn't stop lurching toward his mouth. Matthew knew he had to keep calm; he had a long way to go before he could contact the French Resistance and arrange to get home.

Christmas at Hendre was a seemingly cheerful affair. Everyone sat around the stout oak table with the extra leaves inserted, in the parlour. There was as much going on under the surface of the lively banter as there was on show. Ernie, as inscrutable as ever, watched the faces of those around him as they tucked into their Christmas feast.

Megan and Thomas, he could see, were recovering from the loss of their baby. He noted, the bending of their heads together as if sharing a private joke but the pain was still evident in Megan's eyes and her mother Nancy was carefully watching her daughter with guarded affection. She smiled at Thomas and encouraged him to join in the family festivities and the promise of games after lunch, almost as if she needed to speak to Megan alone. Ernie wondered why?

His eyes flicked across to Carrie who was putting on a brave show for everyone present but whose usual lofty poise and vivaciousness was somewhat diminished and she was not as forthcoming as usual. These were things that most wouldn't notice but Ernie did.

Little Naomi was entranced and somewhat overwhelmed

by everything. Having been used to meagre rations of dried and processed food this all seemed like a dream to her. She chatted happily to young Bethan and it was clear that Naomi had physically recovered from her shocking ordeal but as she chose who to speak to around the table it was apparent that not everyone came into her circle of trust and that he, Ernie, was privileged in that fact.

Sarah sat next to the children. Gone was her sultry seductiveness. She appeared to engage readily with them but was reluctant to converse with anyone else at the table. Laura simply cut her dead by ignoring her as if she wasn't there and Sam never allowed his glance to stray in her direction.

Rose was magnanimous. She behaved with quiet reserve, speaking when spoken to and very little more. Ernie noted her covert glances at John who was understandably reticent to communicate with anyone other than Carrie or himself. But he did spot John's reaction when he and Rose reached together for the bowl of potatoes and their hands touched. John quickly withdrew his hand as if stung and Rose apologised in a shaky voice but no one else was aware of the action that to Ernie highlighted the obvious chemistry between them.

Ernie scratched his stubbly chin as everyone fell onto their plates of food like ravenous tribesmen who hadn't eaten for a week. He helped himself to some potatoes and listened to the bits of chatter that surfaced from them as they cleared their plates.

Naomi looked up questioningly at Ernie and asked, "What's this we're eating?"

"Why, it's roast goose."

"Ain't never ate that before."

"Haven't," corrected Sarah. "Haven't eaten that before."

"No, me neither," said Naomi and giggled. "Is 'em those big white birds?"

"Are they?" said Sarah.

"You tell me, I'm asking the question…" There was a twinkle in the child's eye, as she tried to suppress her mirth, which set Sarah and the children off into giggles.

Ernie, too, found their laughter infectious and the mood in the room shifted and lifted becoming more relaxed.

The Christmas pantomime had been well received. The hall filled each night as those in the surrounding villages came to see and applaud Crynant's latest offering. The local paper had given it a sparkling review and the majority of the cast were disappointed that there were just two performances left.

Megan had stood out in her role of Aladdin and Thomas watched her with pride from the back of the auditorium. He moved to one side as the hall door opened and light from the street gas lamp spilled into the dark theatre. Thomas hurriedly closed it cutting off the source of the light and eyed the stranger. It was no one he recognised.

In the wings, Rose was waiting for her entrance for her scene with the comic policemen as Wishy-Washy and Widow Twanky cavorted on the stage with the mangle routine. John caught the sleeve of his kimono on a protruding nail on the side of the scenery as he somersaulted off. The flat shook. Rose gasped and attempted to steady it. John bounced up but not without ripping his sleeve. Once more he found himself looking directly at Rose. She quickly lowered her eyes as he brushed past her silently cursing.

In seconds Rose swept on stage. John paused to watch her before realising he needed to repair his sleeve and quickly. He dashed to the makeshift dressing room shared with other male members of the cast and tried to find someone to stitch the tear or pin it for him all the while keeping an ear out for the lines that were being said. As the character of Wishy-Washy he had an on stage friendship with the Princess but in real life he was finding it difficult to be around her.

John rummaged around the surfaces unable to find a needle or cotton but he discovered a stash of safety pins that he struggled to try and utilise. Needing someone to do it for him he found himself alone in the room as the other male members of the company were on stage.

John went to try and find someone to help him and walked straight into Rose as she was hurrying off stage. "Can I help?" she whispered.

"Jawch, yes, please. Can you pin this for me or it's going to get caught on everything."

Rose bent her head, took the pins from John and he held his arm up. He allowed himself to study the concentration in her face as she brought the torn ends of the sleeve together. "There that should hold it until you can get it repaired." She brought her head up suddenly and John found himself gazing into Rose's darkly passionate eyes. They stood together for only a moment but in that minute John knew that his own eyes were burning into hers and that he felt something for her.

John gulped and Rose hurriedly turned away, "I have to change."

John whispered, "Thank you," and observed her as she moved away. So absorbed was he in watching her that he almost missed his next cue. The next scene it was if he was some sort of automaton; he delivered his lines but remained inside himself mulling over the feelings that were escalating inside him, which he felt were wrong and too soon. He owed this woman his life but with Jenny only gone a few months, his head told him, it was wrong and he had no right to be thinking of another. John made up his mind that he would not engage in any activity or work on the farm, which involved Rose. If he didn't have to work with her, he could ignore her and blank his feelings out.

At the curtain call he stood between Rose and Mr Segadelli. His throat constricted and he found it difficult to breathe as he held her hand and bowed. All he wanted to do was to turn and gaze at her and bring his own lips down on hers. As the final curtain drew he dropped her hand quickly and rushed off the set to get changed. He had one more performance to get through and then he would be free and there would be no more plays for him at Christmas or any other time. He stopped and turned at the dressing room door surveying the rest of the cast chattering and making their way to get changed. Rose was standing still at the end of the corridor staring at him with a mixture of hurt and disbelief. He abruptly turned and dived inside to the men's room as if it was some kind of refuge. He hardly heard the lively chat and banter from the others but it was just a jumble of meaningless words. He was trying to work out how he could avoid her on the way home. He was used to sitting between Carrie and Rose on the ride up and determined that he would take the reins this time and not sit in the back.

John hung back in the dressing room, dawdling more than usual until everyone had left. He breathed a sigh of relief and wondered if everyone knew he'd got the shine for Rose. He hoped not.

John now changed stepped out and took his tunic costume through to the little workroom where the costume ladies sat ready to effect minor repairs. Mrs Parry was still there, just about to lock up. "John?" John shuffled toward her with his tunic and pointed out the offending sleeve. "Don't worry, Bach. I'll soon remedy that so I will. Give it to me and I'll do it first thing."

John handed her the costume and turned to go coming face to face with Rose who was holding her obi, an oriental sash that had become unstitched. He tried to dodge past her in a fluster and what followed was a strange dance of sidesteps as he attempted to leave. Rose giggled before finally moving aside to let him through. John's face was scarlet as he flew past her and clattered out into the hall.

Mrs Parry looked after him in surprise, "Whatever's got into him? It's like his pants were on fire!"

John clomped into the hall. It was a cold night and the others were waiting inside in the warm until the last possible minute. He frowned as he saw Carrie deep in conversation with a man.

Sam stood up and grinned when he saw John. "Come on. We are all tired out. Not like you to be last. Where's Rose?"

"How should I know?" snapped John and almost bit his tongue. "Last time I saw her she was talking to Mrs Parry... Who's that?" He pointed at the stranger in their midst.

Sam shrugged, "Someone Carrie knows."

"Well I didn't think it was a travelling salesman," he said sarcastically. "There's something familiar about him..."

Carrie spotted John and beckoned him over. She was smiling brightly. "John, I want you to meet Matthew, Matthew Reynolds. We were in France together."

John extended his hand politely and they shook hands. He had a firm grip.

"It was an excellent show, well done!"

"You saw it?"

"Most of it. I think I missed the first five minutes. You were very funny."

John blushed, "Don't think I'll be doing anymore am dram," he said. "I just needed to take my mind off a few things that's all."

Matthew nodded in understanding, "Yes, I was very sorry to hear about our wife."

John struggled to keep a lid on his emotions and rising fury. He felt stabs of jealousy when he saw the way Matthew looked at Carrie. He was angry that his personal tragedy had been revealed in his absence and he was angry with himself at the way he was feeling and behaving. He managed to ask, "Staying locally?"

"Yes, the Star and Garter."

John saw Rose emerge from the back; he nodded curtly and escaped outside into the frosty night air. A muscle pulsed in his cheek as he clambered up and took the reins. His heart was racing; a feeling akin to fear fluttered in his stomach.

The door to the hall squeaked open and the last few members of the company stumbled out onto the road. John tried not to look at anyone but every now and then he would sneak a quick peek at Matthew and Carrie who appeared to be in deep conversation. Rose was standing quietly uncertain where to go. "Hurry up, Carrie. We need to get to our beds," he said gruffly and then regretted his words as Laura tittered.

Sam and Laura hopped aboard as Carrie bade Matthew farewell. As Carrie stepped into the cart Matthew called loud enough for all to hear, "See you tomorrow, then." He strode off jauntily into the darkness, whistling cheerfully.

Rose was still standing awkwardly. Carrie urged her, "Go on Rose. You sit up front with John.

John tensed but knew there was nothing he could do and he tried to maintain his equilibrium as he encouraged Senator into a trot and they made their way back to Hendre Farm.

CHAPTER TWENTY-EIGHT

Assessments and closure

John, tight-lipped, jumped down from the wagon and held Senator steady as the others climbed out seemingly unaware of John's awkwardness. Rose lingered as the others made their way back to the cottage. "Do you want any help, John?"

"No," his reply came too quickly and was too vehement. He checked himself and continued in a better tone, "I can manage. Thank you."

He began to unhitch the wagon and led Senator into the barn. Rose looked puzzled and hurt. She took hold of the cart's wooden shafts and dragged the empty dray to its resting spot close to the roundhouse. She stopped and stared at the barn door where Senator was stabled and unable to help herself she marched into the building. John was in the process of removing the animal's stout leather collar. He looked up in surprise when he saw Rose approaching him. "I said I could manage," he said brusquely.

Rose ignored him, "This is hard enough for one person, besides I need to learn how it's done and what goes where. I've returned the cart to its place."

"Thank you," said John regretting his previous churlishness. "If you really want to help, once I've removed his harness and all the tackle you could give him a good brush down while I get his supper.

Rose nodded and picked up a bucket of items, rug and grooming brush. She coaxed the shire into his stall, flung the rug over the door and began brushing him down. Senator's face was one of ecstasy as he luxuriated in the grooming, which he clearly enjoyed giving the odd overjoyed whinny. She combed the tangles from his mane and tail and his newly brushed coat gleamed in the lamplight. Rose patted the gentle horse before taking the rug and throwing it over him, to keep out the chill of the night. She was nuzzling the gentle shire when John returned with a fresh net of hay and bucket of oats. He strung the hay up on the stable door and hoisted the bucket of oats inside. Senator focused on his food munching contentedly after his night's work.

"He needs water," observed Rose.

"I'll get it." John escaped from the barn and picked up a wooden pail. He dipped it in the water butt and retraced his steps the water slopped as he walked. He was feeling nervous, uncomfortable and confused. He strode to the stable and set down the bucket. Senator bowed his head, dipped his mouth in the vessel and took a long deep draught of water. Rose stepped out with John and securely fastened the door. She paused and leaned over it watching the horse. "He's such a lovely creature. So big and strong and yet so gentle."

"Aye, he is that. We'll soon have to retire him from farm work. Machinery is taking over and he's getting on but he'll still be good for taking us into the village. I can't see that changing or us getting a motor car," said John feeling a little easier.

Rose sighed and stretched. She lifted her arms above her head and yawned, her gingham shirt strained across her breasts. She smiled up at John. "Think I'll call it a night. Lots to do tomorrow apart from the last show. A girl needs her beauty sleep."

John swallowed hard and his voice turned husky, "Don't think you need beauty sleep, Rosie. You are pretty enough as it is." As soon as he said it, he regretted his words.

"Pretty? Why thank you kind, Sir."

John cleared his throat uncomfortably, "Yes, well I'm off to bed, too. Like you said we've got another long day ahead of us. We need our rest." He strutted out of the barn giving Rose no choice but to follow. He bolted the barn securely behind him and stepped off to the house calling, "Good night."

He could feel Rose's eyes on him. He didn't stop and he didn't turn. He hurried to the safety of Hendre.

Carrie was sitting with Ernie enjoying a cup of tea. She looked up at John, "There's a fresh pot made. Plenty left... You were a bit quiet tonight."

John took a mug from the cupboard and poured some tea,

"Got things on my mind." He took the seat opposite Ernie and cradled the beaker warming his cold, chapped sore hands. He could feel Ernie's eyes on him and began to squirm uncomfortably. "Think I'll take this up with me."

"Don't go," pleaded Carrie. "Don't you want to hear my news?"

John stopped and returned to his seat. He never could refuse one of his sister's requests. For too long they'd had no one else in the world but each other. John's hard expression softened, "Well, Cariad. What is it?"

"Matthew has safely returned. He has to go back to Scotland next week to train some Norwegian SOEs for an important operation that could mean the end of the war. That was his last mission in the field. He is taking up a training post in Scotland."

"And that's important to me because…?"

"It's not. Not to you. But it could be to me. I would appreciate it if you could be civil to him the next time you meet."

Ernie jumped in, "Matthew is in love with our Carrie. Now with Michael gone we must afford to be more generous of spirit with her friends."

John had the good grace to look contrite, "Sorry, yes of course, Cariad. Whatever you wish. I am just extremely tired that's all. Sorry. Think I'll go up, now. Night all."

John drained his mug and placed it on the table and retreated through the pine door and up the stairs. He flopped down on his bed and stared at the ceiling. "Duw, Jenny I miss you. I wish you were here with me and Bethan. I wouldn't have my head turned if I had you by my side."

John drew his knees up into a foetal position as if to comfort himself. He turned his head and stared at the wall, which shimmered with frosty patches in the moonlight shafts, which nosily probed their way into the room and sniffed around the wall. An owl hooted somewhere outside and John felt compelled to rise and cross to the window. He intended to draw the drapes on the inquisitive moon but was mesmerised by a beautiful barn owl swooping low along the yard and catching an unsuspecting mouse scampering in search of left

338

over chicken feed. He pulled at one curtain when a movement caught his eye. He saw Rose sitting on the gate to the meadow gazing out into the field. She appeared to be surrounded by an aura of heavenly light. She slowly turned her head and looked back at the farm. Convinced she had seen him he drew the curtain blocking out the curious night. He stopped and peered through a small chink and jumped in shock as Rose's face seemed to ripple and change into that of Jenny. An involuntary cry escaped him and he flung himself back on the bed. "Why? Why had he had that strange vision?"

Without bothering to change his clothes. He lay on the bed fully dressed for sometime before drifting off into a restless sleep.

Carrie chatted with Ernie. Her manner was serious and she questioned her dear friend, "Am I doing the right thing, Ernie? It seems too soon to move on from Michael. Oh, how my heart aches for him but…"

"Matthew is here and now. He wants to court you?"

"Yes."

"Cariad, only you can decide your destiny, the path you want to travel. No one would want to influence you."

"Meet him. Please, Ernie. Meet him. I'll feel a whole lot better if I know you approve. You always told me that my happiness lay in my own back yard."

"And so it does, Cariad. That hasn't changed. What will be will be." Ernie sighed, "Yes, I'll meet the young man. If you like him I'm sure he's a fine person. Now, up those stairs. It's time for bed. I'll wash these up and see you in the morning."

Carrie nodded and slipped across to the old man and kissed him tenderly on his cheek. "Duw, it's like kissing a Brillo pad, so it is. Those whiskers need coming off."

"Jawch, girl," he flustered.

"Don't ever leave us, Ernie. Will you? I couldn't bear it."

Ernie coloured up to his roots under his beret, a permanent fixture on his head, so it seemed. "I'll stay as long as I'm needed. You have my word," and he smiled. His face cracked like parchment and Carrie's eyes filled up. "I'll get the dogs in. It's too cold to be out tonight."

"In the glasshouse, they are. Settled together after their grub."

"Trix always slept in the kitchen. I'll bring them in."

Carrie opened the door and called to the dogs. They trotted into the kitchen glad to be in the warmth and settled on what once was the colourful rag mat, now faded after many washes and had seen better days.

She crossed to the door and looked back fondly at Ernie, "I love you, Ernie Trubshawe. Like a father you've been to me." Her eyes brimmed over with love and tears but before any could fall down her cheeks she vanished through the pine door and up the stairs.

Morning saw the usual hustle and bustle of farm life. John ensured Rose and Laura worked together to take the feed to the sheep. Sam and John saw to the milking before tending the iron fields around Gelli Galed trying to plough the frozen ground. It was tough and the plough often stuck, making it a two-man job.

Sarah was in situ with the children teaching them the piano, which she found easier when John was out of the house and Carrie had made her way into the village. She just had the one house call today and then she was meeting Matthew.

A strange collection of feelings ran through her. She was glad that Matthew had survived but wished in her heart that it had been Michael who had returned. Carrie reprimanded herself, as she knew that was a cruel thought to have.

Carrie scooted away after treating Mrs Ellis who had twisted her ankle when she'd slipped on the icy path outside her house. Carrie pedalled off toward the Star and Garter, where Matthew was waiting. He sat in the bar and Carrie hesitantly entered. It was unusual for a woman to enter a public house alone. She spotted him nursing a beer sitting by the blazing fire and joined him.

He stood up when he saw her. His face creased in smiles and he went to the bar to get her a drink. "What would you like?"

"Um… I'll just have an orange, please."

"Nothing stronger?"

"No, thanks. I have to stage-manage a show tonight. It's the last one. We don't want any mistakes." Carrie sat by the fire and studied Matthew's back. He was certainly tall and looked incredibly strong. As she was admiring him she heard Michael's voice in her head, "Wait for me, Carrie."

Her eyes smarted with tears and she sniffed them back but remained bright eyed, as Matthew returned with her drink. He looked into her sweet open face, "What's wrong?"

"Nothing."

"It doesn't look like nothing."

"I was just thinking of Michael."

"Ah." Matthew fell silent a moment and then looked up, "I'm sorry he's gone. Truly I am but you must forgive me if it also pleases me because now I can try and win you over."

Carrie smiled, "Michael was my first love and will always be in my heart but I promise you I will try…"

"And be my girl?"

Carrie nodded, "But take it slowly."

"I have no choice. I don't have long before I leave for Scotland. The Norwegian SOEs will be vital in putting us back in charge of the war. The sooner it's ended and Hitler is gone, the better."

The two chatted happily until the fire had died down and the landlord came round to toss another couple of logs on the fire and some nutty slack. Carrie stood up, "I must get home, and get ready for tonight. I'll see you at the hall."

Matthew stood up and took her hands. He pulled her into him. She couldn't completely relax but allowed him to hold her. He kissed her lightly resisting the urge to become more passionate. Carrie extricated herself from his grasp and fled.

Taking a large gulp of fresh air after the beery and smoky aroma of the pub, which had clung to her clothes, Carrie climbed on her bike and began the long cycle home. Again Michael's words echoed in her head, "Wait for me, Carrie." With the strength of a demon she pedalled furiously up the Neath Road where she normally would dismount and walk. She turned into The Crescent and freewheeled down the hill. She hoped the breeze blowing in her face would clear her head.

Michael had been forced back down the mine. The work was long and hard. He deemed it to be one of the most dangerous mines in the world. They had already lost some men from their hut. As they travelled below ground in the flimsy cage he joined in with his other compatriots in boldly singing "You are my sunshine." As he sang the words he had a fleeting vision of Carrie in her uniform on her bike and crying. He stopped and whispered into increasing dark, "Wait for me, Carrie."

Shaffer, who was next to him queried, "Carrie? Is that your girl?"

Michael nodded proudly, "Yes and the only one for me."

"I hope my Betty waits for me, too. We'd only been married a few months when I was called up. It's hard not knowing. We thought she might be expecting. If she was, she'd have had it by now." The two fell silent while the others sang and they descended deeper into the pitch black of the passageways leading to the coalface.

The lights were dim as they left the cage and walked along the rocky tunnel. They passed the opening to a newer tunnel that had fallen in when the supporting props had broken and it caved in. They had been unable to rescue Marshall or Field who had been trapped by the ensuing rockslide and Michael was thankful he had got out before them at the end of a thirteen-hour shift. The smell of coal dust filled their nostrils. Their faces became smutty with dust as they dug at the rich vein of coal and loaded the wagons to be hauled back through the tunnel. The place was damp and water dripped where roots from ferns and other vegetation trailed down like tentacles.

The work was long and hard bearing no distinction from slave labour. He tried to sing but was choked up with the sooty particles, which floated and filled the air. He turned to Hicks, "We have to get out of here. Much more of this and we'll die. I don't want to be buried alive."

"You got a plan?"

"Not yet but I will."

The final performance had begun. The hall was packed.

Jack the Marker had taken the tickets and villagers from all around had come to be entertained for the final show. Carrie sat stage right, on the book cueing the lights, curtains and scene changes. It all seemed to be going smoothly.

The curtain came down on the first act and Rose went to check her props for the second act. John, too, had stepped onstage to ensure his bucket of bubbles was ready and the two came face-to-face. Flustered, John stepped back hurriedly into the same flat he had caught his sleeve on before and to his horror it crashed down on Rose. Cast members rushed to right the piece of scenery and John watched in dismay and then hurried to help Rose to her feet. She was somewhat dazed, having caught her head on a stage-weight. She leaned on him as he led her back to the dressing room, leaving Carrie and the others to sort out the mess and glitch in the show. With the curtain drawn and a brief apology to the audience for the small delay stage crew scurried around making the flat safe.

John knocked on the dressing room door not wanting to catch anyone in a state of undress but it seems the whole company had run to the stage to put things right. He sat her in a chair and took a wad of cotton wool from the makeshift counter top and gently dabbed at the trickle of blood that had started to trickle down her cheeks.

"Drat it! I hope it will stop and my make up will cover it."

"It doesn't look too bad. I'll get Carrie to look at it for you, after."

Rose stood up and swayed. She fell against him and this time, John embraced her holding her tight. He looked into her face and brought his lips to hers in a tender kiss before releasing her and stalking out from the room as other cast members came to see if she was okay. Rose looked after John, a faint smile playing on her lips. So, it wasn't her imagination. He did care. She plonked herself back down fending off everyone's questions and patted on some make-up to try and cover the developing bruise.

The play continued and at the final curtain the applause was enthusiastic as the company took their bow. The company danced off stage in a flurry of excitement. Mr Segadelli called,

"We can't let it end like this. We must have a small drink to celebrate. Who's coming to the Star?"

The actors shouted out their agreement and they raced to get changed. Carrie and her team began the big clear up. Mrs Tobin went around congratulating everyone. She turned to the stagehands, "Don't worry if everything's not done tonight. It's getting late and I'm sure you all want that drink. I'll be in tomorrow with some volunteers to finish up. Good job everyone. Well done!"

Folks made their escape.

Matthew was waiting for Carrie. "I'll give you a hand tomorrow. It should be fun. Ready?"

Carrie nodded and took his arm and they walked to the hostelry together. The place was full of happy smiling faces enjoying a small drink. Carrie searched around for Thomas and Megan who were sitting with John who was being unusually quiet.

Laura, Sam and Rose were at another table. Carrie noticed Rose glancing across at John with a hurt expression on her face. John simply averted his eyes and made out he was listening intently to his cousin and Megan chattering together.

Rose suddenly became more animated and turned her back on John and spoke with one of the stage crew who had bought a drink and sat alongside her. Carrie frowned. Something wasn't right. Whatever was going on between them? But she snapped out of this thinking and turned her attention to Matthew.

The days passed quickly and the time soon arrived for Matthew to travel to Scotland. Carrie bade him a fond farewell and wished him a safe and speedy journey. He was travelling to Arisaig where Carrie herself had trained and he was driving in an official car. "I promise I'll write."

"You'd better or I'll be back to haunt you," laughed Matthew as they stood by his vehicle. He put his arms around her and bowed his head to kiss her. The kiss was short and chaste. Matthew whispered, "I will make you love me. I swear. My love is strong and I'll make sure you never get tired of me."

Carrie laughed, "And just how do you propose to do that?"

"With tricks, skulduggery and love. I make this oath in your presence that I will do anything, absolutely anything to make you mine."

Carrie laughed again, "Get on with you. That's a pretty bold statement. I'll hold you to that."

He stooped and kissed her again and this time she was more willing to reciprocate. He stepped inside the car, wound down his window, "Don't forget me, Carrie Llewellyn." He blew her a kiss and set off from the Star.

CHAPTER TWENTY-NINE

1943 – 1944

The ensuing year passed quickly. Naomi returned to school and was thriving. She had formed a strong attachment to Bethan as if she was her own sister and with Sarah who discovered that the child had great musical talent. Exercises and scales were a thing of the past and now she was playing the piano quite beautifully. She had a light touch and a feel for the piano. The house was filled with music once more.

To Carrie things went on much as normal. The aching void in her heart for Michael had not diminished but she had been distracted somewhat by Matthew who wrote regularly and travelled to see her when he was able. They had been able to speak on the telephone once or twice and Matthew had divulged things that would have been censored in any letter. That contact and her work kept her occupied but she was worried by John, who had taken to sitting alone in the evening. He worked in a solitary fashion when it came to the farm. He didn't mix with the Land Girls except for Sarah who was more of a nanny to Bethan and, of course, Ernie..

Carrie confided her concerns to Ernie, "I don't know what's the matter with him. As soon as Bethan is in bed it's as if a light has gone out. His moods are as changeable as the seasons. He's not rude or anything, just not John, our strong dependable John."

"It's been hard for him losing Jenny, Cariad. I can understand his difficulty trying to raise young Bethan who's getting more like her mother in every way. She's a constant reminder of what he's lost."

"But how can we draw him out? He refuses to get involved with any community events ever again. Not even with the next Christmas play, not in any capacity. Even Thomas on his odd visits hasn't been able to resurrect any enthusiasm for anything."

"Cariad, nothing you or I do will make a difference. I feel that in a little while he will have an awakening, you mark my words."

"An awakening? Whatever do you mean? He's not going to get Jesus is he and join the Salvation Army?" she quipped.

Ernie chortled, "No, nothing like that. Besides John doesn't need a new suit." They laughed together at the memory of Ernie's naiveté, when he was in desperate need of new clothes and had joined God's Army for the new suit it provided.

"What can we do?"

"Nothing, Cariad. Let him be. I've a feeling things will change and quite soon."

Carrie frowned, then said acceptingly, "Very well. You always were something of an oracle. I'll trust your word."

"And you, Cariad. What about you?"

Carrie sighed. "Life is good on the district. I enjoy my job, although a part of me still hankers after the nursing I did in London working with the friends I made. Did you know that Lloyd and Pemb are married? Wed in Abergavenny and pulled two witnesses from off the street. Living in Monmouth, they are now, and she's expecting their first baby."

"Aye, you said. You also said they were to be thrown out of their digs once the baby arrived. The landlady refuses to have children in the house."

"I know. Pemb's at her wits' end; I don't know why landlords are so harsh. Just when they need a roof over their head it's to be taken from them."

"They'll be okay. I believe the Governors of the fancy school Lloyd teaches at will find them something. You'll see."

"I hope you're right, Ernie. I hope you're right. What about you? Your daughter?"

"When the war is over that's when decisions will be made. Until then, I'm fine where I am and so is she."

Carrie pursed her lips. She knew when to pursue a subject and when not to. Now was not the time. Whatever plan Ernie had for his future he was not willing to share it yet. She decided to change the subject. "I had another letter from Matthew, yesterday."

"I saw it on the mantelpiece."

"The Norwegian SOEs he trained were highly successful. In fact, some are already heralding it as the greatest success of the war."

"Remind me... What did they do?"

"Their sabotage actions together with the Allied bombing finally destroyed the plant producing heavy water. Operation Gunnerside I think he said."

"He'll be in trouble telling you all this. I thought sensitive information was always blacked out?"

"No, he told me on the phone. He was involved in one failed attempt when he was out there. I'm glad he's in a teaching capacity now and no more missions. Enough lives have been lost."

"Come to think of it I seem to remember reading something about it in the news although a lot of what the papers write is propaganda to keep up the country's morale."

Carrie sighed, "Yes, I expect you're right. You know, we're lucky, here in the country. Oh, I know things are tough with all the rationing but city dwellers have it a lot worse. The bombings and air raids keeping them awake at night., depriving them of sleep. At least, we don't have any terrible air raids or severe shortages on the farm."

Michael's hands were clammy. A bead of sweat dropped from his blackened brow. Using coal dust to black their faces and any visible skin they were camouflaged in the starless night. He and his companions had worked out a plan of escape and the moment was upon them. They timed the route of the searchlight as it flashed around the camp and realised that it was possible to scramble into the roof of their hut through an air vent. The timing had to be precise. Four of them had managed to climb out one at a time.

They could hear the rest of the prisoners being rousted out for parade and roll call while they remained hidden in the roof void. Not surprisingly shouts went up as the German guards began to search for the escapees. They brought ferocious German Shepherd dogs, which barked and slathered in their quest to find the missing men.

Michael and his companions remained silent and frozen as

guards blundered about turning over bunk beds, emptying the cupboards, lifting loose floorboards. They was a big hullaballoo when potato peelings were discovered that had been hidden under the floor. One guard became carried away and fired shots into the boards. Others raised their rifles and fired into the ceiling before stomping out to the next hut. Miraculously, no one was hit. The search was taken further outside the camp. Michael and his fellow escapees remained in their hiding place until the search party had returned and disbanded, and the dogs re-kennelled.

Now came the tricky part clambering from the void onto the roof in the cold night air and avoiding the sweeping searchlight. One at a time they dropped silently from the roof onto the dirt road behind the hut. They had a hundred and twenty yard gap between the back and the perimeter fence.

Hicks had a cutting tool he'd filched from the time he'd spent working on the railway sidings. He'd successfully smuggled it out and sharpened it. It was his job to run ahead and cut the wire. Michael watched anxiously as they waited for him to run. He kept low and threw himself on the ground as the light played around the camp.

Hicks sliced through the thick wire, effectively making a door, which he peeled back and slipped through. He dashed toward a clump of trees and waited. One by one they went. Michael was the last. He returned the wire to the fence. The longer the guards took to discover their escape route the better for them.

Hicks was a useful man as he spoke both Polish and German and was keen to visit his Polish girlfriend who, he insisted, would give them shelter, food and drink. By now the men were tired, hungry and eager for any kind of respite.

Dodging the soldiers they successfully made it to her house. All agreed after a good night's rest they would move on and try and meet the Russian troops they had heard were marching into Poland.

They were just enjoying a warm drink when a German armed 'home guard' walked into the house. He was as surprised as the men and none of Hicks' persuasive chat in both Polish and German could fool the soldier, who covered them with his firearm and marched them into the street amidst the weeping and wailing of the Polish woman. They were handed over to the Wehrmacht.

The men marched reluctantly, constantly prodded in the back by a rifle barrel, to a Division HQ where they were brutally questioned before being pushed into a damp cellar with some Russian Prisoners. They were returned to camp to the rousing cheers and applause of the other inmates.

Their punishment was to be forced back down the mines with its dangerous labyrinth of tunnels, cave ins, rock falls and rats. The short taste of freedom gave them a thirst to escape again and it was not long before they were plotting once more to get away.

Carrie had just finished a cup of tea with Howie Price and had enjoyed a chat. They both had suffered losses in the war and Carrie would listen to Howie talking about his son and she, in turn, felt free to talk about Michael. "I can't believe he's gone. It doesn't seem possible."

"I know what you mean. But at least our last memories of them are good. They were both courageous and did their duty."

"I wear his identity discs. Keep them close to my heart. I don't think I'll ever take them off." She pulled them out from under her uniform and showed him. "Duw, I miss him." And in the safety of Howard Price's front room she sobbed.

Howie placed his thin arms in his threadbare knitted cardigan around her and held her until her weeping subsided. "There, there, Cariad. Life must go on. What about the other young man, Matthew, is it?"

Carrie sniffed and nodded, "We write and he comes to see me when he can but he'll never be Michael."

"No, fach. No one can take your first love's place. But at one time you thought you loved him, too. Remember?"

Carrie nodded, "I know, but..."

"Take advice from an old man, don't deny yourself love because of what you've lost. You cared for him once but cared for Michael more. Now that Michael is gone can't you open your heart to him?"

Carrie took a deep breath, what Howie said made sense. She nodded, "Matthew is a good man. I know. There's truth in what you say. I'm lucky to be given a second chance."

"There's a good girl. Next time he comes to see you, bring him along to meet me."

"I will, Howie, I will," she promised. "And now I must be gone. I've children to see and a report to do for Dr Rees."

Carrie gave the old boy a quick peck on his cheek and left the house. She mounted her bike and sped through the village. Her talk with Howie had done her good and she resolved to open her heart to Matthew the next time she saw him.

John was sitting on Bull Rock surveying the lush green Dulais Valley. Even though nature was in slumber and waiting to wake it was still a beautiful sight. He gazed at his land, the forestation and verdant vegetation. He rubbed his tired eyes, tired from disturbed sleep tormented by dreams he couldn't remember but that left a residual feeling of panic and despair. Bonnie and Prince were at his feet. They bounded through the bracken and snuffled around the rabbit holes and badger runs.

Ernie was milking with Sam, Laura was tending the new born lambs and calves. John had excused himself and taken a walk toward Gelli Galed. He had felt a change in himself this morning. His acute depression that he smothered and disguised around Bethan had dramatically lessened. It was as if the painful emptiness in in the pit of his belly and his anguish torn heart had opened up ready to be filled once more. Over eighteen months had elapsed since Jenny's death and John had denied his feelings, ignored them and now he realised it was time to face what his heart had been telling him.

Crunching footsteps were heard on the cliff top. He looked up and smiled as Rose scrambled down the bank toward the rock. She clambered up beside him.

"I didn't think you'd come," he whispered.

Rose looked out across the valley and down to the now benignly innocent Black River that wove its way through the valley. "It's beautiful. The view here is quite breath taking."

"Even more so when the trees have their coats of leaves."

"They are just beginning to bud. I just love it when

everything explodes into life after the long winter months. But you didn't ask me here to see the view…"

"No." John turned to her and drank in her eyes, her burnished hair. "You're beautiful."

Rose dropped her head shyly, "Thank you. Although, I wouldn't describe myself that way. My features are not even symmetrical."

"Aren't they? I hadn't noticed," murmured John softly.

"Why? Why did you ask me to meet you after all this time? Ever since that kiss you haven't looked at me, barely spoken to me… I don't understand…"

"It's been hard, losing Jenny, with Bethan an' all."

"Yes?"

"I can't deny there's something between us but I was ashamed. It was too soon, it didn't seem right. It was all at the wrong time." John paused; he raised his hand and gently stroked her face with his fingertips. His next words came out in a rush, "If you agree, I think the time is right now."

"Just what am I agreeing to?"

"Rose, will you walk out with me? Take it slowly, steadily, see if it's what we both want and see where it leads?"

Rose studied the sincerity in John's expression and the ice chips in her heart melted. "I was so hurt… I didn't know what to think…"

"And what do you think, now?"

Rose faced John and gently touched his mouth, "My lips burned with your kiss for months."

"Only months?" said John mockingly, "I must be losing my touch."

Rose laughed. It was a rich sound and John felt his heart thump wildly in his chest. She sighed, "What do you expect from me?"

"I make no promises, except that I want to get to know you, find out all about you. As I said, take it slowly, see what happens. I want you to get to know Bethan and then…" he tailed off. "I don't even know your favourite colour."

"It's red. Red is the colour of life, vibrant and alive."

"That's one ticked off the list," he laughed. His face became serious once more, "What do you say, Rose? Will you give this unfathomable thing between us a chance? Will you be my girl?"

Rose slipped her arms around John's neck and nestled her head on his chest, "I think I'd like that... How do we progress? What do we tell people?'

"Nothing. I'll take you to the sixpenny hop next week and we'll take a trip to Neath. Do all the things a young couple should do and that work will allow. What do you say?"

Rose nodded and very gently John bent his head to hers and kissed her softly and tenderly with such emotion that he left her gasping.

"That's sorted, then." John smiled and took her hand to help her down. The dogs came bounding up and wouldn't stop dancing around her until she had petted them. Then they sped off again. "Do you know? I don't even know how old you are, if you have a middle name, your surname, where you are from..."

Rose stopped his mouth with her hand, "All in good time. Let's walk while we still have the sun and it's dry. We can talk on the way. I want to know all about you, too."

John glanced up and a small cloud wisped and changed shape almost resembling a woman's lips turned upward in a smile. He looked across the valley where a small waterfall splashed and clouded with mist. The hint of a rainbow could be seen in the haze. John took it as a good sign. He had a gut feeling that Jenny would approve and had given him her blessing.

Back at Hendre Carrie was amazed to see an official car standing in the yard. Matthew was leaning against it smoking a cigarette. He threw it to the ground and stubbed it out when he caught sight of her wheeling her bike through the gate. He ran toward her. She looked puzzled, "Matthew! Whatever are you doing here? I wasn't expecting you until March."

Matthew took her hands, "I've been called out into the field, one last time."

"But, I thought that was it. You'd be training and teaching now."

"So did I, but now the Russians are on side. They want me

to take another team into Germany. I can't tell you anymore than that."

"But going back... you could be killed."

"I think I've still got a few of my nine lives left." He paused and looked deep into her eyes. "Carrie, marry me. There's nothing to stop you now. You can learn to love me, you can. Marry me before I go away."

Carrie gasped, "When do you leave?"

"In three weeks. I have to return for a week of briefing and final training before the off. I have been granted leave the weekend before we go and just a few days here with you, now. Can we arrange to be wed on that weekend's leave? Please?"

Carrie was flummoxed. Confusion raged in her head, "I..."

"Think about it. I'll be at the Star and Garter. Meet me later tonight and give me your answer, please."

He took her in his arms and brought his lips down on hers and Carrie allowed herself to melt in his arms.

Matthew stepped back into his car and drove off down the track. Carrie watched him with a strange expression on her face. What should she do? She ran into the house calling, "Ernie!"

But Ernie wasn't there.

Michael believed as did all POWs that it was their duty to escape. Their first attempt had been unsuccessful and with the approach of the Russians marching through Poland the German guards were getting the jitters. Two prisoners from another hut had been sent to Colditz Castle after having tried to escape several times and the Germans believed the castle was escape proof. Michael and his stalwart group decided they would try again. Michael believed it would be wrong to wait, that they would try again immediately. The guards would not be expecting that.

They already had their route planned and Michael insisted that the guards would not try so hard to get them back as they valued their own lives too much and with the Russians on the march they would stand a better chance of getting away. Michael still had contacts in France and was prepared to use them. Getting there would be the hard part.

They waited until nightfall. Only two guards manned the watchtowers at the camp entrance. The other watch posts were empty. They already knew the timings of the searchlight and fewer guards patrolled the grounds at night. Several Germans had already deserted and this would be to their advantage.

This time they would wait until after roll call. Once through the perimeter fence they would split up into twos and begin the difficult trek through the freezing cold to the train station. It was their plan to stow aboard a train to Raciborz, taking them into East Germany. Michael was paired with Hicks and the first thing they needed to do was get some different clothing.

The first part of the plan was executed perfectly. On route to the station they skirted villages, marching through the freezing conditions, toward the station. On route they passed a remote farmhouse. Michael and Hicks slipped inside an outbuilding for shelter, which they discovered was a washhouse. Fate was smiling on them, thought Michael as they dispensed with their worn, grubby uniforms and grabbed clothes neatly piled up. It was as if they were expected. Hicks donned a rough striped shirt and black slacks. He changed his socks and replaced his boots, which were still serviceable although the chilblains he suffered were causing him grief. He snatched a heavy overcoat covering an old scarecrow propped inside. He apologised to the straw man, "My need is greater than yours."

Michael changed his shirt and thrust on a big navy fisherman type knit sweater and navy blue felt jacket. He stole grey flannel trousers, which were a little short in length but that didn't worry him. Suitably clothed with their stolen attire they hastened away before they were discovered and hoped the family that had unwittingly supplied their garments wouldn't be too angry. The Poles had no love for the Germans and Michael was sure they wouldn't raise the alarm.

They pressed on through the freezing night, uncertain where they were going or even if they were headed in the right direction. On they trudged, hardly speaking, saving their energy. They decided that if stopped or challenged Hicks would take the lead. He spoke both languages and with his colouring could easily pass for a Pole. Michael would pretend to be his mute cousin.

"What we really need is some money," said Michael.

"What do you propose? Rob a bank?" laughed Hicks.

"I wish... maybe we can ..."

"Do a little B and E?"

"What?"

"Breaking and entering. It's a thought. We may even find some papers, too. That would make our lives much easier," joked Hicks.

They were making good progress in spite of the drifting snow and could just make out the signs of a village ahead. Dim lights could be seen burning in the white blanket of snow.

Michael's hands were now so cold he couldn't feel them. They were painful to touch. He was afraid of frostbite and shoved his hands deep into his pockets to try and generate some feeling. He stumbled along, praying that he wouldn't fall. All he wanted to do was curl up in a corner somewhere, anywhere, and sleep.

They marched on, noting a sign for the railway. "At least we're headed in the right direction."

They skirted the village arriving at another farmhouse. They stepped back into a small copse as a door opened and a young woman hurried out to the barn. "Come on!" urged Hicks and the two stumbled out of the trees and down the bank toward the house. They met the young woman who jumped in fright. Hicks tried to calm her, "Don't be afraid we mean you no harm," he said in Polish.

The young woman made as if to scream and Hicks persisted, "No, please. Can you help?" They exchanged words of which Michael understood nothing and Hicks turned to Michael as the young woman beckoned them to follow.

"It's all right. She hates the Germans. They killed her mother and father, and her brother, stole much of their produce. She's the only one left. And that is because her father hid her away in the loft. She concealed herself behind packing cases otherwise who knows what would have happened?" Hicks and Michael followed her into the house and she bolted the door behind them shutting out the bitter wind and snow.

There was a huge fire in the grate of the kitchen. Logs were stacked either side. Michael took off his jacket to dry and warmed his hands while Hicks continued to talk with the girl.

"They used to patrol the area regularly but she hasn't seen any soldiers for over a week."

The girl said something else and he translated, "She can give us a change of clothes and has her father and brother's papers. We can use these if were stopped but they will need a little doctoring. Meanwhile, she is going to get us something to eat." He rubbed his hands together. Michael sat and looked around at the Spartan surroundings, which were luxurious in comparison with what they were used to.

"What's her name?" asked Michael.

Hicks said something to her and she replied, "Alina"

"Pretty name," said Michael.

"Pretty girl," echoed Hicks.

"Just a thought, does she have any transport or know where we can get some?" Michael began to salivate as Alina began to heat a large stew pan containing a vegetable broth. He watched her as she chopped some carrots and turnips and added them. Hicks continued to talk to her. He translated when he could report something important.

"She's seventeen. As far as transport goes she has a bicycle, which she needs but..." and he teased Michael as he licked his lips ready to reveal some startling information. "There is a motorbike and sidecar, which her parents used."

Michael's eyes lit up, "Can we use it?"

"We can. I have promised her we will reimburse her for it when we get back."

"Indeed we will. I will take her address. Tell her that. What about fuel?"

Hicks spoke again and translated her reply. "Her father had a fuel tank., which was raided by the Germans but, she thinks there may be some left. They didn't find the bike. The family had hidden it in amongst a pile of straw bales. She'll show us after we've eaten."

"Is there anything we can do for her?"

Hicks nodded, "She needs more logs. There's timber in the shed but she finds it very hard to chop the wood."

"I'm not surprised, she's a skinny little thing. Tell her I'll do it after we've eaten and you can take a look at the bike. Can you ride?"

"I can. It was a hobby of mine. You're looking at someone who raced in the Isle of Man TT." Hicks puffed out his chest, proudly.

"That's good, because I can't."

"Then it's sidecar or pillion for you. That's if it has two seats." Hicks turned to Alina and asked her. "We're lucky. There are two seats. It'll be quicker to travel that way than use the sidecar. And," he grinned. "She has a map."

Carrie had tussled with Matthew's proposal. She didn't know whether to accept or not but then the argument in her head continued. Again she remembered the words of the woman in the Angel Hotel, who had believed they were promised. She had urged them to be wed as there were no guarantees he would return from the war. Many Crynant lads had lost their lives, she thought sadly. Startlingly, Thomas' ship HMS Welshman had set sail February 1st transporting stores and personnel from Malta to Alexandria. Two torpedoes of four fired by U-617 had hit her. The ship was blasted in the stern putting the propellers and steering out of action; some of The Welshman's ammunition blew up and there was a huge boiler explosion. She sank two hours later east of Tobruk. One hundred and fifty men perished, sixty lived. The survivors were rescued by destroyers Tetcott and Belvoir and taken to Alexandria but if Thomas had been aboard doing his duty in the engine room. There was no doubt he would have been dead. Once more Carrie thought of Ernie's words, "Everything happens for a reason." It clearly wasn't Thomas' time. The accident although horrific and ending his naval career had in a peculiar way been his saviour.

Carrie was wrestling with this important decision, she thought of Jumbo, and of Michael; good men now lost forever and made up her mind. Matthew was fun. He made her laugh. There was definitely chemistry between them.

She dived into the barn where Ernie used to sleep and found him trying to get a calf off the cow. The remains of the yellow water bag and mucus trailed down, which always preceded the calf and Ernie was trying to help the bellowing animal. "Come and help me, Cariad. Blossom is exhausted, she's been hours more than she should. I've scrubbed up. The feet are just showing, if the nose appears at least the calf is the right way round."

"What do you want me to do?"

"Pass me that rope by there." Carrie fetched the stout three-plied cord. "Now go and calm her from the front, soothe her, talk to her. She's not raging with hormones to be angry, just very, very tired."

Carrie moved to the front of the animal and smoothed the creature down, talking softly as Ernie tied the rope around the little feet and hooves.

"Hold her steady," ordered Ernie as he tugged on the feet with all his might. "That's better, her sides are sinking in. Come on Blossom, one last push." The cow mooed loudly with the effort, Ernie pulled and the calf slipped out with a mess of membranes into the clean straw. "That's a good girl." He checked the calf's airways, which were clear, grabbed a handful of fresh straw and vigorously rubbed the calf clean. "We must get the calf to the teat. The goodness in the colostrum will help the baby fight infection. Give Blossom some water to drink."

Ernie lifted the baby to its mother and the calf readily attached to suckle, while Carrie helped the cow to some fresh water holding the bucket for her. Water slopped over her uniform but she didn't care such was the magic of the birth.

"I never get tired of this," sighed Carrie.

"No, it's one of the most rewarding parts of the job. But, you didn't come here to help." He looked at Carrie's face, "You've made a decision."

Forgoing the railway now they had transport, Michael and Hicks had managed to travel safely unchallenged and undetected through country lanes and between some forty-six small villages. They slept where they could in barns, farmyards, cowsheds and haystacks through Poland and into Germany and on through Czechoslovakia. They were ravenous and ate where they could, and what they could scavenge, stealing potatoes and scraps from pigs.

Michael didn't know why but he felt an urgent need to get home and insisted on pressing on using some of the dangerous daylight hours, to travel in, too. They were weak and fatigued.

"I think we'll save time and stand a better chance going to Switzerland, it's a neutral country we can get a plane home."

"I understood the plan was that we head for Dunkirk," said Hicks. "Why the urgency?"

"I don't know. I can't explain it... Something is telling me we have to hurry."

"I thought you were going to use your contacts in France. Go through the resistance?"

"Originally, yes. But something inside me is yelling, Switzerland."

Hicks shrugged, "Okay, but we need more fuel. We've no money, nothing to barter with. If we don't get any soon we'll have to walk."

Matthew had returned to Scotland a happy man. They had seen the Reverend Richards and applied for a special licence, which had cost Matthew a week's wages. There wasn't time for all the banns to be read but agreed the third ones would be announced directly before the wedding.

Carrie had taken her mother's wedding dress, which her grandmother tailored to fit. Seamstresses who had worked on the Christmas plays made bridesmaid dresses for Megan, Naomi and Bethan.

Hendre was in uproar most of the time with the organisation and planning. The Star and Garter was to be the venue and kind-hearted patients like Howie Price sacrificed their rations so that a cake could be made. Nancy, Megan's mother had offered to bake it. The local farmers had supplied fresh eggs for sandwiches, and Sarah had her now un-manicured hands up to her elbows in making bread.

John was providing pork legally with half a pig that he'd kept for the farm. The Star would use it to make a stew. The wedding feast would not be a feast but it would provide enough refreshment for everyone.

The village was awash with the news that the District Nurse was getting married. Carrie sent a telegram to her friends Pemb and Kirb and hoped they would be able to attend. Everything was being done in such a rush.

The phrase, 'Marry in haste, repent in leisure,' went around and around in Carrie's head and she tried to shrug off the feeling, as the day grew closer. All the talk in the village was of the wedding and everyone wanted to be a part of it. The constant chatter about it gave Carrie the jitters. She put her misgivings down to pre-wedding nerves and listened to the reassuring stories of her patients and how they had suffered similar doubts before their wedding, so that now, Carrie believed she was doing the right thing.

Matthew was arriving later that day. He would stay at the pub and had been warned by all that he was not to see Carrie the night before the wedding. They were to go to the Castle in Neath for one night as their honeymoon before Matthew returned to duty.

Carrie sat chewing a liquorice root deep in thought. Sarah glanced at her, "Whatever is that? It looks like a twig?"

Carrie glanced up and smiled, "I suppose it is, of sorts, I used to munch on these as a kid. Helped me to think."

"Oh. What do you need to think about now?"

"My hair. What on earth can I do with my hair?" She shook her head and the fiery cloud of curls sprung out into a disorderly flaming bush.

"Let me worry about that. I'll do your hair and make-up."

"Make-up? I never wear the stuff."

"On your wedding day – you will."

"I don't think you'll have enough Kirby grips and Vaseline to control this lot." She shook her hair again and it sprung into an even more tangled eruption.

Sarah laughed, "You have amazing hair and I will deal with it. It just needs a firm hand."

"You make it sound like a naughty child."

"So it is in one respect. And don't worry about the veil. I'll be able to fix it, you'll see."

"Right, well…" Carrie thrust out her liquorice root , "Want a chew?"

"Er... no... Thank you." Sarah made her escape into the parlour where Bethan was waiting for her piano lesson.

Michael and Hicks looking very much the worse for wear, fatigued, unwashed, unshaven, and unkempt had filched some petrol from an outlying garage in the dead of night. They had cut through a lock and syphoned enough fuel to keep them going. They had reached the Swiss border and crossed where there were no guards or patrols and pressed on toward Zurich.

They attracted many suspicious glances from the ordinary Swiss people going about their daily work before reaching the outskirts of the town. There, they followed directions to the Rathaus of Zurich housing both the cantonal and city's municipal parliament. It was built on a fundament anchored in the Limmat River.

Hicks leapt off the bike, safely parked it and finding the energy from somewhere ran up the steps, in through the portal to the offices within. Michael followed more slowly. His feet were in a terrible state, blistered with chilblains and it was painful to walk.

As soon as Hicks reached the foyer he was stopped by a male official who demanded to know their business. Hicks babbled in German, explaining their situation and need to return to Britain. The man listened seemingly sympathetic but shook his head ordering them to leave. Michael hobbled over and in French put in an impassioned plea. The man shrugged. Another gentleman joined them followed by another and another. On the periphery of a gathering crowd stood a professionally dressed woman. She listened to Hick's babbling with her head on one side and to Michael's urgent requests.

The second official attempted to bundle them out of the door. People were yelling, shouting instructions and advice. The chaotic babble was fast becoming riotous when the woman called a halt to the impromptu gathering. The crowd of people parted as she walked through them to the two escapees. She gestured to them to follow her. Hicks and Michael hurried after her while the bystanders fell into fervid discussion.

The woman led them into an office and closed the door. She settled at her desk indicating they should sit and spoke in perfect English, "Now, tell me where you have come from and what you want."

Michael and Hicks exchanged a look of relief and launched into a potted version of what had happened to them and the fact that they needed to return to Britain. She paused and surveyed the two men. "You look like you could do with freshening up," she said critically.

"What I wouldn't give for a hot bath, soap and razor," sighed Michael.

"That can be arranged."

"And our clothes," added Hicks.

The woman nodded, "Yes, those can be fixed."

"What about getting home?"

The woman rose. She paced around the office, "As a neutral Swiss territory the allied bombers believe it's safe to fly in our air space. The Germans have pressured us to bring those planes down and land here to prevent them continuing their raids. We have two such planes at the airport."

Michael beamed, "Then we can get home?"

"If you want to take the risk, yes."

"All right!" yelled Hicks. "Let's do it."

"I'll set it up, get the pilots." She wrinkled her nose at the offending odours coming from the two men. "You really do need to get cleaned up," said the woman called Claudia Allenbach. She sat down again and picked up the heavy-duty black telephone.

CHAPTER THIRTY

Wedding Bells

Hendre was busier than a termite mound. Ernie was struggling with his collar and tie. As Megan walked past she ripped the beret from his head. "You are not wearing that to give Carrie away."

Sarah gasped in horror as she saw the old man's wiry grey hair, "Have you had a row with the barber? For goodness sake, I'll get my scissors." Sarah ran up to Carrie's room where Naomi and Bethan sat like little princesses on the bed, dressed in pretty pink taffeta dresses. Carrie was sitting at the dressing table in her dressing gown. She took her mother's locket and placed it around her neck and sighed, "Oh, Mam... Am I doing the right thing? Am I?" she asked herself in the mirror.

"You will look amazing, I promise you."

Bethan looked up, "Can I go and play now?"

"Nooo!" Sarah and Carrie chorused.

"But, I want to play the piano," she complained.

Sarah smiled, "You can play the piano but not outside or on the floor. Understand?"

Bethan nodded and skipped out of the room. Naomi looked up, "Can I go too?"

"Yes, but don't get dirty. Promise?"

"Promise."

Naomi ran out after Bethan and Sarah purred, "I'll just see to Ernie's steel wire tresses, and I'll be back."

Carrie stared into the mirror and whispered, "Oh, Michael. I always thought I would be wearing a wedding dress for you." The glass steamed up in front of her. And a shaft of sunlight beamed through the window reflected off the mirror dazzling her.

She was momentarily dazed by the glare before questioning, "Now, what did that mean? Jawch, I'm getting too much like Ernie, reading signs in everything." She looked up at the ceiling and murmured, "If you're there and watching, give me your blessing and show me I'm right to do this."

A cloud passed the face of the sun and removed the golden glow. Carrie rose and lifted her dress of its hanger, placing it on the bed. "I'm going to need help with this." She shouted downstairs for her friend, "Megan!"

Michael and Hicks had landed in RAF Biggin Hill the previous day. They had finished their debriefing. Michael extended his hand to Hicks, "Thanks. If it hadn't been for you I'd never have got out."

"Likewise. You're a darn good map reader."

They both laughed. Michael asked, "What's next for you? Home?"

"Nah. I don't have anyone left. Family home has gone, blown up. The Forces is all the life I know, now. After a week off, I'll be raring to go again." Hicks looked up, "What about you?"

"I'm headed back to Wales to the farm. According to the authorities my fiancée thinks I'm dead."

"Whoa! You can't just turn up. You'll frighten the life out of her. At least give her some warning. Telephone her."

"No phone all the way out there, just the village exchange."

"Still you ought to let her know. You could send a telegram."

"I could, but I think the news would come better in person. You're right. I'll ring the exchange." Michael paused, "Do you know what you're going to do for the week?"

"I haven't thought…"

"Why don't you come back with me? Meet everyone. There's a couple of very pretty Land Girls," he said with a twinkle in his eye.

"Yeah, why not? Thanks, I'd love to. And you better get on the blower and let your girl know you're alive and kicking. Go on. Get back into the office."

Michael nodded, and retraced his steps to the guardroom, while Hicks idly dragged his feet in the dirt, whistling. They had both been kitted out with new uniforms. Hicks paused to admire his reflection in the window when Michael came flying out in a terrible state. Hicks looked up questioningly. "What's happened?"

"It's Carrie. She's getting married today. I've got to stop the wedding. Apparently, the village is full of it. It was totally unexpected. Come on."

"Can't someone give her the message?"

"No, the operator's in Neath and doesn't finish her shift until six tonight. She's going to try and get through to the village exchange."

"What time's the wedding?"

"Two o'clock. We'll never do it."

Michael was running. He looked around wildly, "Can you drive?"

"Not me, just a bike. Can't we get a train?"

"With the number of changes? We won't get there in time."

Hicks glanced down toward a hangar where a Vincent HRD 1000 cc was standing. "Oh, yes we will!"

The owner of the bike was smoking a cigarette leaning back against the pillion. Hicks charged over to the man. There was a lot of head shaking and wrangling, he pointed across at Michael and the two eventually shook hands. The owner tossed him the keys. Hicks started it up and sped across to Michael. "Hop on! I've promised to get this back to him before Monday and with a wodge of cash."

Michael nodded and sat astride, reputedly, the fastest motorcycle ever built. They skidded off past the hangar and Michael shouted to the man, "I'll see you all right, I promise. Thank you!"

Michael and Hicks proceeded out of the camp. "How do we get there? You'd better direct me. Come on, we've no time to lose."

"Get us out of here. Head for Gloucester to get the ferry at the Old Pier near the village of Aust. Otherwise it's miles round."

"Never heard of it."

"Get on the Woking road through to Reading, Swindon and then Gloucester."

"How do you know that?"

"I don't. I had a good Geography teacher at school."

"Better hope you're right. Now, hang on. I'm stepping it up a notch." Dust and dirt flew up as they hit the road.

"There's a sign!" yelled Michael. "Turn left at the junction. Hurry!"

Back at the telephone exchange in Neath, Anwyn Hopkins, a Crynant woman, was in a dither. She was trying to contact Glenda Pearson in Crynant's Post Office in between handling her usual routing calls. Every time she had a moment spare to ring, the phone was engaged. Anwyn a middle-aged, buxom brunette was becoming more agitated and frustrated as each attempt ended with the engaged signal. She swore softly as she began to sweat and took out her neat lace hankie pushed up her sleeve, more for show that actual use, and dabbed at her brow. "Esgyrn Dafydd, what a to do, oh, Duw!"

Her pal, Carys Mostyn, thirty, a slender platinum blonde looked across at her friend fidgeting in her seat. She put her hand over her operator mouthpiece, "Whatever's the matter, Anwyn? You're acting like you've been attacked by an army of fleas."

"Oh, Duw! I've just spoken to Michael Lawrence, the Englishman who came to the village to run Hendre Farm, now at Gelli Galed."

"So?... Putting you through now, Sir..."

"He's supposed to be dead. Dead, he was. It was reported in the local paper. Oh, yerffyn darn!"

"What? Oh, sorry Sir, not you. I'll check the line again."

"His fiancée, Carrie Llewellyn..."

"District nurse, Carrie Llewellyn?"

"Yes!"

"What about her?"

"Don't you listen to any of the gossip? She's getting married today... We've got to stop her... she must know..."

"Yes, Sir. The line's engaged. Please try later.... Maybe she's changed her mind about this Michael."

"No, no. He was the love of her life. I should know, it was all over the village."

"Ring Crynant get her a message."

"I'm trying. But every time I try it's damn well engaged."

"Cut them off!"

Anwyn was horrified, "I can't do that. I could lose my job."

"Hello? Operator. Yes, ma'am, putting you through now … Ever since that Glenda Pearson took over the Post Office the line's almost always busy. Rumour has it she chats to people all over the world."

"Oh, Holy Mother, what can I do?"

"Try again.

"I've been trying, trying all the time. Oh, Lord…" Anwyn stopped as the clipped footsteps of their manager were heard approaching. Pasty faced, Isaac Humphreys, looking extremely cross marched over to them.

"Everything all right here?" he demanded.

"Yes, thank you," they chorused sweetly.

All conversation ceased and they continued with their jobs as Mr Humphreys hovered around them.

Sarah was teasing Carrie's wild mane into a Rita Hayworth style as she had appeared in Dante's Inferno with Spencer Tracy. Sarah had managed to straighten Carrie's rebellious locks for about four inches from her parting using perming lotion. The rest was allowed to wave softly in subtle curls and tresses around her face.

Carrie had wrinkled her nose, "Open the window! The smell of ammonia in that gunk is enough to kill a rat."

"Wait! Let me get the veil on first," ordered Sarah.

"There's a breeze blowing up. I won't open it far. We don't want you blown to yfflon," said Megan.

"What?" queried Sarah.

"Tatters," translated Megan.

Sarah fiddled with the veil and looked at Carrie in the mirror. "There. What do you think?'

Megan gasped, "Carrie, you look beautiful. Pretty fel llun."

"What?" asked Sarah.

"Pretty as a picture," answered Megan.

"I got the pretty bit…" She eyed Carrie critically, "Just a little more definition in your eyebrows and around your eyes." Sarah took an eye pencil and bent over her to add the finishing touches. "There, now look," she said huskily.

"I don't look like me," said Carrie.

"You do; just a more lovely you."

"Sarah's right," said Megan. "It really brings out the colour of your eyes, just like a film star, you are. All you need now is a band of diamonds, a leopard on a lead, with a coat to match its fur and go walking," joked Megan.

"And where would I put him, great grizzly thing prowling round the house? The dogs'd lose all sense of security," quipped Carrie. The two friends started to giggle.

Sarah stared at them puzzled and then joined in, "Thought you were serious for a moment."

"Right, now stand up. Let's have a look at you. The finished picture."

Sarah and Megan gazed in approval before Megan jumped, "Something missing... Flowers... Carrie what about flowers? We can hardly pick you a bunch of dandelions."

"No," added Sarah. "We don't want you peeing the bed on your wedding night."

The three giggled together again.

"Don't panic! Flowers should be on their way," said Carrie.

"Well, they'd better hurry up! How long have we got?" said Megan looking at her watch.

"Don't worry, they'll be here. John organised it. Besides, we have another two hours yet. I'm ready too early... what do we do until we leave?"

"Pray!" said Carrie.

"The line's still engaged. Damn woman," said Anwyn. "What can we do?"

"The woman's got more chat than a fishwives' convention," said Carys. "It's no good. You'll have to go."

"How?"

"Be sick..."

"What?"

"Pretend to be sick. Faint... anything..."

Anwyn could see her boss frowning and picking his way through the exchange to her. She stood up and flapped her arms around and collapsed to the floor. Carys rose and knelt by her as Mr Humphreys came rushing up. "She ought to go home," said Carys. "She's been feeling rough all morning. Probably going down with something. We don't want the whole exchange going down with it and on top of her you know what." Carys winked.

"Her...? Oh, oh yes, of course. Take her up to the staff room," blustered the man going red in the face with embarrassment. See she gets to the station. I'll pull one of the girls off her break, see if anyone wants some overtime. Go, quickly now, go."

Carys helped her perspiring friend to her feet. Anwyn opened one eye while pretending to groan. She staggered out leaning on her friend and hissed, "Going a bit too far, don't you think? My you know what," she scoffed.

"You know him, one mention of women's troubles and he colours up like a pillar box. Can't move away quickly enough." She helped her friend into her coat and they weaved to the door.

"I'll never live this down," murmured Anwyn.

"But think of the good you'll be doing. Saving romance. Romance and true love. Just like at the pictures," she sighed dreamily.

The two bustled out of the door and ran to Neath station. "When's the next train?"

"Too long," said Anwyn. "You get back, I'll be all right now."

"Good luck." Carys smiled and sighed again, "Ah, how blissfully romantic," and is if her feet grew wings she seemed to glide down the street in a starry-eyed haze.

Hicks and Michael had driven with breath taking speed skirting the major towns and had now left the ferry, which had transported them across the River Severne. They had passed through Newport, by passed Cardiff and Bridgend, and now headed for Maesteg to be followed by Neath and then Crynant.

Hicks had never ridden so fast, yelling out, "Lean!" at every corner they rounded. The bike roared past surprised pedestrians; dogs barked at the machine's throaty booming, vroom engine as if it was an avenging dark angel. The sound echoed under viaducts and it skidded on the roads spraying small stones and dirt up from the wheels.

Michael was gripping Hicks harder than a child on an adventure ride at the fair and resisting the urge to scream. He ducked his head down behind Hick's head to stop bits flying into his eyes.

As they burst into the streets of Neath a church bell chimed. it was now a quarter to two. It was seven and a half miles to Crynant and then on some to St. Margaret's Church. The clock was ticking.

Anwyn was hanging on the door of the carriage as it pulled into the station. She raced out of the door, her coat flapping, shoved her ticket at the astonished guard and ran in an awkward gait as fast as her short legs could move almost tipping over in her shoes. She sprinted, not even knowing she could sprint, up and down the hill. She panted like a dog on heat and although the day was cool her exertions had turned her face as red as a tomato. She huffed and puffed, now feeling nauseous and trying to stop her mid morning snack from escaping her stomach and making an appearance on the street.

On she ran, gulping hard, ignoring the stares of passers by and those she knew, whose comments and questions disappeared behind her into the wind. Her heart was threatening to burst out from her chest and she struggled to breathe. The stitch in her side was now unbearable as she struggled to race onward.

Carrie had processed down the aisle with Ernie now standing stiff and proud behind her. She had joined Matthew at the altar and passed her flowers to Megan. Bethan and Naomi had slipped into the front pew with Sarah. John stood ramrod straight next to Matthew acting as his best man and the Reverend Richards had begun the service. The first hymn had been sung and the introduction made.

Villagers including Mrs Gregory and Howie Price sat with joy watching their district nurse, preparing to say her vows. Some overcome with emotion were openly weeping.

The Reverend Richards stopped and addressed the congregation advising them of the seriousness and sanctity of marriage that should not be entered into lightly. He then went on, "First, I am required to ask those here present if anyone knows a reason why these persons may not lawfully marry, to declare it now or forever hold their peace."

The reverend paused and looked around as the door at the back of the church flew open and Anwyn gasped into view, she could hardly speak but managed to cry, "Stop the wedding!" before she collapsed on the tiled floor in a heaving blubbering heap.

Shocked people whispered and muttered at the display. Carrie turned and hurried to her side, "Why, Anwyn? Why stop the wedding?"

Anwyn wheezed, "He's alive. Michael Lawrence is alive," and then she completely flaked out on the floor. At that same moment there was the throaty roar of a motorbike and more footsteps were heard. Michael entered the church followed by Hicks.

The whispers in the church grew louder as people echoed Anwyn's words, "He's alive. Michael Lawrence is alive."

"Yes, I'm alive, my dear sweet Carrie."

Carrie stood up in disbelief as she laid eyes on Michael's face. She picked up the skirts of her dress and ran into his open arms sobbing with joy and love.

The uproar in the church was unprecedented. No one had ever seen anything like it. Pandemonium ensued. Shuffling feet stilled as guests stood up and moved from their seats to crowd around with their questions.

Matthew made to move forward but John laid a hand on his arm to stop him and shook his head. An unexpected tear squeezed from Ernie's eye and in his funny staccato gait he hastened to help Anwyn up to her feet and into a pew.

Hicks beamed in pleasure and his eyes ranged the church. He grinned even more when he spotted the other young women in the congregation and gave Laura, Rose and Sarah a cheeky salute. Sarah lowered her eyes seductively before raising them again to study the face of this interesting new man.

Megan began the applause, which rippled around the church as Carrie threw her arms around Michael's neck and drew him into a passionate kiss as everyone watched.

Matthew's eyes filled with tears and after one last look at Carrie he removed his buttonhole, which dropped to the floor, walked to the side door of the church and left discretely.

Michael scooped Carrie up in his arms and carried her out of the church followed by the guests bursting with questions and full of excited chatter.

Carrie didn't care. She was in Michael's arms and exactly where she wanted to be. Ernie watched with a soppy expression on his face and John grinned his lopsided smile. For the moment, at least, all was right with the Llewellyns and the future looked bright.

Lightning Source UK Ltd.
Milton Keynes UK
UKHW04f0013130918
328781UK00001B/7/P

9 781910 105474